Circling Senta

L V Madsen

Fenix Publishing
Gaucin, Spain

Copyright © 2014 by LV Madsen

All rights reserved. No part of this publication may be reproduced, distributed or transmitted in any form or by any means, including photocopying, recording, or other electronic or mechanical methods, without the prior written permission of the publisher, except in the case of brief quotations embodied in critical reviews and certain other non-commercial uses permitted by copyright law.

Publisher's Note: This is a work of fiction. Names, characters, places, and incidents are a product of the author's imagination. Locales and public names are sometimes used for atmospheric purposes. Any resemblance to actual people, living or dead, or to businesses, companies, events, institutions, or locales is completely coincidental.

LV Madsen / Fenix Publishing, Gaucin, Andalucía, Spain

http://lvmadsen.com

Cover art: Emma Pathare

Cover design: ebookcoversgalore.com

Book design and formatting: davidrory-publishing. http://davidrory.net

Book Layout ©2013 BookDesignTemplates.com

Circling Senta/ LV Madsen

ISBN 13: 978-1499369526

For Serafina Clarke

Part 1

Wednesday Night was Wagner Night

Wensum Farm, Ringland, Norfolk.

11TH OCTOBER 2008

Astrid tops up my glass.

'I think he may have a point,' she says, glancing at Rhys. She doesn't seem totally convinced, though, and twists a strand of greying hair round her index finger. Hair twiddling. She's been doing that for as long as I can remember, from our earliest childhood days when the curls I envied were a rich dark auburn. I sip the blood red wine.

'But I'm not a writer,' I protest.

Rhys chuckles. 'Come on, Vita. You've got to be better than some of the deluded souls who apply for my courses. At least you read real books.' He gets up from the kitchen table to place another log on the open fire. Outside, the elements have gone wild. A hooligan wind howls around the farm, flinging fistfuls of hail against the window panes.

'*It was a dark and stormy night...*'

My sister smiles indulgently. Rhys ignores my lame little joke and carefully scoops up Jaffa the sleeping ginger tabby from the armchair by the fire before lowering himself slowly onto the hairy cushions. Ooooh mebackmekneemehip. How did we all get to be so old all of a sudden? I study his craggy profile. Is he still handsome, or is it the ghost of handsomeness past that clouds my judgement? Would he seem good-looking to someone who hadn't known him in his youth? He is sixty-one now, but my memory of him as the stocky, strutting, dark-haired, black-eyed Welsh hell-raiser of yore is vivid and powerful. This stiff old crock in his fireside armchair is surely just Rhys acting the part of an old man. The wrinkles and jowls are only the latex confections of a skilful make-up artist and the thick grey hair a cunning toupée. And that paunch is a cushion shoved under his jumper. Got to be. Any minute now he'll leap out of that chair, whip off all the artifice and shout 'Da DAH! Had you fooled.'

He turns to face me.

'Well?'

'I wouldn't know where to start...' I realise that I'm slurring. Astrid notices too and pushes the water jug and the plate with the remaining runny Chaume and crackers towards me.

'At the beginning. *Ab ovo*. First person. That's how most rookie writers start. We can always work on it later and maybe change parts to third person. I'd be more than happy to give you feedback and pointers.'

We?

'Or not,' says Rhys, sensing my reservations. 'Entirely up to you. You can just treat it as a very private exercise in catharsis. Just don't mention the fucking weather on the first page...'

And so I have made a start. If nothing else, it will give me something to focus on while staying with Astrid and Rhys on the farm. Something other than worrying about my flaky teenage son and just doing routine domestic stuff around the house to help my sister. I absolutely cannot work, as the urge to make jewellery has deserted me, and in any case, even if inspiration should return, all my tools and materials are in the studio in Clapham. Hope the place hasn't been burgled...

Where exactly is the beginning?

It all depends how far back I care to go. I stare at the laptop screen and doodle spiral shapes with the cursor but the words I need won't come, because the written word hasn't been my medium for a very long time now. Instead, I end up drawing with crayons on one of Astrid's A3 sketchpads. I turn the paper sideways to form a landscape rectangle. A small cross near the right hand side of the page marks the present; October 2008. Another little cross in the middle of the page marks November 2007. I link the two points by making them equatorial opposites on the circumference of a rather wobbly freehand circle. Above the circle I draw a star, its rays fanning out onto the circumference. I try to imbue it with a hard, evil, cruel and powerful beauty. I stare at the empty circle, the circle of hell, the *annus horribilis.* Then I start to fill it in. I draw a massive fireball of a comet with a flaming tail, about to crash into our house and reduce it to rubble and flames, and then I pencil in names in the smoke clouds; Senta, Toby, Isobel, Tristan, Gerry, Mother and me, Vita. I add Astrid, Rhys, Dylan, Marcus and Ewa right up against the circumference, outside the immediate danger zone. I draw the outline of a coffin around Senta and Toby and a faint one around Tristan. I surround Gerry's with dozens of little question marks, then I cross-hatch my own name. I make Patricia, my mother's name, a little fainter and draw a cloud around it.

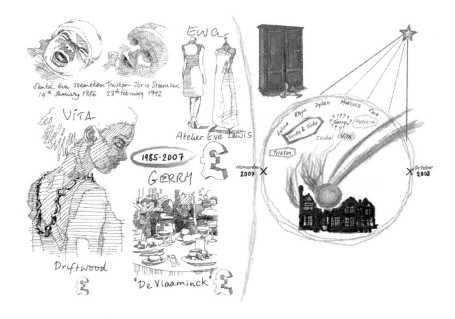

How can I put this into words?

A few days later, Rhys enquires after my progress. I shake my head and smile apologetically. All I've really done is describe my drawing, I tell him, as I show him my sketchpad. 'You have to find both your voice and your audience, Vita,' he says. 'Decide whom you are addressing. If it's a real diary, you can be totally elliptical, because it only has to make sense to you. But for the purpose of catharsis and as an exercise in writing, I think it would be better for you to imagine that you are explaining everything to an outsider. That will help to tidy up your memory cupboards and gain some kind of perspective.'

Back at my laptop, the words still elude me; my muteness frustrates me. I sense the words are there, but imprisoned behind a high wall. I am eloquent enough when I speak, but the words won't form on the screen. I can write about my frustrations, but I can't write about The Topic. And now can't shake off the image of a memory cupboard. I end up drawing it above the circle. It's so stuffed that one of the doors bulges and things half spill out; a flowery sleeve from one of Senta's charity shop dresses, a sandal, the fringe of a silk scarf, a bra cup and the loop of a strap. I pierce the right-hand door with a knife, its blade thrust deep into the wood, which has split. I pick up the crimson crayon but put it down again. Here come the tears again. I sniffle for a bit and pick up Jaffa, this massive ginger blob of a cat. I hug him for comfort – a willing participant if the loud purring is anything to go by – and then put him back on the chair by the fire and go to find Astrid in her studio.

It is late morning and she is standing by the corner window wearing one of Rhys's old denim jackets over a T shirt which comes down to her knees. Her jeans are tucked into paint-splattered Uggs. She has taken off her leather apron and is rolling a joint distractedly, while studying something in the yard. A grey squirrel is flitting around among the hens, stop-starting, sitting up, then rippling along in a diagonal line and dashing up the massive oak tree. The anaemic autumnal sunbeams have caught Astrid's hair, a medusa nest of curls and tendrils piled on top of her head. The ends, where orangey henna is growing out, are on fire. We sink down together into the old bean bag sofa, my little sparrow of a sister, half my size but twice my mental strength, and me, the ungainly, lanky heron. She puts her arm around my shoulder and passes me the joint.

'Don't force yourself with the writing,' she says. 'Rhys can be a bit of a bully. Writing your way out of grief isn't everyone's solution. I don't think it would suit me at all.'

We loll on the bean bag, leaning against each other, toking, and for a sweet while we are little girls again, four and six, me playing with her hair while she strokes my arm and examines my fingers. Astrid the eternal observer. She is always examining something; a foot, a shoe, an ankle, a fingernail. Hands are a new theme for her of late, and have started to appear both in her painting and in the small stone sculptures that she still makes between the commissions for monumental pieces. She has just been on the phone to the Olympic Delivery Authority Arts and Culture people, which is in the process of commissioning works from both new and established sculptors to commemorate the 2012 Olympics. More than a dozen works of art are going to be placed in the Olympic Park itself, and smaller bronze sculptures are also going to be commissioned on the theme of the Paralympics. Astrid has decided to do a gigantic muscular male torso for the park, chiselled out of a massive block of Cornish granite. She started work on it last month. Roughing out the shape with a terrifying electric saw, she was clad head to toe in protective gear, her hard hat and its visor scratched and scored by flying chips of stone, her ears protected from the racket by huge ear muffs, her tiny feet shod in steel-capped boots. She had quite a few accidents in her early years as a sculptor, including cracking a bone in her foot when a large chunk of rock fell on it, and once mashing the joint of her left thumb as she whacked her chisel with a three - pound hammer and missed.

These days, she is much more safety-conscious, though she hates having to wear all the gear. It was terrifying to watch her attack the granite monolith, a ferocious humming bird pecking aggressively at an elephant. This kind of heavy physical work would be exhausting even for a powerfully-built man, but for my sister the effort it requires of her tiny frame is almost superhuman. She feels both flattered and cursed by the Olympic commission, knowing that no matter what she comes up with, most people won't like it, and the criticism will be very public. She is able to switch with enviable ease from sculpting to painting in oils, charcoal sketches, etching and photography. She even makes some jewellery, though it is usually purely playful and rarely of the wearable kind.

She runs her index finger over my knuckles and clutches my hand tightly. The weed leads us gently to lala land and we nod off, curled up together. Eventually, dreamy-brained, dull-blooded, I get up; I have to roll sideways onto my knees to do so. I scrounge a coil of copper picture wire and some pliers and return to the fuggy warmth of the low-ceilinged farmhouse kitchen, the heart of the house, where my laptop screensaver is flicking through a slide show of my 2007 exhibition at Goldsmith's. I look at my burning house drawing on the kitchen table and fix on November 2007.

Unblock yourself, Vita. Let the dam burst. Find your voice...

I pick up a blue crayon instead. November 2007 forms the nexus to the preceding circle, a much larger one, more than twenty times as large, in fact, encompassing 1985 to 2007. I can't draw it to scale on the sheet of A3, so I just hint at its size, drawing a line almost vertically tangential to the left of the *annus horribilis* circle, but with just the slightest hint of a curve to the left as I make it disappear off the top and bottom of the page. Twenty-two years of life, featuring the births of Senta and Tristan, one marriage and three successful commercial ventures. Rags to riches would be an exaggeration, but Gerry, Ewa and I did go from being almost broke all those years ago to our current fortunate status of not having to worry about money, though Gerry is all jittery again these days because of the recent economic slump.

I swap the blue crayon for a Rotring pen, and start to doodle and sketch. Ewa, my Polish business partner, close friend, one-time landlady and next-door neighbour in Clapham has been the most financially successful of the three of us with Atelier Eve Lewis, her couture and grooming business. Next comes Gerry, with De Vlaaminck, his award-winning restaurant. I trail a long way behind with Driftwood, my bespoke jewellery line. I am respected enough in the niche world of artist jewellers, but I don't earn big money. Anyway, we had it, that Thatcherite yuppie dream. Self-made people enjoying prosperity, success, and recognition, all thanks to our own entrepreneurial spirit and hard work. To the outside world, a charmed life, though not without some dark shadows and painful secrets for those inside the circle. Top left, I sketch in the faces of our babies; Senta the screamer, born in 1986, and Tristan, born in 1992, forever googoo gurgling and smiling. Life was kind; Gerry and I even survived a marital crisis brought on by my own stupid jealousy, until April 2008, when the spell broke and everything fell apart. Lady Luck, ever fickle, simply seemed to grow tired of blessing us and decided to move on.

Twenty-two years of happiness is a lot more than most people can ever dream of. This is my personal pep-talk, my mantra, but it fails to console. Grief, we are repeatedly told, has to run its course, and I fear that in our case, that course could well last the rest of our lives. It has hollowed me out. Various distractions organised by Astrid; a holiday on the backwaters of Kerala, hill walking in Scotland, a trip to New York, visits to the Cass Sculpture Foundation Garden at Goodwood, all with Tristan – these have provided brief moments of respite, temporary dams against the swell of despair, but I would be engulfed in blackness again as soon as I was back at Wensum. Gerry appears to be coping better – at least he has carried on cheffing and running his restaurant. He *has* to – he doesn't really have a choice. I've been floundering, precisely because I *do* have a choice. The nature of my job is such that I am not tied to the tyranny of working fixed hours. I have the freedom to be able to work when I feel like it. But those who envy me this freedom don't realise that it has a downside, especially now. It gives me too much time to dwell on the event that has ripped our lives apart. Despite the anti-depressants and the well-meaning but largely useless bereavement counselling, I am still at risk of losing the battle with grief.

While Gerry stayed behind in London to tend to the restaurant, I moved to Astrid and Rhys's farmhouse to monitor an emotionally fragile Tristan, whom we had sent there to get him away from the London drug scene and everything that was associated with the murder of his sister and her friend. I've been at Wensum on and off since May of this year. Tris has started A-levels at Norwich Academy, which counts a string of luminaries among its alumni and has a solid academic reputation. I only hope our boy can live up to that. Getting him accepted at this prestigious place was quite an achievement, given his unpromising background and lack of a single GCSE. We owe it almost entirely to Astrid and Rhys, who managed to convince an understandably apprehensive headmaster. Since then, I have found myself with too much time on my hands and nothing to do other than occasionally flick a duster around the farmhouse and help with grocery shopping, laundry and cooking. I am physically busy, but my unfettered mind has been free to roam dangerously close to the cliff-top of depression. Even if I had all my jewellery making equipment at my disposal here at Wensum, I would still have no desire to create anything. The crafting of decorative baubles all seems absurdly, mockingly, cruelly frivolous.

My main function since April, that of keeping a twenty-four-hour watch over Tristan lest he do something drastic, is now limited to out-of-school hours, and is much helped by the fact that his cousin Marcus has taken him under his wing. They are almost the same age, but Marcus, also at Norwich Academy, and our main reason for sending Tris there, is Head Boy, a year ahead of Tris and something of a model pupil, though not in a nerdy way. More in a rugby-playing, *mens sana in corpore sano* sort of way. They couldn't be more different, these two, with Marcus excelling at the sciences that Tristan abhors, yet they have always got on well. So far, Tris seems to be coping, according to his teachers, though he's often distracted and tired. I hardly dare feel relieved, in case it all goes terribly wrong, so I steel myself for the worst and jump every time my mobile rings in case it's bad news from the school.

The other night, after Tristan and Marcus had gone upstairs to do homework or surf the sewers of the internet, I was talking to Astrid and Rhys about this inability of mine to unwind, this constant fear of further disasters. It was then that Rhys suggested that maybe I should confront what had happened head on by writing about it rather than just waiting for time to bury it. That is how he would tackle it. He offered me the use of his study so that I would have somewhere quiet and undisturbed to concentrate.

I did try sitting at his desk with my laptop, but I found the room distracting and oppressive. The desk has sheaves of papers piled high and threatening to slide onto the floor at the slightest touch. By the desk lamp is a dusty Perspex frame with two picture slots. One contains a faded photograph of a dark-eyed little girl of about six or seven sitting in the entrance of a tree house, legs dangling. This is Louise, Rhys's daughter, the result of an affair with a Canadian artist back in the mid-seventies. The other slot contains a much more recent picture of Louise in her late twenties, together with Dylan and Marcus, taken on her one and only visit to Wensum Farm at the end of 2001. Rhys rarely mentions her; another one of his little mysteries. Then there are the books, all higgledy piggledy on shelves that go right up to the ceiling and overflow in a dozen or more wobbly stacks on the floor. I am not at all tidy, but this kind of mess is too much even for me. I'm sure things have curled up and died behind those books, as there is a musty smell of decay. Maybe a mummified mouse or two, trying to escape from Jaffa's switchblades. Anyway, I felt like an intruder in the lair of a troll, so that experiment didn't last longer than an hour or two. At least the kitchen is neutral territory and I can sit with my laptop at the huge table by the window that overlooks the yard and the driveway, but it does have the disadvantage of being the social hub of the house. Long ago, Rhys claimed what was originally the farm's parlour for his study, so the kitchen has had to double up as the sitting room. It is also the entrance hall, so it can get quite busy at times. However, the real problem lies with me. My years of working as a jeweller, I now realise, have caused my writing skills to atrophy. Years of visualising, moulding, forging and filing gold and silver, these things have gradually deverbalised me. Recall, select, describe... Can I still do it? Maybe I should attempt a graphic novel format, something like *Persepolis?*

Concentrate, Vita. Home in on it.

He said then I said then she said and I replied... All lies, of course. Biographical fiction spun around those facts which just happen to have taken root in one's memory. And if you also invent dialogue, putting words in people's mouths, you create a double distortion, given that memory is a notoriously unreliable mirror. I reach for my sketchpad again. Drawing is so much easier. Marionettes. I start to draw a little Punch and Judy theatre, seen from the inside; the puppet master's view. I sketch in a sea of heads, little more than quick squiggles with froggy boggle eyes. Inside, a pair of hands holds the wooden crosses that manipulate two puppets. I make a huge mess of the hands – can't seem to get them right. I draw the outline of the dolls – very basic, like the articulated wooden figures that are used in art classes. Then I hesitate whether to endow each one with a symbolic feature to make it recognisable; a head of long curly black hair for Senta, a tiny pair of round wire-framed glasses for Toby. But no – I have to present them in language, not images, so I ink their names vertically on their torsos. I draw them entangled in a collapsed heap, their strings slack. Round the inside of the little theatre, in the wings, I draw the other puppets, each with their name spelled out vertically on their backs, each hanging limply by the neck from hooks. It's a tricky perspective, too ambitious for my modest talent, and it results in a crap drawing. I am about to tear it up when Astrid comes into the kitchen. Like a naughty child, I try to cover my sketch with my hand, but she has spotted my manoeuvre and peers over my shoulder. I sigh and move my hand away. 'Oof!' she says. 'Seriously macabre. The stuff of horror flicks.' Actually, she didn't say that, but it did remind her of a scene from a film. That much is true. I had pressed the record button on my laptop the moment I heard her approach from the farmyard, where she's just taken delivery of some animal feed. Here is the transcript:

(Mutt and Doobie are yipyapping and whining behind the double door to the yard, dying to escape and bark at the delivery men. Astrid is outside, waiting for the men to get into their van and drive off before she comes in. As she opens the door, the dogs almost knock her over as they leap out and go haring after the van.)

Astrid: 'Coffee?'

Me: 'Er, no, better not. Had two already.'

Astrid: 'Let's have a look?'

Me: 'It's crap. Can't get the hands right. We're all puppets.'

Astrid: 'Jesus, that's macabre. Dance of Death. Those dolls – they're hanged, not hung?'

Me: 'A fine distinction. Hadn't even crossed my mind.'

Astrid: 'Like that Bergman film, what was it again...'

Me: '*The Seventh Seal*,' playing chess with Death, wasn't it?'

Astrid: 'Yeah, that's the one.' (She kisses me on the parting and briefly massages my stiff shoulder muscles. Her small hands are very strong, as a result of her work.)

Me: 'Help me with the hands?'

Astrid: 'Mmm?'

Me: 'You're brilliant at hands...'

Astrid : 'I think I'd do them... you know... from the front...'

Me: 'The... front?'

Astrid: 'Yeah, audience view. From the... the point of view of the audience.'

(She takes a fresh sheet of A4, turns it portrait way, hesitates and sits down at the kitchen table.)

'You need to model your hands for me... yeah... hold something in each one... here – two pencils... pretend you are... puppeteering.'

(I sit opposite her and pretend to manipulate two imaginary marionettes. She takes the Rotring pen and, after staring intensely at my hands for half a minute or so, starts to sketch. A couple of minutes later she pushes the drawing towards me.)

Astrid: 'Over to you now.'

(The disembodied hands are fantastic, powerful and somehow quite evil.)

Me: 'Great hands...'

(She passes me the pen, and I draw a little theatre with two puppets running across the stage. Senta is running towards the right. I give her a head of long curly black hair and a flowery skirt. Toby is chasing her, trying to stop her, his arms held out. I give him his wire-framed glasses and his favourite checked

sweater. *As I sketch in the heads of the audience, I feel the tears well up again.)*

Astrid: 'Want some lunch? Got smoked mackerel and...' *(opens the fridge, rummages, sucks air through teeth)* some odds and sods for a salad. Bread's a bit stale. We can toast it.'

Me: 'Yeah. Good time for a break.' *(I stop the recording.)*

So there we have it: the truth and my distillation of it, or rather, vice versa. Later that same day, after dinner, I show these last three pages to Astrid and Rhys. Astrid points out that this is what any artist does – you take something, a mood, a situation, an object, a memory, a story, and you transform and reinterpret it. Rhys talks about stylistic conventions and genre, and I find myself tuning him out, as if to protect myself. I fear that too many well-meaning helpful hints will simply block me. I've been trying to think of a name for this genre, this 'me and her' autobiography as a prescription for catharsis. I don't want to be a spinner of rose-tinted tales, a spin-doctor of my own meandering rudderless past. I want to be as truthful as possible, painfully so, embarrassingly so, and if this results in an unflattering self-portrait of a lousy mother and foolish, jealous wife, then let it be my hair shirt. What did Rhys say the other day? "Literature is analysis after the event," or some such quote. More like self-flagellation in my case. These days, when I am not tired – tired despite sleeping long hours, despite invigorating walks with the dogs – I am given to attacks of self-disgust at the way I have allowed myself to bumble and drift through life, screwing up repeatedly in relationships, fucking up as a parent and failing somehow to learn. Yet time and again, a safety net has miraculously appeared at a crucial moment, a solution or opportunity handed to me which I haven't really deserved. Until April 2008, that is, when bad luck finally caught up with me, with us, and dealt us a blow from which we will likely never recover.

The circle of hell, that most recent one, was triggered by the unexpected arrival of a letter from Germany, one Saturday morning in Clapham early last November, not long after my fifty-third birthday. It is a day that I recall with unusual clarity, starting as it did with that letter and finishing in the evening with a hospital drama worthy of a soap opera. Early that morning, Gerry brought me *The Guardian*, a mug of green tea and said letter which had been sent to his restaurant. I immediately recognised the familiar flowing, elegant, self-conscious handwriting and the German stamp, and was amused at the oddness of being addressed so very formally as Frau Vita Rasmussen - Steeneken, c/o De Vlaaminck. The envelope contained a single sheet of white A4 with a word-processed concert schedule for the autumn and winter. Half a dozen dates in December 2007 had been circled. They were performances of *Parsifal* at the Royal Opera House, Covent Garden. Amfortas had been added in brackets. In the margin was a note, written, as always, with a fountain pen, in brown ink. 'Hope we can meet up? W.' The email address at the top had also been underlined. 'Let me know,' he'd added. That was the extent of the message. Deliberately or genuinely casual? Hard to tell.

'A voice from the past,' I said to Gerry, who was rummaging in the wardrobe for his jogging gear. 'From Walter Weiss. He's at Covent Garden next month. Might go and see him.' Gerry pulled a pale blue sweatshirt over his head, raked his fingers through his thick, crinkly grizzling hair and looked at me, as if trying to gauge my sincerity. I put the letter down, feigning indifference, and picked up the paper. An assault of misery... Slaughter in Iraq, meltdown in Pakistan, madman Ahmedinejad threatening nuclear oblivion, Mugabe bankrupting Zimbabwe, the collapse of the dollar under what must surely be the most inept, toxic government the United States has ever seen, and all this rendered relatively trivial by apocalyptic warnings about climate change. I dropped the paper on the floor and slid back down under the covers. 'Wake me up when you get back,' I said. 'I really *must* get out of bed today.'

The wooden stairs creaked and squeaked under his trainers as he bounded down them. Below, Doobie let out her usual volley of yelpy barks as she scrabbled over-excitedly around the tiled entrance hall at the prospect of a pee and a sniff on the Common. The rattle and clunk of the door chain, the turning of a key, the click of the lock, eight heavy footstep crunches on the gravel followed by the squeak and click of the garden gate. Tristan would still have been asleep – no twanging practice riffs on his bass guitar, no cursed hip hop rap crap yet. And Senta – had she even come home that night? Gerry and I had no real need to worry, though. At twenty-one, Senta was a very different person from her troubled younger brother. No pierced tongue, septic tattoos, Vodka-induced black-outs, petty and not-so-petty theft. No gender-bending and pretending to be black. No truancy or drug-taking. Senta was a paragon of old-fashioned rectitude. I don't know who was the more frightening of the two, but somehow Tristan was much easier to understand.

How come Rhys and Astrid's two boys have turned out so sane and balanced, whereas Gerry and I have produced one genius of a daughter handicapped with Asperger's and one delinquent liar of a druggie son? R. and A. would be the first to admit that their own style of parenting was one of benign neglect. In fact, both their boys were totally wild when they were little. I remember one particular occasion when they came to visit us in Clapham. Dylan, who was about five at the time, scribbled all over Senta's bedroom walls with wax crayons, while Marcus insisted on crapping in the flower bed. They were almost feral and totally uninhibited. Could it just be due to the different environments, with Senta and Tristan growing up in London, while their country cousins were free to romp around in the Norfolk woodlands and meadows and go skinny-dipping and fishing in the Wensum? Or is it all just down to genetic luck?

I picked up the concert schedule again and perused the list of engagements for Walter Weiss. After five performances as

Amfortas in *Parsifal* at Covent Garden, he was going back to Munich to do *Fledermaus* in February, then *Tosca* in Dallas in March, followed by *The Flying Dutchman* in Austria in May, *Frau ohne Schatten* in Essen in June, then *Arabella* and *Meistersinger* in Munich in July. He'd have turned fifty-three last summer, and world-wide demand for his rich bass baritone was at its peak. I turned to the entertainment pages in the newspaper and sure enough, there it was; Royal Opera House, Covent Garden. *Parsifal.* Conductor: Bernard Haitink. Walter Weiss as Amfortas, Willard White in the role of the evil magician Klingsor, Petra Lang as Kundry. I didn't recognise the other names, but then again I had not really followed the opera scene for some time.

It was strange; somehow this advertisement had more credibility than Walter's personal schedule with its casual invitation. There it was, all official, out in the public domain for all to see. A wave of sweat-inducing nausea washed over me. Television appearances apart, I hadn't seen Walter in more than twenty years, though I'd loosely followed his career and read about his international acclaim. He'd married and long since divorced a Japanese violinist, with whom he'd had two sons who'd settled in New York where they were pursuing their own budding musical careers. Was there a new partner in his life? I imagined there would be. A famous, attractive and wealthy man is unlikely to remain single for long. A truth universally acknowledged, after all. I had no idea that he knew I was in London. How had he tracked me down? It is true that we had some rather embarrassing unfinished business, but why choose this particular moment to lay those ghosts to rest, after so many years?

15 TH OCTOBER 2008

I pick up the sketchpad and turn to a clean sheet. With the aid of a saucer I draw a perfect circle, and I fill it with a series of cloud shapes. These I fill with time periods and names: Sergio, Raoul, Walter, Claudio, Silke. Florence, Paris, Belo Horizonte, Sifnos, Munich. I stare at the clouds and doodle on them. I add a base to the circle to turn it into a crystal ball and call up my past. I am a medium going into a trance.

Germany... Whenever I think of the murders, my mind travels back to a dark parallel at the end of 1984. I never told Senta about that incident because it was so sordid. She was something of a puritan, so it had seemed pointless to burden her with it. And when she too developed an obsession with Wagner in her late teens, it would simply have been cruel to sully her therapy.

I was living in Munich with Walter the baritone, back in 1984, when, one Saturday morning in dark, dank mid-December, while he was away on the final leg of a tour that had taken in much of Eastern Europe, I had received a sickening shock as I sat poring over the front page of the *Süddeutsche Zeitung* while sipping my breakfast tea. It was the day I learned the meaning of the word '*vorsätslich.*' I had to look it up in Walter's dog-eared Langenscheidts school dictionary. When combined with the noun '*Mord*', as it was that day in the paper, it means premeditated murder. '*Vorsätslicher Mord.*'

I remember picking up the phone to call my friend Claudio, but there was no reply, just his usual crackly answering machine message in German and Italian. I didn't know what to say. I had to ring several times before I could manage to record anything sensible, and then all I could say was 'Call me. I've got to speak to you.' before I choked on the words. Then I remembered. Claudio was going to be working all weekend, and I could think of no easy way, in those pre-mobile phone days, to contact him at the Bavaria Film studios. As I stood wondering whether I should just go to Geiselgasteig and attempt to bluff my way in, the phone rang. It was Elfriede. She too had just heard the news, and was incoherent with shock. She suggested meeting in town at Café Luitpold.

I took the U-Bahn to Marienplatz, the heart of Munich. I was early, so didn't bother changing lines for just one stop to Odeonsplatz. I emerged from the depths into the bustle of the

Christkindlmarkt, the great Christmas market where only the previous evening, muffled in a thick winter coat and woollen scarf, I had browsed among the arts and crafts stalls together with Claudio. Over a glass or two of hot *Glühwein* and big slabs of liver sausage with mustard which we'd bought at one of the food stalls, we decided that the relationship we'd developed of late had to come to an end, given that our respective partners were about to return from their two-month opera tour. Yet my heart had been roiling with confusion. On the one hand I had really started to crave the comforting, square predictability of my relationship with Walter, but on the other I had become far too fond for my own good of Claudio's bohemian wild ways. I recall feeling an entirely irrational stab of jealousy when I realised that he, self-professed libertarian, was genuinely looking forward to being reunited with his girl Silke again. For him, there was no contradiction. An unflattering comparison with a dog came to mind. He'd been only too happy to go walkies with me, but now he was about to leap panting and licking and fawning back into the arms of his true mistress. As we picked over potential Christmas gifts at the craft stalls, I sensed I'd already been consigned to the bulging dustbin of his personal sexual history. I was annoyed with myself for caring, as he'd warned me right from the start against any kind of emotional involvement, so I made a show of being unreservedly enthusiastic about Walter's imminent return. My insincerity must have been pathetically obvious.

I found Elfriede waiting for me in Café Luitpold, a staid, conservative establishment in the Briennerstrasse. She was red-eyed and blotchy-nosed, almost unrecognisable without the heavy make-up she usually favoured, the shock having evidently caused a dramatic lapse in grooming. Her silver-grey hair, normally heavily sprayed and bullied into a neat chignon, was tied back into a careless ponytail. Raggedy wisps straggled out at the side, giving her something of a chic bag lady look.

'*Es ist ja unglaublich,*' she kept repeating in her slow Viennese drawl. 'I can't belief it. To sink that was why she came to our Vaaaagner nights. *Guter Gott!* Could we ever hef guessed what was going on zere? What that poor girl must hef been going sroo? And Otto Schreiber. *So ein Schwein!*' What a pig!

What did we really know about Phailin? Very little, other than the fact that she was a young Thai, not long wed to the much older Otto Schreiber, a wealthy local brewery owner and great Wagner fan who, in his youth, had trained as an opera singer but failed to cut it and ended up going into the family business. It was only from the newspaper that we found out their ages; twenty-three and fifty-nine, she a tiny fine-boned little slip of a thing, he a Bavarian Alp of a man with a massive beer gut, glassy blue eyes and a florid boozer's complexion.

'Should I go to the police? Do you sink they'd want to know about Phailin coming to my Vaaaagner classes?' pondered Elfriede.

I shrugged. I couldn't really see what difference it could possibly make now. According to the newspaper, Phailin had slit Otto Schreiber's throat in his sleep, slaughtering him like a pig before committing suicide by taking rat poison. Their corpses had been found the following day and reported to the police by a hysterical Turkish cleaning lady. Schreiber's Alsatian had already started to gnaw on his master's buttocks.

'Vaaaagner will never be the same for me again,' sighed Elfriede, scraping up the last of her gateau. Her loss of appetite had been but fleeting.

'*Jetzt ist alles verdorben!*'

Now all is ruined... That, I suspected, was quite the worst of it for Elfriede. Not the slaughter of Otto Schreiber and his desperate young bride's dramatic suicide, but the perceived desecration of Wagner's music, now tainted forever in her mind by association with this sordid sexual tragedy.

Wednesday night was our Wagner night, or at least it had been until then. Phailin, Claudio and I, a Thai, an Italian and a half-Danish Brit, would meet at Elfriede Swoboda's apartment in Munich's university quarter, Schwabing, to receive our weekly dose of Wagnerian enlightenment. But I need to press rewind and go further back in time to explain how all this came about.

When Walter and I first met, it was on the Cycladic island of Sifnos in the summer of 1983. I was twenty-eight and had been gipsying around Europe and South America ever since graduating from Bristol with a middling degree in Eng. Lit. I hadn't a clue what to do with my life. I felt overshadowed by my vastly-talented older sister, Astrid, feted by some and reviled by others in the Seventies for her whacky installation art and later a highly controversial winner of the Turner Prize, and so I thought I'd postpone real life by taking a year out to do a bit of travelling. Somehow, one year had stretched into three because I couldn't tear myself away from Florence, followed by two years in Paris, where I just managed to keep solvent by doing a series of odd jobs – some very odd indeed – and became entangled with Raoul, a heart-stoppingly handsome Brazilian who played guitar with a group of musicians from the Cape Verde islands.

I had just discovered to my shock that I was pregnant when Raoul got a call from his mother one evening to say that his father, the owner of a lucrative gem-trading business in Belo Horizonte, had died of a heart attack. This meant that it was incumbent upon Raoul, as the eldest son, to take over the running of the family business. His younger brother Ernesto was ill with HIV which was in the process of turning into full-blown AIDS, and the only other sibling, his younger sister Carla, was studying in Switzerland. Although his mother, Luciana, had always been involved in the running of the business, she had no wish to carry on doing so alone, and pleaded with her eldest son to return. Raoul, who had little interest in the gemstone business, was nonetheless very fond of the financially-carefree lifestyle it had afforded him, as there was no way he could have lived off his earnings just from performing with the band. And so, in the space of a day, as a result of a premature heart attack coinciding with an unplanned, ill-timed pregnancy, fate changed our lives. Raoul decided there was little point in going all the way to Belo Horizonte to attend the funeral, only to return to Paris to pack up and leave for good. Might as well do it all at once. Unlike me, he was unexpectedly delighted at the news of my pregnancy and wouldn't remotely entertain the idea of an abortion. In my confusion, panic and heightened state of vulnerability, I succumbed when he pleaded with me to accompany him back to Brazil and set up home there, despite my misgivings about the future of our relationship.

When, two days after the funeral, I collapsed and miscarried, I felt as if I had let the whole family down. Despite my wish that he should wait until I'd passed the first trimester, Raoul had told them of my pregnancy, mainly to help soften the edges of his mother's grief. Suddenly the tiny candle in her dark night had gone out, and she found her sadness tripled, faced now with the death of her husband, the loss of what would have been her first grandchild, and the fatal illness of her favourite son. She sank into several months of near reclusive depression, and so it was that Raoul found himself having to take over the business largely without the benefit of her knowledge and guidance.

Raoul's father had long ago realised that the child best suited to taking over the family business was most likely to be his daughter, Carla. She was the one with the business acumen, the passion for stones and interest in the workings of the market. It was she who, from her early teens, had spent all her spare time and school holidays at her father's side, observing, learning, helping. In order to consolidate the company's Swiss connections, Carla had been sent, at considerable expense, to do graduate studies in Switzerland, where she stayed with a distant cousin of her father's in Bern. She'd only just spent six months there when her father died, and at a mere twenty-two, the family deemed her too young to take over the business. Raoul, therefore, was prevailed upon to play the part of prince regent. There was a long-serving manager, Ricardo, whose brain he desperately needed to pick. Unfortunately, it was an uncomfortable relationship as Raoul was acutely aware that Ricardo saw him for what he was; an indulged rich boy who was totally out of his depth. Hardly surprising, as Raoul was the first to admit that he'd never shown much interest in the business. I tried my best to help, but it was tough. I barely spoke a word of Portuguese at that stage, I had zero knowledge of the business, or indeed of any business, and I was still reeling from the aftermath of my miscarriage, not to mention of suddenly finding myself in this very foreign land. But we battled on, pored over ledgers with the accountant, familiarised ourselves with the customer base and generally tried to get our heads around the world of gem trading. The company, Geyer Dos Santos, dealt mainly in cut and polished emeralds, with Switzerland as one of its principal customers, due largely to Raoul's late father's Swiss family connections.

 I learnt a lot in a very short space about emeralds. I found out that most stones have flaws, known in the trade as inclusions. Very few of them are perfect, and much fiddling goes on to hide the flaws by oiling stones to fill in and hide the cracks as well as enhancing their colour and sealing them with polymers. Highly-skilled gem cutters are needed to facet the stones because the inclusions and fissures tend to make them brittle. Geyer Dos Santos, however, prided itself on the purity of the stones it traded.

The main competition in South America was from the Cozcuez mine in Columbia, whose emeralds were deemed by experts to be of superior quality to Brazilian ones. Other competition came from the mines of Zaire and Zimbabwe. Geyer Dos Santos also traded in amethyst, aquamarine and topaz, and the sheer ubiquity of these gems, on sale like Smarties all over the state of Minas Gerais, stripped them of their illusory scarcity and radically changed my perception of their value. I had been raised in London in an environment where these misleadingly-named precious stones were and still are highly prized as mementos of very special occasions or else as symbols of the wearer's wealth or status. My mother possessed just one diamond solitaire, predictably in the engagement ring given to her by my father, Sven, and a brooch with a heart-shaped amethyst set in gold, a piece of Victoriana she had inherited from her grandmother. I grew up with the skewed idea that such rocks were extremely valuable and rare commodities. In Brazil, confronted with their abundance, I found the stones lost much of their mystique. I came to realise that this quality had been nothing more than a carefully-nurtured marketing ploy to inflate their perceived value. But it was another altogether darker experience which radically altered my feelings about the whole gem trade.

Once a month or so, Raoul's father would travel up to the two emerald mines in the east of the state which he had acquired in the late seventies. He liked to keep tabs on things and even to participate personally in a spot of prospecting. Carla had visited them a couple of times shortly after Geyer Dos Santos had acquired the mining rights, but none of the other family members had ever been there. Raoul now felt the need to show his face, to assure the manager and the miners that all was well with the company and that it was business as usual, despite the death of the family patriarch. And so we set off, Ricardo the manager, Raoul, Carla and I, in the family's chopper, that must-have accessory of the Brazilian oligarchy, and headed northwest for Itabira, in the richest emerald-producing area of Brazil. Our bird's-eye view of a hilly landscape with patches of lush tropical forest revealed many places where the *garimpeiros*, the independent miners who take their chances and go it alone, had prospected and torn open the land, leaving ugly gashes in the landscape.

The Geyer Dos Santos mines, Minas GDS 1 and 2, were second only in size to the Belmont mine, which was then the biggest in the area. They were extensive, with tunnels that plunged some 200-300 metres vertically beneath the surface, where the miners sought emeralds in the contact zone between biotite schist and granite gneiss. The manager of the first mine, a squat, leathery, bandy-legged man with pale eyes who was probably much younger than he appeared, expressed his condolences at some length before taking us on an inspection tour. He talked in detail to Raoul and Carla about the latest geological surveys, while I, lost in a fog of twangy, nasal Portuguese, wandered off and witnessed the depredations resulting from this activity. The land had been disembowelled and pillaged, and all just to satisfy the frivolous, misguided desires of women thousands of miles away who have no clue about the ugly origins of their much-coveted bling, and probably couldn't care less even if they did. But it was the conditions of the workers and their dependents in the ramshackle huts around the mine which I found even more shocking. Thrown together out of salvaged sheets of rusty corrugated sheet metal, flattened cardboard boxes and dusty lengths of plastic sheeting, these huts had no access to running water or electricity. There were very few families, as most of the miners were either single or else had left wives and children behind in their home villages.

A trio of snot-nosed brown children with matted hair ran around barefoot in filthy clothes while skinny, scabby dogs fought or screwed or scratched at their mangy flea-infested fur, and a sickly baby wailed listlessly. I watched a little girl on her haunches, poking sticks into a pile of dog crap. Pooh sticks Itabira-style, I remember thinking. A couple of care-worn, slovenly women appeared in doorways, babies at their sagging breasts, and stared at me with lethargic, vaguely hostile curiosity. Where was the quid pro quo for these people? For the men folk who risked their lives and their health in the mines, in their search for a certain type of rock? How come there was no reward for them or their families? No decent housing, schools or medical facilities? Shaken and self-conscious, I slunk away and joined the others to visit the crushing and sorting facility where a dozen dark-skinned *pardo* men and women were picking over rough emerald-bearing rock as it moved slowly past them on a conveyer belt. Their job was to spot and select the emeralds. Some eight kilos a month they picked out, Raoul told me, of which only about a fifth was of good quality. I couldn't get over the stark contrast of this solid modern building with its air-conditioned offices and framed posters of the pristine Swiss Alps with the slummy squalor of the miners' flimsy dwellings. Why could they not have spent a little money on decent housing? Wasn't it ultimately also in the company's interest to have healthy workers who were motivated by positive feelings towards their employer rather than these sullen, sickly slum-dwelling drudges? Not only was it inhumane, it didn't even make business sense to me.

Raoul gave me a worried look and asked if I was alright. I told him I wasn't feeling well and went and sat on a chair in a corner. Carla and he continued to talk business with the manager while I tried to come to terms with what I'd just seen. How could this family live with their conscience? How could they enjoy their luxurious penthouse when it came at the expense of such exploitation? How could Luciana justify spending a fortune on pointless plastic surgery? Madame Entitlement, I nick-named Raoul's mother, but the others were no better, just nicer.

I was new to it all, and it sickened me.

Ever since, I have not been able to look at gemstones and simply enjoy the sparkle of their beauty. Instead, whenever I see their shiny facets in some fancy window display on New Bond Street, they reflect images of abject poverty, brutal working conditions and environmental degradation. The experience soured my relationship with Raoul and his family, who showed little concern for the plight of their miners or the damage their operations caused to the environment. Raoul thought I was soft. He pointed out that the miners and sorters employed by GDS were still much better off than the go-it-alone *garimpeiros* who were constantly scouting for new sites to exploit, and who had no security whatsoever. As for the lack of facilities, he blamed the Brazilian taxation system for that. Gems were not taxed at source, he told me, but only upon their final sale as faceted and polished stones, and this meant that the tax revenue stayed wherever the finished product was traded, in the big cities. In our case, it was Belo Horizonte that reaped the profit, whereas the mining village of Itabira remained dirt poor, gaining little or nothing from its mineral wealth, and had no revenue to invest in infrastructure. Besides, miners, often illiterate young men who are migrants from other states and socially the lowest of the low, are not considered worthy of investment. The harsh working conditions, inadequate diet and absence of healthcare mean that they are burnt out by the time they reached their thirties. They are constantly on the move, and it only takes a rumour of a rich new seam or source elsewhere for thousands to pack their bags and migrate overnight like locusts. Still, I thought it was a weaselly excuse for GDS to blame the taxation system.

I felt that, given the handsome profits made by the company, it should be their responsibility to look after their workers rather than that of the town of Itabira. Raoul, however, viewed poverty as a normal, if vaguely regrettable state of affairs for the majority of the human race. He'd grown up with it and become inured to it, and although when I pushed him for his opinion, he thought it was neither good nor just, he accepted it with glib, convenient fatalism. Some people were lucky and escaped it, others were not. As for the poor, when faced with either starvation or exploitation, the choice was an obvious one. That was the way of the world. His favourite saying, which always irritated me immensely, reflected this all too well 'Life is unfair – get used to it.' Such an easy thing to proclaim from a position of privilege. My problem was that I couldn't seem to get used to it. Nor did I want to. I was haunted by what I'd seen – such misery and toil, and for what?

To my surprise, young Carla turned out to be an unexpected secret ally. One evening, shortly before her return to Switzerland, she confided in me and told me of her plans to make radical changes at the mines once she took over. She wanted to turn them into a co-operative, with the workers as stakeholders. She wanted them to have health insurance and pensions. She wanted to build a model worker's village with proper housing, sanitation and a school. Her spell in Switzerland had made her see things differently. She too was now shocked by the contrast between the shameless wealth of the Brazilian fat cats and the desperate poverty of the miners.

This utopian vision won't exactly make you Miss Popularity with Mama Luciana, I remember thinking, but I realise now that Carla was in fact simply in the vanguard of a waxing trend towards greater social consciousness and concern for environmental conservation. Some fifteen years later, instead of GDS going belly up because of Carla's philanthropic excesses, it was to become Brazil's flagship eco-company, held up by President Lula da Silva as an example of a perfect marriage between profitable modern entrepreneurship and social responsibility.

Green emeralds...

After Carla had gone, things turned bleak for me. I couldn't hide my sense of horror at the exploitation that I'd witnessed. Raoul and Mama Luciana thought I was a naïve bleeding heart for my feelings. They had a point; in many ways, I had led a sheltered life. At the time, I simply hadn't realised just how many of the goods thoughtlessly consumed by a privileged first world minority originate from children in the Third World sewing in Dickensian rag-trade sweatshops, from exploited agricultural labour and from workers toiling in unspeakable conditions in stinking tanneries or slaving for less than a dollar a day to produce $200 trainers for top brands.

Gradually, a state of alienation and barely-disguised antipathy grew between me and the Geyer Dos Santos family. At the same time, having miscarried, the decisive factor which had led me to go to Brazil with Raoul was no longer there. I took to spending less time in the business and more wandering aimlessly around the city, but I never felt comfortable there. I wanted to spend time downtown in the Geyer Dos Santos workshops, to escape from the apartment in order to observe the craftsmen who cut and polished the stones, working without masks, heedless of the dust they were breathing into their lungs. Raoul eventually indulged me and gave me a quick tour, but made it clear he didn't want me hanging around there, carping on about poor working conditions and pauper pay.

Before going to Brazil, the poetic name of the city, Belo Horizonte, Portuguese for 'beautiful horizon,' had conjured up National Geographic visions of Edenic natural beauty. Raoul had further fanned the flames of this little fantasy of mine by telling me that Beagá, as locals affectionately call it, was known as the Barcelona of Brazil. I had been to Barcelona, so my expectations were high, but I was soon disillusioned. The city is surrounded by hills, but on the day of our arrival, they were invisible because of the smog. I was surprised to discover that here as well as in Rio, the rich apparently preferred to live in the centre of the town while the poor lived in *favelas;* vast, dense slums that straggled up the surrounding hillsides. If nothing else, the poor enjoyed a great view. That is, whenever a merciful wind chose to liberate the city from the industrial smog that plagued it. Raoul did once or twice drive me, on a clear day, to a large park in the nearby Serra do Curral mountains from which there was indeed a great view of the city, but somehow Beagá and I never did hit it off. Granted, downtown it had some imposing and beautiful wide tree-lined avenues – after all, this was a place that had had been conceived a century ago on an architect's drawing board, carefully planned to impress – but it seemed soulless to me. Brazil's third largest city struck me as an anonymous conglomeration of skyscrapers without a great deal of character. It was completely at odds with my naïve expectation of the country as a land of endless carnival, samba rhythms, uninhibited sensuality and carefree joie de vivre. I'm still not sure to what extent my feelings towards the city were in fact coloured by my increasingly tense relationship with Raoul and his family. Would we have had a better shot at our relationship had we lived, say, in Salvador de Bahia or Rio?

Somehow, I doubt it. It might just have bought us a bit more time before the inevitable split.

A little short of six months after my arrival, I reached a point where I could no longer see any reason to prolong my stay. My relationship with Raoul had grown cold and turned antagonistic and his mother, by then once more actively involved in the business, made it clear that she didn't much care for me and my inconvenient, unworldly liberal scruples. Presided over by the imperious Mama Luciana, the two-storey penthouse with its pool, tennis court, gym, helipad and bevy of servants was sucking the oxygen out of me. I grew to loathe the luxury apartment block in downtown Savassi, bristling with CCTV and armed guards. I left Brazil, barely on speaking terms with Raoul, icily farewelled by Luciana and driven to the airport by a frail but kind, cough-racked Ernesto. I flew to London and then to Athens, heading on impulse for the Greek islands with all my possessions in a little red rucksack. I badly needed to rethink my future. It was, I told myself, high time to stop being a passenger in other people's lives and get behind the steering wheel of my own.

20ᵀᴴ OCTOBER 2008

'Coffee or wine? We've got some decent Bordeaux.'

'Hmmm?'

Rhys grins. Corkscrew in one hand, bottle in the other, he's looking over my shoulder.

'Oh, er coffee. I'm on a roll. Wine will make me dopey.'

'I can see that. Your keyboard's going to go up in smoke.'

An exaggeration, of course. It's taken me almost a week to write these few pages about Munich and Brazil, with constant breaks for doodling, frequent bouts of bursting into tears and being comforted by Astrid, and long phone calls with Gerry, Ewa and Mother in London. I have bent Astrid's picture frame wire into all manner of shapes, indulged in unnecessary dog-walking, too much coffee-making and other self-sought distractions and displacement activities. Still, writing about the events of the 1980s is comparatively easy, because there is no need to shape them. Salient events have already undergone that transformation which occurs when we tell others about the episodes of our life, selecting, editing, filtering, slanting, embroidering, creating jukebox records. Press a given button and out pops the story, already formed, faceted, polished, shining, ready to be retold, cleansed of all inconvenient complexities and unflattering revelations. But wait, I don't want that smoothness. Catharsis requires truthfulness, which requires that the original flaws remain.

If Belo Horizonte had been relatively cool in July, when I left, Greece was stifling. In Athens, the very young, the infirm and the elderly were dying of heatstroke and pollution, but on the Cycladic islands you could always find a cooling breeze. I'd been on Sifnos some six weeks and had got myself a job in the hill fort village of Kastro, serving behind the bar at night in a busy little taverna. I also made some money sketching charcoal portraits, doing watercolours of village scenes and making basic jewellery out of leather, beads and shells, just enough to stay the right side of the breadline. I found the escape from the gilded cage of GDS's ill-gotten wealth utterly liberating.

It was late afternoon and I'd been for a swim. This was both fun and a necessity, given the limitations of my little rented room with its creaky, lumpy bed - (*Room Δωμάτιο Zimmer Chambre* announced the hand-written sign outside the village house.) It had only the most primitive plumbing and the water supply, from a whining hiccoughing tap, was at best intermittent. I was sitting topless on a sloping rock – there was no-one else around in that inaccessible little cove – carefully pouring fresh water from a plastic bottle over my short, salt-caked, sun-bleached hair and combing it through with my fingers when I became aware of a snorkeler. Every now and then a glistening head plastered with dark hair would surface, followed by deeply-tanned shoulders, before plunging back into the glassy depths. He – for it was a man – seemed to be looking for something under the rocks.

I was about to don my bikini top and pick my way back up the precipitous rocky path when he emerged from the turquoise waters, pushing back his mask and shaking his head, the droplets fanning out of his hair into little rainbows.

'Lorelei!' he bellowed, followed by something in German. He had an extraordinarily resonant voice which echoed around the rocks.

I shook my head. Once again I was being mistaken for German. It happened all the time in Greece. 'I'm English!' I hollered back.

He swam towards my rock, found his footing in the shallows and rose out of the water, which now reached to his waist. A big man, this Poseidon, with a powerful, tanned torso. He looked at me more closely, as if disbelieving my non-Germanness, and grinned broadly, flashing very white teeth. He held a harpoon in one hand and with the other he tugged something slithery out of a net bag around his waist. It was an enormous octopus, its tentacles twisting and writhing.

'I vant to ask you if you would like to hev dinner and eat zis...er...*Krake?*' He was stuck for the word.

'Octopus?' I offered.

The following day was a Monday, which was also my night off at the taverna. Walter the snorkeler had told me he was staying with friends in a villa just outside the village. I had often walked past the place on my way to catch the KTEL bus to the main town of Kamares whenever I needed to do some shopping or simply felt the urge to spend a few hours in a more cosmopolitan and anonymous environment. From the road, all you could see was a high white wall overhung with abundant bougainvillea and a wide arch over a rather forbidding, high security sliding metal gate. Above the gate, lapis lazuli-coloured mosaic tiles spelled out the name Arcadia against a white background. This time, about to ring the bell, I noticed a dusty CCTV camera half hidden in the bushes, its round black eye trained on me. Not long after I had first arrived in Kastro, I had asked Nikos, my landlord, who the owners of this place were. 'Rich people from Athens.' he'd said, dismissively. '*Matsomeni. Poli plousi*,' he'd added, rubbing his forefinger and thumb together and pulling a face to indicate an obscene amount of drachmas.

Furious barking and growling erupted the moment I rang the bell. The dog was right behind the gate, poking its glistening snout under the gap, snapping and slavering, hungry for my feet.

'Fasold, *komm hier!*' boomed Walter's baritone. I could hear the dog whining and whimpering subserviently as it reluctantly obeyed.

'It's me, Vita,' I shouted.

'One moment. I just tie him up.'

Arcadia belonged to wealthy Athenians, the Doukas family, owners of a pharmaceutical company, whose daughter, Calliope, was a young lyric soprano with dreams of becoming the next Maria Callas. Her brother, the insufferably spoilt Dimitri, was a playboy who fancied himself a jazz musician with all the trimmings. Calliope had met Walter at a master class for aspiring opera singers held in Milan earlier that year, and had invited him to stay at the villa in the summer. It didn't take me long to suss out the situation. Walter was very good-looking; tall, well-built, dark-haired and hazel-eyed, and had the resonant voice of a god. Calliope was short, pear-shaped, chinless, and apart from a fine, if slightly reedy soprano, blessed with only one thing of beauty; lustrous thick long blue-black hair down to her waist. Nonetheless, she had obviously fancied her chances with Walter. Maybe she was used to getting her way, and had assumed that her wealth would more than compensate for her relative plainness. When Walter approached me with his octopus offer, he'd been staying there just over a week, and on his third night, he'd emerged from the shower to find a naked Calliope in his bed. She'd put a brave face on his polite rejection. He'd offered to leave but she had insisted that he stay on a little longer at Arcadia. No doubt she thought a little perseverance would eventually wear him down.

The three of them had, it seemed, grown a little weary of each other's company, and it was Dimitri who'd suggested that he and Walter go snorkelling, see what they could harpoon, and organise a seafood dinner to which they'd invite a few carefully selected tourists who happened to be staying in Kastro.

The gate slid open smoothly on its rails to reveal a leafy courtyard with tall fig trees and giant oleander bushes. Walter, in white jeans, matching T shirt and flip flops, a vision of nonchalant handsomeness, appeared from a car porch containing a trailer with a speedboat, next to which was a jumble of assorted water skis, windsurf boards and sails, wet suits, flippers and snorkels. He had tethered Fasold the devil Doberman with the spittle-flecked tongue and the gleaming fangs to a pole, and greeted me with a rather formal peck on the cheek, accepting my bottle of retsina with an amused – and I suspected vaguely patronising – smile. He led me towards the villa, a low, austere, blindingly white oblong, very much more Le Corbusier than Cycladic village architecture. It seemed from this side to consist of just one floor and looked quite unprepossessing, but as we entered it, I realised that it was wedge-shaped, built against a steep rocky hillside, so that from the other side it had three floors that gave onto a spectacular series of terraced gardens, culminating in one on a little promontory far below; the villa's very own private peninsula complete with interconnected turquoise swimming pools on three levels, carved into the rocks. It was to this lower terrace that he led me, down flights of steps alongside which ran a little waterfall, engineered to burble soothingly over a bed of pebbles. I mumbled something complimentary to him, and he replied with a dry laugh.

'Ha! Nice to be rich, ja? Well, zat's ze lucky boy over there!' Down below, an even more deeply tanned and very hirsute young man was lolling on a blue and white sun lounger, one foot dangling casually in the lowest and largest of the three pools. He had headphones on and was snapping his fingers and jerking his body to the music on his Walkman.

'Dimitri. Meet our first guest. This is Weeta.'

Dimitri tipped his headphones back and rose to greet me. Mock courteously, he kissed the back of my hand and clicked his bare heels together.

'*Guten Abend Fräulein. Möchten Sie spazieren gehen?*'

'Good evening. Actually I'm English...'

'Oh for God's sake, Dimmi, I told you!'

'Suits me, man, 'cos that's all the German I know. Learnt it from my old man. Sorry ma'am - didn't mean to offend.' This in an American accent.

I loathed Dimitri almost immediately. His greedy, lazy, heavy-lidded eyes were all over me, as if copulation in the near future was already a done deal. At nearly six foot tall, I towered over him, but that did not seem to put him off. I had to fight the urge to push him backwards into his own swimming pool and run all the way back up the steps, through the house, past the devil dog, through the gate and up the dusty path back to my little room in the village. Walter must have sensed my unease and asked me if I'd like a glass of champagne. Just then, we heard the Doberman barking again.

'That'll be the others. Your turn zis time, Dimmi.'

'It's so far,' whined Dimitri, in the voice of a spoilt little child, but off he went, nonetheless, slowly trudging his way up the many steps. I looked at Walter. He was twisting the wire off a bottle of Krug.

'This ... I ... er. . I don't feel comfortable here,' I said, or some such, but my words got lost in the pop of the cork and I watched its trajectory as it plummeted into the darkening Aegean. Walter poured me some of the fizzing pale yellow stuff and clinked his glass against mine.

'Thank you for coming. I'm sorry if the host is a bit ... unmannered. He's OK really, but stupid wiss vimmin.'

I sipped the bubbles and began to feel slightly less edgy.

Not long after, Dimitri reappeared with two Swedes and a French-Canadian girl in tow, all of whom I recognised from the taverna. The Swedes had been in the village about a week and shared a room in my landlord's cousin's house. I had assumed they were gay, as they were always together. They were utterly beautiful; Lars a Nordic God with curly white blond hair and the palest ice-blue eyes; Björn less obviously Nordic, with a pensive, finely sculpted face and dark, brooding, restless eyes. Both were keen wind surfers and divers, and their bodies had been buffed and bronzed by more than two months of travelling around the islands. The girl, Marie-Hélène, was an art student who spent a lot of time sketching scenes in and around the village. She too was beautiful, and looked as if she might be part native American, with green eyes, delicate features and sleek, very straight long dark hair. I wondered if Walter had been sent out by Dimitri with a sort of human shopping list.

We all stood around rather awkwardly as corks popped and more champagne was poured. The Swedes were not great talkers, though highly appreciative of the invitation and unashamedly impressed by the villa and its location. I was chatting to Marie-Hélène when we became aware of a light, clear soprano singing 'Libiam', the opening aria from *La*

Traviata. It was Dimitri's sister, Calliope, theatrically descending the steps in a fluttering, gauzy, floaty white dress, a champagne glass raised in her right hand. One by one we stopped speaking as she approached. When she reached the lowest terrace, she fell silent, took a bow and smiled. We applauded and Dimitri whistled loudly, shouting '*Brava, Brava!*'

Walter filled her glass.

What happened after that? I do recall that the evening seemed never-ending, and that on several occasions I simply wanted to slip away unnoticed, but was at a loss how to get past the Doberman and out through the electronic gates. The alcohol flowed freely and the octopus in red wine was delicious, but the atmosphere was tense and ambiguous. Dimitri, ever drunker, didn't seem able to decide whether to hit on Marie-Hélène or Lars, and at one point had his arms round both of them. Björn was clearly not amused. Meanwhile Calliope was once again trying her luck with Walter, even feeding him selected titbits from her plate. He, however, was trying hard to pay attention to me while at the same time not offending Calliope, and kept attempting to engage the three of us in conversation. At some stage, Calliope claimed to be feeling unwell and insisted that Walter help her up the steps and back to the house. He raised his eyebrows at me, a semi-conspiratorial: *what's-a-man-supposed-to-do expression*, but did his gentlemanly duty and accompanied the wilting maiden up the steps and back to her quarters.

Meanwhile, Dimitri had produced some cocaine, rubbed it into his gums and passed it round for us to sample. I refused, as did Björn, who was concerned lest it should be adulterated with ground glass, but Marie-Hélène and Lars both took some. Dimitri then suggested that we should all go and sit somewhere more comfortable so we could really 'have some fun.' He got up and indicated an enormous wicker sun lounger the size of a generous double bed, strewn with scatter cushions. It was by the edge of the middle pool. Lars and Marie-Hélène followed, but Björn and I stayed at the table. We waited for Walter to reappear but as the minutes crawled past, nothing happened. 'Come and look at the stars with us, you guys,' shouted Dimitri, who'd sandwiched himself between Lars and Marie-Hélène as the three of them sprawled on the lounger. Björn looked at me, grim-faced. 'I don't like the way this is going,' he muttered.

At that moment, I had an idea.

'Dimitri, where do the steps lead? Do they go down to the water?'

'To a little beach. Our private beach.'

'Do you mind if we have a look?'

'Be my guest.'

And so Björn and I made our way down.

'We can swim to the next bay,' he whispered.

'Precisely what I had in mind.'

As it turned out, we didn't need to. There was a rubber dinghy on the little beach; the tender to the Doukas family yacht. We put our shoes in it and carefully lifted it up, to avoid making scraping noises over the pebbles, then lowered it very gently in the water. Björn slid the paddles through the rowlocks and off we went, silently gliding out of the little bay, paddling the dark waters and skirting the headland. We did not speak until we were well into the next bay, aware of how sound travels over water. We beached the dinghy and pulled it well clear of the shore, and then we just sat there for a while. Björn was clearly very upset. I put my arm around his shoulder at which he stiffened and let out a strangled sob. He and Lars had been lovers for two years, but Lars, he told me, swung both ways and could not resist indulging his hetero urges every now and then.

Björn pressed his fists into his eyes, trying to control himself. He finally let himself go, sobbed and wept. I rubbed his shoulders and he blubbed until he was exhausted.

I don't know how long we sat there – half an hour? One hour? Longer? Eventually we made our way back up the rock steps to the village and to our respective lodgings. It must have been very late, as the only sign of life was in the form of skinny, nervous cats, gambolling bats and geckos that staccatoed across the white walls in a manic dart-and-freeze dance under the wall-mounted street lights. I crashed out on my creaky little bed and was just drifting off to sleep when I was roused by a drum-roll of frantic knocks on my door.

'Weeta? Weeta, are you zere? Are you all right?' I was too angry to answer the door to Walter. I got up and opened the shutters a crack so I could speak to him through the window.

'Thenk Gott! You are OK. Is Björn OK? Is he wiss you?'

'He is extremely upset and no, he's not with me.'

'Weeta, I am so sorry.'

'That's too bad. You know, Walter, I am a human being. I am not some plaything for the amusement of bored rich people. Now please go away. I want to get some sleep.' I closed the shutters.

The following evening, Walter came and found me at the taverna. I was serving behind the bar and couldn't get away. I told him I didn't want to speak to him.

'Weeta, please. You must egzept my apologies. I have mooft out of the house. I have a room in the willage now.'

I poured him the Henninger he'd asked for, slid it across the counter with a little dish of olives and carried on serving other customers.

'Weeta, I am not like Dimitri.'

'Birds of a feather!' I shot back, but this got me a puzzled look. He didn't understand the expression.

'I meant that you can judge a person by the company he keeps. You were his guest.'

'Ectually, I was more Calliope's guest.'

I snorted. 'Yeah, and you must have known why she'd invited you.'

He sighed and moved to a corner, where he spent the rest of the evening morosely drinking until the early hours, when we closed the place. Then he, though wobbly on his legs, insisted on walking me home.

'Walter, what do you want from me?' I asked, exasperated.

'I want... I want to spend some time with you. I want to get to know you. I want you to know I'm not a ... decadent shit.'

'You mean you want to fuck me?'

'Of course I want to... fuck you, but that is not the main point.'

'At least you are honest. I like that. Good night.' And I ran off down the narrow alley that led to my little room, scattering scared skinny cats and zigzagging geckos.

Walter was a persistent suitor. He courted me assiduously at the taverna in the weeks that followed. Bit by bit my resistance crumbled. He sang to me – snatches from beautiful arias which, in my ignorance at that time of most things operatic, I failed to recognise. He harpooned another octopus, tenderised it by whacking it on a rock and cooked it for us in a large pan borrowed from the landlord's wife. He even went to Kamares and bought me a tiny gold dolphin on a chain. Adonis, my one-eyed boss at the taverna, couldn't stand it anymore: 'Please, please Vita. This man he try sooo hard to please you. Why you so hard with him? *Yiati, kouklamou?* Where is your heart? Do you have a heart or is it a stone? He is handsome, he is nice. He sing beautiful. He love you. What is your problem?'

My problem was my pride. That, and the fact that I was really rather enjoying my little game of hard-to-get. Yet in the end I gave in, and by mid-August, Walter had managed to persuade me to go to Munich and move in with him. It was not, frankly, as if I had any other plans. Once more, I was playing my life by ear and following a man against my better judgment. It proved to be a hard habit to break.

25ᵀᴴ OCTOBER 2008

'Mu-um?'

Tristan stoops in the kitchen doorway, in a paint-smeared T shirt and old jeans. He's been in Astrid's studio, doing his art homework, which seems to involve a kind of stream-of-consciousness doodling and writing down impressions and reactions to certain stimuli in a huge sketchbook. The theme is Rhythms and Cycles, which sounds like something from a biology textbook chapter about reproduction. It's all about the development of ideas rather than skills, from what I can gather. The stimulation of visual literacy. It seems you can do A-level art these days even if you can't draw to save your life. Oh dear, that sounds so *Daily Mail*...

I am worried by his exceptionally sickly pallor. At sixteen, my boy is already over six feet tall, his hair, a dark blond frizz, has grown back to a more normal length after he shaved off his precious dreadlocks in April. They had been his pride, and the shaving a true act of penance. Frizzy Afro hair apart, which can look pretty cool, especially when tamed with some gel, he is cursed with a jaw-dropping, rather androgynous beauty which attracts gay men. I fear for the safety of his rectum, though less so here in the wilds of Norfolk than in London, but I may well be deluding myself there. If he were gay, that would be another matter altogether, but he's just a tease. Or is he? What do I really know? Should it matter?

'What, darling?'

'Got'nee aspirin or paracetamol? I've got a splitting headache.'

'I'll get you some. Hang on a mo...'

I make my way to the bathroom. I have decided to keep the medicine chest locked, and I don't want Tris to know where I hide the key. Back in the kitchen, I hand him the tablets. He plinks them in a glass, fills it with water and watches them fizz.

'How's it going?' I ask.

'Yeah, good,' he says. He takes a gulp. 'I guess...' he adds, hesitantly. 'What're you writing?' he asks, glancing at my laptop.

'Oh, you know, stuff... about the past.'

'About Senta?'

'Eventually...'

'Ah...Well, I think I'll go to bed. Good night.'

He plods heavily up the creaking stairs.

What crap communicators we became, during his troubled years. Water boatmen, skating over the surface of the pond, ignoring the murk lurking beneath, the monsters in the muddy depths. And yet we used to be so close, he and I, before he reached his teens. Now, grief and guilt have reunited us, but still there is much he keeps to himself. Senta, on the other hand, my late enigma of a daughter, had always been a stranger. Gerry and I used to wonder by what genetic fluke we'd managed to produce such an extraordinary child. In fact, Senta took after Sven, my very tall Danish father, a brilliant civil engineer who'd married an elfin Englishwoman. This particular genetic combination had resulted in my own tall, willowy frame, but without one iota of my father's aptitude for science. By contrast, Astrid , who likewise missed out on the science gene, had inherited Mother's birdlike proportions and a magnification of her artistic talent, but absolutely nothing of Sven's physique other than his very startling cornflower blue eyes.

The genetic cards of scientific and mathematical aptitude along with extreme introversion had skipped a generation and jumped gender, dealt to Senta. She was serious, stubborn, studious to the point of being nerdy, outstanding at maths and the sciences and pathologically private. When quite young, she would often stare at me with what I interpreted as a mixture of curiosity and pity. To her rational, ordered Mensa mind, I must have been the scatty bohemian ignoramus from hell. I couldn't answer her questions. Without having to say anything, she had a way of making me feel that as a parent, I simply wasn't up to the mark, as if I were constantly being judged and found wanting. Her room was the only tidy one in the house, her clothes always fastidiously hung or folded in her wardrobe. Nobody taught her to do that. Not that she cared about the clothes themselves. It was tidiness and organisation that mattered.

In her teens, she had all but given up communicating with us. One day while she was out, when my frustration with her non-communication was at a peak, I went into her room and sat at her immaculate little IKEA desk, just trying to imagine what it was like to be her, trying to get some sense of her, looking for some kind of clue. I leafed through her binders and studied the neatly-written mathematical equations, the top grade physics projects, the beautifully-organised chemistry notes, all quite incomprehensible to my unscientific mind. On her bedside table, a copy of *The Fractal Theory of Nature* by Benoît Mandelbrot, which had been a Christmas present from Sven. Instead of feeling closer to her, I just sensed the chasm between us widening, deepening, becoming vast, unbridgeable. I felt I knew Riita, our Finnish au-pair at the time, better than my own daughter, and wondered where I had gone wrong. I had tried to discuss this non-communication with Gerry, but he was inclined to dismiss it as 'an Aspie teenage phase.' In truth, he was too involved with his thriving restaurant. De Vlaaminck had just been given fulsome praise by *Time Out* and made it into their top twenty of favourite London eateries. With the planning of a television series and tie-in cook book, as well as the possibility of following Jamie Oliver and Gordon Ramsay into the gastro-pub and multiple outlet business, he had neither time nor energy for family problems. He dealt with them by downplaying or ignoring them, leaving me to sort out the mess.

Senta...

How do I write about what happened to you and Toby? And Isobel? It is too raw still. Far too raw.

I will circle a little longer.

28TH OCTOBER 2008

Three days have passed since I wrote that last sentence. For those three days, I have been obsessively active, doing anything rather than sitting and thinking, sinking into gloom. I have taken old Doobie and Mutt, Astrid and Rhys's lurcher-like rescue mongrel, for long windswept, rain-lashed walks along the river and through the woods behind the farm. All the while I would be plugged into Senta's iPod, immersed in Mozart and Wagner from her playlist, allowing the strains to transport me back to my days in Munich, to focus on the past and blot out the pain and confusion of the present.

I spent a day in Norwich with Astrid, doing mindless grocery shopping and visiting the art gallery which exhibits her paintings and some of her smaller sculptures. Astrid, in her younger days the epitome of artistic eccentricity and whackiness, has returned, when not sculpting, to her old love of portrait painting, turning her back on the whole gimmicky contemporary Britart scene represented by the likes of Damien Hirst, Marc Quinn and Tracy Emin. She has long been disenchanted with the unholy trinity of certain collectors, dealer-gallery owners and museum directors who cynically collude to hype and so 'create' certain artists, artificially inflating the value of their stock. However, Astrid's recent portraits are hardly traditional. Of late, they have become increasingly abstract. So much so, in fact, that facial features have given way almost entirely to the representation of a person's perceived mood or character. A painting entitled:

Justin – Cool Anger, is a juxtaposition of the very finest brushwork, delicately detailing minutiae – an ear, a nostril, a fingernail – within an angry vortex of coarse swirls and splodges. 'Does he like it?' I ask, knowing Justin to be one of Marcus's friends.

'Dunno,' she says. 'He's way too cool to express his opinion.'

When I mentioned to Rhys over dinner that I'd got stuck trying to write about Senta, he offered again to look at my writing. It's obvious that he's bursting with curiosity. I tried to put him off as politely as possible. He makes me feel uneasy. Lecturer in Creative Writing, for God's sake...

'You'd inhibit me. You may think it's complete rubbish.'

If he was disappointed by this, he hid it well. He didn't try to change my mind.

'It's so hard to write about her in the past tense,' I tell him.

'Then don't. Use the present. That makes it vivid. Makes it come to life.'

'That's what I want to do. Bring her back to life.'

'Vita,' he sighs, 'that was insensitive of me. I'm really sorry.'

It is hard for people to know how to deal with another person's grief. I wonder how Toby's twin, Isobel, is coping with this. As far as I know, she is still in San Diego where her batty mother lives. She went back there immediately after the memorial service. What is worse, losing your daughter or losing your twin brother? I fear the latter may be even worse, as Toby and Isobel were exceptionally close. I emailed Isobel some months ago, just to say that if she wanted to talk to us, she should simply pick up the phone or come and see us if and when she returned to England. She replied to say she didn't know when she'd be coming back, but would let me know. She's taken time out from her doctoral research at Imperial. She was, as she put it, trying to hang in there. Her mother had persuaded her to have therapy with a specialised counsellor, but Isobel admitted that it hadn't worked for her, and had quit after a couple of sessions. The therapy best suited to her was physical exercise. In her email, she told me that she kept herself active by working out, running, rock climbing and kick boxing. Her mother had taken Toby's death very badly, and from what I could gather, it seemed that Isobel had to provide a great deal of support and consolation. 'You sure know who your friends are at times like this,' she wrote. 'People I thought would be sympathetic have just gone to ground, and others have been fantastic.'

I recognise that phenomenon all too clearly. Some friends tippy-toe around Gerry and me and carefully avoid any mention of the murders. Ironically, this only serves to make us more aware of the elephant in the room. Astrid, not at all talkative by nature, has on occasion suddenly felt the need to keep up a manically bright patter about any old subject that happens to pop into her head in a well-intentioned but misconceived attempt to lift my spirits. In the supermarket in Norwich the other day, this suddenly became unbearable. We were in the pet food section at Tesco's. I'd been feeling rather more down than usual and Astrid had been talking about some exhibition or other, trying to get me involved and enthused. I played along as best I could, my mounting frustration kept in check by my appreciation of her efforts to cheer me up. She picked up a tin of Pedigree Chum.

'Does Doobie like this stuff, or does she prefer something else?'

I stare at her.

'Vita?' She waggles the tin in front of my face. Without taking my eyes off her, I put my hand on hers and guide it slowly back to the shelf to replace the tin.

'It doesn't matter. Doobie will eat anything. For God's sake, stop wittering on!'

For a few seconds, she stares at me, then her bright blue eyes fill with tears. She covers her face with both hands.

'Veets, sometimes I don't know how to ... to deal with this... situation... I... just seem to be fucking things up for you, making you feel worse... I'm so sorry...'

'No, I'm sorry. That was rude of me. Really...' I put my arms around her. It's the first time I ever recall having to console my sister. We snuffle and sob, she weeps in my neck and I press my face into the familiar cannabis scent of her Medusa hair. She's almost a head shorter than me. We separate with an awkward movement and I knock my elbow against the special offer display of Pedigree Chum, which clatters to the ground. We scrabble around, chasing the tins as they roll in all directions. Astrid, on her knees, skinny bum in the air, is trying to retrieve one that has rolled under the shelves. It's a comical sight, and despite myself I start to laugh. She straightens up and looks at me, and her expression of confused astonishment gives way to a tentative smile which broadens into a grin. We are both laughing now; I am on my haunches and I lose my balance, toppling over and sending yet more tins clattering onto the floor. We find ourselves in the grips of pant-wettingly uncontrollable hysterical laughter, attracting furtive looks from fellow shoppers as they nervously push their trolleys past us and turn into the next aisle. A shop assistant, a rosy-cheeked young lad with a gingery bum fluff moustache, shambles over awkwardly and asks if we are alright, telling us not to worry about the tins because he'll pick them up and put them back, that's his job. He gives me a hand and pulls me to my feet. Astrid cannot stop laughing now and there are tears coursing down her cheeks. I help her up and thank the perplexed lad for his assistance. He stares at Astrid. 'You're that sculptor,' he says. 'I remember when you came and talked to us at school.'

'Shit!' she says later. 'This celeb business is really getting to me. I want my anonymity back!' A joke, of course, as hardly anybody outside the art world ever recognises her.

This little episode has brought home to me how much stress I am causing Astrid. Life at my sister's once peaceful farmhouse has been turned upside down, first with the arrival of Tristan, exiled from London back in April and then, some six weeks later, with his grief-sodden, touchy mother and her mood swings. I really should show more sympathy instead of sucking it all up for myself. I must remember that I'm not the only one who's grieving. Think of Isobel. She's only twenty-two... But I barely know her, and that makes it hard to think of her. There's so little for me to focus on. I don't really know what kind of person she is.

I do hope she gets in touch.

I've just spent an hour doing some drawings; recollections of Isobel as I remember her on the three occasions that I met her. The first, in charcoal, was at our house in Clapham one evening, about two years ago, when Isobel and Toby had come back with Senta for coffee after shopping at the farmers' market. Isobel was sitting on the sofa, next to Toby, and both were clutching mugs in an identical pose, two-handedly. Two separate young adults, but still somehow cocooned together by the ghost of a womb. They were about as identical as non-identical opposite sex twins can possibly be, with the same thick floppy dark hair, worn shoulder length. They had perfect white Californian teeth and large brown eyes, except that Toby wore wire-rimmed glasses. There was a wholesome, athletic look about them, with their glowing clear skin. When they stood up, there was quite a height difference between them, with Toby a good six inches

taller, but still shorter than Senta, who, at over six foot, was cursed with the Rasmussen-Steeneken height gene.

The middle drawing was more difficult. I switch to my Rotring pen. This is the Isobel whom I saw in King's Hospital, Camberwell, on April 4th 2008, just after we'd undergone the ordeal of identifying the bodies. It was afterwards, when she was sitting next to Gerry, holding the polystyrene cup of stewed tea a well-meaning nurse had handed to her. She was completely dazed and her hands were trembling as she stared into space. Gerry was on the phone to her father, who was at Frankfurt airport, about to board a plane. Isobel seemed to have lost the power of speech, even the power to cry or sob, and when her father had called her on her mobile, she'd simply handed it to Gerry. She sipped the tea mechanically, again cradling the cup with both hands. She looked like an automaton, malfunctioning for lack of battery power. I have tried to recapture that strange dazed look, that suspended animation. Astrid would have done it a million times better, but Astrid wasn't there.

My third panel shows Isobel on April 12th at Honor Oak crematorium. During the service, she went to pieces and whimpered eerily. She was sitting between her divorced parents, who had each placed an arm around her shoulder, her mother's arm resting lightly on top of her father's. I was diagonally behind her, with Gerry and Tristan. I was afraid she'd do something crazy, throw herself at Toby's coffin or start to

scream, but it was just the animal-like whimpering, a distress that could find no comfort in the brief eulogy, that probably didn't even take in what was being said. This is how I have tried to draw her – the backs of three heads and shoulders, her head slightly inclined towards her balding father, away from her mother's dishevelled blonde bun with its grey roots, the parents' arms trying to give succour to her and to each other.

There was an incident afterwards. Somehow the paparazzi had got wind of the funeral – to this day I don't know how – and saw their chance to make a bit of money out of celebrity misery. The murders had of course been all over the papers. 'Don't react. Don't look up,' Astrid had whispered as we left the crematorium.

Just then, one of them shouted something at Tristan. 'Hey Tristan, how does it feel to be...' Tristan, newly shaven-headed, flared up and shouted 'Fuck off, scumbag!' He lunged out at the man, smashing a fist into his camera. Gerry grabbed Tristan and quickly manhandled him into the black limousine that was waiting for us. And that, of course, was the photo that made it to the front pages of the red tops the following day.

Last night I overheard a snatch of conversation between Astrid and Rhys. They were in the kitchen, he washing the stuff you can't put in the dishwasher, she drying, both with their backs to me. After I'd gone to bed, I had an overwhelming urge to speak to Gerry, so I came padding down the stairs barefoot to retrieve my mobile which I'd left on the kitchen table. They didn't hear me.

A '...to write it down is such a good idea. Everyone has a different way of dealing with death and grief. Yours is writing because that's your thing, but I'm not so sure it's the best way for her. You've no idea how upset she's been these last couple of days. Writing about Senta is just tearing everything open again instead of letting it heal.'

R: 'You don't heal by ignoring things...'

A: 'Yeah, but a wound doesn't heal if you keep scratching at the scab.'

R: 'I won't bug her about the writing, then. Just let it fizzle out. Leave it up to her. Don't want her to think she should do this just to please me, for Christ's sake!'

A: 'I've already suggested that she might like to do some painting. I've set up an easel for her in the studio, but she seems to prefer drawing, doodling. It's quite good, actually'

R: 'What, the writing? You've read it?'

A: 'God no, some of the drawings. I haven't a clue about the writing.'

I tiptoe back upstairs to the guest bedroom and the huge double bed and check the time. It's gone eleven; the rush hour will be long over at De Vlaaminck. In fact, when he answers his mobile, Gerry has just got back to Clapham and is next door at Ewa's. Since my move to Wensum, Gerry has not wanted to spend time alone in our house, so he has been staying next door with Ewa and Salvatore in one of Ewa's spare rooms. Strange how our life as a couple has gone full circle. After a brief exchange of news; problems with the over-familiarity of one of the new waiters, the performance of the new Hobart dishwasher, the dreaded imminent Health and Safety inspection, there is a silence, and we both start to cry. In the first months after Senta's death, this was the way all our calls went. Recently, we've been able to manage the odd call without blubbing, but we are both feeling raw at the moment. It waxes and wanes, this grief, much like my hot flushes and attacks of sweating, and it is as unpredictable as it is uncontrollable.

My bedroom door opens and Tristan comes in. He is wearing a pair of his cousin Marcus's pyjamas. He's heard me talking. I hand the mobile to him and he chats to Gerry about this and that, about school, about an art competition which he hadn't mentioned to me. We are only just beginning to appreciate that he has considerable artistic talent. In our family, everybody can draw or paint to some extent, ranging from the ultra-talented Astrid through to mother and myself, and including Gerry who, though completely untrained, does a nice line in illustrating his hand-written menus with highly idiosyncratic drawings. Senta too could draw, though it was always photographically representational. Her diagrams and technical drawings were of a superhuman accuracy. Anyway, this is one of the reasons why Tristan's talent had seemed like no big deal. Yet of late, with Astrid's encouragement and positive, supportive noises from his art teachers at school, he is spending more and more time in his aunt's studio. He has been producing some rather striking, if disturbing work; Picasso-ish body shapes, contorted and haunting, but also beatific renaissance Madonna faces. I can hear Gerry making the required parental feedback noises, encouraging, soothing, praising. I know how difficult Gerry finds it to do this, how he has to struggle to overcome his resentment of Tristan. When the call is over, Tris curls up into a ball on the bed.

'Mind if I stay here?'

I stroke his woolly hair.

'Of course not, my love. Get under the covers.'

This is by no means unusual, though Tristan likes to keep up the pretence that it is. His excuse is that his frequent nightmares wake Marcus, whose bedroom he officially shares. Usually he waits till Marcus has fallen asleep before slinking out of the room and into my bed. Very early in the morning he reverses the process, before Marcus wakes up. He would hate his cousin to think he's a mama's boy. Little does he know that Marcus is fully aware of it and has mentioned it to Astrid, who has told me.

Astrid has sworn Marcus to secrecy, and as far as I know, Marcus has kept his word. He's a real brick, with a maturity well beyond his years.

30ᵀᴴ OCTOBER 2008

What *is* going on in Tristan's head these days? Although communication has improved, I still find it hard to tell. We have all tried so hard to assuage his feelings of guilt, but I'm not at all sure that we have convinced him, maybe because we are not entirely convinced ourselves. He won't talk about it – that's his way of dealing with it, but he has these screaming, sweating, thrashing, panic-riddled nightmares, and has taken to making slashes on his thighs and upper arms with a razor blade. He sees a therapist in Norwich once a week, but whenever I ask him how things are going, he just shrugs or mumbles something non-committal. Marcus won't divulge anything to me about Tristan's state of mind either. It is hard to tell whether this is out of a sense of loyalty to Tristan or just a male unwillingness to discuss emotions. Some months ago, when the self-harm business first came to light, I asked Marcus if Tristan had talked to him about it.

'It doesn't help, you know.'

'Talking doesn't help?' I say, incredulous.

'He doesn't want to talk about it. Not to me, anyway. Maybe to the shrink. I don't know. Or maybe to Lucy.'

Then he went out to feed the hens, and I heard the sound of Tristan practising riffs on his bass guitar. I wish he'd find himself some band mates at school.

Tomorrow I have a meeting with his teachers. I only hope they haven't given up on him. However, we do have a fall-back plan – Astrid has offered to tutor him through his A-Levels in

Art and Art History, and Rhys and I between us can help him with his A-level English, but it's hardly ideal. What we really want for him, and what we've been counselled to do, is to keep him in a school environment to have the social contact and distraction that comes from being with his peers. Cooped up with us at Wensum all the time would not be conducive to psychological health and healing.

Fingers crossed.

1ST NOVEMBER 2008

Meeting nowhere near as bad as I had feared. Tristan came along, most reluctantly. He hates this kind of thing and so does his mother, as I know that I too am under scrutiny and my performance will be discussed and graded afterwards. Would I get a B Minus? Or a C Plus? We assemble at a round table in the Headmaster's study; Dr Stanton, Miss Critchley, Ross Henderson and Joshua Kellerman. Henderson and Hannah Critchley were very complimentary about Tristan's artistic talent. Kellerman was less effusive about T's performance in his English lit. classes. It's the usual story – lack of discipline, an inability to meet deadlines, difficulty in concentrating, very good essays alternating with very poor ones. Still, he appears to be holding his own, and is polite and pleasant to his teachers. I decide not to mention the fact that this very politeness, as noted at his previous school, is a trick of his to keep them off his back. The general opinion is that he seems fragile but is just about coping.

Tris was twitchy and monosyllabic whenever they tried to involve him in the discussion. He suddenly seemed alarmingly immature, arms folded defensively, hugging himself. Afterwards he told me he felt he was being dissected, like a lab rat. I know the feeling.

What a contrast with his sister. How can two siblings turn out to be so totally different?

In the last five or six years of her life, Senta had become more and more interested in all things ecological and environmental, and gradually our back garden in Clapham had been turned into a miniature organic farm which she tended in all weathers and with her characteristically dogged dedication. The rose bushes and herbaceous border plants were ruthlessly replaced with rows of cabbages, runner beans and tomatoes. I rather resented it at first. The lovely old eglantine was uprooted and the bed along the south-facing garden wall was planted with brambles and raspberries. Right at the back of the garden, she hammered together a hen-house with a fifteen-foot run which was soon inhabited by three light Sussex hens, a present from Astrid and Rhys.

With this little farm to look after, it should hardly have come as a surprise to us that Senta showed no inclination to leave home and set up on her own once she had graduated, something which I had secretly hoped she would do. I should have known better, for Senta loved nothing more than the security of routine, continuity and all things familiar. She managed to persuade Gerry and me to buy as much produce as possible from the Clapham farmer's market every Sunday instead of enriching her pet hate, the supermarket chains. We went along with it because we did not have a convincing argument against it. We could afford it and as I worked from home, I was not able to resort to the excuses of many of our friends who worked long office hours and for whom low cost and the convenience of the supermarkets won a guilty victory over environmental correctness.

Having sailed through her bachelor's degree with a First, Senta was awarded a doctoral research scholarship by Imperial. At the end of her first post-graduate year, in the summer of 2006, she got to know the Hobbs twins, who were similarly involved in research into global warming and its effects on the Greenland ice sheet. The following summer, they did part of their research together with scientists from the University of

Washington in that most inhospitable part of the world. The findings, which indicated that glaciers were indeed moving faster, were alarming, if hardly surprising.

Gerry and I were delighted that Senta finally seemed to have formed a real friendship. She took to spending more and more time with Toby and Isobel Hobbs, who were both members of the Unitarian Church. Senta, the ultra-rational scientist, daughter of parents who simply took atheism for granted as self-evident and who thought rather dismissively of the religious as deluded eccentrics, became interested in Unitarianism.

Much to our astonishment, she would make the journey to the Unitarian Church in Kensington every Sunday and meet up with the Hobbs twins. When we quizzed her about this, she was cagey, reluctant to give much of an explanation. 'Just interested,' she'd say, with a dismissive shrug. Was this the price of friendship with Toby and Isobel? No doubt it was a factor, but we also gradually gathered from the crumbs of conversation she would occasionally dole out that she was searching for a moral compass, and Unitarianism, this broadest, most tolerant, most inclusive of churches, was simply the closest fit she'd been able to find to date, having already investigated Buddhism, Secular Humanism and various other faith-isms. She'd been shaken by the death of Sven, her grandfather and mentor, in March of 2007, and had become even more than usually withdrawn. The Unitarian Church seemed to fill some kind of gap.

Gerry and I were puzzled and concerned. In our ignorance, we had originally confused the Unitarian Church with the Unification Church of the loony Moonies. Was she in the process of being suckered into some sinister cult which had sniffed out her state of heightened vulnerability? Her reluctance to explain Unitarianism to us did not help, partly I suspect because she knew it would not sit well with our deeply-held secular values. It was then that I started to read up on Unitarianism on the internet, and realised that I had got it completely wrong. This was no cult, but rather an ultra-enlightened, liberal form of Christianity which rejected the concept of the trinity and shunned both creed and formula. Unitarians see no contradiction between science and faith – indeed, they see them as complementary, and it was easy to see how this view would have appealed to Senta. She took to spending more and more time with Toby and Isobel, Tobybel or Isotobe, as Tristan nicknamed them, and when she did come home, she would withdraw even more than usual into silence and keep to her room.

Gerry and I knew we had to make allowances for her Asperger's and found ways of working around it as much as possible. Tristan, however, found it exasperating and often refused to indulge her. 'You taken some vow of silence, like a Trappist nun or somefink?' he said to her one day.

'Trappists are monks, for your information,' she had snapped back. 'The nuns are known as *Trappistines*.'

'Oh look, everybody, it *speaks*. It has a *tongue*,' he had taunted her, pulling a face. But Senta would have regained her composure by then and gone back to her usual habit of ignoring her brother.

Just as Gerry and I had reached the nadir of despair with her non-communication, she started to change. It is one of the many things I now wish I could discuss with Isobel, as she might be able to tell us how this transformation came about. It's as if Senta had suddenly decided to become a normal human being and impose a complete personality change on herself. Did this have a religious base? I think so, but again, I can't be sure. We had become so used to not asking personal questions for fear of pushing the wrong buttons that it proved a hard habit to break. What is more, Gerry and I were convinced that Senta would not be able to keep it up. Still, we marvelled at the apparent thaw it had brought about in her relationship with us. She became less judgmental, less severe, more humble, altogether more human, though I could never quite shake off the feeling that she somehow still regarded us as lesser beings, now worthy of her compassion and indulgence instead of her distant intellectual disdain. She had simply opted for a different way of dealing with us. Was Toby in any sense her boyfriend? Again, only Isobel would know now. I have no idea and neither Gerry nor I has ever dared ask Senta, for fear of getting one of her old death ray looks. Tristan, on the other hand, had rather foolishly taken to baiting her – he found the new user-friendly Senta even harder to cope with than the original – and on such occasions, a flash of the old sarky Senta could suddenly flare up.

'That Yank who was here the other day, is he your boyfriend, then?' Tris was foolish enough to ask one day when the three of us were having dinner together. At first, Senta didn't reply, pretending not to have heard.

'Well?'

'Well what?'

'Is he?' he persisted.

'Is he *what*?'

'Your boyfriend! Do you sleep with him? Do you have S.E.X?'

'I don't see how that's any of your business.'

He mimicked her haughty tone, but she ignored him.

'God, you're so fucking... prissy!'

'Lovely fish pie, Mum,' she said to me.

Tristan glowered at her with loathing and frustration. I seem to recall that he pushed his plate away and thundered off upstairs to his room, muttering curses, while Senta continued to eat in her careful, infuriatingly measured, chew-every-mouthful-twenty-times way.

'Do you have to snub him like that, darling?'

'Mum! My private life is really none of my nosy prurient little brother's business.'

Well, she did have a point.

Senta... she could be very difficult to deal with, even in her newly compassionate Unitarian incarnation. Whenever I asked her about her research, she would reply politely, much as one might make conversation with an elderly, senescent and none too bright maiden aunt. There were many times when I wanted to scream at her, to shake her and beg her to be natural, to drop the façade, to open up, but I knew that this would only bring on a massive anxiety attack. It was because of her neurological condition, I would console myself, but I never quite believed the diagnosis of mild autism. High Functioning Asperger's, they called it later. It made her sound like a sophisticated robot rather than a human being. Deep down I remained irrationally convinced that it was all my fault and that I had somehow failed to find a way into her because I hadn't tried hard enough.

Senta, solitary Senta, my unfathomable Aspie Lite of a daughter, my eternal enigma. Composed, aloof, saddled with an alienating IQ, a prisoner of her own brilliance.

3ʳᵈ NOVEMBER 2008

I've fashioned a miniature bird cage out of a length of Astrid's picture wire, complete with tiny door. The bottom consists of an inverted crown cork. Too big for an earring and an awkward shape for a brooch. Could hang it in a Christmas tree. I'll make a little swing perch inside it and leave the door open.

Rhys came home this evening with a brand-new 42-inch plasma screen TV to replace the little old telly which has been on the blink for some months now. I have in fact been existing – not unhappily – in a TV vacuum since the summer and have taken to reading the online edition of the broadsheets. Astrid, Rhys and the boys have TV in their bedrooms, but with the US elections imminent and all the excitement surrounding the ever greater likelihood of an Obama victory, Rhys wants to involve the boys more in world politics and current affairs, and stop them from disappearing upstairs to play mindless computer games and watch dumb programmes as soon as they have finished eating. Astrid, however, insists on the TV being switched off while we eat, so the plan is that from now on, we all gather round the table and watch the evening news together, then have dinner, which is mainly prepared by me. What I can see happening, though, is that the boys will prefer this flash new television to their own, and will spend the rest of the evening in the kitchen, channel hopping. This means I will no longer have the peace and quiet that I need to concentrate on writing after dinner. I know I shouldn't grumble, as I have the daytime to write in, but more than ever I crave a study of my own. I've tried typing in the bedroom before, at the little old dressing table by the window, and I've even taken the laptop to bed, but I like the homeliness of the kitchen, the warmth, the big table, the nearness of Astrid and the easy access to coffee. Let's hope that the novelty soon wears off.

MUNICH, MID-SEPTEMBER 1983

Back to my rudderless past, so different from the way Senta would have led her life, had fate granted her the opportunity. I'd just taken the ferry from the Cycladic dream island of Sifnos to the grim, industrial Athenian port of Piraeus. From there I travelled by underground to the sweaty chaos of Athens airport and flew to the silent Teutonic efficiency of Munich-Riem. Walter was at the airport to meet me with an old-fashioned beribboned bouquet of flowers. Munich was looking particularly seductive, as autumn had started to tint the many trees in shades of russet and gold.

Walter had a few more weeks of holiday before he had to be back at university for what he hoped was his final year of an economics degree he'd started eight years before at the age of twenty. I found it rather odd that he should still be studying, given that most students in Britain graduate in their early twenties, but in Germany the system was very different. For a start, first degrees were much longer, so studying for five or six years was not unusual. In addition, Walter would take time out every now and then to pursue his career and gain experience as a singer by going on tours with a travelling opera company. The degree in economics had been his father's precondition for supporting his only son's musical aspirations, but Walter, who did not lack academic ability, hated economics and frequently had to retake his exams. Still, in many ways he did lead a life of considerable privilege. His paternal grandparents had left his parents a beautiful sunny apartment in Haidhausen, a trendy residential area of central Munich. The parents, however, were already comfortably ensconced in a villa in exclusive leafy suburban Grünwald, so Walter ended up as the fortunate occupant of the three-bedroom apartment. He did have a lodger to help with the bills, but gave him notice just before my arrival. The price we had to pay for this privacy was poverty. We were flat broke at the start of our time together in Munich, and Walter was reduced to selling his car, an old VW Beetle, to tide us over.

Those early weeks were wondrous, despite the shortage of money. When we weren't in bed, making love, we were out and about, cycling around a radiant, sunny Munich as Walter introduced me to the magic of the English Gardens and the crystal-clear Isar, quite the most miraculously clean river I have ever seen run through any city. In the beer garden under the Chinese Tower, we ate huge salty pretzels and quaffed quantities of Weissbier served by strapping waitresses whose heaving bosoms were precariously contained in tight Dirndl frocks, while we listened to big beefy Bavarians in *Lederhosen* playing their traditional oom-pah music on highly-polished tubas, trumpets and clarinets. Everywhere we went, we would bump into Walter's cousins, old school friends and acquaintances, for Walter was a native *Münchner*.

I was enthralled by it all at first; Munich was so orderly, so clean, so beautiful, and in those aspects so very different from the places I'd lived in since leaving England. Unlike Brazil, there wasn't the undertow of casual violence, the constant fear of being mugged out on the streets, the stark difference between the rich, in their high security bastions safely isolated from the rest of humanity, and the poor in their slums. The centre of the city in particular had something of a film set appearance about it, a toy town with pristine chocolate-box building façades which looked as if they had only just been built and freshly painted. Nearly all of it was in fact post-war reconstruction in the original style, hence the strange new-oldness of the place, but in the suburbs too, many of the buildings were immaculate. '*Sanierung*,' Walter explained to me. This was the process of renovating anything that looked even vaguely dilapidated, ripping out all the old fittings and replacing plumbing and wiring. The result was buildings that looked brand new because they had undergone a kind of age-defying plastic surgery, yet retained many of the architectural features of their original epoch. There was something disconcerting about it.

In late September, I had my first experience of live opera. Mindful of the fact that he was dealing with a complete novice, Walter had carefully chosen something he thought would win me over and hopefully whet my appetite for more. He was in the habit of going to almost every opera performed in Munich, often making do with the gods, where there were some very cheap seats from which you couldn't even see the stage. Listening seats for the penniless but truly dedicated. However, for this special occasion, he had somehow got hold of two excellent seats on the balcony. The opera he'd chosen for my initiation to the art to which he hoped to dedicate his life was *The Magic Flute.* He had played me recordings of it in the flat and serenaded me with some of Papageno's arias, so when the curtain rose, I was already familiar with the strange nonsensical story and some of its divine music.

It was an irresistible seduction. I sat, spellbound, in the midst of my epiphany, as Wolfgang Brendel's Papageno clowned around in his costume of feathers, but when the Slovakian coloratura soprano Edita Gruberova, the Queen of the Night, sang her *Eine Holle Rache* aria vertically spread-eagled in a huge hoop, precariously suspended above the stage, I felt tears well up at the unearthly beauty of her voice. Her notes were taut threads of pure spun crystal, radiating from her mouth. I had not realised that the human larynx was capable of producing such gorgeous sound, such perfection and at such amazing volume. Only later did I find out that Gruberova was considered to be one of the greatest interpreters of the role, and none of the many subsequent productions I have seen, including ones at Covent Garden, has ever come near to thrilling me as much as that one did. I was hooked, and back in the flat I listened again and again to Walter's 1960's recording with the rich, confident voices of Elizabeth Schwarzkopf and Walter Berry. I read the libretto, learnt the lyrics and puzzled over the nonsense of the tale. I even tentatively tried out my own voice when nobody was around, and wondered if it could be trained to produce a better sound, but concluded that sadly it really didn't have the makings of anything more than a quavering schoolgirl soprano.

The university semester started, and Walter reluctantly resumed his studies. We were so broke by the end of that month, as the paltry monthly allowance that Walter received from his father was intended to be topped up by rent from a flatmate, that we had to sacrifice our precious privacy. And so we were joined by an old school friend of Walter's named Günter, who was studying at TUM, Munich's prestigious technical university. His rent put food on our table and helped to pay the utility bills, but precious little besides, and I was beginning to get twitchy. I wanted to get a job but was hampered by my lack of German, which I hadn't touched since a very mediocre O-level twelve years earlier. I couldn't even apply for the humblest of jobs without at least a working knowledge of the language, so I set about brushing it up with great determination. I watched hours of bad German television. Soap operas were especially useful because they were rich in dialogue, and Dallas dubbed in German was a favourite, because the uptight and formal-sounding German sounded so comically wrong coming out of relaxed Texan mouths made for drawling. I also listened to banal talk shows on local radio and diligently pored over grammar books, reacquainting myself with the prepositions governing the dative and accusative. That aside, I dutifully prepared thrifty, dull but worthy meals out of brown rice, lentils, nuts and raisins in an effort to make ends meet.

That month we saw *The Marriage of Figaro*, and once again, Walter had prepared me well by playing me extracts from his recordings. I loved it, but not quite as much as *The Magic Flute*, possibly because we had lousy seats way up in the gods, which were all we could afford. Walter had a large LP collection of opera recordings by illustrious singers and famous conductors past and present. Apart from listening over and over to the *Flute* and *Figaro*, I tried to listen to *Tristan and Isolde*, both for the German and in order to understand what it was Walter was so passionate about, for his greatest love was Wagner, not Mozart or the Italians. However, appreciation of Wagner eluded me and I told Walter that it just sounded like a bullying, hysterical, bombastic assault of sound with no clear beginning or ending. This earned me a rueful smile. 'Don't listen to Wagner yet,' he advised. 'You're not ready. That time will come.' He wouldn't elaborate and this annoyed me, but I took his advice and started on Verdi and Puccini instead, putting my Wagnerian experiment on hold.

It wasn't long before I became seriously restless and frustrated by our penury. One evening Günter's elder sister, Ulrike, complimented me on a lapis lazuli bead necklace that I was wearing and which I had assembled myself. I explained that I used to make simple craft jewellery when I lived in Greece and had also learnt a thing or two about the gem trade while in Brazil. I knew how to assemble stuff; nothing highly skilled, just working with beads, shells, leather and wire, with a pair of pliers as my main tool. She mentioned that she was a self-employed silversmith and so, through this fortuitous encounter, the next chapter in my life began.

Ulrike worked out of a cousin's garage which she had turned into a workshop. It was in an unfashionable and rather drab suburb of Munich called Giesing, near a cemetery. She specialised in hollowware, making objects like vases, bowls, wine goblets, teapots and milk jugs, but she also did repairs and occasionally made items of jewellery. Some of it was work for retailers, but quite a lot was directly commissioned by customers. She'd been in the business for more than fifteen years then, had a well-established customer base and made a good living out of it, not least because only a fraction was ever declared to the tax man. Three times a week I would cycle out there and spend the day with her, helping her with routine cleaning and polishing of silver teapots and other antique heirlooms that she was restoring or plating. In this way, I did a sort of unofficial apprenticeship as she showed me how to work with silver. Ulrike was congenial, generous with both her time and her knowledge, enormously talkative and not particularly at home in English, so I was exposed to large doses of Bavarian-accented German while at the same time learning about soldering and polishing, adding to the little knowledge I'd gleaned in Brazil.

By late November it was getting unpleasantly cold and damp. The workshop had no heating except for a wholly inadequate smelly little electric stove. The only thing to do was wrap up warm and wear thick socks and boots. Alas, I had no money for this, and did not want to reveal to Ulrike just how broke I was. Günter's rent paid for the groceries and the utility bills, but that was all. So Walter had to take in a second lodger, a music student. Silke Nass was then a promising young lyric soprano, originally from Dresden, who had been introduced to him by their mutual voice coach. We were fortunate in that both Günter and Silke were model lodgers – at least initially – but the apartment did suddenly become very crowded. Although there were three bedrooms, there was only one bathroom. Still, Silke's rent contribution meant that I was finally able to buy a pair of fleece-lined boots, a couple of thick woollen sweaters and a much-needed winter jacket.

The increased rent money also meant Walter and I could afford tickets for decent seats at the National Theatre. In early December, he took me to see *The Flying Dutchman*, which he deemed a suitable introduction to Wagner. Once again, he was right. If *The Magic Flute* had enthralled me, something about this Wagner opera took me straight to heaven. The great Swedish soprano Catarina Ligendza sang the part of Senta and Franz Ferdinand Nentwig was cast as the eponymous Dutchman. The sets were extraordinary; props shrouded in sheets and hawsers strung across the stage, but it was the powerful voices and soaring emotion that really captured me. Was it because I wished I was more like Senta – yes, I named my daughter after her – that I envied the romantic intensity of her love and her willingness to make the ultimate sacrifice? Was it the contrast with the undemanding, comfortable, already sexually routine nature of my relationship with Walter?

The only obvious cloud – and initially it was a very small one – was Silke's presence in our lives. She and Günter had come with us to see the Dutchman, and in the interval, over glasses of *Sekt* which we couldn't really afford, she irritated me by harping on about Ligendza's poor pronunciation of German, and dragging the two men into a pointless discussion as to whether non-native speakers of German should even be 'allowed' to sing Wagner. Walter at least had the courage to make gentle fun of this opinion, reminding her that Birgit Nilsson, another Swede, had been one of the greatest Wagnerian sopranos of her day. Günter, duly intimidated, just smiled sheepishly, cowed by Silke's flash-eyed forcefulness.

7TH NOVEMBER 2008

Just had to take some time out. Thinking about *The Flying Dutchman* brought Senta back to me, and for an eerie moment I was convinced that she was in the house; that if only I willed it hard enough, I could make her materialise and enter the kitchen, like a scene from a magic realism film, as if nothing had happened. I was staring hard at the door that leads to the studio, when it opened and in came Astrid. I started and promptly burst into tears. Without saying anything, she comes over to me and hugs me.

'I'm losing my mind...'

'Shhh, don't worry. You'll find it again,' she says as she massages my shoulders with her tiny, powerful hands. They smell of turpentine.

Spent the late morning and early afternoon preparing finger food for Bonfire Night which we are celebrating two days late so that there are no worries about getting up for school the next day. Marcus had the idea of inviting his and Tristan's school friends as well as the kids from the neighbouring farm to a party at Wensum. I have no idea how many bodies this will result in – could be anything between ten and twenty.

I have wrapped King Edwards in foil to bake in the embers. Tris and Marcus have made a guy by adapting a scarecrow, dressed him in old pyjamas and given him a George Bush mask which they found in a joke shop in Norwich.

Dubya and his Neocon rabble are history now. Barack Obama has been elected, which has given us unrepentant liberals the warm fuzzies here at Wensum. Tristan is slipping back into his black persona, having temporarily played it down after the murders. He's bought himself an Obama 'Yes We Can' T shirt and goes round telling people he's proud to be black. They see a green-eyed pale face with a halo of fair hair and must think he's quite mad.

With the mess Obama's inherited – two hideously expensive, highly unpopular unwinnable wars and an economic meltdown on an unprecedented scale – he certainly has his work cut out.

8TH NOVEMBER 2008

About thirty kids showed up. It didn't rain, luckily, so they were able to stay in the yard and have fireworks which unfortunately scared the daylights out of the dogs and birds. Astrid had rounded up the hens, shooed them into the barn and locked the door, but they freaked out nonetheless from all the noise. This morning the place was a sight – feathers and shit everywhere, but with senior hen Bessie the only casualty, on her back, legs in the air. Mother Superior, Astrid had nicknamed her. She reckoned the hen was ten years old and hadn't laid an egg since she was three. We buried her in the rose garden and marked her grave with pebbles, aware of the fact that, should they ever find out, our farming neighbours would think we were completely bonkers.

The kids, only just over half of whom were from Norwich Academy, the others being hangers-on and an assortment of girl- and boyfriends, had come with supplies of booze, mainly spirits, beer and Bacardi Breezers, judging from the debris, as well as a massive boom box which blasted out head-banging Techno. It was impossible to control, and we were rather concerned as most of them are in the sixteen to seventeen age range and therefore under age.

Rhys was in an annoying told-you-so mood today. *Told you we'd get loads of gate crashers. Told you they'd get pissed and turn it into some kind of re-enactment of Skins. Told you we'd have to ferry people home because they're too fucking pissed to drive Daddy's car back.* He was right, of course, and that's what made it all the more infuriating. Astrid and Gerry ended up as the taxi service. Others drove themselves home when they probably shouldn't have. Very few were picked up, which made me wonder whether they'd even told their parents where they were going. As they'd mostly parked outside the gates, there was little we could do to stop them from driving off other than to try and dissuade them and ply them with strong coffee. I was left to deal with the drunks. I had to minister to a couple of them who got violently sick and puked their guts out in the hedges and the yard. Three of them, all lads, passed out cold and had to spend the night on the kitchen floor. Marcus and Tristan were just about sober enough to help clean up the yard, with the help of Tristan's shadow, the pointlessly faithful and utterly sober Lucy whom we later found mopping the filthy outdoor loo floor.

Lucy Bligh, the scholarship girl from the farm up the road at Weston Green. She's a sweet girl and obviously totally besotted with Tristan. I so want to warn her off, but daren't interfere. He has a lot of female fans, a regular babe magnet, to quote Marcus, who doesn't do badly himself on that front, having inherited Rhys's brooding dark Welsh looks. I am convinced that in some sick way Tristan's association with Senta's murder adds to his appeal. Last night, the girls were vying for his attention, but he only seemed interested in one; the only dark-skinned girl at the party, the beautiful Laura who is in the year above him at school and who has an older boyfriend already at university. She is not interested in Tristan, but is probably vaguely flattered by his attention. Amazing how white this part of the world is. Laura stood out as something exotic and unusual, whereas in London, just 100 miles down the road, she would almost have been the norm. I observed his attempts at courtship, but she kept giving him the slip, disappearing to go to the loo, going into the kitchen to offer help, joining other groups. At one point, I spotted Tris surrounded by three girls, but watching Laura as she chatted to Rhys. I was glad her boyfriend wasn't there – it could have ended up in a brawl.

All this reminds me of being embarrassingly sick and hung over many years ago in Munich...

Christmas 1983 came, and with it my first invitation to Walter's parents' Grünwald villa on Christmas Eve. It had begun to bother me that I'd been in Munich for four months without having been introduced to them, but when at last it did happen, I realised why he'd spared me the experience. They were extremely formal, and while they tried to put me at ease, achieved the exact opposite. Walter's father, Johann, asked me if I spoke Danish, and when I told him I only knew half a dozen words and phrases, he got on his soapbox about how it should be every parent's duty to pass on their native tongue to their children. His mother was Polish, and had raised him bilingually. He in turn had passed his Polish on to Walter. My father, Sven, didn't think Danish would be much use to Astrid and me, so apart from teaching us a few greetings and formulaic phrases, he didn't bother, and I wondered what use Polish really was to Walter. Johann had poured me a stiff gin and tonic upon arrival, and surreptitiously topped up my glass several times, doubtless in a misguided attempt to get me to relax. Meanwhile, Walter's mother, Hannelore, was visibly wincing at my German and the mess I was making of my articles and case endings, even correcting me, which did little for my confidence. By the time we sat down for our *Heiligabend* supper, a rich feast starring an enormous roast goose, almost obscenely sumptuous after so many months of lean pauper cuisine, I had to hold onto the edge of the table. The gin had gone straight to my head, and everything was swaying and swirling around me. Walter, realising what had happened, kept topping up my water glass, but it was too late. I had to excuse myself and only just made it to the loo on time to throw up.

'Is she pregnant?' I heard Hannelore ask Walter in a stage whisper as I dashed out of the room with as much decorum as I could muster.

Once again, not a promising start...

The following January, Walter told me he'd heard that the Canadians were opening a consulate in Munich and were looking for tri-lingual local hires. I didn't rate my chances, but was so desperate for paid work that I submitted an application which stressed my proficiency in French and what I optimistically termed my 'working knowledge' of German. I was amazed to be called for interview.

The building, on exclusive Maximiliansplatz, was impressive, bank-like and solidly Germanic, but the interview was totally New World informal. I was vetted by a Vice-Consul in shirt sleeves who had a girlie calendar on his office wall, and given the briefest of oral German tests by his local assistant. My job was to consist of sitting in a bullet-proof glass box in the lobby, operating the telephone switchboard and the security doors that allowed access from the lobby to the offices. As the receptionist, I was to be the first point of contact for the public, he stressed, so I should be a polite, presentable and helpful 'people person.'

The consulate concerned itself primarily with trade, so there was relatively little conventional consular work apart from passport renewal, the issuing of citizenship certificates or the occasional repatriation of a Canadian corpse, often a casualty of overindulgence at the Oktoberfest. Emigration enquiries were dealt with by the embassy in Bonn. As far as jobs went, it was very undemanding, but the pay was quite generous and the staff, consisting of just ten people, five Canadians and five locally-employed Germans, were pleasant enough. Fortunately, it didn't exactly stretch my limited linguistic abilities, as the vast majority of phone calls were in English. Every now and then I'd have to do battle with Quebecois French, which on occasions I found very hard to understand.

In between putting calls through, I had a lot of time just to sit and read, and I used it to peruse some of the books Ulrike had lent me on jewellery making and design, while doodling my own ideas in an exercise book. I missed her company, but still saw her in her garage studio on Saturday afternoons, when I would take her my own tentative designs and my questions about their feasibility. Bit by bit I formed the idea of a collection inspired by memories of Sifnos. It was to consist of bead necklaces, brooches and earrings made of silver, with turquoise and lapis lazuli to suggest the sea and the bright blue and dazzling white of traditional Cycladic architecture. I also had an idea for flat wooden wall cabinets fitted with hooks, little containers and sections inside for storage. I bought a supply of cheap Romanian-made key cabinets from IKEA and modified them, painting the doors with blue and white Cycladic scenes, both abstract and representational. Ulrike was of great help, particularly when it came to realising the silverwork.

When, a few months later, I had finished two dozen sets of jewellery and a number of painted storage cabinets, she persuaded an acquaintance to place a selection in the window of his bookshop in Schwabing, the university district, as part of a display of travel guides and coffee table books about Greece. The window display was eye-catching, complete with stripy canvas deckchair, next to which was a small table with a book on the Greek islands, a tube of sunscreen and a pair of sunglasses. A navy blue beach towel had been carefully crunched into peaks and troughs, on which samples of my jewellery were displayed. Next to it was one of the painted storage cabinets, the little door tantalisingly left ajar, showing glimpses of more necklaces and earrings. At that dark, rainy, depressing time of year, it evoked a powerful yearning for carefree summer holidays in the Med.

Ulrike also got me an interview with a journalist friend who wrote a piece on me for a local paper, accompanied by half a dozen photographs of my designs. As a result, my little collection sold out within a matter of weeks, which did wonders for my confidence. The cabinets in particular were a surprise hit. I can only think they appealed to a certain Germanic desire for order. No more tangled necklaces and earrings. Women seemed to like the simple designs of the Hellas Collection. The journalist who'd interviewed me for the newspaper article had quite wrongly attributed this plain style to my Nordic origins, whereas in fact it had arisen out of necessity rather than choice. The designs were simple basic shapes because I had not, at the time, mastered the requisite skills to produce anything more complex. I could only do very simple casting, the kind shown to me by Ulrike, carving out shapes in cuttlefish bone. The items were not particularly expensive, so I did not make much money out of my success, especially as the shop took its cut too, but it was a very encouraging start to my career as a jewellery maker in a highly competitive market, and provided me with just about enough cash to buy further supplies and pay back Ulrike for the materials she'd so generously provided. When I suggested to Walter that we could now afford to give notice to one of our two lodgers as I had a regular pay cheque from the Canadian Consulate and could make extra money with my jewellery, I had assumed he'd choose Silke. He didn't. He wanted her to stay, so they could continue to sing duets and talk music. It was poor Günter who was told to start looking for somewhere else to live.

I had increasingly come to find Silke hard to take; for one, she was fanatical about protecting her voice and terrified of catching a cold. When I went down with laryngitis in February, she treated me like a leper and went about the flat in a surgical mask. Although when she'd first moved in, she'd kept herself very much in the background, it wasn't long before she started to spend more and more time with Walter. There were evenings when I felt completely cut out of the conversation, not just because I was limited by my poor German, but because the subject was invariably opera and ranged from gossip and bitching about people I didn't know to heated discussions on technique and interpretation. They practised heart-meltingly beautiful duets together, with Günter dropping by to accompany them on the piano. Yes, I was jealous. She made me feel insecure and insignificant.

The German word for jewellery is *Schmuck,* which sounds bad enough to English ears, but Silke had a way of saying the word, while almost wrinkling her nose, that made it sound like a particularly unpleasant variety of dog shit. She was confident, haughty, and beautiful in an old-fashioned, voluptuous way; large-breasted with a narrow waist and broad hips; a real womanly hourglass figure. By contrast, I was very *gamine.* Boyish, slender, small breasts, narrow hips, spidery long legs. I'd started to grow my hair just to look a bit more feminine, though Walter tried to discourage this. Like Astrid in her younger days, Silke had long, thick glossy auburn hair, which I greatly envied. My resentment of her grew day by day, though I went out of my way to be nothing but polite. Then one day I just lost it spectacularly. Silke was very tidy, and my own untidiness grated on her nerves. I could tell from the expression on her face whenever she walked into the kitchen and found the sugar bowl or the coffee jar in the wrong place. One evening I was working at the kitchen table, preparing a top-up order of the Hellas designs for the bookshop in Schwabing. I was polishing the items and wrapping them up in tissue paper. Walter was in the bathroom, warbling Wagner under the shower. Silke came into the kitchen, took one look at the mess and sighed, muttering something under her breath. For some reason, I suddenly flipped. I felt that Silke looked down on my craft and considered me little more than a mediocre dilettante, which touched a raw nerve. I lost my cool and a lava flow of fury erupted from my lips.

'If you have a problem with it, just fuck off out of here!' I snapped. 'We don't need your rent any more.' Her pale green eyes nearly popped out of their sockets and she flushed a blotchy crimson. She opened her mouth to say something, changed her mind, turned on her heel and stormed out.

'Fucking drama queen!' I shouted after her, for good measure, finally venting months of pent-up irritation and jealousy: 'Arrogant bitch!' Not long after, I heard the front door slam. The next day, she came back, collected her possessions and moved in with her Italian boyfriend, Claudio, a cameraman who worked at the Bavaria Film Studios.

Walter was livid. He barely spoke to me for a week.

My screen saver comes on after five minutes of inactivity. I got fed up with the Goldsmiths' gallery and have reverted to one which consists of a continuous loop of family photographs, to help me to focus and not linger too long in the 1980s. Among them, there is one of Senta in the back garden in Clapham, tending the hens, taken just over a year ago in the summer of 2007, the last summer of her life. I was in my studio in the garden and had my camera to hand. I opened the window and called her name, and the resulting picture captures her with an expression that hovers between surprise and mild irritation. She has half-turned towards me, a bag of her homemade organic chicken feed in her right hand. The old shorts reveal long slender brown legs. My beautiful daughter with her mass of dark ringlets. She lacked any trace of vanity, never bothered with make-up and dressed with genuine carelessness. Her beauty was all the more striking because of it. She didn't have to try; it triumphed loudly over the crappy thrift shop clothes, a rose on a dung hill.

My lovely girl... what on earth did you think you were going to achieve that day in Godforsaken Peckham...

Astrid has just come into the kitchen and spots me staring at the screen.

'Writer's block?'

I nod, without taking my eyes off the photograph. She fires up the percolator and brings me a mug of coffee.

'Bit parky in here. Shall I put another log on the fire?'

I give her a blank look. I'm with Senta at the moment. Astrid glances at the screen, smiles, raises a hand to show understanding and returns to her studio, where she's preparing for a sculpture workshop with half a dozen art students from NUCA who are due here tomorrow.

After lunch, we had an interesting little experience with Yvonne Townsend, mother of Rory, one of the lads who drank himself sick last night and slept on the kitchen floor. His mother, a superannuated British Airways flight attendant, decided, quite unannounced, to pay us a little visit in her shiny pillar- box red BMW convertible. She kicked off with a waterfall of apologies for her son's behaviour and any inconvenience this may have caused us, thanking us profusely for taking the trouble to drop him off back home. In fact, it was Rhys who'd done so on his way to work this morning. I rather suspect her main motive for driving out to Wensum was to check out our set-up. Astrid is a well-known local figure in certain circles, and there are plenty of people in the area who would love to be able to claim that they know her socially and drop her name into their conversation. They are also curious to see the Funky Farm and the weird and wonderful sculptures that line the driveway and populate the courtyard. Yvonne Townsend, all chunky gold, cashmere and blonde highlights, was obviously dying to see the place. I introduced myself very briefly, by first name only, but did not mention that I was Tristan's mother or Astrid's sister. Most of the parents and pupils in Tristan's year must know why he is here, thanks to Gerry's fame and the media frenzy that followed Senta and Toby's murder. The whole school probably knows about it. Anyway, the last thing I wanted was for anyone even to allude to The Topic. I busied myself making espresso while she went on to complain to Astrid about young people today, binge drinking spirits and doing drugs. (Had she caught a whiff of cannabis?) Apparently everything was going to the dogs and Norwich was not the nice town it used to be. All the while her eyes were darting around the kitchen, taking in the Campbell's soup can chandelier, the little Venus de Milo miniature with the Barbie Doll head on the window sill, the cartoon of Thatcher being rogered up the jacksy by a huge pig with Ronald Reagan's grinning face; all the weird and wonderful things that I barely notice any more because I have got used to them over the years. I happened to glance out of the kitchen window at this point and caught Mutt peeing on the front tyre of the Beamer while Godfrey the capon had hopped onto the bonnet where he was strutting about like a pompous comic book general.

Meanwhile, Astrid was just letting the woman talk, tossing in the occasional I see and yes and I know. I put their little yellow cups on the table but kept myself apart by sitting down in a fireside armchair instead of joining them. I could still observe them, reflected in the mirror on the chimney breast. There followed a short lull in Yvonne Townsend's monologue as she sipped her coffee. Astrid, who was becoming irritated, then switched fully into Medusa mode, which famously involves sitting stock-still and staring unblinkingly at the person struggling to make conversation, without saying a word herself. I recognised the tactic from many a past experience. Yvonne Townsend probably misread it for artistic eccentricity. She may even have thought that Astrid was grateful for her visit and her apology. In any case, she cleared her throat and launched into Part 2. Maybe, she said, steepling her fingers to show off bright red nail polish to match the car, maybe, with all due respect, it hadn't been such a wise idea to hold a party out here, because teenagers being teenagers, they were bound to take advantage of the fact that it was seven miles outside Norwich and therefore a nice distance from their parents and from the police. Maybe, just maybe it had been a little... naïve of Astrid and Rhys to allow this to happen? What if some of those kids who had driven back in their parents' cars had had accidents? Of course we were very lucky that this hadn't actually happened, but just imagine... Oh, and did we know that so and so's son had had an accident on the Fakenham Road just the other week, having driven his father's car into a ditch? He was badly concussed, but it could so easily have been much worse.

Astrid just continued to stare at her. Yvonne Townsend's expensively foundationed cheeks had flushed pink and she started to fiddle nervously with the slack of her Rolex watch strap. In the silence that followed, as she waited in vain for some sort of response from Astrid, I held my breath. 'Well, she went on, 'I'd better not take any more of your time because I'm sure you are very busy, I mean you must be very... er... busy with commissions and all that...' Any sarcasm intended at the beginning of her utterance had evaporated by the end as Astrid continued quite simply to stare at her. She got up, grabbed her outsize Louis Vuitton tote, and bade us an awkward goodbye which Astrid, who remained seated, acknowledged with the merest hint of a nod. I got up and opened the door to let her out.

We watched her make her way to the car and shoo Godfrey off the bonnet with a swipe of her handbag. Not a wise move, as Godfrey took fright and squirted a streak of shit on her car as he flapped to safety while Mutt and Doobie yipyapped their familiar doggie duet.

'Well, I hope madam feels better now she's got that off her silicone-inflated tits,' said Astrid. 'Or maybe she'll come back and accuse us of not teaching our chickens good manners!'

'I don't know how you do it. I would have lost my rag,' I said.

She smiled. 'Not worth it, Veets. The silent approach is far more effective and energy-efficient with a silly cow like that. Shall we have a smoke?'

9TH NOVEMBER 2008

It's my 54th birthday. I had told everyone that I didn't want to celebrate, but Rhys insisted on taking us all out for a pub lunch at the Old Lodge, which I actually ended up enjoying. Gerry came late yesterday morning, on his Harley. We had all been sitting in the kitchen having our Sunday breakfast and reading the papers when Doobie suddenly started to whine, cocking her head and wagging her tail, while Mutt just gave her his puzzled look. 'She's heard the bike.' I tell the others. And true enough, thirty seconds later, Gerry comes roaring up the driveway and the terrified hens flap, squawk and scuttle for cover like scandalised old ladies who have just had their bottoms pinched by a perv in a dirty mac. He had brought a birthday cake, which was a bit shaken up, as well as a present from Ewa, a beautiful moss green pashmina of the finest quality, from her own range. I had a long phone call with Mother too. I sense she is getting lonely. Two of her closest friends have died in the past couple of months, which has left her in a reflective mood. Must make sure she doesn't slip back into a state of depression. We will have to see if she can be persuaded to move a little closer to us.

Reading yesterday's musings has reminded me of that other bitch, though she wasn't exactly silly... Silke Nass. I wonder how Astrid would have dealt with her? No doubt not by letting rip the way I had. The eviction of Silke Nass. Sounds like the title of a Fassbinder film: *The Bitter Tears of Petra von Kant. The Eviction of Silke Nass.* Looking back, might this have marked the beginning of the end, or is that just another example of our tendency to reorder and reclassify the past into neat beginning, middle and end phases that never actually existed? Was there ever really a beginning? Did I ever really love Walter? Certainly there was a powerful physical attraction, but when I moved to Munich and into his flat, we'd only known each other for a little over four weeks, and those had been spent in the idyllic surroundings of Sifnos, where reality was suspended by being on holiday and the blinding hormonal high of a new relationship. And in Kastro, we were both foreigners. Munich, by contrast, was Walter's stamping ground, but a place where I did not know a soul.

It had been different in Italy and France. I had gone to Florence for the art, learned passable Italian and worked in a dodgy language school as an equally dodgy English teacher. I had my own minuscule *monolocale* studio flat and jealously safeguarded my independence from any of the men I became involved with. In Paris, too, I'd had my own little modest bolt hole in Porte des Lilas while Raoul the Brazilian lived with two musicians and a smackhead transvestite, Danny the Tranny, in a *louche* little backstreet in Montmartre. Yet in Munich I had started to feel much as I had in Belo Horizonte, the common factor being my lack of independence, my foreignness, and being linguistically hobbled.

Walter rarely mentioned Silke after my infamous outburst, but I knew they still got together to practise duets at the house of Walter's voice coach and in a nearby church, by kind permission of the local music-loving priest. I remained, I am embarrassed to admit, corrosively, pathologically jealous and suspicious of Silke. She was talented, alluring and had a truly powerful, rich, dramatic soprano. She and Walter shared a particular passion for Mozart and Wagner which further fuelled my insecurities. True, I was trying hard to learn all I could about opera, but I was starting from zero and I didn't have their musical background. Grade three on the piano was as far as I'd managed to progress at school, before begging my mother to allow me to stop so that I could escape the combined sarcasm and halitosis of my piano teacher, the crabby Miss Ball, concert pianist manquée.

Mother and Sven had a typically middle-class smattering of classical LPs; a box set of Beethoven's symphonies, Mendelssohn's violin concerto in E Minor and some recordings of Arthur Rubinstein playing Chopin, but they were hardly what you'd call dedicated music lovers and neither could play an instrument. I'd never been to an opera before coming to Munich, and suddenly there I was, surrounded by singers and musicians whose lifeblood was classical music and opera. On evenings when Walter invited other singers back to the flat for wine and song, I felt totally inadequate; a non-person, politely greeted, briefly once-overed and then pretty much ignored. I was doubly handicapped, for although my German was improving by leaps and bounds, it was a long way off being good enough for more complex topics of conversation. I'd retreat into the room Silke had vacated, read library books about design and doodle ideas. Meanwhile, I decided to abandon my Mozart phase for a while and force myself to listen more systematically to Wagner. But whereas I adored *The Flying Dutchman*, and learned to love *The Mastersingers of Nuremburg*, I couldn't get my head around *Parsifal* or *Tristan and Isolde*. I confessed my problems to Walter. He was both flattered and vaguely amused at my attempts to understand his passion, and I in turn was touched by the fact that he genuinely didn't expect me to show any interest in his music.

Around that time, there was a performance of *Tristan and Isolde* at the National Theatre. Walter didn't want me to come; he didn't think I was ready for a five-hour Wagner opera, but I knew that Silke would be going, so I badgered him into taking me, telling him that a live performance would help me to appreciate the opera better. He remained unconvinced, especially as he could only afford the seats in the gods, from where you could not see the stage, but he got me a ticket anyway. I remember it started in the afternoon. At the Consulate I had to pretend that I had a dental appointment in order to get there in time, and I went straight from work, in my drably formal office garb. I met Silke and Walter in the lobby. Walter was in his usual jeans and sweater but Silke was in an emerald green woollen dress with plunging neckline which accentuated her voluptuous figure. She offered me a perfumed cheek to kiss. I had long since apologised to her for my outburst, but we continued to dislike each other as much as ever beneath the thinnest veneer of politeness. I felt plain and ungainly next to her, and kicked myself for not having had the foresight to pack a change of clothing to slip into in the theatre's loos.

Walter was right. I found *Tristan and Isolde* a mind-and-bum-numbing drag, though I am sure that not being able to see the action on stage, combined with my feelings of inferiority, jealousy and resentment of Silke, played a part in this. The gods were packed with Wagner aficionados who sat, eyes closed, entranced, as the music transported them. At one point I dropped my programme and my seat creaked as I bent down to pick it up. This drew disapproving looks and frowns from those around me, almost as if I'd farted in church. I started to get more and more annoyed at what seemed to me like an unhealthy form of pseudo-religious worship of Wagner. Next to me, Walter and Silke sat with their eyes closed, soaking up the sounds which so singularly failed to thrill me. By the time the first interval arrived, I was ready to flee. Sheer pig-headedness made me stick it out and pretend to appreciate it. I didn't want Walter to have the satisfaction of knowing that he had been right, but more than anything, I didn't want Silke to think I was a philistine. Why did I care so much about their opinions? The thing is, I have always cared too much about other people's opinions, while at the same time pretending the opposite. It comes from a lack of self-confidence rooted in an inferiority complex, partly the result of feeling utterly overshadowed by Astrid.

I did, eventually, learn to appreciate and even love *Tristan and Isolde*, but our children did not thank me for saddling them with what they considered to be embarrassingly pretentious names. Pointing out that Moon Unit, Zowie or Heavenly Hirani Tiger Lily would have been a lot harder to live with simply cut no ice. For the longest time, Tristan wanted to be known as Stan, and would go to great lengths to keep his real name a secret to avoid the ridicule of his peers. In fact it is only now, in the Lower Sixth at his new school, that he has reverted to his real name.

Senta was less bothered. The inevitable Senta/Santa jokes annoyed her a bit, but on the whole she couldn't have cared less about other people's opinions in her pre-Unitarian days. No, that isn't true. By saying she couldn't care less, I don't mean to imply that it was a deliberate choice. It was rather a genuine insensitivity to the feelings and opinions of other people. Outstanding though she was academically, she had no social antennae for such things, no matter how hard she tried. That, in the end, was to prove her undoing.

Just had to endure Rhys banging on about the whole sorry subprime mortgage business and trying to explain the cause of it all to the boys over my humble macaroni ham and cheese dinner. This was triggered by the news of China's announcement of a massive economic stimulus package. I really wouldn't mind his explanations, but it's the irritating pomposity that goes with it, and the assumption, somehow implicit, that the rest of us are all complete idiots. I glanced at Astrid a couple of times, and noticed that she had tuned out. That's how she copes with Rhys when he switches to lecture mode. Marcus was polite as ever, but I could see his feet twitching impatiently under the table. I miss Gerry. I miss home. I miss my own space.

I must not whinge...

10ᵀᴴ NOVEMBER 2008

I am plugged into Senta's iPod, listening to *Don Giovanni* to help transport me back to Munich, the late spring of 1984 and the decline of the vinyl era. Walter, Silke and a couple of other aspiring singers gave a well-attended and enthusiastically-received recital in the church where they'd been practising all these months. I don't recall the full repertoire, but shall never forget their Don Giovanni / Zerlina duet: *Là ci darem la mano* or their, by then perfected and polished, Papageno / Pamina duet from *The Magic Flute*. To my untrained ear, their voices were magnificent, soaring and swooping and looping the loop, exuberant dare-devil swallows on a summer's eve.

I felt terrifically proud of Walter, but alas, along with this pride, my jealousy of Silke grew correspondingly uglier, fed as always by a familiar sense of my own inadequacy. I couldn't sing. I couldn't compete. I was a chirruping sparrow in the company of full-throated nightingales. I was in agony as they performed that duet from *Don Giovanni,* with Walter all hot lust and Silke, magnificent in a figure-hugging ruby-coloured taffeta dress, faking coy trepidation. Faking? It certainly didn't seem like it. I was churned up with a sickening mixture of awe, admiration and toxic suspicion. It was beautiful and it hurt like hell. Why couldn't I just enjoy Walter and Silke's talent? Walter had never seemed bothered by my lack of musical ability, and had even intimated on occasions that he wasn't sure he ever wanted a relationship with another musician or singer because it would be too intense. Too intense? So did that mean that our relationship was comfortably relaxed and lukewarm, like an old shoe?

Oh dear, how a jealous mindset can and will twist anything into the blackest possible interpretation.

Mozart and Wagner... I had absolutely no trouble with the former, or even with early and middle-period Wagner. Methodically I worked my way through Walter's collection of recordings and became familiar with every single aria from *The Magic Flute*, *Un Ballo in Maschera*, *Così fan Tutte* and *Don Giovanni*, these four being my favourites. I copied them onto cassette and listened to them on my Walkman as I made my way to work.

I went to see Milos Forman's *Amadeus* several times at the cinema and worked my way through Walter's dog-eared copy of Deutsch's Mozart biography with the help of a dictionary. Meanwhile, I doodled my second collection of baubles in idle moments between putting through calls and pressing buttons to open doors to the inner sanctum of the Canadian Consulate. I thought of this collection as my Mozart collection, but it was very much an abstract representation. No silver quavers on chains, no little flutes or masonic symbols. Instead, while listening to Mozart and with Ulrike's invaluable technical assistance, I made silver pendants and earrings in the shape of starbursts of delicate exuberance. By the end of May, with a lot of help from Ulrike, I'd produced just over one hundred earrings and pendants. This time, one of the trendiest boutiques in Haidhausen had agreed to display them, thanks to my previous sales record and press coverage. The only problem was the name. What was I to call this collection? Mozart was out; I couldn't expect people to make the connection.

'How do you feel when you listen to Mozart?' Ulrike asked me. I waited for the adjectives to pop up in my brain. Blissed out. Humbled. Enchanted in the most literal sense of the word. High. Transformed. Ecstatic.

'Stop! Ecstatic! *Dass ist Perfekt!*' she said. 'You can call it *'Die Ekstase Kollection!'* I should add that this was well before the heyday of the little rave pill. At the time, I merely thought it sounded vaguely sexual, suggestive of a massive climax, a suitable name for a Beate Uhse sex toy. I shared my reservations with Ulrike.

'*Nah und?* What is wrong wiss zat?' she said.

So... *Ekstase* it was. Another interview was arranged, this time with the women's glossy, *Burda*, and I duly delivered the collection to the boutique, along with another fifty wooden cupboards, the doors painted midnight blue with star bursts and comets. Within a month, every item had been sold. It seemed women loved the fact that the items, though hardly expensive, were a guaranteed limited edition of local manufacture. The *Burda* coverage, though little more than a quarter page, had a great deal to do with it too. Without it, I doubt very much whether I would have sold more than a dozen items. This time round, I made rather more money too, as the boutique had suggested prices I would never have dared ask myself. My God, I had blundered across something I had a knack for. The problem was, it seemed so trivial. Next to the musical talents of Walter, Silke and their crowd, it seemed utterly insignificant. I tried to explain this to Ulrike one day. She was so astonished that she stopped soldering, put her propane torch down and turned round to face me. '*Du bist ja verrückt, oder!*' Are you nuts or what? My God! You've just produced this beautiful stuff and it's sold really well, and now you are complaining about it being only a trivial achievement. What do you want? A commission from Princess Deeana for a teeara?'

Walter was delighted for me. We celebrated together with Ulrike and her husband by blowing what seemed back then a large amount of money on a gourmet meal at the Rue des Halles, a swanky French restaurant on the corner of our street, at which I'd often cast a longing glance or two in our penniless days. Still, as soon as the initial euphoria had passed, the old ogre of perceived inadequacy reared its head again. Nothing could convince me that my miraculously successful ability to produce baubles that for some utterly mysterious reason appealed to some of Munich's moneyed-but-arty *Schicki Micki* crowd was anything other than fluke, a flash in the pan, and in no way equal to the magic of Silke Nass's divine, powerful, sexually-charged lyric soprano.

June came and Walter flunked one of his exams, which put him in a dark mood for a while, as it was the only thing now standing in the way of his economics degree. He went off to a singing master class for a couple of weeks, with – so I subsequently discovered – Silke Nass. This was to be the cause of our first major argument upon his return.

Me: 'You never told me *she* was going to be there.'

W: (looking perplexed) 'You never asked. Anyway, so what!'

I hated myself for sulking, for behaving in this way. I knew it was ridiculous but I couldn't seem to stop myself. Walter, seeking to placate me and reassure me of his affections, suggested we go back to Sifnos for a holiday. I took two weeks' leave from the Canadian Consulate and off we went.

I think we both knew that this was unwise; that we should at least have chosen a different destination. There was no way we could turn the clock back, erase the intervening twelve months and recapture the past. In the village of Kastro, things had changed. The taverna where I had worked was being managed by a middle-aged German hippy couple while one-eyed Adonis was in hospital in Athens, being treated for a kidney condition. The room we rented was noisy. It was too close to the taverna and suffocatingly hot, as it faced south. The bedbugs drove us crazy and were a complete passion killer. The bathroom was home to a family of cockroaches and stank of drains. We stuck it for just a couple of days before decamping and taking the ferry to Santorini.

Santorini... a crescent-shaped volcanic island with black sand. Walter and I stayed in brand new soulless rooms with glaring fluorescent lights in a little concrete box of a house whose flat roof bristled with rusty reinforcing rods. Still, at least the plumbing worked and the beds were comfortable and bug-free. We had left the ghosts of Kastro behind, and in the days that followed, managed to go some way towards repairing the cracks that had appeared in our relationship, gluing the pieces with a cocktail of sex, retsina, *kalamares, taramasalata* and – for me at least – the heavenly absence of Silke Nass and the whole opera crowd.

I made a vow to myself to keep the ogre jealousy on a very short leash in future.

12TH NOVEMBER 2008

'Mum, we're off to the cinema with Lucy.'

'What's on?'

'*The Dark Knight.*'

'Got some money?'

'Yeah. I'm good. Dad gave me some the other day.'

'Got your mobile, Marcus?'

'Yup.' He fishes it out of his pocket to show me.

'Don't be home too late. Remember it's a school day tomorrow.'

'Yeah. No worries.'

Marcus passed his driving test only last week, which means the boys are no longer dependent on us or on infrequent, inadequate rural bus services to ferry them in and out of Norwich. Fortunately Marcus is a level-headed, reliable boy, but nothing can compensate for his lack of experience as a driver. Good thing there isn't much traffic around here, but that accident on the Fakenham Road that Yvonne Townsend mentioned the other day continues to haunt me. Tristan is now bugging me about driving lessons. I'm not in favour, and nor is Gerry, because we think he is too unstable, yet we know we need to show him that we have faith in him, and this is, after all, an important rite of passage into the adult world. Next summer, we've told him. Next summer you can have lessons. By then, we hope he will have stabilised and matured a bit more.

Art may be going well, but he is none too happy with some of the stuff he has to study for English. He reserves a particular loathing for *La Belle Dame sans Merci* and *The Eve of St Agnes*. ('All this fucking consummation stuff. One big wank!') Rhys has been trying to help him, and has at least managed to rekindle his interest in *The Great Gatsby* by showing him the old film with Redford and Mia Farrow. The truth is, Tris is no reader. He relates far better to film and image than he does to the written word. I can't remember when he last read anything for pleasure, and we're beginning to think that A-level English was not the best choice.

Tristan... What headaches he caused us in London before we finally rusticated him to Wensum six months ago. By contrast, Gerry and I never once had to worry about Senta, other than a bit of light-hearted concern about the fact that, in her teens, she so rarely seemed to show any inclination towards the usual adolescent interests. No sexual experimentation, it would appear, almost certainly no drugs, and as far as we could gather, no rock'n roll either.

Tristan had, unlike Senta, been a wonderfully uncomplicated, cheerful and affectionate child. He'd shown a certain amount of academic promise earlier – not in his sister's league, but good enough to get him into Westminster, where he was a day boy. Then something happened as he hit his teens. Our angelic, parent-pleasing boy soprano was brutally mugged by a flash flood of hormones and within a matter of months, sex and drugs had replaced Maths and French. At fifteen, his girlfriend has been an 'older woman' of seventeen, much to Gerry's amusement. Ashley from Stockwell; a tall athletic Jamaican Brit whom Tris had met in some club that neither of them should have been in, given that they were both under age. Ashley seemed to buy Tristan's chosen black identity. He had taken to dying his frizzy blondish hair black and persuaded her to braid it into corn rows. We joked that he was a Michael Jackson in reverse. Any mention of Jackson used to rile him, as he despised him for being what he called a traitor to his own race.

However, much more worrying was Tristan's habit of flirting with men. His ambiguous looks – he'd taken to wearing eyeliner – attracted men, and I feared that one of these days things would get out of control and someone would beat him up and worse for his ceaseless prick teasing. As for drugs, that had been, if anything, an even bigger worry. Gerry and I had turned a blind eye to his cannabis consumption – it would have been hypocritical to do otherwise – but he'd been caught smoking skunk and heroin with his classmate Sam and his elder brother, Josh, in their parents' garage. The three of them had also drunk themselves into near oblivion on vodka on more than one occasion. Suffice it to say we were worried sick.

All three boys, on advice from their headmaster, were sent to a counsellor and had half a dozen sessions which appeared to have little effect. I just had no idea what he was up to any more. Gone were the confidences, the little intimacies, the hours he would spend with me, drawing and chatting about anything and everything. Puberty had thrown the switch and he had clammed up and become secretive and gauche with me, even downright hostile and rude at times. At least these days there's no rudeness and hostility any more, but he's still holding a lot back. There is a kind of mute animal warmth between us now, but not much real emotional closeness. He rarely confides in me. I do worry if he'll ever be able to cope with life again once this whole elaborate family and school support system is removed.

MUNICH, SEPTEMBER 1984

Loss of intimacy...

What Walter and I regained on holiday on the island of Santorini back in 1984 soon ebbed away back in rainy autumnal Munich. He auditioned for the Bavarian State Opera and was told to try again the following year. Fortunately, his self-confidence was somewhat restored when he got the part of Figaro in a touring production of *The Barber of Seville*. I was much less thrilled to discover that Silke Nass had got the part of Rosina, but I kept my vow of not showing jealousy, even though it practically tore a hole in my stomach. They were to be on the road for ten weeks, touring the provincial theatres of Austria, Hungary, Romania, Bulgaria, then back through Poland, what was then East Germany, the northern part of the old West Germany and back down into Bavaria, so that the cast could be reunited with their families for Christmas.

Rehearsals were held that September in Vienna. Walter invited me up for the last pre-tour weekend, and advised me to contact the tour manager, a Munich-based Berliner, Torsten Freitag, a tall, gaunt-faced, Slavic-looking man in his late twenties, who would be able to give me a lift to Vienna that same weekend. As we drove along the Munich to Salzburg Autobahn, Torsten did little to put my mind at ease about the manifold temptations of opera singers on tour. As maniac death wish drivers screamed past us in their Porsches and BMWs, Torsten, a veteran of these operatic tours, that particular one being his eighth, told me about his job. Among other things, it consisted of driving the lorry that contained the props and acting as stage manager. This, given the run-down state of many east-European theatres, required considerable ingenuity and improvisational skills as a handyman, carpenter and electrician. Romania was so impoverished that he had even brought along his own supply of paint and brushes and a very comprehensive first aid kit. He conjured up a picture of Hieronymus Bosch-esque misery, with some peasants in the countryside still shod in rags for lack of shoes.

'I suppose you get ... certain situations... when people are on the road together for ten weeks?' I fished. I remember that he laughed darkly at my euphemism. Maybe my German sounded clumsy. He'd witnessed them all – affairs among the cast, of singers with singers, of singers with members of the orchestra, of everybody with the corps de ballet, of one night stands with locals, not to mention the jealousies, sulks and shouting matches that would inevitably ensue.

'Are you worried about Walter?' he asked suddenly, with disconcerting directness.

'Well, yes, I guess I am...'

'I think it's something you have to accept with theatre people. They're constantly exposed to temptation, especially when they're away from home. In any case, their first love is the stage itself. That doesn't leave much room for anything else.'

'You're not exactly putting my mind at rest.'

'Well, actually, I was on tour with your handsome Walter last year, and I think he was one of the few who always slept alone, though he could have had his pick of women. The first violinist was after him, as was the prettiest ballerina from the corps de ballet, and a Polish soprano, but he didn't seem interested. My God, even I used to come back to my room in the early hours and have to toss a ballerina or two out of my bed. But I'm a realist and I know damn well that what most of them are after is a chance to defect to the West. We West-German males are just a passport to freedom and a potential meal ticket.'

Silke Nass wasn't on tour with them last year, though.

'Do you know Silke Nass?' I ask.

Another one of his mirthless laughs.

'Not well. Did a tour two years ago. Not very friendly. Very cold. Very ambitious. A real ice queen but a wonderful voice.'

I spent the rest of the journey nursing dark thoughts about her.

18TH NOVEMBER 2008

Gerry has just returned to London, having left partner Sal and sous-chef Sandrine to run the restaurant. Still no buyer for our house. The market is lousy right now, and the media doom-mongers bang on relentlessly about recession, lay-offs, the credit crunch and negative equity.

We still haven't cleared out Senta's room. I know we are going to have to do it one of these days, and both Ewa and Astrid have offered their physical and moral support.

Strangely enough, so far De Vlaaminck seems to be recession-proof, but Gerry fears there may well be a delayed effect. He has concocted a special dessert, the Credit Crunch, a variation on *tiramisù*, but with nuts and a layer of bittersweet chocolate. It's going down well, apparently. Being within walking distance of the Houses of Parliament means the restaurant has always been able to rely on the custom of government people from both sides of the House. The only time when takings really dip significantly is during summer parliamentary recess. Gerry has taken to closing the place down for the whole month of August while the rest of central London gorges on tourist cash. September is slack too, but in October it's hectic once more, with parliament back in session.

He doesn't look well, which is hardly surprising. There are dark circles under his eyes and since last April, he's started smoking again. Rhys is a Born Again Non-Smoker and Astrid only ever does spliffs in her studio, so when Gerry comes to Wensum, he has to keep nipping out to the barn, followed each time by dire warnings about the consequences of burning cigarette ends landing on straw. But the real danger lies in the continued tension between Gerry and Tristan.

At dinner time on Saturday there was no sign of Tris, and it's at times like this that I regret our decision, back in April, to confiscate his mobile. Marcus told us he'd gone to see Lucy. He stayed away all weekend, leaving only a brief message on my voice mail, and I think Gerry, though annoyed, was also guiltily relieved. The last time he was at Wensum, they had a massive argument triggered by Tristan cracking his fingers, a habit, as Tristan is well aware, that gets on his father's nerves. It was just a tiny spark that ignited a conflagration. Astrid, Marcus, Rhys and I ended up leaving them to their shouting match in the kitchen and seeking refuge in various remote corners of the farmhouse.

These days Gerry, so gentle and laid back by nature, harbours a rumbling volcano of anger inside him which he cannot always control. Senta had been his favourite, and I remain convinced that Tristan's teenage truancy and experiments with sex and drugs had been in part attempts to gain his father's attention. Gerry doesn't have much time for my kitchen sink psychology and simplistically blames Tristan for Senta's murder. He knows this isn't fair, but it is in danger of becoming his default mode. It has taken a lot of persuasion by our bereavement counsellor as well as by Astrid, Rhys, Ewa and me to make him realise that nothing good can come from burdening Tristan with guilt. Wrecking his life will not bring Senta and Toby back. He knows this, but can't seem to control the urge to blame Tris. It's causing friction between us too.

I feel sorry for Lucy, destined to be Tristan's sort-of-but-not-quite girlfriend. Little Lucy with her incongruous urban hair, dyed raven black, and the tiny blue nostril-stud which sits oddly with her healthy apple-cheeked farmer's daughter looks and old-fashioned, soft, rounded body. She and Tris are in the same A-level art group, but her main passion is for Latin and Greek, which is what she hopes to study at Cambridge. If she gets accepted, she will be the first member in the history of the Bligh family to go to university. I get the impression that farmer Bligh, though proud of his daughter, doesn't quite know what to make of her, and that is something I can sympathise with. That she is besotted with Tris is obvious, as is the fact, to me at least, that it will never be reciprocated. He likes her well enough, but doesn't fancy her, though he probably sleeps with her nonetheless. To him, she is an adoring sympathetic ear, a comforting refuge, a fuckbuddy, someone to stay with when Gerry comes to the farm and usurps his place in the matrimonial bed. I don't like to admit it, but Tristan is a bit of a user, and seems to think that being screwed up and having issues gives him the right to ride roughshod over the feelings of others. My inclination is to warn the girl, but I know I shouldn't meddle. At most I can have another go at Tristan about not using people, but beyond that, I have to let them learn from their own mistakes. Sadly it's the only way.

Later that night, in bed, as Gerry pulled me into his arms and as an autopilot erection, ever ready like a boy scout and no respecter of circumstances, stiffened against my thigh, he asked me about my writing and if it was helping. I guess it has, in that it gives me something to do, trying to make sense out of my messy, rambling life. On the other hand, I am still not able to confront The Topic. I am circling, procrastinating, pursuing tangents, seeking refuge by rooting around in various pockets of my past.

Tristan asked me the other day if my laptop was password-protected. 'Why, did you want to read what I've written?' I said.

'No, but Uncle Rhys might,' he said. He'd spotted him hovering around in the kitchen with a memory stick in his hand, looking shifty. But Tristan has a habit of half making things up, or interpreting anything ambiguous in the most negative or sensational light. He has a talent for making the truth sound like a lie, and vice versa. He's a bit of a stirrer, and believing him on a previous occasion very nearly caused our already rocking marital boat to capsize.

VIENNA, SEPTEMBER 1984

In a rainy, grey Vienna, the tour group had assembled in a small theatre and was in a flurry of organisational activity and stress-induced histrionics. Costumes had to be altered by a harassed elderly wardrobe mistress, the first violin feared she was going down with 'flu and one of the singers had an infected toe. Silke Nass had lost a gold bracelet which had disappeared from her dressing room, and suspected one of the stage hands, Walter feared he was getting a cold, and the Bulgarian conductor, a stocky man with a lion's mane of white hair, was being condescendingly sarcastic to the rather wooden Polish baritone who had the role of Count Almaviva. All par for the course, so Torsten assured me. I decided to sit through the rehearsal, but after an hour or more of stop and start, shouting, tantrums and an overdose of Silke Nass's tauntingly gorgeous voice and quivering bosom, I decided I would brave the wet weather and go for a stroll around the city. As I headed for the exit, a familiar-looking man smiled at me and got up from the back row. He came over to me and held his hand out.

'Claudio Richter, remember? How are you?'

Silke's partner, boyfriend, lover. The Italian cameraman. We shook hands. I'd seen him before, fleetingly, on occasions when he'd come to collect Silke from the flat, and once at the recital in the church in Haidhausen. A feeling of awkwardness came over me. Would he be well-disposed towards me? Maybe Silke hadn't told him that I had been the cause of her moving out of Walter's flat? Or maybe he was pleased because it meant she had finally moved in with him? I told Claudio I needed some fresh air, and to my surprise, he offered to accompany me, saying he was dying for a cigarette and knew of a great traditional coffee house. We had no umbrellas and were confronted with relentless autumn rain. Skirting the shop fronts, we hurried along until we reached Café Schwarzenberg. We found a table by the window and watched the red and white trams trundle past.

Over a *mélange* coffee and rich wedges of gateau, Claudio lit his much-craved cigarette and was delighted to discover that he could speak Italian with me. Although his German was excellent – he came from the city of Bolzano, in that part of Northern Italy called South Tirol, where many inhabitants are bilingual in German and Italian – he much preferred to speak the latter. He told me a little about his work at the Bavaria Film Studios, how, two years before, he'd been working on a production of *Parsifal* and had met Silke, who had a minor role as a flower girl. '*Mia piccola strega tedesca*', he called her, affectionately, my little German witch. That's witch with a 'b', I remember thinking, and not so little either. His droopy dark eyes became dreamy as he mentioned her, and a little smile played around his lips. I uttered some compliment about her voice, and he instantly waxed rapturous. *Una voce magnifica*... honeyed, silken, pure, soaring...

How did he feel about his little German witch going on a ten-week tour with my handsome wizard? He hesitated a while, drew on his cigarette and bounced the question back at me. But I asked you first. Ah, no, you tell me. No really, how do *you* feel about it?

'Aren't you jealous?' I remember asking him. He smiled a slow worldly smile. He had heavy hooded eyelids which made him look permanently sleepy. his teeth were tobacco-stained and he had a five o'clock shadow. Roguish and unkempt, a handsome tramp who'd clean up nicely. His thick hair already had quite a lot of grey in it and was beginning to recede. It was tied back in a ponytail.

He told me he didn't feel very Latin. In any case, where he came from, people tended to be rather more Germanic in temperament. He lectured me on jealousy. Jealousy was the greatest destroyer of relationships. Jealousy was not about fearing the loss of one's lover to a rival, but a measure of one's own insecurities. An ugly form of egotism, base, cancerous and destructive.

'So how do you cope with it?' I persisted.

Another cigarette. (Couldn't smoke those in Silke's presence!) And a second *mélange*.

'Maybe I'm a bit masochistic. Maybe I even enjoy it.' he confided. His eyes danced as he scrutinised my reaction. I must have looked puzzled.

'You're surprised, I think. Well, look at it like this. *La bellissima* Silke won't be with me forever. She is very, very ambitious, and sooner or later she'll hook up with some big fish, some *pezzo grosso* who can further her career. I have no illusions about that. At the moment I'm... useful to her. I'm more than ten years older. I'm separated from my wife. Silke lost her father in a mining accident when she was only four years old, and she had a hellish childhood. Now she looks to men for protection, father substitutes, yet at the same time she doesn't fully trust them. I'm part father, part lover. Silke needs the illusion of freedom. For now, she likes to... live in my tree, if you like. A bird of passage.'

'I wish I could be so philosophical about Walter.'

'When I was your age, *cara*, I wasn't quite so philosophical either. I learnt my lessons from my marriage.'

Did he feel in any way inferior when surrounded by musicians? Did he feel they looked down on him? Or worse, did he feel... invisible in their presence? This question seemed odd to him. In fact, he appeared to find it faintly ridiculous. Why did I feel like that? Wasn't I artistic? Didn't I make beautiful jewellery? Yes, I argued, but moulding, twisting and soldering pieces of metal wasn't quite up there with being able to thrill an audience with a stunning Mozart aria.

'Ah – if you will look at it that way. How negative you are. *Dio mio.* Why do you have such a problem with your self-esteem? And you are a very beautiful woman. *Una vera bellezza!*'

I blushed and he laughed, but I was genuinely irritated. Physical beauty may be a wonderful gift, but it is transient and certainly no substitute for talent. Besides which, I didn't consider myself beautiful.

What *did* I want out of my relationship with Walter, he asked. Marriage? Babies? The illusion of security? Claudio had put the question gently enough, but that didn't stop it from hitting home hard. It seems ridiculous to me now, but aged twenty-nine, I was beginning to feel old. I had left behind me a ten-year trail of relationships which had soared and then fizzled or crashed. The urge to settle down had become stronger, but I spent a lot of time fretting over a nagging fear that once again I'd got involved with the wrong person, that Walter and I were not really right for each other. And yet... he was handsome, gifted, intelligent, an attentive if rather unimaginative lover, a highly sociable and respected man with many friends. So what was missing exactly? Frankly, I suspected he wasn't really all that interested in me as an individual. I kind of fitted a template of the type of woman he wanted by his side. Attractive, a little bit bohemian, intelligent enough; a very presentable accessory. But he rarely asked me questions about myself, my past, my views, my feelings. As if he wasn't really interested in getting to know me. Whenever I tried to ask him the sort of questions I'd like to have been asked by him, questions about his childhood, his relationship with his parents, his previous girlfriends, he'd more often than not give the shortest possible answer and make it plain that the subject was simply too trivial or dull to be of further interest. I'd spoken to Ulrike about this on one occasion. She'd just shrugged: '*Ach Weeta*. A lot of men are like that, surely. We women are far more into sharing intimacies. Our whole way of thinking is different. It's yet another one of God's bad jokes.'

Claudio waved his hand before my eyes, to draw me out of my little reverie. '*Allora?*' he prompted me. Well?

I shrugged. I couldn't answer his question. I suppose what I wanted was certainty that staying with Walter was right, and for Walter to want to understand me a bit better. Should I learn to compromise and not expect too much? Was I simply unrealistically demanding?

'It's stopped raining,' Claudio remarked, wiping the condensation off the steamed up window pane. 'Let's go for a walk.'

We left the old-fashioned, comforting warmth of the café and turned our collars up to walk along the Ringstrasse. It was still hardly the weather for sightseeing, and puddles shimmered on the deserted streets. Although it was a Saturday afternoon, the shops were shut, creating an oddly provincial air for a capital city. The massive, imposing grey stone buildings were a reminder that this sleepy place was the decapitated head of a once mighty empire. It was affluent, full of elegant shop windows displaying luxury goods, it was immaculately well-preserved and clean, and yet it was somehow entirely lacking in humour and warmth. No doubt my mood and the grim weather combined to play their part, but I did not take to Vienna and found it slightly sinister. A snatch of lyrics from a Joni Mitchell song kept going through my head. Something about some European city being 'too old and cold and settled in its ways.' I don't think she was singing about Vienna, but she might as well have been.

It started to rain again, and on impulse, we decided to go into a cinema we happened to spot across the road. Woody Allen's *Zelig* was showing. It was most bizarre to watch it dubbed in German. There can't have been more than a dozen people in the audience. I let out a deep sigh as we sank into our seats, and Claudio took my hand. He held it for the duration of the film. I didn't know what to make of this – was he making a pass or just trying to show some misguided compassion? Did it mean anything at all? I glanced at his profile, but unlike me, he seemed utterly absorbed in the film. After a while, I thought he'd actually forgotten he was still holding my hand, but when I tried, very carefully, to wriggle free, he tightened his grip.

Why didn't I ask him to let go?

'How do you remember what people said?' Tristan has snuck up behind me and is peering over my shoulder. It's something I cannot bear. Normally I sit with my back to the wall to prevent it. It's pure self-consciousness, but today Jaffa has installed himself on my usual chair and I don't have the heart to evict his old bones.

'You make it up.' I say.

'Then it's fiction.'

'Yeah.'

'I thought you were, like, writing real stuff. Autobiographical.'

'Well, it is and it isn't,' I say, wishy-washily.

He looks unconvinced.

'Darling, the past is what we choose to remember,' I say.

'Jesus, Mum! You're beginning to sound like Uncle Rhys.'

'Bog off!' I say, playfully.

He smiles, and for a moment he looks genuinely happy. Then he disappears into the studio.

A glimpse of happiness, of normality. I ought to celebrate that somehow before it evaporates.

20TH NOVEMBER 2008

Have gone down with a stinking cold, the kind that gives opera singers nightmares. Am typing this in bed, under an electric blanket – a recent purchase of mine – with tissues and paracetamol close at hand and a pint mug of tea supplied by Astrid. Have just been on the phone to Gerry, who is similarly indisposed at Ewa's. He was bemoaning the fact that, inconvenience apart, he hates being ill because it gives him too much time to brood. He's been trying to read, but Gerry's never been a particularly avid reader. My books are too heavy for his taste, so he's trying to read some of Ewa's. He's tried and failed with Barbara Taylor Bradford and Maeve Binchey. Sal has promised to lend him *The Audacity of Hope*, when he's finished with it, which should be more to his liking.

He's getting nervous about the now imminent broadcast of his two Christmas episodes on BBC2. Much of the footage was shot a year ago in Belgium, and features Senta in several of the scenes. We both dread watching it. It's not just the effect that this brutal reminder of our loss will have on our emotions, raking everything up again, but the fact that viewers will be reminded of Senta's murder, which may trigger a new wave of condolences and well-intended but painful enquiries about how we are coping. Quite apart from dreading the broadcast, Gerry is now fretting more and more about the effect of the economic slump on the restaurant. So far so good, but he keeps saying it can't last. To cheer him up, I remind him that last year when his series went on air, it was followed by a sharp increase in bookings. 'Ach, ya, Vita, but dat was before de economy went down de pluckhole. I sink people will start staying at home or going to cheaper places, you know, pizzerias, Greek tavernas...'

'Not your customer base. They're a totally different category.' I tell him. But he's just not in the mood for consolation.

Greek tavernas...

VIENNA, SEPTEMBER 1984

That evening before the start of the tour in Vienna, Walter and I went out for what was meant to be a final pre-tour romantic dinner *à deux* in a small Greek restaurant. We'd just ordered our meal when who should appear but Silke, Claudio, Gyorgy the lion-maned Bulgarian conductor and the wooden and lispingly camp Polish tenor, Paweł Something-ski. I cursed under my breath, but to my exasperation, Walter didn't seem at all to mind the invasion of our last evening alone in two and a half months. On the contrary, he even suggested that we push our tables together. I tried to read Silke's reaction. She had a sort of frozen half smile which could have hidden any number of emotions. Did she know Claudio and I had been out that same afternoon? Claudio was brazen. He came over, kissed me on both cheeks with a casual '*Ciao bella,*' and sat down opposite me with a sly wink. Silke and I brushed cheeks, coolly, exchanging minimal clipped greetings with arctic politeness and Medusa eyes. Walter introduced me to the other two. I was fuming, but determined not to show it, yet in my head, I thought I heard the death-knell of our relationship.

We all drank too much, even though the retsina was awful – odd how it only ever seems to taste right in Greece. Conversation went on in three languages and occasionally lapsed into English. Walter and Paweł spoke in Polish, Gyorgy, the director, was conversing in German with Silke. Claudio and I spoke in Italian, what little we did say to each other. Inevitably, the main topic of discussion was opera; this production, past productions, their highs and lows, what was going on in Milan, in London, in New York, who was hot and who was not. Then the sacred name of Wagner cropped up. Walter alluded to the fact that I was having a little difficulty coming to grips with the great man's music. All eyes were on me, briefly, as if I were some kind of leper. Silke's green eyes glinted superciliously. Then Claudio admitted that he'd never cared much for Wagner either. Music with the specific gravity of a ship's anchor; hours of hysterical warbling and thunderous booming.

Silke beamed an icy stare at Claudio and then shifted her gaze to me: 'I sink you need to have a Tcherman soul to understent Vaaaagner.' This in English, for everyone's benefit. Brief silence, then Gyorgy cleared his throat: 'I don't agree, Silke. I am not German, but I love Wagner. But I think that, almost more than with any other composer, you have to understand what he was trying to do, what his philosophy was. Then at least you can appreciate what a *genius* the man was. But to say you have to be German... no, that seems a little chauvinistic to me.'

I could have kissed the man.

The meal ended in a wrangle over the bill. Back at our modest hotel, Walter and I had an awkward night together, both of us determined to pretend that nothing was wrong. His mind was already on tour, so conversation was more strained than usual and our lovemaking was mechanical, alienating instead of bonding and comforting. I told him about my unexpected cinema outing with Claudio and tried to gauge his reaction. He froze and gave me a strange look. For a moment, I thought he might be jealous. Claudio, he said, was '*ein interessanter Typ.*' I wanted to know more, but he was unwilling to expand, and I decided not to probe for fear of provoking a scene on our last evening together. I wondered what he would have said if I told him about the hand holding.

The following day, Claudio offered me a lift back to Munich in his dirty red Alfa Spyder. It would be dishonest of me now to pretend that all manner of ignoble fantasies to do with revenge on Silke did not go through my mind, but I tried to suppress them. Walter's description of Claudio as '*ein interessanter Typ*' suddenly struck me as intriguing and deeply ambiguous. There was a touch of something louche and vaguely amoral about Claudio. He reminded me of a tomcat; sleek, slinky, sexual, independent, casual, cool, unknowable, attractive. Very attractive. No way, I said to myself. Don't even *think* about it...

As we hurtled along the Autobahn in torrential rain, I brought up the subject of Wagner, and Silke's comment about the German soul. Claudio told me he knew of a woman in Munich who held weekly classes in Wagner appreciation at her apartment. He was thinking of signing up, to see whether a greater understanding might help him, if not to like, then at least to appreciate Silke's favourite composer. He too was irritated by this belief of Silke's, that one couldn't appreciate Wagner if one wasn't German. As if we non-Germans were not quite evolved, not quite civilised enough to appreciate Wagner's genius. How did I feel about signing up for the Wagner class? I thought it would be a great idea.

When we reached the flat in Haidhausen, I did not invite him in. In the car, I scribbled my telephone number on the back of a supermarket till receipt and handed it to him. He smiled and squeezed my knee. '*Ciao bella. Ci vediamo.*'

23ʳᴰ NOVEMBER 2008

Tristan is in a complete state again. Every time I think he's getting a bit better, he has a relapse and seems worse than before. Therapy doesn't appear to be very effective, but who knows how much worse he might be without it. Sometimes I fear for his sanity, because he doesn't seem able to find a way of coping with what he perceives as his guilt, but at least he has never once mentioned suicide. Not, however, that I consider this to be in any way grounds for complacency, and the possibility haunts me constantly.

'When is it going to stop?' he moans, as he sits up in bed and I hand him a glass of water. He's woken us both in the middle of the night with his thrashing and mumbling, in the throes of yet another nightmare.

'Why can't I have pills for this kind of thing? It's driving me fucking nuts.'

'Darling, the last thing you want is pills. You of all people should know that drugs are not the solution.'

'Doctor's pills, Mum. They're like... different?'

'Do you want me to take you back to see Dr Hemming again?'

'Yeah, no, dunno. Maybe...'

'Try and get some sleep, darling. It's gone 3:30 and you've got to get up for school tomorrow.'

'Fucking school,' he mutters, then turns his back to me, pulls the duvet up and sighs deeply. Sleep is treacherous territory for his disturbed mind, not the balmy restorative oblivion it should be, but a dark, dank, cavernous dungeon haunted by visions of syringes, of knives and of blood-soaked slaughter. At school they think he's narcoleptic. He keeps falling asleep in class.

On the day when I received Walter's concert schedule, that Saturday last November in Clapham, we had a major scare with Tristan. It was Doobie's excited barking that woke me up. Tristan had just come home. I glanced at my alarm clock. Gone six in the evening. Instead of getting up, as had been my intention earlier that day, I'd fallen asleep again. My sketchpad was on the floor and my pencils were scattered around the bed. Damn! Get up. Have a shower, become a fully-functioning parent again. Set your troubled teenage son a good example. I leapt up, not wanting him to see me sluttishly dishevelled, undressed and still in bed. A dull ache in my abdomen reminded me that all was not healed yet down under. I carefully straightened the duvet, opened a window, hastily stashed some discarded clothes in the wardrobe and, just as he was clumping up the stairs, locked myself in the bathroom and got under the shower.

I was surprised to find that the kitchen had been tidied up. Presumably the mess had got too much for Senta. She'd even mopped the floor and put Doobie's gunky bowl to soak in the sink. Should I feel grateful or ashamed? Since the departure in June of our most recent cleaner, a sulky little Slovak girl who cleaned like a demon, the house had gradually turned into a tip. We'd hired an Albanian, a plump, dark-haired girl in her late teens, who was absolutely brilliant, if a little over-enthusiastic with the cleaning products, but who, after a couple of weeks, simply vanished. Then we had a Pole, Małgosia, who was pleasant enough but clumsy and none too thorough. She kept breaking things, then hiding the evidence, hoping we wouldn't notice. Six weeks and half a dozen breakages later, we terminated her services. Since then, nobody. Of course, I'd been recuperating from my operation. I am not one for housework at the best of times, but right then it was simply impossible to do much, as I was not supposed to lift anything. I decided guilt was an entirely inappropriate sentiment under the circumstances – I should just be grateful to Senta and remember to thank her for cleaning up.

Tristan and his friend, the tall, bespectacled Sam, were in the kitchen. Sam, with his Buddy Holly face, who always looked so serious and studious. Hard to believe the things he got up to. Their presence here at that time of day on a Saturday meant only one thing – they were hungry, and Sam was rather partial to our non-kosher food. I looked in the fridge. For the past three months, Gerry had been bringing back leftovers from the restaurant every night, so that I wouldn't have to cook. I lifted the lid off a large terracotta pot.

'Some kind of carbonnade. I'm afraid it looks like it might be pork,' I said, out of mock-concern for Sam. It was a game I played with him.

'No worries, Mrs S. Yahweh will forgive, I'm sure. He must know pork is clean these days!'

We ate at the dining table. Sam tried to make conversation with me, which I found endearing. Tristan, my darling son, made no effort whatsoever. Sam asked me if I'd designed a new collection yet. I told him I'd only just started sketching some designs earlier today, shapes vaguely inspired by winter themes. Just then, Tristan's mobile rang. He checked the number, raised his eyebrows and decided not to answer.

'That reminds me. Dad forgot his mobile here today,' I say.

'Yeah? Ah well, never mind. He's got another one, hasn't he. A little Nokia.'

'Oh, has he? I... had forgotten about that,' I reply.

Tristan shot me an ambiguous look. Forgotten? I didn't know anything about this second mobile, but wasn't going to let on. Why hadn't Gerry mentioned anything to me?

Tris and Sam stayed in for a while to play some apocalyptic and hideously violent video game. As I stashed the plates in the dishwasher, I could only think of one thing. What possible reason could Gerry have for a second mobile if he weren't up to something he didn't want me to know about?

Back in the bedroom, I remember undressing and examining myself stark naked in the full-length mirror. This vanity seems quite ridiculous in retrospect, yet these dark days I'd give anything to have the luxury of such trivial concerns. Not bad for fifty-three, I remember thinking, but still... undeniably fifty-three. Apart from a slackness of the belly from two pregnancies, and that new, very red scar from the navel down to the pubic bone, I still have a good figure and particularly good legs, though I'd begun to notice a tiny web of blue veins spreading at the back of my knees. As for breasts... well, definitely not very pert, following two lots of breast feeding, but still quite presentable, especially when cantilevered by a good bra. Neck and jaw line... signs of sagging when I lower my chin to my chest, but quite passable still when I hold my head up. I have high cheekbones which help to hold things in place. Face... crow's feet aplenty and smile lines around the mouth. Don't mind those – at my age I do not even wish to look like an eighteen-year-old. But what I do hate are those little vertical lines that have started to appear round my lips, into which lipstick likes to bleed. Cat's arse syndrome. Should I resort to Botox and collagen?

My God, did I really consider that? I believe I did... But in fact the only truly frightful thing about my appearance at that time was my hair. During my thirties, my once blond hair faded to a sort of dirty dishwater colour, and I went through phases of dying it jet black, magenta red and platinum blonde in an assortment of styles, just about everything from boyishly short to a severe asymmetrical bob. For the past ten years or so, I'd given up on it, hoping it would turn a low maintenance shade of elegant, artistic silvery grey, but instead it was a limp salt-and-pepper mess with some faded strands of anaemic gold. I tended to wear it up rather carelessly in a messy bun or in a ponytail.

Staring at it in the mirror, that day just over a year ago when we had no inkling of what was about to befall us, it suddenly, instantly became the focus of an obsession. Something had to be done about it – immediately. How could I have been so blind about this? It was this dowdy hair that made me look haggard, scrawny, old before my time. On impulse, I picked up my mobile and called the always immaculately-coiffed Ewa. What was the number of her hairdresser?

'Vitka darlink, it's seven thirty on a Saturday evenink. Even Damian can't help you now. How about Monday mornink first think? Can you bear to wait that lonk?'

I pulled on a thick sweater and a pair of Uggs and poured myself a generous glass of Pinot Noir which I took to the studio, the large garden shed where I made my jewellery. It was not exactly warm in there, so I turned on the radiators, stretched out on the ancient creaky sun lounger, rolled myself a large spliff and wondered how to confront Gerry.

At some point later in the evening, there was an urgent knock on the studio door. Senta didn't wait for my answer but came straight in. She was holding my mobile as if it were a dead rat.

'Oh God, Mum! Why do you have to be off your face right now of all times. Here, it's Dad for you.' She thrust my mobile at me. She was unusually agitated. That was obvious to me even in my drugged state. And when Senta got stressed, she was prone to fits. It's an Aspie thing.

'Vita? I just had a phone call here at de restaurant...'

'Yeah?'

'It was Martin McCullough's father. He told me dat when he came home just now, he found Martin and Sam in a panic because Tris had collapsed and they didn't know what to do, so he called an ambulance.'

Martin McCullough... the one person both Sam and Tristan had been forbidden from seeing. Martin had been expelled from school for drugs and petty theft. He was an only child, and his mother had left when he was very young. He lived with his father, a QC, in an apartment on Cheyne Walk. The problem was, Martin was on his own all day, neither studying nor working, and seemed to have developed a serious drug habit.

'I can't leave the restaurant at dis time. You have to go.'

'Jesus...Which hospital?'

I cringe with shame as I recall this now...

Woozy from the weed and wine, I had to force myself to engage with ugly, brutal reality. Senta was still standing over me. She had a look of pure disgust on her face.

'Car or tube?'

'Car. You drive.'

'At least brush your teeth before we leave, Mum. Change your clothes – they smell of dope. And drink some water. I will make you a double espresso while you get changed.'

On the way to St Thomas's, I was in an absolute funk. What had Tris, Sam and Martin been up to? Had they been dabbling again? Chasing the dragon? Sniffing? Shooting up? Smoking skunk? It had to be one of those, surely. At the same time, I was scared stiff that a doctor or nurse would immediately spot my own state of intoxication, although the shock had gone some way to sobering me up. What kind of example was I to my son? I started to cry.

'I'm a lousy mother. I should have tried harder to reach out to him. I've failed him. I've failed your brother.'

Senta stared straight ahead as she clutched the steering wheel.

'Stop beating yourself up over him, Mum. This isn't your fault. We are all free to make certain choices.' Her voice was the usual unemotional cool monotone.

'Yes, but look at what kind of example we've been to him. Your father and I, between us, we're not much cop as parents. A dope smoking mother and a career-obsessed never-at-home telly chef for a father.'

Senta set her jaw.

'This isn't about you. For God's sake, Mum, this is about Tristan. Why must you always blame yourself for everything. It's a kind of... vanity. You just do it to invite denial and consolation.'

I didn't know how to hit that particular spin back. She'd obviously been reading some Teach Yourself Psychobabble book. I lowered the window to suck some cold damp London air into my lungs.

'He'll grow out if it, Mum,' she said, to break the silence.

'If he doesn't kill himself first.'

'He's just being a bit of a drama queen. Attention-seeking, I think they call it.'

'So he's not getting enough attention?'

'I don't know. I don't really understand these things.'

I let it rest there. It was true, Senta had little real understanding of human psychology, though she was often able to fool people for a short while. I'd certainly tried to give Tristan plenty of attention, but whenever I attempted to talk to him, he'd ignore me, brush me off or reply in grunted monosyllables. Senta herself had also been particularly uncommunicative at that age, which, we were warned, was entirely to be expected from an Aspie, but unlike Tristan, she had done nothing to provoke us. She simply locked herself away and communicated almost exclusively with Grandpa Sven, the only member of our family who was on a remotely similar intellectual wavelength. Even then, the few snatches of telephone conversations with him that I overheard were about her studies, about scientific topics or articles she wanted to discuss, never about personal or emotional problems.

Tristan, on the other hand, quite apart from dabbling in drugs and skiving off school, was nicking things and sticking studs through his tongue and rings through his navel as well as getting septic tattoos in dodgy parlours where they were not too particular about checking the age of their clients. And he was telling lies.

On the ward, I spotted Martin McCullough and his father with a rather fierce-looking nurse. Martin was showing great interest in his shoes. No sign of Sam. McCullough senior looked up as we approached.

'Mrs Steeneken...'

I ignored him and turned to the nurse. 'Where's my son?'

'In the operating theatre. Having his appendix out.'

'His appendix? He has appendicitis? Oh, thank God for that!'

'Mum!' Senta moaned, pinching my arm hard.

'Well, it's not that trivial. If an appendix bursts, you can be in serious trouble,' the nurse explained to me, her head cocked sideways, her pale eyes narrowed, flickering with suspicion and disapproval. My reaction must have seemed utterly bizarre, even callous to her, and no doubt I'd have been able to control it better had I not been under the influence.

'My mother means... I mean, the reason why... er, well, my brother's been dabbling in drugs of late, and...'

'Oh,' said the nurse giving me the stink eye, 'now I understand.' Could she smell the weed on me? Had the smell lingered in my hair? Did she really think I'd supplied drugs to my own son?

McCullough Senior shot me an *Aha!* look that put me straight in the dock.

24TH NOVEMBER 2008

My God! Have just discovered that Tristan is in the school choir! Would have thought that was extremely uncool, but what do I know. He probably wouldn't have told me if Rhys hadn't enquired about the school's apparently famous carol service over dinner. Marcus then said that Tris would know, because he's in the choir. In the Norwich Academy Choral Society. I can't believe it. It's like a throwback to the good old days when he was an angelic boy soprano at Westminster, singing the solo in 'Once in Royal David's City' and making his mother weep silly sentimental tears.

'Really? You're in the school choir?' I say to Tris.

'Yeah. It's no big deal,' he says, blushing scarlet.

Something tells me all is not lost, and a little vestige of the angel boy is still alive and well.

The days that followed Tristan's appendectomy a year ago were the sweetest. Convalescing at home, he was meek as a lamb, all his childhood vulnerability having returned for a brief visit before saying its final farewells. He admitted that he'd been doing a line of coke with Martin and Sam when the pain in his abdomen, which had been nagging away at him for some time, suddenly became unbearable. I sat at his bedside and we made a pact – we would both give up drugs. And wine drinking, for me, was to be restricted to a glass or two at the weekend and only at meal times. I knew it was going to be hellishly hard for me, but how else could I set an example?

I tidied, dusted and vacuumed his room for him while he watched from his bed. I was ashamed of the fact that I had not set foot in there in many months. I had kidded myself that this was out of some kind of respect for his privacy, but in truth I knew it was really out of fear for what I might discover. What I did find was mostly predictable and innocuous; encrusted mugs and plates, mouldy trainers, piles of dirty laundry. The porn mags I was convinced he'd have stashed under his bed proved to be a figment of my imagination, but then again, I suppose that stuff is all over the internet these days. God knows what sick stuff he accesses on his laptop.

I went through all his things in his presence, and found no trace of drugs other than a small lump of cannabis which we ceremoniously flushed down the loo, along with my own supply. The last thing to sort out was the debris of childhood. He opted to keep Rupert Bear, Action Man and an assortment of Corgi toys, but was happy to let the rest go to the Oxfam shop.

A week later, Tristan was back at school and I decided to go ahead with my planned transformation. With hindsight, this was clearly triggered not just by my suspicion that Gerry was having an affair, but by Walter's note. I wanted to prove to both of them that I was still attractive. Pathetic and vain, I know, but I wanted to feel better about myself, to reclaim, at the age of fifty-three, what could be salvaged of my sexuality.

When I came home from Damian's, Ewa's hideously expensive hairdresser, I was feeling girlishly rejuvenated. Damian's expression had been one of barely-disguised horror as he squeamishly fingered my straggly salt-and-pepper locks. Sizing up my slender physique and small features, he decided on a blonde retro look à la Twiggy circa 1967, though less sleek than Sassoon's original, to make it a little more 'age appropriate.' The result was a dramatic change. The asymmetrical blond bob took years off me and awakened the lust for a shopping spree, which I indulged that very afternoon. I was suddenly determined to shed the mud and sludge colours I'd been wearing of late with something a lot more vibrant and positive. Lime green, white, watermelon red.

Gerry was home when I got back, Monday being his only day off. I opened the door, wondering how he'd react, only to walk straight into a father and son slanging match. Tristan, supposedly back at school after his week-long convalescence, had been playing truant yet again and the school had phoned to find out if our son was genuinely sick or just skiving. Gerry had been in all day, so he knew Tris was out. When he tried phoning him, he heard Tristan's mobile ring in the bedroom. He'd left it at home, no doubt deliberately. At tea time, the prodigal had reappeared, pretending to have spent a fruitful day at school. Gerry had let rip. He still hadn't learned that shouting at Tris got you nowhere. He would simply retreat into a sullen silence and refuse to answer questions with anything other than an infuriating shrug or a mocking smile. It was an ignoble relief to see that Tristan could be just as rude to Gerry as to me. The last year or so, I'd borne the brunt of his teenage moods. Gerry, who was in De Vlaaminck or at the BBC every evening bar one, had been smugly convinced that I simply didn't know how to handle Tristan, when in fact he was simply rarely there to do so. Lately, Tris had developed the annoying habit of riling Gerry by quietly mocking his Flemish accent, which was guaranteed to push Gerry's buttons. I found them in the kitchen – Tristan foraging in the fridge while Gerry, red in the face, was leaning against the sink. I stood in the doorway.

'Let's hear what your mudder hess to say about dis,' growled Gerry, who'd heard me come home. His accent always got stronger when he was agitated. Then he looked up and saw me.

'*A maai!*' he exclaimed, his expression switching from anger to pure bug-eyed amazement.

Tris retrieved a ToxiCola from the fridge, popped the ring pull and looked up. His cheeks were flushed and his eyes had a feverish shine.

'Jesus Mum! What have you gone and done to yourself!' They were both gawping, in surprise rather than admiration. Gerry seemed pleased with my new look, but it was hard to change mood so suddenly from argument to compliment. He poured himself a glass of water and took a swig, then composed himself and switched gears.

'Glad you are feeling more like your old self. So what brought all dis on?'

I shrugged and smiled. Tristan snuck past me into the living room. Gerry made me an espresso and we sat down at the kitchen table. He took my hand and looked into my eyes. His, I noticed, were bloodshot and tired. I wanted to ask him about the second mobile business, but the fact that he'd only just had a shouting match with Tristan and said something nice to me put me off. I decided to leave it for the time being.

'Well?' he said, eyeing my hair.

'Oh, you know, I just felt like a change. Sick of being sick and sad,' I said, lamely. In fact I was sick of being fifty-three and invisible. Sick of being a frump. Sick of the lack of passion and excitement in my life. Sick of myself, of being uninspired and uninspiring, of working with a business partner whose vision I had long ceased to share. Of designing pseudo-chic accessories for wannabe socialites. Saddened by my son's recklessness, my daughter's remoteness, my husband's apparent infidelities, my new sexlessness and the advent of old age. My God, that haircut and those new threads had their work cut out.

We heard the front door lock click quietly into its slot. Tristan had slipped away. He had told Gerry he'd started feeling unwell on the way to school, so had spent the day with his old friend Dominic who'd dropped out of school only a month ago, much to his parents' despair. Gut ache, Tris claimed. Probably connected with his appendectomy. Hadn't wanted to come all the way back home. Decided that Dom's place was more convenient, just round the corner from the school. Very convenient for a day of Play Station, surfing the net for porn and doing some dope, Gerry had said to him.

Gerry and I stared at each other. What were we supposed to do with Tristan? How could we reclaim him? He seemed to think nothing of making promises and breaking them immediately. He lied. He stole. He had, in the space of eighteen months, gone from being a sweet-natured parent-pleasing angel to a complete shit. Complicating this was the fact that it was his GCSE year; not a good time to be farting around.

'Maybe we should ask Senta to take him along to one of her Unitarian meetings,' Gerry suggested. At that, we both burst out laughing. The sun had peeked through the clouds after a thunderstorm, but it didn't stick around for long. Gerry had some meeting with the producers of his series. An evening meeting? Or a little rendez-vous with some floozy? If not Sandrine the sous-chef, then some other little cheffette on the make? Or was it some producer at the Beeb? Was it an affair that had given him the impetus finally to do something about his waistline?

'Don't forget your mobiles.' I said, a throwaway sort of comment as he left the kitchen to go upstairs and get changed.

'Uhuh.'

That was it. 'Uhuh'. I wondered if he'd heard me properly. I let it go. I didn't have the energy. Or maybe it was just plain fear.

27TH NOVEMBER 2008
AROUND 3 AM. (COMPLETE INSOMNIA)

Shocking news this evening. Terrorists are attacking various locations in Bombay/Mumbai, mainly, it would seem, ones frequented by foreigners. They are in the Taj Mahal hotel, where they appear to have embarked on an insane shooting spree. The sight of all that blood and carnage has completely freaked me out, and whereas Tristan and the others just sat and stared mutely at the television screen, I had to leave the kitchen. I went into Astrid's studio and curled up in the foetal position on the bean bag sofa. No tears came, which is bad, as tears provide release. I'd just gone rigid. I felt suicidal. I wanted to fall asleep and never wake up again. I could see no way out of my unhappiness, and that triggered a toxic fog of despair. Astrid followed me and sat next to me, stroking my hair. Then Tris joined us and sat on the floor, leaning his head against my legs. A couple of minutes later, Rhys and Marcus came with mugs of tea. We didn't speak. Sometimes it is better that way. We huddled together mutely for consolation and warmth, like a litter of abandoned puppies.

I still cannot write about Senta's murder or the funeral. Or not yet anyway. Grief has no cure, but time will gradually diminish it, so we have been promised, by Astrid and Rhys, by Ewa, by well-meaning friends, by the kind but useless grief counsellor recommended to us by the police. And by Jenny Burrows who lost her own son, and who runs a South London counselling group for the parents of murdered children. There is, she pointed out, no noun to describe a parent who has lost a child. A child without a parent is an orphan, and we have the words widow and widower for bereaved spouses, but there is a gap in the English language for those of us who have lost a child, whether through illness, suicide, accident or murder. Maybe it's too awful to have a noun of its own, or maybe it is simply too banal. Not so long ago, before the days of vaccinations, antibiotics and sophisticated surgery, it would have been all too common for children to die young. You had as many as you could bear, to ensure at least some would survive. After all, Mother Nature culled the weak without mercy.

Eight months have passed since her murder; December is round the corner and we face the first Christmas without her, but I have yet to experience that promised diminution. I do find, however, that the times when I do not actively think about Senta and Toby are getting longer, and I even experience the briefest spells of happiness, but as soon as I become aware of them, I am sucked back into a searing, sickening vortex of loss.

Gerry's reactions are often ones of incomprehension and anger: 'Why Senta? Why her? Why my daughter? Why our extraordinary girl? *Waarom?*' Strange, but this is one question I never ask myself. Gerry has always considered himself an atheist, yet it seems he has retained some illogical vestige of belief in divine justice, and therefore in the divine. Gerry's god is of the Old Testament variety; irascible, fickle and jealous, and he hurls abuse at Him. I envy Gerry the luxury of this punch ball. I don't have anything to smash or curse or vilify. I'm just punching the air. I just feel empty and I harbour a deeply ignoble fear, one I daren't share with anyone because it seems so selfish. It is the fear that our lives and that of Isobel and her parents have been wrecked forever, and that we will never know true happiness again. Every now and then this feeling engulfs me, and it has not dimmed in the slightest. It crashes over me like a tidal wave each time. I mourn, yet I try hard not to indulge my grief for fear that it will destroy me. But where exactly is the line between mourning and wallowing in grief? There is no line, of course. Just a grey zone. You have to find your own balance.

That is the hardest thing.

28ᵀᴴ NOVEMBER 2008

Rhys has lent me a couple of books about creative writing. I am reluctant to read them lest I should discover that I am complete crap at it. I still doodle a lot on a sketchpad which I keep next to the laptop. I was just looking at the circle drawings I made last month, with those dates and facts contained in the circles. Missing, significantly, are the dates of the deaths. That of Phailin and Otto in December 1984, and that of Senta and Toby on April 4th 2008. Three knifings and a suicide. I now baulk at the sight of knives – not ordinary cutlery, but cook's knives, carving knives; anything with a vicious blade and a sharp point. Astrid and Rhys had their kitchen knives hanging from a magnetic strip by the range. Astrid caught me staring at them one day back in May, a few days after I'd moved in. The next day they had disappeared. She'd put them out of sight in one of the kitchen drawers.

Christmas... what a nightmare prospect. Can't face sending cards with just three names on them. No presents this year, Astrid has suggested. Just donations to the Aspie charity, the Asperger's Syndrome Foundation. Heaven knows they deserve it, for all the help and support they've provided to us over the years.

30TH NOVEMBER 2008

These recollections, along with another little incident involving Tristan, have brought on a powerful urge to escape from the farm and the louring, headache-inducing pewter-coloured clouds of a Norfolk autumn. I am simply gagging for London. Ungrateful though it may sound, I have started to long more and more for my own surroundings, my own house, my studio shed, my life back in Clapham with Gerry and Ewa and our friends. Old customers have been asking for commissions, and I have had to turn them down. Astrid and Rhys have been wonderful in their support of us and I don't know how we could have coped without them, but I'm beginning to tire of a life spent between the guest bedroom and the kitchen table. The prospect of having to stay here for the next year and a half to monitor Tristan while he limps through the sixth form is depressing, but I daren't admit it to anyone because it seems so un-maternal, so thankless of me. Yet another thing to feel guilty about.

Two nights ago, Tris had done the usual post-midnight bed switch. He was thrashing about in his dream, and I was steeling myself for the screams and shouts that so often erupt from his nightmares, when instead, he rolled over and grabbed me, panting, and came on my thigh. I don't know which one of us was more embarrassed. I tried desperately to make light of it, but he was mortified. When I came back from cleaning myself up in the bathroom, he'd gone. There was no sign of him in the room he shares with Marcus and I eventually found him in Astrid's studio, hunched up and shivering on the bean bag sofa.

There was no persuading him back to his own bed, let alone mine. No amount of me saying things like 'Don't be silly, it's just a reflex, you were dreaming,' made the slightest bit of difference. He was too embarrassed even to look me in the eye. He seemed to want to indulge his embarrassment.

The studio was cold – far too cold to sleep in without half a dozen blankets or quilts, and in the middle of the night I could hardly go barging into Astrid and Rhys's bedroom asking for spare ones. In the end, we dragged the bean bag sofa into the kitchen and placed it, much to the annoyance of the dogs, in front of the range, which was blasting out heat. I promised Tris we'd sort something out for him the following day, though I hadn't a clue what. Of course he's made me swear not to tell anyone what happened.

The next morning, I simply told Astrid that his nightmares were too much for me to cope with, without going into any detail. We moved his single bed from Marcus's room into what used to be Dylan's room. The bed in there is covered in junk and boxes of stuff from his student days, boxes that have never been unpacked and sorted. He will have to do something about them when he comes home for Christmas. Sleeping arrangements promise to be tricky, as Mother will be here too. Putting Tris in Dylan's room seems like the best solution, yet I worry about not being there to comfort him when he has a nightmare, and wonder about getting one of those monitoring devices that we had when Senta and Tris were babies. Astrid doesn't like the idea. She reckons it'll just infantilise Tristan and make him more dependent on me. I find that rather harsh. I console myself with the thought that I should in any case be able to hear him, as Dylan's room is next door to mine and the bed is just the other side of the wall.

3RD DECEMBER 2008

Just back from a brief jail break. With Christmas approaching, I find myself teetering on the edge of panicky depression, wondering how we are going to cope. I just wish we could fast forward through to the summer of 2009, past what would have been Senta's 23rd birthday on January 18th. Past the anniversary from hell in April. I am also finding winter time on the farm to be rather claustrophobic. The weather is so grim right now that I don't even feel like taking the dogs for walks by the river. I was getting a real case of cabin fever, made worse by the incident with Tristan, and had to escape. Astrid encouraged this and salved my conscience about abandoning Tristan by promising to sleep with her bedroom door ajar, so she could listen out for any nightmares and provide the necessary words of comfort. Tris would have to scream very loud, as Astrid sleeps like the dead. I'd have to rely on Rhys waking her up.

I took the train to Liverpool Street and spent three days in London, catching up with Ewa, seeing Mother and visiting my jewellery guru, Susanna di Maggio. Despite the usual Christmas trappings, London is in the grip of a very sober mood, and it doesn't take long ere the topic of the economic situation rears its head in conversation. Gerry has the bug quite badly too, but both Ewa and Susanna are only marginally affected so far. In fact, Susanna told me a funny thing. Her customers are coming to her, saying that they now want to 'invest' in gold rather than spend money on things of a more ephemeral nature. Ewa too has heard talk of 'investing in classic pieces.' It's as if customers feel guilty about spending on luxuries when thousands are losing their jobs, and want to justify what might be perceived as Marie-Antoinette-ish extravagance.

I stayed at Ewa's in the bedroom that Gerry and I used to share when we first met, all those years ago. It's where Gerry has been sleeping for the past six months or so, rather than come home late at night to our eerily-deserted house. The room still contains the same double bed, which brought back happy memories of nights of passion but also made us cry. Curled up together for comfort and consolation under the thick duvet, we talked about our house and about the need to brace ourselves and sort out Senta's things. House prices are plummeting, and the recommended asking price of just under two million which the estate agent seemed so confident about back in May now seems hopelessly optimistic. In fact, Gerry and I were both beginning to have our doubts about the wisdom of putting the house on the market, irrespective of the economic meltdown. We had both thought it would be wise to make a completely new start, rather than stay on in the same place and learn to live with constant reminders of the times when Senta was still with us. Now we are not so sure. We have both, unbeknownst to each other, started to miss the place and long for our familiar surroundings.

Yesterday morning we did it. Ewa, Gerry and I went through the connecting gate in the back garden wall which we had put in some twenty years ago to enable easier access to each other's houses. Our house was remarkably tidy as Ewa had arranged for a team of cleaners to blitz the place after the estate agent had hinted darkly that the mess did little to create a favourable impression on potential buyers. Senta's room was the only one she had instructed them not to touch, but it would have been the only immaculate one in the house anyway. The three of us climbed the stairs and stood in the middle of her little realm. A thin layer of dust had settled over her desk. In the corner of the window frame, quivering in a wintry sunbeam, was a large spider's web. Senta was fascinated by such things and would have studied the geometry of its structure with a magnifying glass. She told me once that a web was believed to mimic a pattern resembling those that are reflected by certain flowers in UV light. Insects on the look-out for their preferred flower would see the web in UV and fly into the sticky trap. She'd have studied the spider and taxonomied it into its correct arachnid class. This particular spider seemed to have abandoned its post for lack of prey, and the weak winter sun showed only dust on the sagging silvery threads. Ewa catches me staring at it and before I can put a hand out to stop her, she's taken a swipe at it, causing it to stick to her fingers. Gerry put his arms around us, but ironically he was the one who was overwhelmed with emotion and had to sit down on the bed, burying his face in his hands.

'What do you want me to do?' Ewa asked me softly. Shall we take clothes out of wardrobe? Take them to charity shop?'

I nodded and went in search of a couple of suitcases in the attic. Ewa and I did the packing. She took the bedclothes to put in her washing machine. Gerry, choking back his tears, picked up Senta's post-grad library card and wandered off round the house on a tour of inspection. He couldn't bear to stay in the room. When we had finished this saddest of tasks and come downstairs, he was on his haunches in the back garden, inspecting Senta's now neglected, overgrown vegetable patch. He'd harvested some rosemary for the restaurant. He came in, crushing the needles between forefinger and thumb and inhaling the scent: 'Remember how she loved dis smell?' he said, as he held his fingers under my nose, and we both had to fight the tears again.

Meanwhile, Ewa was inspecting the kitchen doorpost, running her finger along it. I thought for a moment that she was checking to see if the cleaners had done their job properly, but in fact she'd found our old growth chart; a series of little horizontal pencil lines for Senta and Tristan, recording their height on each birthday. Senta's last measurement was on 14 - 01 - 2005 – 1 metre and 83 centimetres. Tristan's was on 28 - 02 - 2007- 1 metre 81. He's a couple of centimetres taller than that now. I looked at Gerry. 'I don't think I can bear to sell this place, Ger. It's too much a part of us.'

'Ja. Too much a part of us,' he echoed. 'I feel dat too. Let's take it off de market.'

Ewa smiled and kissed us both. 'I'm so glad, darlinks. Come back with me and I will make us some nice coffee and I send Anya to get cakes.'

I had a bad experience on the way back to catch the train to Norwich. I was on the tube when a couple of black teenage lads got on and sat down opposite me. I have tried hard to bury my memories of the murder trial, but the paler of the two reminded me of Laron Grant. They didn't look particularly threatening, clad in the ubiquitous generic urban teen uniform of the beanie, slouching in their seats, affecting an attitude of cool indifference while plugged into their iPods. A year ago their presence would scarcely have registered with me, but now I started to tremble, sweat and feel sick. There was just one more stop to go, and when I got up at Liverpool Street, my legs were shaking. I was completely disorientated and had to find somewhere to sit down and compose myself before I could board the train.

Back in September, Laron Deangelo Grant was sentenced to 12 years and 6 months for voluntary manslaughter. Aged seventeen and eight months, he was still a minor at the time of the stabbings.

How am I going to survive in London if I react like this every time I see a black teenage boy?

4TH DECEMBER 2008

If Tris had any nightmares during my absence, they hadn't woken Rhys, and unlike Astrid, he would surely have heard any screams or shouts. Tris phoned me when I was in London and asked me to bring back some beads and earring hooks so he could make a little Christmas present for Lucy. I am rather touched by this. Yesterday evening he sat at the kitchen table with me, selecting, arranging, rearranging and threading lapis, amber and moss agate beads onto two little wire coils and attaching them to hooks. Then he scrounged some coloured tissue paper from Astrid, wrapped the earrings in it and placed them in a tiny wooden box. On the lid he'd painted a duck with a drooping wing.

'Who is the lame duck?' I ask.

'Who do you think?' he mumbles. 'Not Lucy!'

'It's a nice idea,' I say.

'It's the least I can do. I've been a right shit to her.'

'Why?' I ask.

He shrugs. 'She's such a doormat. That's the problem. Sometimes I just want her to tell me to fuck off!'

'Maybe you should break up with her,' I suggest.

'She's not my girlfriend.'

'You sleep with her, don't you?'

'Does that make her my girlfriend?' The idea seems outlandish to him.

'What do you think?'

'Hmmm... I don't love her... I like her. I don't find her very attractive.'

'Attractive enough to fuck. You are using her. You know she's crazy about you.'

'Yeah!' He smiles and holds up the little box. 'So this is my way of saying I'm sorry.'

'One day the boot will be on the other foot,' I tell him. 'Some girl you are in love with will play cat and mouse with your heart. Then you'll know how Lucy feels.'

'Yeah, I'm a shit. I know...' He gets up and heads for the stairs.

'Tris, you need to become responsible for your actions and learn to be a little more considerate. It's part of growing up.'

He sighs, more out of irritation than contrition, and plods off.

5TH DECEMBER 2008

Just reread yesterday's entry. So much about Tristan reminds me of myself. It was quite strange to watch him fiddling with pliers and beads, much as I used to do many years ago. As for admonishing him for his behaviour, how hypocritical of me. I have hardly been a model of rectitude myself, especially in my Munich days, and I was ten years older than Tristan is now.

Gerry's first Christmas episode is on tonight. It's going to be hard to watch that footage, shot in mid-December 2007, of Gerry and Senta together, looking at how Belgians prepare for Christmas. Mother told me on the phone that she has decided not to watch and to have an early night instead. Gerry is going to watch it with Ewa, Sal and a bottle of brandy. How I wish we could suffer this together. Instead, I will be here with Tristan, Marcus, Astrid and Rhys.

It's going to be tough.

6TH DECEMBER 2008

Tristan decided he couldn't face it either, so he went out to Norwich with Marcus last night while Astrid, Rhys and I sat in the kitchen in front of the big screen, sipping the mulled wine I'd concocted and nibbling the spicy Belgian *speculoos* biscuits that Gerry had brought on his last visit. The scenes shot in the family restaurant in Brussels, showing a carefree Gerry joking with his old papa while Senta chats with Arnaud, the sous-chef, in her funny mix of French and Flemish; those scenes were too much for me. I wept and wept, silently, but could not tear myself away. Rhys offered to turn the TV off and Astrid held my hand. 'Don't torture yourself,' she said. 'Don't watch if you can't cope with it.'

Yet they understand my need to watch. If I don't, I'll always be left wondering what was in those two programmes. At the same time, I am churned up by this reminder of our past happiness, just a year ago, and my own idiotic behaviour at around the same time which almost cost us our marriage. That is something I have never even confessed to Astrid.

Some things are just too embarrassing.

MUNICH, AUTUMN 1984

Back from Vienna, I'd been faced with an empty flat. I had often dreamt of this in the crowded days when both Silke and Günter had lodged there. Now, instead of feeling liberated, I felt depressed. The Biedermeier furniture that Walter had inherited may have been pieces of the highest craftsmanship, but it simply wasn't my taste. Nor were the gloomy landscape paintings or the dark dusty velvet curtains, and I felt frustrated by the fact that I could not change anything about the décor to reflect my own preference for lighter, plainer Scandinavian stuff. I felt trapped in someone else's past. This was just not a young person's flat. At least Walter's bedroom was a little better – he'd long got rid of the old bed and bought a modern king-size double, but granny's mahogany wardrobe was still there, and it exuded a mothbally smell every time you opened the doors with their creaky hinges. I reprimanded myself for these feelings. A place like this, in Haidhausen, was a luxury well beyond most people's means.

Although I had met a lot of people through Walter, I had few friends I could call my own in Munich, apart from Ulrike, but she was married and had two young children, so was not exactly free to hang out with in the evenings or at weekends. Some of my colleagues at the Canadian Consulate were pleasant enough, but much older and all married. Fear of loneliness gripped my throat and turned my stomach. Looking back now, I realise how ill at ease I was with my own company. I needed people around me to stop me from dwelling on the glaringly obvious fact that I was not happy. *Pas bien dans ma peau.* Was it me? Was it my faltering relationship with Walter? What was the matter with me? Was I simply incapable of happiness? Was it some fatal flaw in my character? I got out my sketchpad and started to draw, but couldn't produce anything other than flowers with complex, twisting roots and nasty thorns in a sort of evil *Jugendstil* meets Arthur Rackham. I scrunched up the pages in frustration.

A week had passed without a sign of life from Walter. He had warned me that contacting me could be difficult because of the generally poor state of the telephone networks in Eastern Europe and the difficulty of even finding a functioning phone to call from. When the phone did ring, one Monday evening, I leapt up to answer it, thinking it was him, but instead it was Claudio, wanting to tell me that the first Wagner class was that Wednesday evening at Frau Elfriede Swoboda's flat in the Schellingstrasse in Schwabing, not far from his own place. He offered to meet at the Josephsplatz underground station exit at seven o'clock.

The woman who opened the door to us was in her sixties, plump, carefully and conservatively dressed in dark colours and sensible shoes. She had thick, picture-book silver granny hair, severely groomed into an immaculate chignon. Strangely at odds with this image of unimaginative bourgeois respectability, however, was her make-up. Her face was covered in a thick layer of foundation that was an unnatural pink, and her eyes were heavily made up with emerald green eye shadow and black eyeliner, making her look rather like an ageing flamenco dancer. We introduced ourselves, shook hands and followed her into the sitting room, a temple dedicated to Wagner. Everywhere you looked, there were prints of the man, framed Bayreuth programmes and old concert posters. There was a library of biographies and a massive collection of LPs, not just of Wagner, but of Verdi, Mozart, Bach and assorted lesser musical immortals. A gleaming black Steinway baby grand stood in a corner, its lid propped open. She seated us around a large dining table and poured us honey-sweetened herbal tea from a flask into little glasses in silver holders. We mentioned our recent visit to Vienna, her native city, which prompted a brief gush of nostalgic, misty-eyed girlhood recollections. Although she had lived in Munich for more than thirty years, she had retained her slow Austrian drawl, which, mercifully for me, meant her German was relatively easy to understand.

We had not been chatting long when the bell announced the arrival of the third and final member of our little class. We could hear Elfriede talk to a man with a booming Bavarian voice, but when she came back to the sitting room a few minutes later, she was accompanied only by a tiny, exquisitely beautiful, doll-like young Asian woman. Phailin was Thai, all of twenty-three, and had been married to Otto Schreiber for just under a year. I later learned that this had caused quite a few raised eyebrows among Munich society. Otto Schreiber was a wealthy local brewery owner in his fifties, with three children from his previous marriage, all older than Phailin. A corpulent cradle-snatcher with a catalogue bride.

Elfriede introduced us and we shook hands with Phailin. Hers was tiny, frail and limp, lacking confidence. She was dressed in a little wool Chanel-style suit with a pink silk blouse and black pumps, and her sleek black hair was swept up into a bun. The clothes and hairstyle seemed too old for her, but maybe that was the intention. She looked like a little twelve-year-old girl playing dress-up. Her German was very basic – I wondered how she was going to be able to follow the libretto and Elfriede's explanations. Her English was a little better, but so accented sometimes that it was hard to make out what she was saying. Elfriede expressed her concern about this, but Phailin just smiled. 'I just risten to music – is no plobrem.'

The problem, as any serious Wagnerite will tell you, is that the lyrics and the music are designed to be one. Wagner wrote all his own librettos, and the relationship between the words, their meaning, their stress patterns and the music itself is famously one great indivisible. Elfriede offered to translate and explain things in English, but I could see she was less than happy with this. On one occasion, when we were waiting for Phailin to arrive, she confessed that she would never have accepted Phailin on the course had she realised how poor her German was. She felt Otto Schreiber had misled her. Later she was of course to rue the day she'd been talked into taking her.

What did we do in that first session? Well, Elfriede asked us each why we wanted to study Wagner and what we hoped to get out of her course. It turned out that we all appeared to have much the same motive. Claudio and I both wanted to be able to understand what so held Walter and Silke in thrall. I also felt that studying Wagner might give me some insight into the nature of the German soul and help me feel less like an outsider. Claudio, however, claimed to be more interested in the music theory side of things. Why was Wagner considered 'superior' by some to his great Italian contemporary, Verdi? What aspect of compositional expertise was it that justified this hallowed status? Why was it considered among so many of the German opera crowd to be more sophisticated to like the chromatic Wagner rather than the diatonic Verdi?

'And you, Phailin?' asked Elfriede, switching to English.

She smiled sweetly and fingered a large sapphire pendant that graced her slender neck. 'My husban wan me to undastan Wagna,' she smiled.

As we stepped out into the windy autumnal night after our first class, a dark Mercedes drew up and an enormously fat man heaved his bulk out from behind the steering wheel; Otto Schreiber. He rang the entry phone bell. The door lock buzzed and clicked open. He'd come to collect his tiny bride, who'd stayed behind with Elfriede after we'd left. Presumably he wanted to find out what kind of progress she'd managed to make.

'A butterfly and an elephant!' Claudio remarked. He invited me back to his flat, in nearby Neureutherstrasse, but I declined, giving my need to get up early tomorrow morning to go to work as an excuse. He just smiled his annoying, unnerving smile.

'*Ciao bella, allora.* See you same time next week, then!'

With that, he gave me a cheeky pat on the bum and crossed the road.

Elfriede had lent us cassette copies of Deryck Cooke's introduction in English to the *Ring der Niebelungen*, Wagner's massive opera cycle consisting of *Das Rheingold*, *Die Walküre*, *Siegfried* and finally, *Götterdämmerung*. Our homework was to listen to it. This I did with grim determination. I ordered the librettos from Hugendubel on Marienplatz and I took the Cooke cassette to work with me. I listened to it with my Walkman in the bulletproof glass reception cubicle while manning the switchboard. This initially earned me disapproving looks from my boss, the Vice Consul, but when I assured him that I could quickly push the headphones over my head and round my neck if anyone came through the front door, he let me be. It wasn't, frankly, as if the consulate was particularly busy. The number of daily visitors could be counted on the fingers of one hand.

It was a good thing that I had Messrs Wagner and Cooke to occupy my waking moments, as I would have been bored stupid otherwise. There really wasn't a great deal for me to do at the Consulate. The Vice-Consul's assistant, a friendly young woman from Augsburg, showed me how to process passports. It seems like another age in these days of biometric wizardry. Canadian passports had the bearer's details typed on an old-fashioned manual typewriter and the photo, which had to show the bearer's signature on a white strip at the bottom, was simply glued in, without any kind of seal to prevent tampering. We would then sandwich the passports between two telephone directories and sit on them to flatten them before they were issued. How endearingly amateurish this now seems, in this post-9/11 age of hi-tech passports and paranoia about terrorism. At the time, typewriters were also gradually being replaced with word processors, but nobody knew how to use the new technology properly and my admin colleagues were sent on training courses from which I was excluded as I could not be freed from the shackles of the switchboard. I didn't care. I sat and listened and soaked up the fascinating information that Deryck Cooke imparted in his soothing mellifluous voice, and bit by bit I felt myself getting sucked in, bedazzled and seduced.

Phone calls from Walter were rare, as predicted. Twice, to my immense frustration, he managed to phone on Wednesday night while I was at Elfriede's Wagner class. I returned to the empty flat to find the red light blinking on the answering machine. The messages were crackly, full of static, strange clicks and pinging and hissing sounds. As far as I could work out, their content was reassuring yet blandly uninformative. The tour was going well, reviews in local newspapers were fulsome in their praise, Torsten Freitag had fallen backwards into the orchestra pit in Gyor and broken his thumb. The weather was lousy and the food was a mixed bag. Was I OK? He missed me.

Ich liebe dich, mein Schatz.

Had he been to bed with Silke Nass? Had the witch seduced the wizard?

I think it must have been some time in late October when Claudio invited me over one Saturday to listen to a recording of excerpts from *Das Rheingold* on his brand new Bang and

Olufsen stereo. It was my first visit to his lair, and I was a little nervous. I'd brought a bottle of Gewürztraminer, and fretted over the possibility that this might send out the wrong message and make this encounter seem too much like a date. He was clean-shaven for a change and his shoulder length hair, usually tied back in a rather greasy ponytail, was loose and shiny. When he kissed me on the cheek, I could smell some kind of lemony aftershave. I was both slightly alarmed and excited by these signs of grooming, which seemed to be for my benefit. Or was I flattering myself? Maybe Saturday night was his grooming night? Maybe he had intended to go out on the town after our little Wagnerian homework session?

His apartment, a studio flat, consisted of one large room with a raised platform in one corner on which lay a double mattress with rumpled bedclothes. The walls, painted a silvery grey, were covered in large black and white photographs, mainly stills from his work at the film studios, including one of Silke as a flower maiden in *Tristan and Isolde*, looking uncharacteristically vulnerable. His only piece of conventional furniture was a large glass coffee table in the middle of the room, strewn with bills, photographs and trade magazines. Instead of sofas or armchairs, he had large floor cushions. Camera equipment was everywhere, even in the bathroom, which doubled as a dark room. He proudly showed me his new stereo before disappearing into the kitchen to uncork the bottle, returning with a dish of olives and some sliced salami.

'How do two of you manage in one small flat,' I asked, surprised at the lack of anything that might testify to Silke's presence. No clothes, no shoes, no make-up in the bathroom. Had she taken it all on tour?

'We don't. She stayed one month and moved out – the flat above this one became vacant, so she took that.' He clinked his glass against mine and offered me an olive. He'd only heard once from Silke since the start of the tour. She'd called from some place on the Hungarian-Romanian border. Everything was alright apart from minor niggles, so it seemed. He didn't expect much communication while she was away. We chatted inconsequentially for a bit, then he got up to put on the record, which I imagine probably came from Silke's collection. It was an old recording from the sixties with Karl Böhm conducting a stellar cast, including Birgit Nilsson and Wolfgang Windgassen. I have the same recording at home in Clapham. Senta used to listen to it a lot.

Claudio was about to lower the stylus when he changed his mind. He went to the kitchen, returned with an old-fashioned biscuit tin and sank down again on his cushion. He held the tin up.

'Share a joint? I find it really improves my appreciation of Wagner.'

I sort of half nodded, half shrugged, not wanting to seem too keen. I was no stranger to weed even then, but could take it or leave it. He fashioned a roach out of a tram ticket and rolled the joint with an experienced hand. Then he pulled his floor cushion a little closer to mine to ease the sharing and put on the record. We toked and closed our eyes to the sound of the beautiful, drug-enhanced gentle swell of the Rheingold Prelude.

How long did we spend like this? I have no idea. Ten minutes? Half an hour? I don't recall, but at a certain point we both got the giggles. We must have finished the joint. Claudio got up and retrieved something from a shelf above his bed. When he turned round, he had glove puppets on his hands; one of Miss Piggy and one of Kermit the Frog. He kneeled in front of me and made Miss Piggy mime to the sounds of the Rhine Maidens singing: '*Wallala, Laialeia, Leialei,*' while Kermit swooned and squirmed, gurning grotesquely to the part of Alberich. I couldn't stop laughing. I was in hysterical tears.

Claudio rolled over on his back and Miss Piggy continued her aria to the fawning appreciation of the frog. I had to beg Claudio to stop, or I was going to choke. He turned round – Miss Piggy was singing right in my face now, with Kermit all atremble on my shoulder.

'Stop it! I can't stand it anymore. Claudio, *ti prego!*'

He shed the puppets, put his arms around me and pulled me close, burying his face in my neck.

'This is totally wrong,' I mumbled unconvincingly, half-heartedly clinging to some vestige, some pretence of moral scruple.

'Hmmm...' he said, as his mouth found my lips and his hands wandered under my sweater and over my crotch. 'You are absolutely right! Please tell me to stop at once!'

I didn't. I couldn't...

Looking back, I can say with confidence that he was one of the most experienced, imaginative lovers I have ever had. Our lovemaking left me breathless, flushed, hopelessly excited while he teased, dawdled, nibbled, kissed and introduced me, among other things, to the extraordinarily erotic sensation of having my toes sucked. I was stoned and drunk and astonished that, aged nearly twenty-nine, I still had so much to learn about lovemaking. The contrast with Walter's predictable routine was cruel. Or was my memory playing tricks on me?

Much later, our desires slaked, my body sticky and sweaty, abuzz with endorphins, we got the munchies and went out for a pizza in the nearby Osteria Italiana, close to Elfriede's apartment. It had once, so Claudio informed me, been one of Hitler's favourite restaurants, but he'd taken me there for its convenience rather than its infamy. My head was in a mess. I was in a post-orgasmic stupor, yet Claudio seemed cool, as if this kind of sex was the order of the day in his life. I couldn't even concentrate on the menu; he had to order for me.

'What's with you, *cara*,' he asked, after a while.

'I'm ... confused. Did you... plan this all along? I mean, did you plan to fuck me this evening?'

He took my hand: 'Plan, no, not exactly. But I did dream about it. I did hope it would happen. Do you feel bad?'

I shook my head: 'Just tell me you are not doing this to get back at Silke.' He looked at me, wide-eyed with what appeared to be genuine astonishment.

'*Dio mio, cara*, why should I want to do that?'

'Because she's probably fucking Walter.'

'You are joking, no?'

The very notion seemed outrageously far-fetched to him. He tucked into his pizza. 'Why, did *you* by any chance want to have sex with *me* to get back at Walter or Silke?'

I shook my head. I told him I wasn't that calculating, yet I knew that this was not entirely true. Revenge, I realised, was not actually my motive, but rather a sort of bonus. He poured me some water and I tried to shake off my stupor.

'I don't think you need to be afraid of Walter and Silke getting involved with each other,' he said, after a while.

I wasn't so sure. I'd seen how they'd looked at each other when they were singing duets. The attraction seemed all too real.

'That's acting, for God's sake.' Claudio snorted, when I mentioned it. 'It's simply part of what they have to do when they are singing love stuff. I don't think they are really attracted to each other. And anyway, if they are, they are. It would just be a tour thing.'

'Doesn't that bug you? That possibility?'

'Aren't you being a bit of a hypocrite?'

I was. I didn't know what to say to that. After a while, he smiled: 'I can't let these things bother me, *cara*. As you now know, I'm not cut out for monogamy. Silke knows that. I love her, but I know she's going to leave me and move on to better things. She is... *una cometa*, passing through my life.'

There seemed no bitterness in this observation, just pragmatic acceptance. You couldn't call it resignation, as that would have implied some lost battle. He put his knife and fork down and looked at me, about to say something.

'What?' I prompted him.

He shook his head.

'Your Walter... he isn't really the right type for you either, you know.'

This annoyed me, probably because I knew it was true.

'Why do you say that?' I asked, not bothering to hide the pique in my voice. 'Do you think I'm not good enough for him because I'm not a musician?'

'Oh *Dio mio*, there we go again. Out comes the inferiority complex. No, of course I don't think that. On the contrary, in fact. It's just...'

'What? Is there some dark secret I should know about?'

'OK, *basta!* Enough of this, let's drop it. Are you going to have an espresso?'

That's where we left it, and as we sobered up my mood turned sour and reflective. He wanted me to stay the night but I insisted on going home. Somehow, I felt I'd allowed myself to be played with.

Vita the salmon and Claudio the fly fisherman.

8TH DECEMBER 2008

Just had an interesting interruption while I was reading over my Munich musings. Marcus was in the kitchen and peered briefly over my shoulder, mug of tea in hand. Jaffa has pinched my chair again. Sensing that he's making me uncomfortable, Marcus tips a protesting Jaffa off the chair and sits down opposite me.

'Are you writing about Senta?' he asks.

His question surprises me. Marcus is rather shy and has never shown much interest in what his aunt does. He is great with Tris, but a little awkward around me. He is a handsome lad, blessed with his father's looks, but much taller. His elder brother Dylan has been less fortunate in the looks department, turning out pint-sized and slight as a jockey, just like Astrid.

'Hmmm...' I reply. 'That's the idea, but so far it's more about my past than about her. It wasn't my intention, but it's the way it's turned out. It's as if I'm not ready to write about Senta yet. I'm circling and digressing. But there is a connection. It's to do with Wagner.'

He nods, sips his tea. 'Yeah, she was into Wagner, wasn't she. I never understood that.'

'She wasn't really *into* him. Not in the way that you might be into certain types of music. It was one of her experiments with human emotion. She thought that she might be able to re-programme her brain to understand and tolerate emotion if she listened to a lot of Wagner.'

'Oh yeah, the autism and all that...' He shakes his head.

'Asperger's', I correct him, pedantically.

'Did it work? The Wagner cure?'

I shake my head: 'Mind you, she could have done another PhD on Wagner as a result...'

He changes tack: 'How do you know that what you remember is accurate?'

I tell him that it doesn't really matter, because I'm hardly writing a history textbook. In any case, we could get into a great philosophical debate here. You know, how reliable is anybody's memory? No two people have exactly the same memory of a given event. It's all filtered and distorted by our individual perception, and then if the events took place a long time ago, there's all the stuff you simply forget, for whatever reason.

'I'm playing with the past,' I tell him. 'It's like puppetry. I'm learning to write. It's a whole new skill.'

'Has Dad been any help?'

'He's offered, but I think he'd intimidate me.'

Marcus grins. 'Yeah, I know what you mean! No shit! I asked him for help with a T. S. Eliot essay once. Never again!'

'How's Tris doing?' I ask, as casually as possible.

He peers into his mug, puts it down, pushes it from his right to his left hand and back again: 'OK, I think. He doesn't say a whole lot. I guess he's OK. He has his art. That's good.'

Silence for a while. Then: 'It's going to be a weird Chrismas...'

'Hmmm...' I say.

'I miss the way it was before. Everything's all... fucked up now. Like everybody's affected by it.'

This is the first time Marcus has spoken to me about the fall-out from Senta's murder. Once again, I realise that I have tended to underestimate how much grief this has caused the entire family. And Marcus, as Tristan's self-appointed guardian angel, has had to shoulder a fair share of it. I want to get up and hug him, but sense he might not appreciate it. He's not very touchy-feely.

'Marcus,' I say, 'I want you to know that I am incredibly grateful for everything you are doing and have done for Tristan. Please don't ever think I take that for granted.'

He looks at me with his fine dark eyes and his lop-sided smile.

'You're welcome, Aunt V.'

Aunt V... He rarely calls me that. Usually he avoids using my name altogether. Must have been my rather formal expression of gratitude that prompted such a response. His guardianship of Tristan has forced him into a sudden maturity. He is no longer the silent, adult-averse teenager that I recall from six months ago. I wonder when Tristan will stop thinking of himself as the centre of the universe and start taking an interest in other people? I suppose the earrings for Lucy are a start.

Tristan... how did we end up with such a liar and a stirrer of a son? Marcus has gone out to the barn and left his mobile on the kitchen table next to mine. 'Dad has two mobiles,' Tristan had told me last November. He'd mentioned it so casually, as if it was nothing. Was it a deliberate attempt to sow mischief and create friction between his parents? I dare not ask him, because I know he would only deny it, and I wouldn't believe him, so I'd be no closer to the truth. It was the day I'd had my hair cut Twiggy-style and walked in on an argument between Gerry and Tristan, who'd been caught skiving off school yet again. Tristan had given us the slip and Gerry had gone upstairs to get changed, while I sat in the kitchen, silently cursing both husband and son.

Later that same evening, Gerry reappeared in the kitchen doorway. He'd changed into new jeans and a primrose yellow sweater. He smelled of expensive aftershave.

'So... what are we going to do about dis son of ours?' he asked, rattling his keys. 'Had any brilliant ideas? He's so sneaky – dat trick of leaving his mobile so he couldn't be contacted...'

I shot him a dark look. 'Yes, the advent of the mobile has brought with it whole new possibilities of deception and detection.'

Gerry didn't react at all to this barb. He just gave me a blank look. After a while he said, 'Yeah, that's how de police traced de Glasgow bombers, wasn't it, from de records on deir mobiles in dat car dey left outside de Kensington nightclub with de nail bomb dat didn't explote.'

Once again, I remember coming to within an inch of confronting him, but when he returned to the subject of Tristan, I decided to put the responsibilities of parenthood before marital dry-cleaning. We discussed the options. Another serious tête-à-tête? Yet another meeting with the headmaster, maybe with an ultimatum this time? One more incident would be followed by expulsion. Moving him to another school? Sending him to boarding school? (A thought I found unbearable.) More counselling... no, we knew that was a waste of time, but maybe it was the counsellor. Should we try and find another one? Grounding him didn't work – we'd tried that, and he'd simply disobeyed us. We'd stopped his pocket money; that didn't seem to have any effect either, and just made us worry that it might tempt him to steal again. Lock him up in his room and leave him there for three years, until he'd matured sufficiently to rejoin the human race? Not feasible, but oh so tempting...

Gerry kissed me on the cheek, patted my new hair and went out. Off somewhere by cab or tube, not on his Harley. Why? Because the bike was a dead give-away? Because lots of people recognised it? Because he didn't want to arrive wherever it was all crumpled and sweaty? I remember reaching for a bottle of Chablis, then, remembering my promise, slowly, carefully, very reluctantly putting it back in the fridge.

Tris may have been a liar and a mischief maker, but he was still pretty much an open book back then, even if some of the print was illegible. Senta was the complete opposite. She had been diagnosed with Asperger's, albeit a mild form, and it supposedly explained why her emotional intelligence was at best underdeveloped. For many years I refused to believe the diagnosis, which seemed so slippery and vague, but she definitely ticked some of the boxes. I listen to a lot of classical music, particularly opera, and although she liked the soothing predictability of baroque music, she found Wagner and indeed any overtly emotional music threatening. Bach and Handel were no problem, but the emotional and romantic stuff seemed to cause some kind of circuit to blow, and could trigger a complete meltdown. When she was quite young, five or six years old, she completely freaked out one day when she came back from spending time at Ewa's next door and walked into *Götterdämmerung* turned up full volume. She put both hands over her ears and screamed and screamed until she was quite puce in the face. I had gone out into the garden to fetch the washing in, and suddenly became aware of the screams piercing the singing. She stood in the middle of the sitting room in her little yellow summer dress, beside herself, shaking with anger, an explosive attack of pure rage which she was prone to in those years. Trying to calm her down was difficult, as she would lash out and kick if you tried to touch her. I turned the music off, muttered soothing words and watched her decompress slowly, as the hysterical convulsed sobbing died away.

It is quite an art, dealing with an Aspie in a rage. As a parent, your instinct is to hug the child and offer the soothing comfort of your body. Instead, you have to wait patiently, calmly, until the red heat has gone out of the fit, and then try to distract the child. I would offer her a tumbler of her favourite homemade lemonade and then coax her into the garden to look at flowers or insects, which were the source of endless fascination and amazing knowledge in one so young. I was advised not to ask her why she'd freaked out, for fear of bringing on a second fit. I soon learnt only to listen to Wagner through headphones.

Years later, around the time when she started her undergraduate studies at Imperial, she decided to try and teach herself the rules of *normal* behaviour and human interaction. She forced herself to listen systematically to every single opera in my Wagner collection to confront and exorcise her phobia. It must have been agony for her. Just as I had thought an appreciation of Wagner would help me to understand Walter and relate better to all things German, so Senta thought Wagner would help her tolerate displays of emotion.

We were both wrong.

9TH DECEMBER 2008

Christmas cards are arriving by the dozen now. Astrid has a habit of not displaying them which I've always found rather rude. She gives them a cursory glance and tosses them onto a pile on the kitchen table. The commercialism and the platitudes annoy her. It was the boys who decided to put the cards on display. Yesterday evening, they attached lengths of string with drawing pins to the kitchen ceiling beams and fixed the cards onto the string with staples. They made no distinction between beautifully designed, hand-made cards from fellow artists and the crassest of cheap economy pack Santas. The cards were all given equal treatment, juxtaposed indiscriminately. I found it endearing.

Tomorrow is the school carol service at the cathedral. We are all going to go. Meanwhile, I will revisit a spiritual experience of a different kind.

After that evening in Munich of whoopie, weed, wine and Wagner with Claudio, I was mightily confused. The Sunday that followed, he didn't call me and I stubbornly resisted the urge to contact him. He had made it all too clear that this little episode was not to be misinterpreted as the beginning of a relationship. I too wanted very much to feel cool and casual about the whole thing, but in my heart of hearts I just felt like a fool, so I tried to distract myself with various activities. I got out my sketchpad and half-heartedly made some earring designs. I attempted to read the libretto of *The Ring* with the help of Walter's dictionary, but couldn't keep my mind on it. Memories of

Claudio's skilled, unhurried lovemaking kept sabotaging my concentration, arousing me all over again. In the end, I went out and mooched aimlessly through a gloomily autumnal Munich. I crossed the Isar at the Max-Joseph bridge and wandered around the English Garden to the Chinese Tower, recalling the happier times Walter and I had spent there the previous September when I'd first arrived in Germany. But the autumn beer garden was deserted, the café shuttered, and it was drizzling steadily. Had I actually been happier then, or just more wilfully deluded, seduced by the newness of the experience, the beauty of the place, the gorgeous late summer weather?

I must have walked four or five miles north, trudging much of the way along the little burbling stream that runs all the way from the English Garden towards the suburb of Ismaning. All the while I tried to chase away my bleak thoughts about Walter by recalling the many good times we'd enjoyed. Trips to Munich's magical *Viktualienmarkt* to choose the freshest, tastiest, most wholesome-looking specimens of fruit and vegetables I've ever seen; being introduced to the fattening delights of the *Butterbretze*, a massive pretzel topped with big salt crystals, sliced open and thickly buttered; lolling by the banks of the Isar somewhere near Thalkirchen, where it was very shallow, Walter reading to me from *Die Unendliche Geschichte* while I was mesmerised by two topless, big-breasted, totally uninhibited women who were throwing a beach ball to each other in the middle of the glassy clear river. And, of course, being introduced to the world of opera through *The Magic Flute*. Yet... no sooner had I taken strength from these memories, than I would plunge again into muddled thoughts about Claudio, Silke, Germany and above all, myself. What was I doing with my life? I was nearly twenty-nine, adrift in this beautiful but curiously impenetrable city with its sinister past, doing a mundane job and floundering in a wobbly relationship.

My caper with Claudio only seemed to confirm this. Even though he'd denied it, I couldn't help suspecting he had to derive some sense of satisfaction from his little conquest and I was annoyed at myself for allowing it to happen.

The drizzle turned into driving rain, so I headed out of the park, heavily forested at this point, into Ismaning and took the S Bahn to the centre of town. Not wanting to go back to the empty flat, I contemplated phoning Ulrike, but decided against disturbing her family Sunday. Instead, I spent the rest of the afternoon in the Alte Pinakothek with the good burghers of Munich, distractedly gazing at masterpieces from four centuries of European painting, while at the same time feeling they deserved much closer attention than I seemed able to give in my agitated state of mind. Among the couples and earnest middle-class families I recall a searing sense of loneliness and alienation; a dawning realisation that I would never really feel at home in Munich. For the first time, I actually felt homesick for England.

When I got back, there was a note taped to the front door. It was from Frau Wiedmeyer downstairs, reminding me that I had neglected my staircase cleaning duties, and at the same time drawing my attention for the umpteenth time to regulation number 17b that forbids flat dwellers to flush their toilets between the hours of 10:00 pm and 6:00 am, to avoid disturbing the neighbours. There was in fact a rota for staircase cleaning pinned up on a notice board in the entrance hall. There were eight flats that shared the same staircase, and every week it was the turn of a different neighbour to sweep the stairs and water the plants on the landings. In Walter's absence, I'd completely forgotten about this. Frau Wiedmeyer, cantankerous and interfering old bat that she was, always banging her broom on the ceiling whenever Walter or Silke practised their scales, had even plonked the dustpan and brush against the wall by

Walter's front door. A wave of irrational loathing for all things German swept over me.

Early November came, and with it my 30th birthday. Walter sent a dozen red roses – something, I later found out, he'd had the foresight to arrange with Ulrike before going on tour – and called me from somewhere in Romania. It was a dreadful line; I could barely make out what he was saying, but it was very comforting just to get a sign of life from him. It also made me feel profoundly guilty.

At about the same time, *The Mastersingers of Nuremberg*, late period Wagner and relatively light – if a five-hour long opera can ever really be deemed light – was on at the National Theatre in Munich. Elfriede, Claudio, Phailin, Otto Schreiber and I went to see it. I'd spent the preceding weeks preparing myself by listening to extracts of the *Mastersingers*. Walter had a much-loved but crackly old recording conducted by Herbert von Karajan. Its jolliness meant that it was a pleasant change from *The Ring*.

Otto had bought great tickets in the stalls for all of us, and treated us to glasses of champagne in the interval. Phailin was exquisite in a shell pink silk shift, with pearls in her hair. Otto had dressed his beer and sausages bulk in a smart tailor-made suit, but still managed to look like a pig, with his florid face, feverish little blue eyes and flabby cheeks. As we stood around, making polite conversation and sipping our drinks, a succession of people came up to greet Otto and Phailin. I couldn't help wondering what they really thought of them behind their polite smiles and their very formal modes of address.

I greatly enjoyed the performance, and afterwards Claudio invited me for a drink. I didn't care much for the bars in the centre of town, nor did I want to go back to his place. On impulse, I invited him back to the flat. My territory now, I reasoned. I'd have things under control there. While I uncorked a bottle of chilled white wine, he wandered around the now messy flat, browsed through the record collection and ran his finger along the piano keyboard.

'Nice stuff.' he said, stroking a little walnut table. 'Silke mentioned there was some amazing Biedermeier. Must be worth a bit.'

I explained the granny history and handed him his glass. He sat down on the sofa, so I made a point of sitting in the armchair opposite him, safely out of reach. He mentioned he'd had a couple more calls from Silke. All seemed well with her, but predictably the weather and the food were both lousy. Equally predictably, the hotel accommodation left much to be desired. No real news, basically. He asked if I'd put on the Charlie Mingus LP he'd spotted.

'*Che bel culo che hai!*' he said. What a great arse you have! This as I bent over to lower the stylus onto the record.

I sighed. 'Claudio, for heaven's sake...' and plonked myself down in the armchair.

'*Dio mio, cara*, you are blushing!' he smiled. 'Why so far away? Come and sit next to me.' And he patted the space on the sofa beside him. Grandma Cornthwaite would do that whenever she invited her old spaniel, slobby Bobby, to sit next to her, but only after she'd carefully covered the seat cushions with an old tea towel she kept under the sofa expressly for that purpose. No wonder it had turned Mother into a bohemian.

'Claudio, we didn't come back here to have sex... I ... I really don't want a repetition of what happened in your place a couple of weeks ago.'

His expression was a mix of astonishment, puzzlement and hurt.

'Didn't you enjoy it? Wasn't it good?'

I tried to explain that it was not a question of physical satisfaction but of guilt, of wanting to be faithful to Walter. That it all felt a bit shoddy. Yet I knew that once again this wasn't the whole truth. Had I been more honest, I would have said it was that I sensed Claudio really didn't care much about me beyond having a good fuck, and that this had simply hurt my pride. I was too vain and too much of an emotional control freak for a casual relationship. This explanation triggered a long, well-polished spiel by Claudio about his sexual philosophy. What it all boiled down to was his refusal to subscribe to monogamy and his belief that the only golden rules were A -to make this abundantly clear to his women; B - to try and make sure that nobody got hurt and C - providing A and B had been met, to share the maximum amount of physical pleasure two people could get from their bodies.

'What if you fall in love?' I asked. 'Would you want your partner to screw around? Would you not be horribly jealous and insecure? Would you not live in fear that if she screws around, one of those casual relationships might flower into something more serious, threatening your own relationship?'

He pondered for a while. Yes, he conceded, jealousy was a big problem, a stupid, base but all-too-human sentiment. Discretion was therefore of paramount importance.

'That's not discretion. That's what I call cheating.'

'It's not cheating if you both play by the same rules, *cara*. It's... respect.'

'Respect?' I shrieked. '*Ma stai scherzando!*' You've got to be kidding. He was clearly put out by my reaction, and we fell silent for a while, allowing Mingus to doodle in our ears. Funny, I loved Mingus, but my head was still full of Wagner, and Mingus seemed to jar. After a while, Claudio had collected his thoughts. He put his glass down and had another stab at explaining his take on things. Sex, he maintained, was one of the greatest gifts people could share. If you got good sex regularly, it benefited both your body and your mind. He found it worked best for him if he got the greatest possible variety; different bodies, different appetites, different desires, different places. He trotted out the old thing about being very fond of steak but not wanting to eat it every day. I rolled my eyes, which annoyed him.

'I'm just being honest, Vita. Don't act all superior.'

I apologised insincerely and poured him some more wine.

'Can't we just be friends?' I asked.

'Sure, *cara, come vuoi,* whatever you want. I'm at your service.' He said it so sweetly, got up and mock-courteously took my hand and planted a kiss on it. I pulled it away and sought refuge again in my old person's armchair. Biedermeier. Old Biddy-meier...

'At least let me take some photographs of you some time. Promise?'

I laughed. I'd heard that one before: 'Yeah, sure. Are you going to make me a star?'

He ignored my sarcasm. 'No, just make you a gift of some beautiful pictures to treasure when you are old and wrinkly.'

He let his head roll back and closed his eyes while his fingers drummed along to the rambling rhythms of the jazz. When we'd listened to both sides of the LP, he got up to leave. Was I secretly, shamefully, perversely disappointed that he'd shown such a take-it-or-leave-it attitude? At the front door, he kissed me very briefly on the lips, ran his index finger along my cheek, winked at me and made for the stairs. I heard him bounce down them, the soles of his shoes squeaking on the wooden steps. Lithe as a cat, off into the night for a spot of mousing. I'm stupid, I thought. Sex with no strings attached would have been brilliant, especially with such an experienced lover who also happened to be rather good company. I nearly ran out after him, but my pride held me back.

Pride and fear.

10TH DECEMBER 2008

The school carol service was moving and magnificently atmospheric. Even we three out-and-out atheists were moved, but the glorious cathedral setting makes it difficult not to be. I wept as I watched a once-more angelic-looking Tristan, now with the tenors, sing the familiar carols. What ruined the effect a little afterwards was Tristan asking me, as we drove home, if he could spend some time in London during the Christmas holidays. I'd just praised the beauty and simplicity of the service and the singing when he struck with his question. It's awful, but I half suspect that he may have joined the choir just to soften me up for it. I'm holding firm on this one, though. He can't go back to London until next summer, and even that is conditional on his progress here in Norwich. He protests meekly about missing his friends, and I have to remind him that it will take some time before we are convinced that we can fully trust him again, and that we are not ready to put him to the test yet. To soften the blow, I suggest that he might like to invite a friend to stay at the farm during the Easter vacation.

'At the farm?' he says, 'Are you serious?'

'Why not?'

'I couldn't invite them to the farm, for God's sake! Like, what would we *do*?'

I had to smile at that. Wensum Farm is clearly not a cool address for a London boy. How things have changed. He used to love coming here when he was little...

For a brief while, back in Munich, I gave up all attempts at design. The muse just wasn't there. I was preoccupied with a number of things, not least trying to understand what exactly it was I wanted out of life and out of my relationship with Walter. His absence and my undemanding job at the Canadian Consulate left me ample time both for navel gazing and Wagner studies. Whenever I came across things I didn't understand, I would phone Elfriede for explanations and we would often discuss them again in our Wagner class. I sensed her delight at my questions, and Claudio's mild amusement. Did he think I was playing teacher's pet? He himself rarely had questions, and didn't share my obsession with wanting to know all manner of biographical detail about Wagner. He was attentive enough during the sessions, but Wagner hadn't cast a spell over him as he had over me.

As for Phailin, who knows what she was thinking. She always turned up on time, chauffeur-driven, looking doll-like in expensive little pastel suits, matching bags and shoes, her grooming immaculate. Once, Claudio and I invited her for a drink after class, but she declined with her polite, sweet smile, saying she didn't want to keep the chauffeur waiting. Another time, I couldn't help noticing that her foundation had been applied in an unusually thick layer. Was that a bruised cheekbone she was trying to disguise? I mentioned it to Claudio. He'd noticed that she was limping slightly, but then again, she was wearing precariously high-heeled shoes. We thought nothing more of it.

The Ring der Nibelungen had me well and truly in its spell by then. On my Walkman, I listened over and over to the cassette that Elfriede had issued to us of Deryck Cooke's introduction to the Ring Cycle. I was amused by his pronunciation of *Nibelungen* as Nibble-lungen. I fell in love with his beautifully modulated voice, and his clear explanations of some of the many *Leitmotivs* helped to guide me through the monumentally long passages of the full opera. Slowly I felt myself becoming hooked. In the evenings, as I eased the needle carefully onto the precious vinyl, I imagined what it must be like to be addicted to heroin. *The Ring* became my drug – I listened to it over breakfast, on my way to work, at work whenever possible, and again in the evening. Soon, Elfriede's class wasn't enough. I decided that nothing short of listening to every single music drama Wagner had ever composed would suffice to gain a complete understanding of the man and his work. Walter only had the middle and late period works, so I bought recordings of *Die Feen, Das Liebesverbot* and *Rienzi*. I didn't want home-made cassette copies with handwritten indexes in blobby biro of the kind that Elfriede had supplied us with; I wanted to *own* these records. As it turned out, I didn't much like the early stuff – it was charming enough, but it just wasn't real Wagner for me. My God, it verged on the frivolous.

Thanks to Elfriede's classes and Deryck Cooke's guide, what had once been a sort of decibel blur, the impenetrable wall of emotional hollering I'd complained of before my enlightenment, now came gradually into sharper focus. It reminded me of getting my first pair of glasses once I realised, when learning to drive at the age of seventeen, that I couldn't read the number plate of the car in front at the required distance. Only this time, it was my ears that were being attuned. I got tremendous satisfaction out of being able to distinguish leading themes and appreciate the extraordinary marriage of the lyrics and the music. I would read the libretto as I listened. I became obsessed with wanting, by hook or by crook, to obtain tickets for the July 1985 performance of the Ring Cycle at the opera house in Bayreuth, which Wagner had designed to his own specifications to meet the needs of his music dramas. Elfriede herself had only managed to attend two performances there to date, and told me that my chances were extremely slim. Some half a million people chased after 50, 000 festival tickets every year, so you had to send in an order and repeat your request every year. If you were lucky, you got tickets after seven or eight years. Forget to put in your order one year, and you were automatically moved to the back of the queue again. I realised that I didn't stand a chance.

One Sunday in mid-November, I even took the train to Bayreuth, just to walk around this Wagnerian temple and see what it looked like, if only from the outside. I really had it bad. The music wasn't enough. I was also fascinated by the man himself, his belief in the supreme importance of love, his phenomenal sex-drive and compulsive philandering, and his paradoxical devotion to his second wife, Cosima von Bulow, who was Liszt's illegitimate daughter. Then there was his friendship with Nietzsche, their shared admiration and intimate knowledge of the works of Schopenhauer, his radical politicking, his exile in Switzerland, his repugnant, virulent anti-Semitism and the long, demoralising years of waiting before his genius was finally recognised. I became terribly eroticised by certain passages of *Siegfried*, and couldn't stand to listen to them at work, where I could be interrupted at any moment by the switchboard or by some hapless Canadian who had lost a passport.

One Wednesday in late November, while sipping one of Elfriede's honeyed herbal concoctions as we listened to the passage where Brunnhilde and Siegfried sing *Ewig war ich, ewig bin ich,* I felt my hormones surging and my juices starting to flow. Claudio's eyes were on me – could he smell my need, like a dog with a bitch in heat? Was it so obvious? His foot brushed against mine under the table. He smiled and winked, which made me blush, and made him smile all the more. Fortunately Elfriede was oblivious, as she always listened to Wagner with her eyes closed. Did Phailin notice? Hard to tell. After the class, while Phailin waited for her chauffeur to ring the bell, Claudio and I got in the tiny lift instead of taking the stairs as we normally did, and simply fell on each other. I don't know how we made it back to his flat with our clothes on.

Our sex back there was wordless, intense, liberating and cathartic. We coupled over and over to the soaring voices of Birgit Nilsson and Wolfgang Windgassen, both of us seemingly insatiable. Later, our appetites finally satisfied, Claudio opened a bottle of wine and appeared with his Leica. I still have some of the beautiful black and white photographs that were taken of me that evening. Out of several hundred he selected a set of six, and gave me both the prints and the negatives. One of them now hangs in De Vlaaminck. It shows me for the beautiful waif that I was in those days, sitting naked on Claudio's rumpled sweaty bed mattress, a sheet pulled between my legs and over one shoulder, toga-like, one hand dangling by the side of the bed as I looked slightly to the right of the camera. Senta once asked me if I was 'on' something at the time, but I wasn't. I didn't need to be. The beatific dream-like expression was purely post-coital, endorphin enhanced. I don't know what Gerry makes of this photo, which, to my knowledge, still hangs above the dessert buffet at De Vlaaminck. He has never probed me about the circumstances under which it was taken. He probably guessed, it hardly takes a genius to do so. I admire his lack of jealousy, his unquestioning acceptance of my past.

From that moment on, my relationship with Claudio changed. Two or three times a week in the remaining three weeks before Walter and Silke's return, I'd meet him at his flat for sex, wine, weed and Wagner. On one occasion I couldn't wait and turned up without phoning him first. Outside his front door, I could hear the incongruous strains of steamy Bossa Nova, bringing back memories of hot Brazilian nights. Claudio was with a Brazilian girl, Sonia, whose athletic, bronzed body I remember well. It was the first time I'd joined in a threesome and my first and only experience of sex with a woman. God almighty, it was wild. No Wagner that time, just João and Astrud Gilberto spinning their sultry magic, their horizontal music, made for carefree casual sex. I was glad about that – I wanted to keep Wagner for Claudio and me. I didn't want to share him with anyone who didn't understand the music. In a way, sex with Claudio to the sound of Wagner was already a kind of threesome. I was making love to Wagner too.

A side effect of this explosion of uninhibited and experimental sex was a sudden return of the muse. I started designing again, this time inspired by my erotic experiences. *Erotik* I called it, representations of genitalia, breasts, mouths, buttocks, but subtle, slightly abstract, not immediately obvious. I worked with silver, and this time I did not draw anything first, but played with the metal. I found it frustrating not to be able devote more time to it. Saturdays were not enough. I was totally driven. It would have been wonderful to have something available for Christmas, but I knew that time was very tight. Ulrike was a great help, and made at least two thirds of the collection of twenty-four pieces, just following my examples. She'd advised me to keep the collection small, not just out of time-driven necessity, but to appeal to the snobbery of the limited edition crowd. She was puzzled by the sudden change in me, but what could I say? Her brother, Günter, was after all a close friend of Walter's. I burned to confide in her, just to be able to talk to someone about Claudio, but I decided against it.

Too risky.

13TH DECEMBER 2008

Erotic reveries of the past brutally interrupted by a dose of reality – the usual daily chore of cooking for five. After all these months, I have the routine down pat now. I almost wrote: 'to a fine art', but that would be a lie, as my cooking remains fairly basic.

The boys' Christmas holidays start in a few days time, and I'm wondering how I'm going to find the peace and quiet to write, as the kitchen will be turning into Piccadilly Circus. Maybe I can get them to do some of the cooking and other chores. They should at least know the basics of cookery if they don't want to live off baked beans and pizza once they start their studies. Astrid admits to having been remiss in this respect, as Dylan could neither boil an egg nor iron a shirt when he left home. I think Astrid may have accidentally boiled an egg at some stage in her life, though I doubt she has ever ironed a shirt. Rhys does all the ironing. Says he enjoys it because it gives him time to think. Wish it had that effect on me. All I can think of when ironing is how much rather I'd be doing almost anything else.

Interesting news item last night. At a news conference in Baghdad, in which the now thankfully ex-president Dubya was fielding questions, a journalist hurled his shoes at him and called him a dog. Dubya deftly dodged the shoes, which went whizzing past his head. The journo was immediately whisked away and arrested, but millions of Iraqis will no doubt lionise him for this act. The boys thought it was pretty cool too.

'I hope the shoes had dogshit on them,' Rhys said. 'Pity they missed.'

I wonder what will happen to the journalist? Prison and torture, no doubt.

Mid-December in Munich there came a turn in my sexual tide. Claudio seemed intent on enticing me into ever more adventurous situations, trying to beef up my sexual portfolio. I'd enjoyed the unexpected experience with Sonia, though I had no particular wish to repeat it. I tolerated his latest desire to watch erotic films projected onto the ceiling while we were having sex, but I drew the line one evening when he introduced me to a very tall Nigerian man, Eboa, and said he wanted to watch us making out. That was it for me. Really all I wanted was just Claudio and Wagner, and I felt this was going way too far. They were good about it, though clearly disappointed.

We went out for a meal instead, in an Argentinean steakhouse, as if this was the most normal thing in the world; as if I'd just turned down an offer for double glazing. Eboa 'Just call me Hans' turned out to be a doctoral student in economics on a scholarship at Munich university. I wondered whether he knew Walter. I found it strange to think their paths might have crossed.

I didn't see Claudio again till the next Wagner class. I somehow felt embarrassed and I was also a little scared that this sex thing was getting out of hand. After class, we went for a beer – I didn't want to go back to his flat. He was puzzled by my attitude.

'*Cara*, I would never force anything on you. You must only ever do what you feel like doing when you make love. Don't be angry with me.' He took my chin between forefinger and thumb and looked me in the eyes: 'Believe me!'

I did. Claudio had opened doors for me, but had never pushed me through them.

'I believe you,' I said, and brushed a kiss on his lips. He held my hand and we sipped our beers in silence in the smoky tavern.

Claudio offered to take photographs of my little *Erotik* collection, and came to Ulrike's garage studio with his dirty red Alfa full of camera equipment the Saturday after the Eboa incident. I like to think he felt a little guilty, and wanted to do something to atone for having upset me. He was as much taken with the chaotic studio as with my baubles, and took some beautifully atmospheric pictures of Ulrike as she soldered a handle onto a silver jug, and of me as I hammered a ring on a mandrel. He suggested that the best way to display the jewellery would be on a model. He held a silver pendant against my neck and peered through his viewfinder. Too pale. Not enough contrast. Darker skin would be better. Sonia! Sonia would be perfect. I felt a pang of jealousy but realised he was right. My silver things would indeed come into their own much more against Sonia's dewy *café au lait* skin. He took a dozen pieces and drove off to track her down. I stayed with Ulrike.

'That's Silke Nass's guy, isn't it?' she asked me, while buffing up the silver jug. I nodded, trying not to blush, but she looked up and guessed.

'Aha... now I understand...'

I felt uncomfortable and foolish.

The following Wednesday was the last Wagner class before Christmas, and the last one before Walter and Silke's return to Munich. After that evening with Eboa, one door too far for me, I'd had no more trysts with Claudio. I had started to long for Walter's return and the rather prosaic, conservative normality of our lovemaking. I had been dabbling in something dangerous, something I felt could take me over if I let it, but I wasn't going to. I am sure this resistance was related to my age. I was in my thirtieth year, and the urge to settle down with someone dependable and to have babies was becoming stronger by the day. Had I attended the Claudio Richter Academy of Sexual Adventure when I was younger, I might have felt very differently and taken a longer and more leisurely stroll on the wild side.

Elfriede had prepared delicious *Glühwein* and baked *Lebkuchen* biscuits which we guzzled while listening to act 3 of *Götterdämmerung*. Phailin was absent – Otto Schreiber had phoned to say she had a touch of the 'flu. Claudio and I tried to probe Elfriede a bit to gauge her feelings about the Schreiber marriage, but she would not be drawn into gossip. She had known Otto Schreiber for years from the local Wagner Appreciation Society. He was, she reminded us, the archetypal local pillar of society, *ein guter Mensch*, involved in all manner of charitable causes, and I vaguely wondered if she'd ever fancied him herself in his younger, slimmer years. All she would do was pull a face and admit she didn't really approve, and yes, it was a little... unseemly. Such a tiny young shrimp of a girl plucked from a totally different culture to satisfy the jaded sexual palate of this blubber bag of a beer billionaire. My words, of course, but I'm sure she shared that opinion.

Afterwards, Claudio invited me back to his place to have a look at the photographs he'd taken. The black and white prints, about fifty of them, were suspended with pegs from clothes lines which crisscrossed the living room. The pictures taken in Ulrike's studio were classics of *chiaroscuro*, especially the one of Ulrike soldering the jug handle. But the real surprise was the photos of Sonia and ... Eboa. The Sonia pictures were striking enough, seductive and powerful, but you tended to notice the woman more than the jewellery. When I pointed this out to

Claudio, he laughed. 'But that's what is supposed to do, isn't it? Enhance the beauty of the wearer?'

He had a point. I remember Grandma Cornthwaite once wistfully remarking that when she was younger, people would compliment her on her looks, but as she grew old, they would compliment her on her clothes. No matter. The photographs I could not take my eyes from were those of Eboa alone and of Eboa with Sonia. It would never have occurred to me to employ a man to model women's jewellery, but Claudio had not used him as one might a conventional model, rather as a human sculpture. Eboa had lain naked and face down on Claudio's bed, his beautiful smooth black skin a striking contrast with the peaks and troughs of the crumpled white sheets. Claudio had taken close-ups of the breast-shaped earrings displayed on one of Eboa's muscular buttocks, so that it looked at first as if they were perched on a dark hill. The silver chain with the buttocks pendant was not on Eboa's chest, but on his back, between his shoulder blades. He'd turned his head sideways so that you could see his proud profile. Then there was a close-up of Sonia's breast pressed against Eboa's muscular shoulder, my silver lips pendant peeking out between them. Yet another showed a close-up of their two arms, Eboa's mighty muscles effortlessly arm-wrestling Sonia, almost pushing her right back. His middle finger was sticking up, provocatively, and from it dangled my breasts pendant. But it was the shot of the ring in the shape of labia that had been Claudio's *pièce de résistance*. He had rested it on Eboa's pillowy lower lip. His nostrils flared like an angry bull but his eyes were closed, which gave his face a mask-like quality, as if in deep meditation. A paradox of power and calm, of raw masculine sexuality and the most delicate of caresses.

'But these are spectacular,' I exclaimed, and hugged Claudio. 'They are good enough for an exhibition, surely. Far too good just to be used just for advertising purposes.' He smiled wolfishly; it was obvious that he was very pleased with these pictures himself. Then it occurred to me. Had he, Eboa and Sonia enjoyed a little threesome before, during or after this spot of creative, erotic modelling? I didn't want to ask. I was sure I knew the answer, but I didn't want to have it confirmed. I didn't want to know for sure. I realise now that this in itself was telling, as it showed that I was beginning to get possessive about Claudio, and that, clearly, was not a good idea.

When I showed Ulrike some copies of the Eboa series, she went into a state of rapture. She had an interesting way of doing this. Instead of loud exclamations of praise, she became extremely quiet, as if overwhelmed and unable to find words. She placed them against the studio wall, lit a cigarette and just stared at them with a slow smile.

'Let's aim to get a limited edition of your *Erotik* out by Easter of next year. Meanwhile, we need to get one of the big fashion magazines like Burda to see this and do another interview with you.'

I was touched to see her enjoyment of my success. No envy evident at all, maybe because she'd had a large part in it, having taught me so many of the secrets of her craft. I would give her full credit in any interview. However, Christmas was approaching, so we decided to leave the publicity side of things to the New Year. I realised I also needed to discuss the use of the pictures with Claudio.

The details of Phailin's suicide following her slitting of Otto Schreiber's throat became public in dribs and drabs in the week that followed the discovery of their corpses. Phailin had left a detailed suicide note which had to be translated from Thai into German. The tabloids guzzled it up with screaming headlines – a sex scandal of monumental proportions and perversity.

According to Phailin's note, Otto Schreiber had subjected her to stomach-churning humiliation, forcing her to participate in the most depraved sexual practices with other men and women which he liked to watch and film. He didn't participate physically because, Phailin revealed, he was impotent. No 'Willy's little helper' blue pills back then. His sexual theme of the moment had been Wagner, the Ring Cycle, to be precise... He would play excerpts from *The Ring* on his stereo while Phailin was made to enact a sexualised version of the scenes with men and women from the porn industry whom Schreiber had hired for the purpose. He would, it seems, have paroxysms of guilt about this afterwards, and reward Phailin with diamonds and expensive designer clothes, while sending fat cheques back to her family in Chiang-Mai. However, there had come a point when Phailin could take no more, and it was when he had wanted to include a Doberman in the orgy. That was when she finally decided to put an end to her abuse, and his murder followed by her suicide – out of shame, because she felt irredeemably defiled – had seemed the only way out.

My reaction was one of horror compounded by unease. Wagner had sexualised me too, but not quite, I liked to think, into the realm of the seriously perverse. It was hardly something I could confide to Elfriede, for whom listening to Wagner was nothing short of a sacrament. After I'd met up with her in Café Luitpold to discuss the shocking news, I was at my wits' end. Claudio was working that weekend, trying to meet a deadline at Bavaria Film Studios. Later, I found out that he'd only learned of the deaths that evening. I went back to the flat and phoned Ulrike; no answer. Then I remembered she'd gone to Berlin to spend the Christmas period with her in-laws. What was I to do? I didn't know anyone of my colleagues well enough to seek their emotional support, certainly not at the weekend.

I couldn't bear the thought of being alone with this news. Rifling though the papers on Walter's desk, I found the tour schedule. They were in Rosenheim for three days, about fifty km south-east of Munich. Theater am Marktplatz, Innstrasse. Their last stop before disbanding and returning to their homes for Christmas. It was early afternoon when I reached Munich Central Station and caught a train. Half an hour later I was in Rosenheim. I had no idea where the cast might be staying. As poorly-paid unknowns, they tended to go for the cheaper options, whenever possible staying as guests with the local theatre crowd who understood all about the life of musicians on a shoestring budget. I found the theatre, but it was closed. Round the back was Torsten Freitag's props lorry, but no sign of him or anyone else. I'd have to wait. It was cold, so I sought refuge in a café, tried to calm myself and considered my options. On reflection, I decided it would be selfish, even downright irresponsible, to spring this news on Walter before a performance. I knew how much he suffered from stage fright, and how he liked to empty his mind, rest and meditate before going on stage. I decided the best thing to do would be to make my way to the theatre as soon as the box office opened and see if I could buy a ticket, then catch Walter after the performance.

Somehow I managed to kill the next three or four hours. I lingered in the café, then went and walked around the deserted town, without taking in what I saw. Try as I might, I could not clear my mind of images of Phailin in various forms of humiliation, then of her stabbing a cook's knife into an obscenely snoring Otto Schreiber's fat pink throat. Why had I ignored the signs? Why hadn't we realised that something was going on that time she showed up on a Wednesday evening with a limp and a bruised cheekbone? Why hadn't we made more of an effort to draw her out? When the box-office opened, I was told that the performance was sold out, but that people sometimes turned up with a spare ticket intended for a partner or friend who had been unable to make it. The woman kindly suggested I try my luck that way. This was indeed how I found a ticket; a well-dressed, silver-haired elderly gentleman had a spare one because his wife was indisposed. He looked me up and down with barely disguised disapproval. The good people of Rosenheim had dressed up for the occasion, the ladies all fur, perfume and pearls, but I was in jeans, scuffed boots and an old anorak, minus make-up and minus *Schmuck.*

I can remember very little about the performance itself. Walter and Silke's voices were rich and pure, and received generous applause, but Paweł, the wooden Polish tenor who had the part of Count Almaviva, sounded strained and a little awkward. I wondered whether he was unwell. His hesitant, colourless delivery contrasted with the confident tones of the other leads. The audience was clearly not impressed, but at least they refrained from booing. When the curtain call came, the poor man's performance was damned with a faint, polite applause that quickly faded away, whereas Walter and especially Silke received not just lengthy applause, but numerous calls of 'Bravo!'

My heart went out to Paweł, a feeling that was not to last long... After the last curtain call, I made my way onto the stage and slipped into the wings. A stage hand pointed me in the direction of the dressing rooms, and I caught a glimpse of Silke taking off her wig, pulling pins out of her long auburn hair and shaking it loose as she disappeared through a dressing room door, nonchalantly trailing a large bouquet that a little girl in a Dirndl dress had handed to her. Somebody pointed out Walter's door and I knocked, but there was no answer. As I stood there, hesitating, I became aware of sounds of distress coming from within – sobbing and murmurings from one person, comforting noises from another. It obviously wasn't Silke, as I'd just seen her disappear into another dressing room. I hovered a while, uncertain what to do, but started to attract the attention of stage hands who must have taken me for some deluded fan, so I carefully opened the door.

Walter, naked to the waist, stood with his back to me in the middle of the small room. He was in a tight embrace with Paweł, the tenor, who was sobbing, his stage make-up badly smudged. He had one hand on Walter's buttock, and with the other, he was fondling Walter's hair. Paweł looked up; I think he was too upset to be startled by my presence. Did he even recognise me? He'd only ever seen me that evening in the Greek taverna in Vienna. Without even bothering to close the door, I retreated. I ran all the way back to the railway station and all I could think was how come Walter hadn't told me. So that is what Claudio had hinted at, and not just Claudio but Torsten Freitag too. Suddenly, the pieces fell into place.

This man likes both meat and fish. Can you cope with that?

I decided I couldn't. Back in Munich, I packed up my few belongings, posted notes to Ulrike and Claudio in which I promised to contact them and explain my sudden departure, left an apologetic message on the answering machine of the Canadian Consulate and caught a plane back to England the following day before Walter returned. I left him without so much as an explanatory note. I was just in time to spend Christmas with a surprised but ever-hospitable Astrid and Rhys at a draughty and uncomfortable Wensum Farm, which they had bought that summer. It still stank of pigs and the only warm room was the kitchen.

19TH DECEMBER 2008

The boys' holidays have started, and they've gone to nearby Taverham to buy a Christmas tree. Tristan's school report was a relief, after the dreadful ones that he had at Westminster. A bit of a curate's egg nonetheless. Praise from his art teachers, Miss Critchley and Mr Henderson, but Dr Kellerman is more restrained, implying between the lines that Tristan's heart really isn't in Eng. Lit. Well, given his past, it is good enough for Gerry and me. It's just great that he has at last discovered something for which he has both talent and passion, something which absorbs him and which nourishes his depleted self-esteem.

I have temporarily decamped to a corner of Astrid's studio, as the kitchen promises to be bedlam for the next couple of weeks. This is not an ideal solution, as Astrid doesn't feel the cold and the studio is arctic. I simply do not understand how her skinny little body can function so differently from mine. Even as a child, she never wanted to wear a jumper or a scarf in winter and on our summer holidays, she would happily frolic in the cold North Sea surf off the Danish coast while I huddled under a large beach towel and could barely get myself to paddle in the shallows. At this time of the year, she does wear Uggs to keep her feet warm, but by April she's back in flip flops. It's unbelievable.

I now have a trestle table in the corner and a fan heater that blasts hot air onto my feet. I can't see into the yard from here, so at least one distraction has gone, but it has been replaced by another one; Astrid's music. She has an impressive sound system in here, and likes to play stuff at full volume. This morning it was Philip Glass and Gotan Project which I quite like, though not this loud. She also likes rap, which I am dreading. Though it may not seem so at first, she is quite discriminating and constantly exploring new stuff, new sounds. Avant garde jazz, the stuff that's totally off the wall, is another favourite. I think I shall just have to take the dogs for a walk when she puts that on. I haven't the nerve to ask her to listen through headphones, and in any case, I know she doesn't like listening in that way.

Of late, she has been agonising more and more over her Olympic commission and regrets having accepted it. She doesn't like the Olympic Games, or rather what they have become; this multi-million pound business which favours those who have access to sophisticated performance-enhancing drugs that cannot be detected. This massive waste of money. She is toying with the idea of withdrawing from the project, but she can't quite get herself to do it. The massive male granite torso she's been chiselling away at, destined for the Olympic Park, looks like a piece of Soviet era art. She is dwarfed by it. She stands there, looking at it, her arms folded, perplexed.

'Well, it certainly shows your ambivalence,' I say.

'Hmmm... I'm thinking I should have used marble. Or a big block of salt!'

'But it's going to be outside, isn't it? The elements would erode it.'

'Precisely! That's the idea. The ridiculous impermanence of all that training, all that effort. In the end, as soon as you neglect it, it all goes to waste. It turns to fat. It's all so pointless.'

'That's exactly what some people say about modern art.'

'Yeah, don't I know it...'

'So are you going to order marble and start again?'

She shrugs: 'I think I'll give it a rest and see how I feel after Christmas. I have this idea for a huge hollow male torso – just a thin carapace of grotesque rippling muscles on the outside, front and back, but open at the sides, so you can see through it, see that there is nothing inside.'

'That'll go down well,' I say.

'That's the problem... Oh sod it, Veets. Share a spliff?'

It was hardly surprising that I should be a little apprehensive about meeting Walter again almost exactly a year ago. That in itself was almost exactly twenty-three years after the Rosenheim incident. In the immediate aftermath, I had wavered between absolute certainty about his bisexuality and an equally convincing fear that I might have completely misinterpreted the situation. What if Paweł was just a gay man with a crush on Walter, desperately seeking consolation after a dud performance? But then my own suspicions and dozens of oblique comments and allusions made by others over the past couple of years would suddenly surface insidiously and incline me in the opposite direction. These days, I suspect I had other motives for my flight that I was only dimly aware of or loath to admit at the time. I knew that our relationship wasn't strong enough and I also knew that I didn't want to stay in Germany. This incident was simply the convenient excuse I needed to beat a retreat. When had bisexuality ever really bothered me? I had no strong feelings about it. I'd had a taste of it with Sonia and Claudio, and that had been enjoyable, but on the whole I preferred heterosexual partnerships. Did a relationship with a bisexual partner presuppose any greater risks of infidelity than one with a heterosexual one? Possibly, but I must be honest here. I left because I saw no future for myself with Walter, because I no longer wanted to be with him. Because I had suddenly begun to see him as a privileged, pompous prat.

Why had he suggested meeting up and why on earth had I accepted? What did I hope to achieve by seeing him again? My motives were murky. I told myself I wanted the chance to talk about Rosenheim and the immature way I had reacted. I wanted to admit that I had used it as an excuse to run away. I knew that if I had felt more for Walter, I would at the very least have stayed to talk things over. I had another motive for wanting to see him too, a truly ignoble one. By meeting up with Walter, I was getting back at Gerry for spending so little time at home and for possibly having an affair. At the same time, there was also a strong element of personal vanity. I was trying to prove that I was still a desirable woman, despite my age. It all seems ridiculous and immature with hindsight, and it does not cast me in a very flattering light.

A dull English winter's day; coldish and punctuated by unconvincing sunny spells, gusts of bone-chilling wind and unpleasant little showers. No matter how hard I tried not to, I could only think of *Parsifal* and my imminent meeting with Walter.

To distract myself, I made a proper breakfast of bacon and eggs, freshly squeezed orange juice and filter coffee with a pinch of cinnamon for Tristan, Senta and myself. It was something I hadn't done in a very long time, and which understandably came as a pleasant surprise to them. As a reward, Senta wore her sweet, encouraging, indulgent expression. Tris said nothing, but his appetite was a most eloquent spokesman. We sat at the dining room table with our spoils, absorbed in various parts of the Sunday papers, Tris reading the music reviews, Senta whizzing through a sudoko. How long had it been since we had last shared a Sunday breakfast like this? Even so, the family was not complete. Gerry had already left before 10 o'clock to go to the restaurant. Did I feel guilty? Not nearly enough, probably. We were together, yet all three in our separate worlds. I had no idea what was going on in their heads, and they had not the faintest notion of my inner turmoil.

'I'm going to the opera this afternoon...'

'Oh? This afternoon? A matinee? What are you going to see?' (Senta)

'Munch munch munch' (Tristan)

'*Parsifal.* Royal Opera House. Old friend of mine's in it. Meeting him afterwards for dinner.'

Oh how casual and insignificant I made it sound.

'Walter Weiss?' (Senta)

(More munching and coffee slurping from Tristan.)

'Yes. Him. Old friend from my Munich days.'

'That'll be nice for you, Mum. Very long opera, though.'(Senta)

I felt for her. She had an Aspie thing about large numbers of people in confined spaces. Theatres, cinemas, lecture halls and crowded trains could bring her out into an almost uncontrollable panic. Her mobile bleeps. A text message – from Toby? Or Isobel? – which brings a smile to her face. She texts back, thumbs flying over the keys.

'You'll have to get your own meal this evening. There's paté in the fridge. And salad. Tristan, did you hear me?'

'Yeah! Cool. No worries.'

At about half past one, I leave the house because I simply can't bear to wait any longer. I've put a lot of thought into my appearance, but don't want it to show. I'm in black, except for a top of the palest gold raw silk. Black trousers worn over black boots and from my own collection, a necklace of lapis lazuli and gold beads with matching drop earrings. I am carefully made up. I put on my calf-length black leather coat and fling a gold and maroon cashmere shawl round my neck before grabbing Gerry's enormous black umbrella. The look I'm aiming for is casual but classy. Above all, I don't want to look as if I'm trying too hard. I take the Northern Line and get out at Leicester Square to avoid the claustrophobia of the cattle truck lifts at Covent Garden tube station. I'm far too early, so I wander up Piccadilly to Waterstone's and go through the motions of looking at books. I poke around in the Eagle Place shops and I drink an insipid cappuccino in a little café where three bored, pale-faced Polish girls skulk listlessly behind the counter. I take out my mobile, delete all the old messages and weed out the deceased, the no longer required and the who-on-earth-is-that-agains.

Eventually, having dallied enough, I make my way back to Leicester Square. It is raining again, and the area around Trocadero looks particularly tawdry, the pavements sticky with the remains of junk food, chewing gum and pigeon shit, yet inexplicably crowded with smiling tourists. James Street. Human statues under umbrellas, jugglers, a man, his head poked through a hole in the bottom of a pet carrier box, pretending to be a talking dog. The back entrance of the opera house is just round the corner. My stomach lurches. You are too old for this kind of nonsense, Vita. You are fifty-three, not twenty-three. For heaven's sake, woman, get a grip...

I take the Bow Street entrance and leave my coat in the cloak room, then head for the Hamlyn Hall, the old greenhouse, where I buy an overpriced glass of Sauvignon to give my hands something to do and take the edge off my nerves. The place is busy with an international crowd spanning the generations and wearing anything from ripped jeans and sweaters to evening gowns, mink stoles and dinner jackets. Next to me, leaning against the circular Perrier bar, I recognise a young Russian customer of Ewa's, wearing a pale grey Thai silk dress and a pair of my emerald pendant earrings which flash and dazzle as she talks to an elderly and rather portly compatriot. He has just bought them a statement bottle of champagne which sits on the counter in an ice bucket. She looks elegant and sophisticated, a carefully cultivated highly-groomed but rather hard-edged look which is typical of many of Ewa's self-conscious clientele. But then I spot her shoes. Oh dear, those ridiculous little red-soled Louboutins with their impossible heels that render the wearer knock-kneed and struggling to keep a balance. Style is a tough thing to get right when you are a nouveau riche from Omsk or Tomsk or whatever Godforsaken Siberian hellhole this woman has clawed her way out of.

I take my seat in the centre of the Grand Tier. I am amazed at my own nervousness. My hands are sweaty and my stomach feels uneasy. When the orchestral prelude starts, a kind of nausea washes over me and brings with it memories of Elfriede, Claudio and Phailin. I can't really concentrate and am impatient to see and hear Walter. He finally appears about twenty minutes after the start as the mortally wounded Amfortas, carried on a litter by his knights. His distinctive baritone is richer than ever as he launches into '*Recht so. Habt Dank.*'

I scrutinise him carefully, but under all the stage make-up and the costume folds it is hard to make out what he actually looks like. Has he piled on a lot of weight or is it merely padding? Is his hair really grey and straggly, or is that a wig? Knowing someone in the cast of an opera or a play can be a distraction. I find myself losing concentration, fixing on Walter, as all manner of memories from my Munich days bubble up. I have to force myself back to the opera every now and then. Willard White as Klingsor and Petra Lange as Kundry are magnificent, despite having to make do with the most minimal, dullest of sets. Ralph Gerber as Parsifal, the blameless fool made wise through pity, is less impressive. He is a handsome man, but his voice seems to lack the power needed for the part.

After the performance, I make my way to Floral Street. Maryn's is crowded. I ask for a booking in the name of Weiss or Wise, and am ushered to a nook behind a screen, where a table has been laid for six.

'I was expecting a table for two. There must be some mistake.' He goes back and consults the bookings on his screen.

'No Madame. Mr Wise booked zees table for seex. Would you care for a dreenk?'

I sit down and re-examine my assumptions. Had Walter ever promised a dinner for two? Had he even intimated it? Was it unreasonable of me to have assumed it? Disappointment, confusion, embarrassment, anger at myself – all swirled round, rose up, swelled, shrank, merged, disappeared and reappeared in different configurations.

Gin and tonic. Not my usual aperitif, but I need something strong. I can't see the door from where I am sitting. A good thing, maybe, as I'd only be staring. I'm poking morosely at my slice of lemon, trying to understand myself, when two men are ushered into the nook. The handsome Parsifal himself and someone I don't recognise.

'Hallo! You are Frau Steeneken? Weeta?' I nod and am immediately reminded of Walter. Germans often struggle with my name. They either say Feeta or Weeta. We shake hands. 'I'm Ralph Gerber. Walter has told me about you. He is delayed a liddle, but will be here shortly. This is Werner Gluck, my understudy. Werner, may I present you Frau Weeta Steeneken, an old friend of Walter's. Well, not old, you know. I mean, from a long time ago.'

Ralph Gerber is even better looking close up than from a distance. He oozes an easy, experienced, old world charm all over me, treating me to the full gaze of his dark eyes as if intent on hypnosis. Is he doing this because Walter is late and he feels sorry for me, or is he just a compulsive flirt? He has the looks of an old-fashioned matinee idol, a dimple in the chin, dark hair slicked back, curling at the collar. Improbably white teeth that must surely have been bleached or veneered. I find it in myself to compliment him on his performance and he beams, muttering some self-deprecating reply. And what did I think of the production? A bit... static, I venture, wary of causing offence.

'Haha! Static! Tja, there we have it, a real British understatement, is that not so, Werner?'

Werner nods. 'Visually dull for the audience,' he admits.

As Ralph Gerber turns the full beam of his charm on me, I cannot help but feel flattered. While awaiting the arrival of Walter, he asks me how we'd met and what Walter was like in those days, but quickly switches to questions about the present. So I am a jeweller? He has never met one of those before. What is it exactly that I do and who buys my designs? Anyone famous? What are my designs like? Did I design my necklace? It is magnificent. Why did I become a jeweller in the first place? And where do I work? In Clapham? What a coincidence! That's where he has a flat that he uses as his London base – a sort of musicians' time-share, in Macauley Avenue, off Clapham Common. That's just round the corner from the Rasmussen-Steeneken residence. Well well well...

His flirting is not subtle, yet there is nothing vulgar in it. It is stagey. He is adept at using that most successful of tactics: making the object of one's attention feel like the most important person in the room. Despite the cynical little voice in my head, I still feel myself getting suckered in. When did I last get flirted with like this, especially by a handsome man some twenty years younger than me? I couldn't remember.

Another quarter of an hour passes ere Walter arrives with two women in tow. He doesn't so much arrive as erupt. We cannot see the door for the screen, but we hear his great booming baritone and thundering theatrical laugh: 'Weiss. Ja. Tibble für zix.' I imagine the diners looking up in surprise, then quickly away again. London cool. Don't show you're impressed. Celebrity gawping is strictly for tourists and country cousins. This place is for people who are too subtle for The Ivy, for those who want to fly below the paparazzi radar. Or pretend that they want to do so because they can't actually get a table at The Ivy.

'Weeta!'

I get up and we embrace; a great bear hug.

'Let me look at you! Beautiful as always and so slim! I am afraid now I am neizer!'

He pats his considerable paunch and smoothes his thick grey hair. There's a tiny trace of greasepaint under one of his earlobes.

'We must drink to this, Weeta. Waiter! A bottle of Krug! *Libiam!*' He introduces me to the two women, a cellist and a violinist, an Austrian and a Czech, then lowers his bulk into the seat next to mine. It creaks precariously under his weight. It occurs to me that the last thing I want to do is drink champagne, but it would seem churlish to refuse. In truth, I am not feeling too well. I do a quick tally; one glass of wine before I left home, another three at the opera and two stiff G and Ts here, all on a nervous empty stomach. I need to be careful.

The Austrian cellist has taken the seat opposite Walter and is smiling at me. A fine-featured, creamy-skinned woman in her early thirties at most, with thick dark hair piled loosely on top of her head and very conservative one carat diamond stud earrings.

She looks at Walter, then at me again, and says something in German to the violinist diagonally opposite her. Something of subliminal subtlety in her body language betrays involvement with Walter.

Really... What had I expected?

We order. Can't remember what. Fish, I think. Maryn's specialises in seafood, so it must have been fish. Walter duly bombards me with all manner of predictable bio questions. He clutches my hand; not privately, furtively, but publicly, on top of the table. Turns out he'd discovered my whereabouts quite by accident. Ulrike had told him that she'd found an article in a trade magazine which had mentioned me and the fact that I worked in Clapham and was married to Gerard Steeneken the Belgian restaurateur and telly chef. All he needed to do then was send a letter to the restaurant.

I'd long lost contact with Ulrike, which was shameful of me, I know...

20TH DECEMBER 2008

How did I feel exactly? I'm sitting here in Astrid's studio, trying to recall it, but am constantly interrupted by banal thoughts. Did I remember to take my Cipralex? Must buy deodorant. What to cook for the evening meal? I'm so tired of thinking up dinner for five people every day, three of whom, the men, have serious appetites that also require daily puddings. Astrid suggested chicken for this evening, but she wants one of our own plump free range Sussex hens. No way I could catch and kill one - will have to leave that to Marcus. And the car is making a strange knocking sound. Something to do with the tappets, according to Rhys. Must get it seen to. Must contact Isobel... Christ almighty, life is a never-ending to-do list.

Astrid's jazz – this time it's Miles Davis's *Bitches Brew* – drives me out of the studio. Mutt and Doobie really don't need a walk, as they are free to roam and run around outside the farm all day, but I like having them with me when I go down to the river. They are so uncomplicated and full of joy, the way Mutt hares around while arthritic Doobie hobbles after him, both of them snuffling and sniffing and wagging their tails and peeing and crapping with expressions of total doggie bliss on their faces.

God, what an idiot I was last year...

Werner Gluck chats with the Czech violinist opposite him. They are seated at the end of the table. Maybe they too are a couple. Walter meanwhile showers me with bonhomie while Paula, the Austrian cellist, smiles her discreet but smug Mona Lisa smile, chops her food into ridiculously tiny pieces and eats with irritating prissiness. She only drinks mineral water and has no more than a tiny token sip from her glass of our celebratory champagne. When I bend down to pick up my napkin, I notice that the tip of her navy blue court shoe is resting against Walter's ankle.

Walter dredges up names from the past and tells me what has happened to whom. His parents have both died. He himself is divorced but has two fine sons who are making it as jazz musicians in New York. Ulrike is still silversmithing, her two boys have both graduated from T.U.M., Munich's prestigious technical university. Her daughter has just had a baby. Oh, and Günter married a Canadian and lives in Vancouver. Not quite sure what he does there exactly. Something to do with producing documentaries.

'And Silke Nass?' I ask, feigning ignorance. Paula looks up from her decimated food, darts a quick glance at me, then at Walter.

'Well,' says Walter, 'a glittering career. She's at the Met now. The Great Diva. Up in the pantheon with Netrebko, Fleming and Te Kanawa. Tja, zat doesn't surprise anybody really.' He offers to refill my glass but I cover it with my hand. I am feeling seriously queasy by now. I excuse myself and make for the loo where I spend an apparent eternity being violently sick. At one point, both Paula and the Czech girl come in and knock on the cubicle door to ask me if I'm alright. Stupid question, but I guess it's what one invariably asks under those circumstances. I tell them not to worry; to give me ten minutes or so to recover before I rejoin them. I ask them to bring me a glass of water so that I can rinse the hideous sourness out of my mouth.

As I stand in front of the mirror brushing my hair and studying the sickly lard-like pallor of my sweaty face, I know I cannot go back. I need fresh air, or what passes for it in central London. I need to get away from these people and from the smell of rich food. As I emerge from the loo, I bump into Ralph Gerber, on his way to the gents. He puts a hand on my arm, gives me a 'sympathetic look full of understanding' which now only annoys me. Drama school stuff.

'I'm going out for some fresh air. Can you tell the others? I just need to get away from the smell of food for ten minutes or so.'

'I will come wiss you, if you like. Make sure you are OK.'

I shake my head: 'No need for that, but thanks anyway.'

He smiles, reaches into his breast pocket and pulls out a business card. He places it in my hand and closes his fingers over mine, very briefly.

'Contact me if you want. You know where to find me.' And he disappears through the grey door.

Once outside in the cold, damp night air, I walk down Bow Street and Lancaster Place, heading for the Thames. Half way across Waterloo Bridge, I stop and gaze at the view up river. To the left is that new addition to the skyline, the London Eye. Typical Londoner that I am, I've never been on it. Further down to the right, beyond the cable stays that fan down to hold up those two other architectural parvenus, the Hungerford footbridges, are the golden floodlit towers of the Houses of Parliament and Big Ben.

I reach into my coat pocket and retrieve the little white cardboard rectangle. Ralph Gerber. Embossed letters; tasteful dark green. An email address, a German mobile number and an agent's website. I fold it neatly lengthwise and bend two of the ends over to make a tiny aeroplane, then I launch it into the scaly blackness of the river. It zigzags drunkenly downwards and the wind carries it away, under the bridge and out to sea.

When I got home that evening, I was in a very dark frame of mind. Tristan and Senta were both out and Gerry was still at the restaurant. Only Doobie was there, but her enthusiastic greeting turned into a simpering whine when she sensed my mood. I drank copious amounts of water, showered at length and lay on the bed, staring wide-eyed, sickly sober, into the dark. I woke up some hours later to the sound of creaking floorboards. Gerry was tiptoeing around the bedroom in the dark.

'I'm awake. You can turn the light on.'

He clicked his bedside light on and turned the shade towards the wall.

'Are you alright?'

'Are you having an affair?' I ask.

'What?'

'Are you having an affair? Not that I'd blame you...'

'What de hell...'

'You have two mobiles. Are you having an affair? Just answer my question.'

'I do not hef two mobiles. What are you talking about?'

'You haven't answered my question.'

'I don't understand your question.'

'Which part of "Are you having an affair?" do you not understand?

'What? I am *not* heffing an affair!'

'Have you had an affair recently?'

'Yaysus, darling, what is dis? De inquisition? Did somesing heppen dis evening?'

'Answer my question.'

'No!'

'Is that "No, I'm not answering your question" or "No, I have not had an affair recently?"'

'Oh for God's sake! No, I hef not het an affair recently. Now are you going to ask me if I've ever sought of heffing one? If I've ever looked with sexy soughts at another woman?'

'Tristan says that you have two mobiles. Why haven't you mentioned that to me?'

'Because I don't hef two mobiles!'

'Why would he lie?'

At this, Gerry shot me a dark look and sank down heavily into the clothes-strewn armchair in the corner of the room.

'I sink we have a misunderstanding, Vita.'

'You think...'

'Ya, I sink maybe he saw Danuta's mobile. She'd left it behind after her lunchtime shift, so I brought it home to take round to Ewa's. But dat was more than a month ago.'

Danuta... one of the Polish waitresses who lodges with Ewa. I covered my face with my hands.

'I'd like to believe you...'

'Yaysus, now you accuse me of lying too?'

'Gerry, I don't know what to believe anymore.'

He got up and slowly headed for the door.

'Where...'

'I'm going out. I need to get away from you for a while. *Godverdomme*, this is crazy. You and Tristan are bose crazy.'

Doobie clattered up the stairs, padded into the bedroom, pushed her wet nose into my neck and gave me a quick lick. I stroked her head and pulled her onto the bed.

'I've really fucked up, Doobs.' I mumbled, caressing her floppy ears. She whimpered sympathetically and beat her tail against my legs. 'I'm fifty-three years old and I haven't grown up yet. I'm making the same stupid mistakes I made twenty-five years ago. I still haven't got my jealousy under control. I still don't know a good thing when I see it. Maybe this time I really have pushed him too far.'

Doobie licked my hands.

That night, I once again made several promises to myself. Number one was to apologise to Gerry and beg him to give our marriage another chance. Two was to make a greater effort with Senta and Tristan. Three was to learn to accept the inevitable onslaught of the ageing process, not by fanning the embers of my sexual attractiveness through misguided trysts with old lovers or affairs with younger men, nor by espousing pseudo-artistic drab sexlessness, but by making some kind of balanced peace with my middle-aged self. Finally, I would return to my craft, which had languished too long in the doldrums.

Gold, silver and stones. Creation.

The following morning, I found a message from Walter on my voicemail, enquiring after my well-being. After dithering for a while, I finally decided it would be very rude not to call back. I apologised profusely, attributed my nausea to not being used to drinking so much, and babbled inconsequentially about this and that. He didn't mention Rosenheim, to my relief.

Neither of us suggested meeting again.

Gerry returned in the late morning, after I had sent him several increasingly desperate text messages. We were both spent. He was absolutely exhausted, having walked for miles during the cold, damp night. He flopped down on the sofa, hands behind his head, eyes closed, stubble-chinned, hair in an unkempt frizz.

'Where have you been?' I asked, gently, carefully.

'Does it metter?'

'No. I... I'm just ... trying to find a way in.'

'What?'

'You know...'

'Vita, I spent de night making luff to several of my non-existent girlfriends, OK? Just don't ask me which ones.' He says this very quietly, without a trace of anger or sarcasm.

He rubs his eyes and looks at me. 'I am exhausted. I need to sleep.'

'Forgive me...'

'My God, Vita, when do you sink I'd have time for an affair even if I wanted to hef one? These days, I'm only ever in one of sree places – at home, at de restaurant or at de BBC studios. Or going from one to de odder... And now, I'm going to bed for a couple of hours. There's a private booking this evening – I can't let Sandrine do everysing on her own and Salvatore's gone to Naples for his fadder's birsday. He is eighty.'

It's the bloody restaurant that's your real mistress, I thought to myself, and immediately hated myself for thinking it.

'Come on,' he said, as if reading my mind. 'You know it can't be nine to five wiss weekends off.' He got up slowly, stiff-limbed. 'We talk tomorrow, OK.'

I watched him trudge up the stairs, followed by a whimpering Doobie.

The following day, Monday, we stayed in bed late and talked, though it wasn't much of a talk. I apologised again. He just looked at me with a deep, wounded weariness and a disillusionment which scared me. I hugged him and buried my face in his neck, but he remained passive, barely responding. He wouldn't have done this to punish me – to do so would simply never have occurred to him, and that is what made it all the more frightening. Our marriage was in jeopardy. We rarely argued, but also lacked the opportunity to do so because we spent so little time together. The August holidays were the exception, but he desperately needed those to recover from the relentless stress of running De Vlaminck. We generally spent them in a rented house in the Ardennes, with Senta and Tristan. The Belgian relatives would come and go. For the past two years, Senta had not joined us, going off instead to do fieldwork for her doctoral research, so it would just be Tris and one or two of his Belgian cousins. But it was never just us.

'We need to go away, just the two of us, even if it's only for a week,' I mumbled.

To my surprise and unspeakable relief, he nodded.

'Maybe I can find something on the internet? One of those last minute deals?'

Our marriage was saved, rather improbably, by a week on Lanzarote in a perfectly banal villa with wobbly cane furniture and garish amateur oil paintings of local scenes featuring bright turquoise seas by the British dentist who owned the place. A week of sleeping, eating out, making love and splashing about in the pool. A week without Senta, Tristan and De Vlaminck. All responsibilities and worries on hold.

A whole week just for us.

When we got back to a rain-sodden London, I resumed long overdue contact with Ulrike. At the end of February, she told me in an email that Walter and Paula had got married in Vienna.

At the beginning of June 2008, Paula gave birth to a girl, Angelika Gisèle.

A circle had closed behind me and another had opened. One might reasonably expect a lot of soul-searching in the wake of such experiences, of such wilful stupidity, but my main feeling was one of relief. I felt liberated from my delusions and humbly grateful to have salvaged Gerry's faith in me, in us.

A couple of days before Christmas, Gerry went to Brussels and Bruges with Senta and a BBC film crew to record footage of Belgian Christmas preparations for what became the *In Memoriam* episodes finally broadcast two weeks ago.

Christmas 2007 was to be the last one with Senta and the first without Sven, who had died of a stroke a few days short of his eighty-second birthday. It is the only time I have ever seen Senta seriously out of sorts, as she had been closer to her grandfather than to any of us. Gerry and I were strong once more, although I still sensed a certain wary reserve on his part. I feared he would never really have total faith in me again, and I only had myself to blame for that.

As usual, we spent Christmas with Astrid and Rhys on the farm, Wensum being the only place large enough to accommodate all twelve of us. Dylan was home from Cambridge and Mother, in her first year of widowhood, travelled up with us from Wimbledon. Ewa, her stepson Andrew and his wife also joined us. Senta insisted on going to church in Taverham on Christmas Eve. Gerry, Mother and Ewa went with her. Why could I not have indulged her with my presence just for once?

The Christmas meal was the usual feast of seasonal excess; a succulent free range Norfolk turkey prepared by Gerry, too much booze, too much Christmas pudding, too much of everything. Our focus was on Mother, 2007 being her first Christmas without Sven. Of all people, it was Senta who succeeded in distracting her. Senta, who hated posing even for photographs, persuaded her grandmother that she would like nothing more than to have her portrait painted by her. Astrid prepared a canvas in the studio, and Mother, who hadn't picked up a brush since Sven's death, asked Senta what sort of pose she had in mind. Senta, of course, didn't have a clue. In the end, Mother asked her to fetch whatever book she was reading at that moment and make herself comfortable in the studio. That is how she had started to portray her, seated on the old bean bag sofa, legs drawn up to her left, her long black gipsy hair loose about her shoulders, reading a hardback copy of *A Philosophy of Unitarian Universalism*, which she is holding in both hands. It had been a request Christmas present from me.

Mother never finished the portrait.

Curiosity suddenly overwhelms me. I turn round and ask Astrid to show me the unfinished picture. It is stacked against a wall, under a sheet of bubble wrap.

'Are you sure...'

'Yes, and don't blame yourself if I get upset,' I say.

She removes the plastic and lifts the canvas onto an easel, then stands and looks at it for a while, arms akimbo. I pull my chair up and sit down opposite it, about six feet away. The outlines are all there; the shape of Senta's head, cocked slightly to one side, the book, her stockinged feet peeping out from underneath her long skirt. It was a dark-green bell-shaped corduroy one which Ewa had made for her birthday. She took to wearing it with a pair of old black biker boots, which was, I'm sure, not in the least how Ewa would have envisaged it. The only colour was on Senta's face, on her forehead, where there were a few experimental dabs of the palest beige. Rhys had taken a photograph of Senta as she posed on the sofa, so Mother could finish the portrait at a later date, but neither Astrid nor I could remember ever seeing it downloaded. We thought it would probably still be on Rhys's camera.

'Would you be prepared to finish it for me?' I ask, at last.

She stands and looks at the picture a while, winding and unwinding tendrils of her hennaed hair around her index finger.

'It's not mine to finish, really. It's Mother's.'

'She's never going to finish it. You know that.'

'I'd have to ask her permission.'

'Please...'

'But... what would you want me to do? Copy Mother's style?'

'No, your own style. Oh, whatever feels right.'

'Wouldn't you like to finish it yourself?'

'Come on. I'm no good with oils. I haven't done any oils since A-levels.'

'Look, I need to think about it. I'm not totally comfortable with the idea,' she says.

'Don't feel you have to,' I say.

'Hmmm... I'll think about it Veets, but I just don't know if I can do it. Maybe we should just leave it unfinished. After all, her life was unfinished.'

22ND DECEMBER 2008

Mother and Gerry will be here tomorrow, so today we've been sorting out the sleeping arrangements. Mother will get Dylan's old room; Dylan will share with Marcus, and Tristan wants to sleep in the kitchen. He doesn't want to be with Dylan and Marcus in case he has one of his nightmares again, so he has proposed dragging the bean bag sofa from the studio into the kitchen at night and putting it near the range.

'What if you have a nightmare?' I ask, when we are alone.

'Don't worry, Mum,' he sighs. 'The dogs will be with me. If I get a really bad one, they'll start barking and then everybody will wake up.'

The boys have offered to cook dinner this evening. I can't wait to see the results. Dylan currently has a Greek girlfriend, Irini, who has apparently taught him how to make a mean moussaka. Marcus and Tristan are going to have a go at a Delia Smith apple crumble. Lucy, who has finally been invited round for dinner, has offered to make a salad. Astrid and I decide to stay well away from the kitchen.

Rhys has gone to see his sister in London.

23RD DECEMBER 2008

Writing time reduced to near zero at the moment. Last night's meal was a bit hit and miss. Dylan had made enough moussaka for a small army, but it was on the dry side. Of course the poor old range got the blame – that 'medieval piece of shit!' In London he and Irini have a *civilised, modern* electric oven. However, Marcus and Tristan's crumble was a success, even if the custard was a tad lumpy. Lucy's salad was a work of art, so beautifully arranged that it seemed like a shame to mess it up with a serving spoon. Astrid and I showered them with praise and opened a pre-Christmas bottle of fizz to celebrate what we rather optimistically hoped would be the first of many more such occasions.

Mother and Gerry arrived this afternoon. Mother has brought the cat with her. Maggie Scratcher has become a bony old crock old and diabetic to boot, so Mother does not want to leave her on her own. Poor old Mags has the squitters, probably caused by the car journey and made worse by the sound of Mutt and Doobie barking excitedly at the smell of a strange cat. She will have to stay in the bedroom with her litter tray to avoid being bothered by Jaffa and the dogs. Mother will have the joys of stinking cat pooh to contend with. Astrid did try to persuade her to leave Maggie in Wimbledon and ask the neighbours to come in and feed her, but Mother wouldn't hear of it.

'Don't forget that Maggie Scratcher is a link with Sven and Senta,' I say, after Mother has gone upstairs to unpack.

'Yes, I know...'

'Remember Senta found her as a tiny kitten when she was out walking on Wimbledon Common? With Sven?'

'Yeah,' she says, wearily, twisting her hair into a knot and fastening it on top of her head. 'Yeah, the neighbour's dog heard tiny little miaows coming from under a hedge... I know... '

Maggie Scratcher... Grandma had given her that name. Maggie Scratcher, Milk Snatcher. Mother loathed Mrs T. , who wasn't even PM any more at the time.

27ᵀᴴ DECEMBER 2008

Thank God this much-dreaded Christmas is over. I'm worried about Gerry, who isn't at all well and complains of chest pains. On top of grieving for Senta, he is stressed out about the future of the restaurant. It is not at all like him to see the glass half empty. We didn't want to let him do the cooking this year so that he can have a bit of a rest instead of the usual busman's holiday. However, as Rhys has turned what was once the parlour into his study, the kitchen also functions as sitting and dining room, and Gerry cannot bear to sit and watch us messing around amateurishly with food.

We had our Christmas meal on Christmas Eve, a continental tradition that Gerry has introduced. Rhys had to take Gerry to The Swan to get him out of our way for a couple of hours, but as soon as they had returned, he was peering over our shoulders again, lifting the lids off pans and poking his nose in the oven. Mother joked about tying him to a chair, and Dylan finally succeeded in distracting him with a game of draughts. We sat down to our meal of roast duck at around nine o'clock, with a recording of carols from Norwich Cathedral on the CD player. Both Rhys and Gerry were well-oiled by then, and there was none of the usual banter among the boys. Mother's thoughts appeared to be elsewhere and I found myself on the verge of tears again. Astrid opened a dusty bottle of Margaux, filled the glasses and asked if anyone wanted to propose a toast. It was Dylan who raised his glass.

'To Barack Obama. One of the few good things to have happened to the world this year.'

We all raised our glasses and drank to him.

'He sure is going to need all de support he can get,' muttered Gerry.

We ate in silence. In a way, it was wonderful that nobody felt the need to pretend that all was well. No fake merriment, no Christmas crackers with silly jokes and paper hats. We hit the brandy afterwards and got completely wasted. Mother had to go up the stairs on her bottom.

Christmas Day was dedicated to the nursing of shocking hangovers.

The day she arrived, one of the first things Mother had asked, after we'd all sat in the kitchen with our mugs of tea, was how Astrid was progressing with her commission. Astrid grimaced and told her that she hadn't touched the chisel in a while, that she wasn't even sure that she wanted to finish the granite torso. Mother asked if she could see the unfinished work, so we all trooped into the studio. The first thing she saw was her own unfinished portrait of Senta. I could see Astrid flinch, and I cursed myself for not having put it away. Mother goes up to it and strokes Senta's face, and then the tears come. I persuade her to sit down on my desk chair, at the trestle table where I have been writing.

'My God,' she says, after a while, 'I'd quite forgotten about that.' She sips the glass of water that Tristan has fetched for her.

'I don't suppose you'd want to finish it?' I ask, softly.

She shakes her head and suddenly looks very old. 'No, dear, that would kill me. But if either of you two would like to...'

Astrid and I look at each other, then speak at the same time.

'I can't finish what you've started,' says Astrid.

'I'm no good with oils,' I say.

There is a brief silence, then:

'Grandma... can I... finish it? I mean... would you... '

We all stare at Tristan. He breaks the silence by clearing his throat and cracking his knuckles. Just as well Gerry wasn't in the studio. Mother smiles. 'If you want to, Trissie. Why not. I hear from your aunt that you are becoming quite an artist.'

Tristan smiles nervously. We go back to the kitchen, leaving Mother and Astrid to look at the granite monolith.

This afternoon, we were discussing with Mother whether she would like to move to Clapham rather than continue to rattle around a large house in inconvenient Wimbledon. As Gerry and I have now taken our house off the market, new possibilities have opened up. Marcus has a conditional offer for a place at LSE, and would be able to stay with us in Senta's old room; the perfect way to compensate Astrid and Rhys for letting Tris and me stay with them at Wensum. Mother could move in with us in Clapham, always provided she can be persuaded, or sell the Wimbledon house and buy a smaller place nearby. Astrid wants her to stay on at the farm for a couple of months after Christmas but Mother is clearly not keen and concerned about how Maggie Scratcher would react to being cooped up in the guest room all that time. I don't think Mother is quite ready to let go of her house just yet, and that is something I can really understand now, but at least we've sown the seeds of an idea.

28 TH DECEMBER 2008

This morning Tristan was asking about the photograph that Rhys had taken of Senta as she posed for Mother last Christmas, but Rhys had left in the early hours to see his brother in Swansea. He isn't due back till January 2nd. I brewed some coffee for the three of us, and when I returned to the studio, Astrid was on the phone to Rhys, perched on her work bench amid the clutter of tools, rags and dog-eared artist's supplies catalogues. Did he remember the photograph? Where was it? Where was his camera? She disappeared upstairs and we could hear the floorboards creak above our heads. After five minutes of rummaging, she reappeared with the Nikon and a download lead, which we plugged into her laptop. Senta'spicture is number 67 out of nearly 200 that have never been deleted. Astrid was briefly distracted by the other pictures; there are rather a lot of a pretty young woman with striking pale red hair.

'Who's that?' Tristan asks.

'Oh, Emily, one of the students on his course. I think your uncle may have had a thing with her a few months ago.' She says this so matter-of-factly, very calmly, as if it were no more than a head cold.

'No shit?' says Tristan, not sure how to react to this revelation. He probably can't imagine that a man as ancient as his uncle should even think of sex, let alone have a fling with a beautiful and very much younger girl.

'You take it well,' I say to Astrid. I kind of wish she hadn't mentioned it in front of Tristan, who is not known for his discretion.

She shrugs. 'He's had so many over the years. And I've been no saint either.'

Tristan gulps and stares at her. His aunt, and uncle... adulterers! He clearly finds it hard to believe. Astrid takes the mouse, selects Senta's image, crops it, enlarges it and prints it off. We sit there with our coffee and look at Senta. I can't help thinking it's a pity that she wasn't looking at the camera with her beautiful amber eyes, but Astrid disagrees, and she has a point. After all, Senta had great difficulty in making and maintaining eye contact. As a teenager, she forced herself to do it, but would break off after a split second and settle her gaze on your mouth or neck. Astrid continues to gaze at the photograph. She likes the tilt of the head, the look of tranquil absorption on the face, the way the wavy mass of dark hair tumbles over her shoulders. I feel my tears surge. I have to get up and blow my nose, dry my eyes with a cold wet face flannel. When I return, Tris is still staring at the photograph. It's as if he wants to drink in the image, tattoo it on his retinas.

Astrid turns to me: 'I'd like to paint her too, but I have to do it my way. It will be an impression, an abstraction.'

29ᵀᴴ DECEMBER 2008

Astrid has swapped her chisel for a brush and made a start on her portrait of Senta early this morning. All I can say right now is that it's very swirly. Black, grey and white swirls, very coarse brushwork. A large empty oval remains at the centre of the canvas. No sign yet of any activity from Tristan. Maybe I shouldn't hold my breath. Maybe he just said it for effect. That is not a kind thing to say, but it would be true to character.

Meanwhile, Mother is getting a case of what she calls the Wensum Clozzies – a kind of claustrophobia that she develops whenever she spends more than three consecutive days on the farm. She is a city person, so late this morning, at her behest, Astrid and I take her to Norwich for the requisite tonic of hustle and bustle and a visit to Jarrolds department store, where the post-Christmas sale is in full swing, which perked her up immediately.

This afternoon, back at the farm, Astrid is working on her canvas. I can't concentrate.

'What do you think about as you paint?' I ask.

'Oh God,' she moans. 'You sound like some journalist.'

'Well, when you started painting this morning, what were you thinking of?'

'You know, Veets, it may sound perverse, but when I'm painting, I don't seem to be thinking of anything. I mean, obviously I must be, but I'm not aware of it. It's kind of... pre-verbal, non-verbal, whatever. I get these kinds of questions from journalists, and I never know what to say. "Where does your inspiration come from?" That kind of thing.'

'When I think of Tristan, the image of Tristan, I see something opaque, orangey, shimmery, with purple edges and dark splodgy stains,' I say.

'In that case, I guess Senta is energy for me. Intense energy and frustration. Burning up, like a star. That and beauty. Nothing splodgy, for sure, but a lot of mystery.'

'Solitude?'

'Yes, that too. Very much so.'

'Transparent or opaque?'

'Opaque. Unseizable.'

'Do you think she was ever happy?'

'I don't know. Did you ever ask her?'

That made me think. I'm pretty sure I only ever asked her if she was happy with or about a particular thing or situation. Happy about getting a puppy. Happy about some birthday present, about going on holiday. But I don't think I ever asked her whether she was happy about life in general. I'm sure the question would have met with incomprehension. She'd have asked me to define happiness. I'd long learned to avoid questions about emotions.

It was like asking a blind person to describe a rainbow.

NEW YEAR'S EVE 2008

This morning, Mother asked me how I managed not to go stir-crazy on the farm. I had already told her about my writing, but I don't think she had appreciated the role it has played in keeping me sane. Whilst she's been here, I haven't been able to do much, which must have given her the mistaken impression that it is only a little spot of occasional diary-keeping. 'Do you feel,' she asked, 'that it has helped to tame your grief by writing about her?' I had to confess that I had managed to write some 64, 000 words (I have just checked!) without systematically describing her life, let alone confronting the circumstances surrounding her murder. Without addressing The Topic, but fleshing out background details which were more about myself than about Senta. Circling The Topic, jumping around in time.

'Why don't you pretend you are talking to her? That way you'd be addressing her directly. It would give you a different focus altogether. Make it more about her.'

I have pondered this unexpected piece of advice for a while and have decided to give it a try, without consulting Rhys.

Part 2

Portrait of an Enigma

3ʳᵈ JANUARY 2009

The Wensum Farm where I sought refuge for Christmas twenty five years ago, after my hasty departure from Munich, was a very different place from the one that you knew and loved so much. The farmhouse, damp and draughty, was freezing – your aunt and uncle had bought it in the late summer, and nothing much in the way of renovations had been done to it yet. They had both wanted to move away from London; Rhys because he'd got a post as a lecturer in Creative Writing at a Norwich college, and Astrid because she needed space for a proper studio. They did not have the slightest knowledge of or interest in farming, and their only venture in that direction was the purchase of half a dozen pied Suffolk hens, so that they could have fresh eggs. They didn't have a clue how to wring a bird's neck, and once the hens were given names, killing and eating them became more and more difficult.

Wensum had originally been a pig farm, and the acrid smell, a nauseating mix of hydrogen sulphide and ammonia, lingered long after the last porkers had gone to meet their fate. Astrid and Rhys grew inured to it, but it always smacked me in the nostrils and made my eyes water whenever I drove through the gates and into the yard in those early years, past Astrid's tribute sculpture, a life-size pig fashioned out of layer upon layer of chicken mesh. It wasn't until the sties were converted into Astrid's enormous studio that the lingering stench finally vanished, though very occasionally you can still catch the merest ghost of a whiff even now.

The only warm part of the house was the large, low-ceilinged kitchen with its open fire at one end and ancient blackened range at the other. Your grandparents had to stay in Wimbledon that December, as Grandma had a touch of bronchitis and wasn't well enough to travel, let alone shiver all night in a draughty, unheated bedroom on the farm. The three of us visited them between hangovers in the festive limbo between Christmas and the New Year, and I remember with gratitude the relief I felt that neither asked me any loaded, judgemental questions about the reasons for my sudden return to England and my lack of a job. They were quite simply pleased to see me. I have tried so hard to be non-judgemental with you and Tristan, but know I have only partly succeeded, in that I have, most of the time, managed to keep my opinions to myself.

That year, Astrid, Rhys and I celebrated Christmas very quietly on the farm, with a great deal of Beaujolais and a meal thrown together from a raid on a Norwich deli. Neither Astrid nor Rhys was interested in cooking, and none of us had any clue what to do with a range, though over the years, Astrid, who had initially hated the thing, did eventually get the hang of it. My bedroom was so cold that the frost drew flowers on the inside of the window panes. I dragged my mattress and bedding into the kitchen every night and slept under several duvets, wearing thermal long johns and at least three insulating layers of T-shirts as I huddled against the range.

One night I woke up to find your uncle Rhys leaning over me, stroking my hair. He'd been drinking – he drank heavily in those days and I could smell brandy on his breath. Next thing I knew he was trying to kiss me, shoving his tongue down my throat, his stubble scraping my face. He was strong as an ox, still playing rugby regularly, and if I hadn't been cocooned in all those layers of clothing, he might have succeeded in raping me. I struggled and struggled and eventually managed to put my knee in his groin. That put an end to it.

'You bastard! You fucking bastard!' I hissed at him.

'Silly bitch!' he groaned as he clutched himself. 'As if your sister would care!'

'What the hell makes you think I would welcome your advances?'

'Whoa! Calm down! Don't get on your moral high horse.'

And with that, he sloped off upstairs and back to bed. Astrid, being the heaviest sleeper I have ever known, would not have heard any of this, and I have never breathed a word to anyone about it. This, of course, is how abusers so often get away with their abuse. The victims dare not speak for fear of destroying a marriage, a family or, more selfishly, of ostracising themselves. Your uncle apologised to me the following day, but blamed it on the booze, which rather undermined the sincerity of his apology.

I have never entirely trusted him since, though he has only ever been very correct with me. Super correct in fact. He dare not even greet me with a peck on the cheek. I don't suppose you would have noticed that, though our *froideur* has not gone unnoticed among the others. I think Astrid suspected something, but for whatever reason, chose not to open a can of worms.

The New Year rolled round, I was thirty years old, unemployed and broke. What was I to do? Even if the incident with Rhys had never happened, I couldn't remain at Wensum indefinitely, and staying with your grandparents was totally out of the question. Rhys and Astrid's stock was sky high at the time – Rhys's novel *Ashes* had been well-received by the people who mattered to him – Amis, Barnes and Co, and got respectable reviews in *The New Statesman* and the *TLS*. Although it only sold moderately well, a very substantial cheque arrived when the film rights were sold and Meryl Streep fleshed out the lead part of Myfanwy, doing what sounded to me like a plausible Swansea accent, though Rhys claimed it was merely passable. When the film came out, some three years after the novel, and Streep was once more nominated for an Oscar, Rhys's mood plummeted from ecstasy to mortification thanks to a bitchy comment from one prominent critic who insisted that the film was so much better than the novel. But the film also revived the demand for the novel, which promptly reappeared in a new *now a major motion picture edition*, featuring a tormented-looking Streep on the cover. Rhys made an amount of money undreamt of by most authors, but I don't think anything could have compensated for those humiliating comments. I suspect he secretly cursed the film, and Streep in particular. Still, this money financed the conversion of Wensum Farm from an inhospitable, damp, primitive pile into the place you knew; the double-glazed, centrally-heated, white-walled, airy, slate-floored place it is now, with its glass-ceilinged studio.

Astrid too was much in demand at the time for her sculpture, though she was only too happy to remain aloof from the London social scene. She is much like you in some respects. Not good at making social chit chat. When dragooned into attending a party, she would take a glass of wine and then find the nearest nook to hide away. She's not shy; my God, she can be very forceful, even aggressive, but she doesn't have any conversational opening gambits and prefers to observe other people. They, in turn, often don't even notice the tiny bird-like woman with the wild hair and the startling blue eyes. Sometimes at parties and functions, people would ask to be introduced to her and almost invariably they would tell her that they had imagined her to be a tall woman, that photographs they'd seen – head and shoulders portraits – had given them that impression. She is without doubt the tallest short person I have ever known. Tall by virtue of her personality and her talent.

'What is it you want to do with your life?' Rhys had asked me one evening, as we huddled round the open fire in the kitchen. It was before The Incident. A reasonable question, asked in a gentle tone, but I was no closer to answering it than I had been when I first set out on my travels nearly eight years earlier. Compared to Astrid and Rhys, I felt like a complete failure, and unlike you, I never had any clear plans, no career dreams, no special talent, no obvious path to follow. I could sketch a bit and knew a little about English Lit. and the jewellery trade, but that was it. How do you make a living out of that? I wasn't even able to teach English in a secondary school, as I didn't have a post-graduate teaching qualification. I didn't even have a TEFL qualification. However, I was in desperate need of a job. In the end, it was Astrid who hit on a temporary solution. A friend of a friend had been left by her husband and was struggling to pay the mortgage on her large house on Clapham Common North. Though her two stepchildren had long left home, the woman was determined to hang on to the house rather than sell up and buy something smaller. She had already rented one room out to a single man who worked nearby, and still had a second room to let to a suitable tenant. Astrid explained the situation to her and offered to pay my first month's rent while I looked for a job, any job. A Mc-Job if need be. Tesco shelf stacker, cashier, launderette manager, dog-walker, house sitter, call centre drudge, whatever.

There was an opening for a waiter or waitress in a French restaurant off Clapham High Street, the woman had told Astrid. The same restaurant where her lodger worked as a sous-chef. He'd happened to mention the vacancy to her the previous day. However, as far as she knew, the restaurant normally hired staff through a catering employment agency, but it was worth a try, she thought. I remember thinking I didn't stand a chance, as I had no experience as a waitress except for a spell of serving behind the bar in Adonis's *taverna* on Sifnos. Well, the rest you know. The other lodger was your father, Gerard Steeneken, then working at hyper-trendy Notre Table on Clapham Park Road, a place much favoured by the yuppies. Our landlady was your beloved other 'Aunt', Ewa Kwiatkowska-Lewis, ambitious, feisty and extremely angry with her ex-husband and determined not to slide back into the mire of provincial Polish poverty from which she'd struggled so hard all those years to escape.

Looking back now, it is the almost indecent speed of our courtship that amazes me. Within a week of meeting your father, we were lovers, and it was very fortunate for us that Ewa was broad-minded about this. When I first saw him, on my second morning at Ewa's, when we all had breakfast together – black coffee, a glass of revolting-looking green spirulina and a fistful of vitamins and supplements for Ewa – I thought Gerry might be South-American, possibly Brazilian. When Ewa introduced us, he stood up to shake my hand. I was immediately taken with this very tall, powerfully-built man, quite a bit taller even than me. I was intrigued by his beautiful café-au-lait skin and by his crinkly dark hair, which he wore very short. Then there were those eyes of a surprising, luminous blue-green and those fleshy lips which revealed a dazzling smile. His hands too amazed me, because they were covered in dozens of scars and burn marks, the legacy of many an accident in the kitchen. When he told me he was Belgian, I thought he was having me on at first, but the Flemish accent was all too convincing.

'I know what you are sinking. It woss hanky panky in de Congo! My grendmudder woss Congolese.' His eyes twinkled wickedly as he said this.

I was very embarrassed that he'd read my mind, and I blushed beetroot. Hanky panky in the Congo! It had been an expression he'd learnt in the restaurant when he'd explained his racially-mixed origins to a British colleague. He laughed, a wonderful throaty laugh, and I think that was the moment when I tumbled over the edge of restraint and fell in lustful love with him.

We'd known each other all of two minutes. I got the waitressing job without being asked a single question about my experience.

Your father had already spent two years in London by then. He had fallen for an English girl whom he'd met on holiday in France and had followed back to her homeland. Caroline Kroll had just obtained her law degree and was doing her training with a firm of solicitors. As you know, your father had learnt to cook from your grandfather, in the family restaurant in Brussels. Initially, Opa Steeneken had hoped that his son would return home, once his infatuation with the little English lawyer-to-be had run its course, but in this he was to be disappointed. Gerry and Caroline lasted a year and a half. What exactly caused them to break up has never been clear to me, as your father, to his credit, has always been very discreet about previous relationships, but it appears to have been due to her excessive jealousy and her conviction that he was having it away with every waitress in London the moment her back was turned. Then there were the notoriously anti-social hours of his work, which meant that he was nearly always out when she was at home. It can't have helped that Caroline's parents were apparently unimpressed with their daughter's choice of a boyfriend. Not enough status. Possibly also some prejudice against his mixed race.

When your father and I met, he'd only been lodging chez Ewa for a couple of months. Caroline had given him his marching orders from the Kilburn grot pad amid scenes of theatrical jealousy. She'd thrown his stereo, his only possession of any value, out of the third floor window of the sitting room onto the pavement. It wasn't Gerry who told me about all this, but Ewa, and she'd heard about it from someone who knew someone. Anyway, your father, whether out of discretion, loyalty to Caroline, embarrassment or simple determination to put it all behind him, would not talk about it. Remembering how corrosive, futile and misdirected my jealousy had been in previous relationships, I vowed once more to keep the beast under control, sadly with mixed success. Even though I keep it muzzled and tethered to a post, I can't seem to stop it from snarling and straining at the leash.

For the next three months or so, Gerry cheffed while I waitressed at Notre Table. We continued to lodge with Ewa, but took to renting the entire top floor of her house instead of the two rooms we'd previously occupied. This gave both parties a greater measure of privacy, but we still had to share a kitchen. It wasn't a problem, as your father and I ate in the restaurant and invariably got up late, having breakfast around 11:00, by which time Ewa had long finished in her kitchen. She seemed to exist on a cocktail of health food store supplements, black coffee, yoghurt and water. Those were the days when she still smoked , using a six-inch black cigarette holder to prevent the nicotine from staining her manicured fingers.

Our relationship with her gradually changed from that of landlady/tenants to a friendship on equal footing. She was in her mid-forties then, and for twenty-five years had been the financially-pampered wife of a wealthy property developer, a wide boy done well from the East End who had made money through various dubious deals. She had first got to know him when she, fresh from Białystok in Eastern Poland was taken on by him as nanny to his two young children, shortly after his wife, Jill, had died of leukemia. Now he, nearing retirement age, had traded Ewa in for a twenty-six-year-old friend of his daughter Sylvia's, and disappeared to Puerto Banus on the Costa del Sol, leaving behind a trail of debts, a son and daughter who had disowned him and no alimony whatsoever for Ewa. Under the circumstances, she was lucky to keep the house. It was ultimately destined for the son and daughter, but there was an all-important clause which Ewa had insisted on not long after she had got married that gave her the right to have sole use of the house for as long as she lived. As you know, she has remained on excellent terms with her stepchildren, who still dote on her.

Your aunt Ewa was determined never to become dependent on any man again, and was consumed with an ambition to make something of her life, to become Someone. I don't know how much of this you knew, but you tended not to ask questions about people's past, and she may not have volunteered the information. She had learned to sew much in the same way that your father had learned to cook. Her mother had been a seamstress, and from a very young age, Ewa had grown up surrounded by the paraphernalia of dressmaking, pattern cutting and the sound, until late in the night, of the rocking rhythm and hum of her mother's old treadle-operated Singer sewing machine. It was in her London years that Ewa assiduously cultivated a taste for conventional bourgeois chic. You'll recall that she liked an understated, severe form of elegance and had a near pathological horror of kitsch and vulgarity. Her wardrobe rarely departed from a palette of black, grey, navy, beige, taupe, cream and aubergine, with the occasional flash of magenta or emerald green. Equally predictable, her favoured fabrics were rich silks, cashmere and linen. She abhorred what she called the East European slut look of tight, cheap, skimpy, shiny synthetic clothes, chipped nail polish and too much make-up. Currently, particular ire is reserved for the deplorably casual fashion of flip flops, tattoos, bare midriffs, 'rinks in the navel' and nose and tongue studs, though the biggest offence of all in Ewa's book of fashion no-no's is the thong. Especially when black, looped sluttishly over lardy English hips for all to see, and disappearing under a pair of low slung white bumsters or visible through transparent skirts or trousers. And don't get her started on the subject of scruffy, druggy models. She has no time for anyone who designs the unwearable for the unfazeable. These include luminaries such as Vivienne Westwood and Christian Lacroix. 'They are just makink fun of women, darlink.' She loves Armani and Jill Sander and Jaeger as long as they don't do naughty things and deviate too much from respectable understated conservatism. Punk was an aberration, as was Kate Moss's early heroin chic look 'That toast rack from Treblinka,' Ewa called her, ever-allergic to PC.

Grotty hair is another pet hate, especially the obviously dyed and half-grown-out variety like your aunt Astrid's. I've only ever known Ewa's own hair, late period Thatcher golden blonde, to be swept up into a perfect chignon with never a trace of grey at the roots. Even now, approaching seventy, she stands ramrod straight, like a ballet dancer, has a dress size six and harbours a pathological horror of fat. Both her mother and her grandmother had been big plump women who had lost their waists even before they were out of their teens. 'Too much pottaitos and sausages in Powland,' Ewa would say, pronouncing the words with a curl of the lip and investing them with such contempt that it always made us laugh. If all the years in London have taught her to how to camouflage her humble origins with the accoutrements of material wealth and style, she retains a tin ear for the English language, and her accent and near article-free grammar never seem to improve. I love it and used to imitate it for Gerry's amusement, though I wouldn't dream of making fun of Ewa to her face. Remember how Tristan, who has always called her Anteva, pronounced as if it were one word? 'Aunt' or 'Auntie' was not allowed – too fuddy duddy. He used to have us in stitches with his mimicry? Even you seemed to find it amusing... or was it one of those instances where you were laughing because you realised it was what 'normal' people did?

Ewa adored you, and you liked being around her. I was both grateful and jealous, as well as puzzled. For a long time I believed that it was my ignorance of science and the natural world that frustrated you, but Ewa wasn't very knowledgeable in that area either. Once I asked Ewa what you talked about, and she told me that often you didn't talk at all. You liked to hang out in the *atelier* and observe how things were done. To you, all processes and skills were equally interesting – you never did have any intellectual snobbery. You thought pattern cutting and learning to use a sewing machine or do the delicate beading on an evening dress were just as interesting as understanding the complexities of physics. The only time I ever recall Ewa getting cross with you was when you took one of the sewing machines apart to fix it and lost some vital screw which disappeared between the floorboards.

One rainy Monday in April 1985, four months after my move to London, I was having coffee with Ewa in what she insisted on calling her drawink room. She was finishing off some alterations to a black evening dress for one of her half dozen or so regular clients. Since her divorce, this had been one of the ways she'd managed to make a little money, but it was obvious that she found the business rather infra dig. She hung the dress on the tailor's dummy and fussed at its stiff taffeta folds.

'What kind of ugly design this. Not flatterink, no,' she grumbled. She pinned in the baggy waist. 'That much better, no?'

I nodded. Had she ever designed dresses? Yes, as a young girl, she was always drawing impossibly elegant models in evening gowns, inspired by photos found in dog-eared copies of *Vogue* and *Burda* which had somehow found their way, through many hands, from West Germany to Eastern Poland. She knew how to cut patterns, but there was not much call for chic evening wear in Białystok. Her mother mainly did alterations and repairs, and made decent, hard-wearing, frumpy clothes for the middle-aged matrons of the local commie bigwigs; ladies with sagging bosoms and large derrieres.

'How about going into the dress design business?' I suggested. 'I could design the accessories to go with your collections.'

That's how Atelier Eve Lewis came about. The tiny acorn that grew into an oak tree, which in turn fathered spin-off saplings around the world. Hard to believe, but those were the origins of what is now this global fashion forest with its highly lucrative lines in accessories and perfumes. A world in which I feel quite uncomfortable.

Your father was enthusiastic and encouraged our plans wholeheartedly. Within days, our imagination had built a fashion empire that stretched from London to Tokyo and included Paris, Milan and New York. Ewa didn't want anything to do with Poland. When I suggested it, she looked at me as if I'd taken leave of my senses. This was 1985, and it was impossible to imagine the historic changes that were about to take place in Eastern Europe with Lech Wałesa's Solidarnośź, and Gorbachov's perestroika policy, the rusting of the Iron Curtain and the dismantling of the Berlin Wall.

Our problem was venture capital. We didn't have any. It may have been the heyday of the yuppie era, but we couldn't get a bank loan because we didn't have the necessary collateral. The house ultimately belonged to Ewa's step children, Sylvia and Andrew, and she was reluctant to approach them as loan guarantors. In the end it was Astrid who lent us an interest-free twenty grand and came up with the concept of serious exclusivity. Forget having a fancy shop, of doing international collections twice a year, of employing expensive models. Make a virtue out of necessity. Build up a word-of-mouth reputation for tailor-made sophisticated high-end clothes. Not quite one hundred percent hideously expensive hand-stitched haute couture – sewing machines would still have their place – but highly-skilled tailoring nonetheless. The idea was to appeal to women on the make who are unsure about how to put a classy, discreet look together; the sort who are out to ensnare a billionaire. And to the first wives from provincial nowhere whose husbands have made it big, and who want to upgrade their appearance to fit in with a new milieu, to reduce their chances of being traded in for a younger, hotter model. Ewa knew all about that particular female insecurity. Give wardrobe advice. Combine it with grooming, deportment and even elocution. Nowadays you'd call it Life Coaching.

Pygmalion – the works.

With Astrid's money, we refurbished the 'drawink' room and turned it into Eve Lewis's Atelier, then at Gerry's suggestion changed that round to the posher-sounding Atelier Eve Lewis. He suggested Louis instead of Lewis, but Ewa wanted her married name in there; her all-important claim to Englishness, even if it did belong to the bastard ex. No froggification, thank you. She wanted a sophisticated English rose image. We decided on a mixture of the antique and the modern. We bought that white office desk and the matching leather swivel chair that you and Tris liked to spin around on until you were so dizzy that you were almost sick. We also got two smaller matching leather armchairs for the clients. We removed the rather frumpy ceiling lamp and replaced it with a sleek, modern Italian one. Ewa also chose that matching standard lamp with an enormous arched swivel arm. She kept the burgundy leather Chesterfield and the Persian carpet. Her sewing machine and cutting table went in the dining room which became her new workshop, out of sight from clients. Such an environment full of sewing clutter just wasn't chic enough. One problem was deciding what to put on the walls of the atelier. Ewa wanted fashion prints; I suggested that she should make her own, but she claimed that the kind of sketches she made would not be suitable for this purpose. Something bold, colourful and stylish was required. In the end, I had an idea. Who, I asked Ewa, is your idea of the epitome of feminine elegance? 'Audrey Hepburn. Breakfast at Tiffany's,' she said, without a second's hesitation.

I sought out some postcards of the young swan-necked, doe-eyed Audrey in a souvenir junk shop on Oxford Street that, in addition to Charles and Diana mugs, Union Jack and Mind the Gap T-shirts and policeman's helmets, sold posters and postcards of film stars past and present. Back at Ewa's, I made some sketches, and then settled on the final composition that you would remember and which is still there today. It consists of three Audreys; a central one standing face on and two either side of her, one looking over the head of the middle Audrey and the other looking down with an elegant incline of that long neck. I left the bodies as faint window dummy outlines and showed the sketch to Ewa. I wanted her to design the dresses. 'But it's still going to be too small,' she protested.

'No no,' I explained, from this sketch I will make a life size mural of the three Audreys.'

'Mural? You mean you paint on my wall?'

I nodded.

'But... my beautiful expensive William Morris wallpaper, darlink!'

'I'd like to paint over that wallpaper. Paint it all white. That will make the room much lighter at the same time. Then I'll paint the Audrey mural.'

'I have to think about it, Vitka.'

She went out to do some grocery shopping on Clapham High Street. Half an hour later, she came back, popped her head round the door: 'Let's do it, Vitka. You start paintink wall. I design dresses for Audrey. Where is sketch?'

At first I thought it was the paint that was making me queasy, but paint had never had that effect on me before. I had inexplicable and uncharacteristic bouts of sudden exhaustion, as if my limbs were filled with sand. Suddenly I couldn't stand the smell of coffee or garlic.

You had announced your arrival...

It wasn't a very convenient time to get pregnant, but an abortion was out of the question. I was expecting Ewa to be put out, but she wasn't. Congratulations, she said, and meant it. You are lucky. You are blessed. She hugged me with surprising intensity and shed a tear or two which mystified me. She didn't allude to it any further, but was considerate around me, drank her coffee and smoked in another room. I wanted to ask her if she'd ever wanted children herself, but felt the question was too delicate. It wasn't until well after you were born that she told me her story.

Your father was delighted and wanted us to get married. I don't recall him ever actually proposing. He just asked me when I wanted to do it; before the bump showed or after the birth. I opted for the latter. I felt our financial situation was too precarious at that point to be thinking about a wedding. First we had to nurture the newborn Atelier Eve Lewis, then you, and only then should we worry about formalities.

Ewa sketched the outfits for the Audrey mural. Middle Audrey got that floor-length sleeveless slinky silver-grey fishtail gown and high-heeled burgundy peep toe shoes. Left-hand side Audrey wore a moss green tailored suit with high-waisted trousers. Her right hand was on her hip, which she pushed out, holding open her jacket with her left hand to show off a white blouse with a pussycat bow at the neck, as favoured at the time by Mrs T. and Princess Diana. Remember how Tristan used to imitate the pose in a queeny way for a laugh? Ewa loved both ladies, though she felt Mrs T. could do with a little fashion advice and a diet to de-frumpify her. The remaining Audrey was in a knee-length golden cocktail number, cinched at the waist with a wide belt and with a low v-neck to flatter her most famous feature, her long swan-like neck. Ewa had changed the position of the left arm so that this Audrey now held her hand a little distance from her left ear, fingers back, elegantly displaying a cigarette in a long black holder. At least she'd resisted the temptation to give her opera gloves. All three Audreys wore their dark hair swept up.

'You decide on *accessoirrrres*, Vitka.' Anglophile though she was, she always uses the French word, and rolls the 'r'.

Over the next couple of weeks, between bouts of morning sickness, I transferred the sketches to the wall. If I'd had *carte blanche*, I would have opted for something slightly cartoonish in the style of Roy Lichtenstein or Andy Warhol, but I had to bear in mind the likely taste of Ewa's target customers, so I played it safe, reined myself in and went for a more conventional interpretation. I worked in the afternoons, once my nausea had subsided. I had to give up waitressing as it was too exhausting with you inside me, and I was fearful of another miscarriage after my Brazilian experience. Luckily for us, around this time Alain, the chef at Notre Table and Gerry's immediate superior, was given the boot. When on form, he was unbeatable according to Gerry, but his behaviour had become increasingly erratic. He was Corsican, and predictably they all called him Napoleon behind his back. He was moody, could be vile-tempered and frequently reduced his staff to tears. Shouting and swearing are not uncommon in the tense atmosphere of restaurant kitchens, but Alain raised this to new heights of bilingual obscenity. Your father couldn't be more different and loathed this kind of diva behaviour. We discovered that Gerry's predecessor had left because Alain had 'accidentally' stabbed him in the hand with a knife in a fit of rage. Alain, it transpired, had become heavily addicted to cocaine. When, on two successive and particularly busy weekends, he failed to show up and Gerry had to hold the fort, the owner, an elderly Hungarian émigré, gave him his marching orders and asked Gerry to take over. He was delighted, and the increase in salary was very welcome.

The '*accessoirrrres*' Ewa asked me to paint onto the Audreys had to be very conservative, as they had to go with the image of restrained good taste. Accordingly, I gave middle Audrey a pearl choker and cocktail Audrey got the thinnest of gold chains from which I dangled a small gold crescent moon with a sparkling diamond on its chin. Moss green Audrey, her beautiful neck criminally concealed by the mumsy pussy cat bow, got a small star-shaped diamond brooch on the lapel of her jacket. Ewa was happy. I know now that she'd had misgivings at the start because of our very different tastes in clothes and jewellery, but this reassured her that I could adapt my style to complement hers. It was to become second nature over the years, but in the end it led to my designing my own radically different line under a different name with a completely separate identity.

Next, Ewa decided to design a collection for spring of the following year, as it was far too late to do anything for the winter of 1985, especially as she had to do all the sewing herself. She decided she would make just nine outfits; three for evening, three for work and three 'casual.' However, Ewa's idea of the term was somewhat different from mine, consisting as it did – and still does– of blazers, cashmere cardigans, silk blouses, linen skirts and pumps or penny loafers. Her aim was to show her collection at a private function with champagne and canapés, hosted by some well-connected wealthy middle-aged lady who would invite no more than a dozen carefully selected friends of similar ilk to attend. A sort of up-market Tupperware party. I had assumed that Ewa would make these outfits in larger sizes; 14 upwards, as I thought this was likely to match the figures of her target demographic, but here she proved to be much more perceptive than me about client psychology. She tailored her selection on a dummy adjusted to a perfect size 12; and instead of larger models, she asked her svelte and stylish step daughter, Sylvia, who was in her thirties at the time, and a tall and slender Polish friend, Agnieszka, in her forties and very well-preserved, to do the modelling. Both women had excellent posture, good legs and the desired proportions, yet they were not impossibly young catwalk queens with attitude. Looks and figure-wise, they were well above average but without being intimidating. Most importantly, they did not exude the message that the clothes they modelled would only look good on teenage stick insects. Instead, they reassured and inspired. This was precisely the effect that canny Ewa was striving for.

The next six months were frantic. As you grew in my belly, the nausea left and took the intolerance for garlic and coffee with it. As my small breasts tripled in cup size, I pored over library books – not on childbirth and its aftermath, but on jewellery design. I searched London for someone who could turn my sketches into reality. Before I dreamt up anything to go with Ewa's first collection, I had to know what exactly she was designing. Ewa wanted necklaces and brooches only at this stage. The two of us had just had our meal one evening in the kitchen when talk of jewellery led me to reminisce about Brazil and the Dickensian horrors I'd witnessed the first time I visited the Geyer Dos Santos mine in Itabira. I remember the silence that hung between us as Ewa realised the extent to which I detested the whole ugly gem trade. I'd talked myself into a corner. A jewellery designer who disliked stones? Not possible.

Ewa studied me carefully as I clutched the elegant little coffee cup, feeling awkward.

'You can work with paste, darlink. Gold must be real gold; no substitute for that. Can be recycled gold. But stones, you can use paste. Very good synthetic stones nowadays. You cannot tell if real or fake, only with meecroskop.'

'But the kind of clientele you have in mind will want the real thing, surely?'

'Ha. No, Vitka. We market it as exclusive costume jewellery. Advantage: if someone robs or mugs, no big loss. That's how we sell to these ladies. That is Atelier Eve Lewis *accessoirrrres* Unique Sales Point.'

Unique Sales Point. A marketing term she'd learnt from her ex-husband, the bounder. Everything always had to have a USP.

Ewa drew and you grew inside me. Gerry cheffed happily, and the atmosphere at Notre Table changed from one of fear and stressed-out misery to something much lighter and sunnier, though the pressure of having to maintain peak performance at all times always remained. Your father coped with it by giving up smoking, keeping fit with a regular morning jog and doing hatha yoga exercises. Grandma and Sven came up from Wimbledon to meet Gerry and we all went up to the farm in Norfolk to see your aunt and uncle. Astrid was pregnant with Dylan at the time, and we were to give birth within four days of each other. As Astrid and I ballooned, Grandma seemed to be getting tinier and skinnier every time I saw her, more and more bird-like. Recently I've noticed that your aunt too is becoming more and more desiccated and sinewy now that she is in her mid-fifties.

Grandpa Sven was much taken with your father, as was Astrid, but Rhys was a little put out. He had, I suspect, become used to being the alpha male of the family, a position cemented by the critical success of his novel, *Ashes*, which had given him a degree of confidence verging on swagger. Now suddenly his perceived place in the family hierarchy was threatened by this genial, handsome, imposing Belgian who towered over him. 'What a dish, my love!' your grandma had joked, as she winked at me and pinched my arm. Rhys did not know how to cope with your father, and I don't think they've ever really been that comfortable in each other's company. Rhys had a habit of raising conversational topics that Gerry knew nothing about or had no interest in, British politics, cricket, rugby and English literature being favourites. It used to infuriate me the way he tried to score points off Gerry in this childish way. Gerry just let it slide off him with a smile; he either genuinely did not notice or just ignored the barbs, and invariably it was your uncle who ended up looking foolish.

If they worried about the absence of wedding rings, your grandparents didn't let on. They declared themselves delighted with the prospect of imminent double grandparenthood. Your aunt and uncle weren't married either. They never did bother with that particular formality. Both Dylan and Marcus have our Danish surname, Rasmussen. Better than plain old Jones, Astrid had said to me once, by way of explanation. Your father never could get his head around that. It's one of the few things he remains old-fashioned about. Children should have their father's name. None of this women's lib hairy armpits denim dungarees mother's maiden name crap!

As my abdomen grew tight as a drum and my navel popped out, I sat at home in Clapham, wearing leggings and baggy T-shirts as I put together stylish understated bits of costume jewellery for ladies who lunch. Out of necessity, I kept things very simple; strings of cultured pearls which I assembled myself, interspersed with gold beads, and brooches also made of loops of pearls. However, proper collections, not ones cobbled together, needed far more lead time. Ewa even let me buy some items, time being so short.

It was a time of great contentedness, and I was grateful for having finally had the flukish good fortune to land on my feet. Ewa, Gerry and I had become a tight-knit unit and this closeness further increased after you were born. Ewa adored you as if you were her own, and was endlessly tolerant of your nightly crying fits. I was amazed to witness this unsuspected maternal instinct in a woman I had assumed to be far too vain and fastidious to want to change nappies and rinse baby sick off the back of her silk blouses and cashmere sweaters. How wrong I was.

By mid-January, the little collection of clothes and *accessoires* was ready. Ewa had found the perfect hostess, the wife of a Bulgarian diplomat who lived in a large house in Notting Hill, and who had duly invited a dozen diplomatic consorts, mainly fellow East Europeans, who varied widely in age, dress size and degree of chic. Ewa's hope was that these ladies, if suitably impressed, would spread the word, and that their diplomatic status would confer a certain cachet on their recommendations. I was the size of a whale – you were born just ten days later. I hadn't really wanted to attend. I just longed to stay at home with my feet up, but Ewa really wanted me there. When she showed me the eau-de-nil silk dress she'd secretly made for me (I remembered admiring the material some months back, but had assumed it was for her collection) I knew I couldn't back out. The dress, very plain, very loose, was absolutely gorgeous, even though it would never have occurred to me to buy something like that for myself. It was gathered under the bust and allowed ample space for my huge belly. What I hadn't realised was quite what my role was to be at this little show.

Gerry had done the catering. After lengthy discussions, Ewa agreed that a Scandinavian style buffet of *gravad laks*, caviar and *smörgåsbord* would be suitable. Nothing English, because English food... well, Ewa didn't have a very high opinion of it. And Polish food? She laughed so hard at this suggestion that I thought she was going to dislocate her jaw. French? Italian? Hmm, yes, maybe.

A Scandinavian seafood buffet?

Brilliant! That would be a little different. We don't want any culinary clichés.

Ewa, Sylvia and I arrived at the house in Sylvia's little red VW Golf, the precious collection sheathed in flimsy dry cleaning bags and draped carefully over Ewa's lap. It was around midday and our hostess, Youliana, was busy preparing the reception room. This consisted mainly of issuing imperious instructions to a uniformed Filipina maid and a rather formally-dressed young lad who was shifting furniture around. It was a very large, rather gloomy rectangular room, with a grand piano by a bay window with burgundy velvet curtains. Ewa introduced Youliana to Sylvia and me. We were given a heavily bejewelled hand to shake, and were greeted with a measured, professional, vermilion-lipped smile. Youliana was slender and vivacious, an expensively preserved fifty-year-old, but there was something very tough about her. She looked a bit like a steely, gimlet-eyed version of Dame Margot Fonteyn.

Not long after, one of the waiters from Notre Table arrived in the restaurant's minivan with the lunch, and proceeded to set it out on a white linen table cloth spread over the large, claw-footed mahogany dining table. He had brought twelve bottles of Krug 1985 and an equal number of ice buckets. Gerry reckoned we might get through six bottles, but Ewa was determined to create an impression of generosity and wealth. Long-stemmed pink roses were delivered for the table, ordered by Youliana.

Ewa unpacked the collection. She had brought her own iron and steamer but had to borrow an ironing board. Youliana offered the services of the maid for the ironing, which Ewa politely refused, trying to keep the look of sheer horror off her face. Once Youliana had left the room, Sylvia burst into a fit of the giggles. She knew her stepmother would never ever have let anyone else iron the clothes she had personally designed and made.

The ladies started arriving shortly after one o'clock. Russian, Czech and Yugoslav, but also Japanese and Korean. Aged between thirty and sixty at a guess, and mostly dolled up for the occasion. I remained seated on a dining chair by the piano in my silk eau-de-nil confection, feeling like a complete outsider. Thoughts of my sexual adventures with Claudio just over a year ago flashed before me. Yes, the same Claudio who came to visit us with Ulrike when you were little. The man who had taken that photograph of me which hangs in De Vlaaminck. He had been your mother's sexual Svengali all those years ago. If he could see me now... I'd gone from apprentice bohemian libertine to pseudo-bourgeoise, yet the bohemian episode had really only been just that; an episode, a little adventure. I still didn't really know which world I fitted into. It wasn't bohemia, but I also knew it certainly wasn't this brittle artifice of careful image culture that Ewa so aspired to.

The ladies shook hands and air-kissed, smiled and chatted, helping themselves casually to the glasses of champagne that the maid was offering from a silver tray, while Elena and Ewa, who was groomed to the nines even by her own high standards, did the rounds, Ewa trying hard to make polite small talk which I suspect she'd learned from a book. As I sipped mineral water – I really could have done with some champagne just to cope with the situation, but that was out of the question – I observed it all from my corner, this little comedy of manners. And how had Ewa managed to penetrate this particular social circle? It had been via her hairdresser, of all people. She had discussed her launch plan with Damian, Coiffeur to the Right Demographic, and he had proposed it to Youliana, another regular customer of his. Ewa had told Damian about her concept for a total grooming service to go with the clothes collection, and invited him to be the 'hair consultant.' Your aunt Ewa has one hell of a brass neck and an amazing talent for networking, but she makes sure there's always something in it for other people. Mutual back scratching. Ewa doesn't just use people. There's always a quo for each quid.

Lunch was elegantly nibbled at, coffee served and the ladies invited to sit down in a horseshoe-shaped configuration of chairs, facing the door. Not exactly a catwalk, but the best we could do. In an adjacent room, Ewa was helping Agnieszka and Sylvia into their clothes while I unpacked the '*accessoires*' in the reception room and handed out the dainty little printed order forms and silver pencils. The true function of the young lad who'd helped to shift the furniture now became apparent when he sat down at the grand piano, propped up the lid, and with a few warm-up scales, started to play anodyne wallpaper music, keeping his foot well down on the damper pedal. Ewa popped her head round the door and held up three fingers to me.

Three minutes to go till blast-off.

It was my task to read out Ewa's descriptions of the garments, to be a sort of catwalk compère. I really hadn't wanted to do it, convinced that it would be much better coming from the designer in person. After all, who could be more knowledgeable than Ewa herself? But Ewa was self-conscious about her strong Polish accent, and she didn't think that the voice of Ewa Kwiatkowska from Białystok went at all well with the desired image of Atelier Eve Lewis. I thought this was silly, given that everybody invited spoke English with some kind of accent, but no, she was adamant. She wanted a neutral-to-posh (but definitely leaning towards posh) English voice. Sylvia would have been good too, but she was modelling. So, Vitka, darlink, please, you do this for me, no? Please?

So there I was, a stranded eau-de-nil whale, with you trampling my bladder, playing football inside my belly as I shuffled Ewa's little cards with the descriptions and read them out to the tinklings of *Tie a Yellow Ribbon Round the Old Oak Tree*.

'Agnes (Not Agnieszka, darlink!) is wearing a navy and taupe trouser suit of light wool and an ivory silk blouse.'

I wanted to giggle and when Agnieszka winked at me, I nearly lost my composure.

We ended up with twenty-three orders for the spring.

Ewa was delighted. We celebrated at home that evening and I allowed myself half a glass of champagne. I don't think it did you any damage. Ewa was already worrying about the next thing. She had to find highly skilled assistant seamstresses and buy more sewing machines. We were down to our last five thousand borrowed pounds by then and on a financial tightrope. It was both thrilling and terrifying.

Don't look down. Look straight ahead and keep going.

The babies arrived. First Dylan, on January 10th, by caesarean. Then you, on January 14th via the normal route. A hellish birth despite an epidural, and an experience I swore I'd never go through again. Your father had been present when I went into labour, but when I cursed him between fits of projectile vomiting and threatened to deck him one as he tried to comfort me by holding my hand, he decided to sit it out in the waiting room. A nurse had to reassure him that women often scolded and cursed their menfolk at such times.

Senta... I'd chosen your name long before you were born, as soon as I found out I was carrying a girl. My obsession with Wagner had waned, but I still loved the music and names of some of his characters. Senta – she who sacrifices all for love in *The Flying Dutchman*. My God, little could we have known... It is also, quite coincidentally, the third person singular polite imperative form of the verb 'sentire', to listen or feel, in Italian. Ironic really, as you never listened much to people unless they happened to be imparting information of specific interest to you. As for feelings, you found it almost impossible to express them, which is not of course, to say that you didn't have them. We chose Eva for your middle name, opting for the English spelling. Senta Eva Steeneken. Ewa was your godmother, but as none of us believe in the Almighty, Ewa restyled herself as your godless mother. The whole thing was unofficial, as you were never baptised. The non-baptism and the godless motherhood were duly celebrated with more champagne in Ewa's office, in the company of Sylvia and Andrew and their spouses. You hollered most of the time; you only stopped when I offered you my breast.

The first three or so years with you were particularly difficult. You were a tiny little insomniac screamer, much given to spectacular tantrums, and there were times when I really regretted motherhood. Times when I came within an inch of doing something dreadful to you, when I had to walk away and pummel a pillow or kick a wall, when I found myself filled with hatred and frustration, afraid of what I might do if I lost control of myself. You refused to go to sleep in your own cot, and insisted on sleeping with us. I resisted this with all my might, but in the end you won the battle by wearing us down through sheer exhaustion. I sometimes wonder how I would have managed without Ewa's help. She had a way with you, of rocking you and calming you and singing lullabies to you in Polish. 'Lulaj maluniu' was an endearment of Ewa's, which she would utter over and over when trying to rock you to sleep Once, after a particularly prolonged screaming fit late one afternoon when you were about six months old, after I'd held you in my arms until they ached and walked you round and round the house and up and down the corridor, my ears ringing as you yelled, I burst into tears. 'I'm a lousy mother,' I blubbed to Ewa. 'Shhh,' she said, and, putting aside her sketches, pushed her reading glasses onto her head and took you from me. She rocked you gently and murmured nonsense into your ear. Within minutes, you had dozed off, and your little face, from being a blotchy red and contorted with anger, gave way to an expression of bliss. Ewa sat down with you in the big white leather armchair behind the desk.

'You're so good with her... so good with children, Ewa...'

She stroked your cheek.

'I think Senta feel your tension. Relax, Vitka.'

I slumped down into one of the customer chairs on the other side of the desk.

'You know Vitka, I never tell you this, but I wanted very much a baby. But I could not. '

'Oh?'

'My mother, back in Białystok, she was widow. I was eleven and my father died. He survived war, then died drinkink too much. His older brother Witek, he not married and come to live with Mama and me. To help with rent. Then he started to... you know...' Her voice trailed off with a sigh. She couldn't finish the sentence. She looked at me, waiting for the penny to drop. You were asleep in her arms, the perfect cherub.

'Oh no, Ewa, no, no...'

'Six years he did that to me. Horrible. Horrible. He was nice to me, buy me presents and sweets, take me on outinks. That was my reward for keepink secret, for not tellink Mama. Two times I am pregnant. First time abortion on farm. I am fifteen. Not good. Much pain, much blood. Then he is more careful. Second time I am seventeen. He no touch me for many months and I think at last it stop. But then one evenink he come to me. I miss my period. I tell Mama. She scream on me: "You tellink lies. Uncle Witek not do such filthy thinks. 'Ty dziwko!'. It means 'you slut.' She say: "Which boy? Tell me, tell me." And she hittink me. I don't know what to do. I go to priest. He say I must have baby. It is... *wola Boża*, will of God. I say no no. It was uncle Witek's *kutas*. Not will of God. If that is will of God I want nothink to do with God. Now priest is shoutink. I go home, wait till Mama go out for shoppink, I pack some clothes, take her savinks from biscuit tin in kitchen, go to station, take train to Warszawa. It was 1959.'

She paused, put her little finger against your rosebud lips. You tried to suckle it in your sleep. Meanwhile I had started to weep silently at this revelation, this unexpected avalanche of past suffering.

'In Warszawa, I stay with my cousin Marta. She find nurse for me. All illegal in Poland, of course. Very dangerous. I stay with Marta some time, then contact other cousin, Marta sister Basia, in London, in Ealink. I just want to leave Poland, communism, misery. I wanted new life. Forget about Białystok, mama, uncle Witek. Basia try to fix visitor visa for me. No easy. In fact I come to England illegal. That is other story – I will tell some time, Vitka. Anyway, in Ealink I stay with Basia and do jobs. Anythink. Washink dishes in restaurant. Cleanink lady at

BBC. Waitress in Lyons Corner House. All time learnink English. Then baby sittink for one nice couple. They see I am good with children. They have friend who need nanny because his wife dead. Cancer of blood. Leukaemia. He has two children, a girl, she is ten, and a boy, he is seven. That's when I come here to this house. Sleep in dinink room. Sylvia, Andrew and Harry upstairs. Sylvia in your room, Andrew in Gerry old room. Harry in back bedroom. Children very upset and missink mama, specially little Andrew. Harry not know how to be father really. He always away on some business, some crooked deal. He buy them lot of presents. Always presents. He is generous and kind but he know nothing about raisink children. Nothink. Jill his wife, she doink all that. One hundred percent mama, you know. Anyway, children and I slowly learn to trust. I love them. Then we have very good relationship, but I wanted own babies too. Harry and I marry in 1962. Many many tries but no baby. Many visits to gy... gyna... specialists. They say too much damages inside from bad abortion. Also maybe psychological. So...'

She rocked you gently from side to side. You were still asleep. She got up and handed you over to me. She was always like that with you, gentle yet business-like. She didn't crowd you. She didn't get upset if you hollered.

'Oh Ewa, Jesus Christ...'

She smiled. 'No *Jezus Chrystus*, Vitka. Remember I am godless mother. Now I will make some coffee for you and me.'

Did she ever tell you this? I have no idea, because if she had, you wouldn't necessarily have mentioned it to me anyway, even if she'd also told you that I knew. This was not out of a sense of discretion or delicacy on your part, but rather out of a lack of interest. I don't think Ewa's past, no matter how dramatic, how painful, would have meant much to you. This may sound damning, but it was said to be a feature of your Asperger's. What interested you about Ewa was mainly connected with processes. The process of couture. Later it was to be the same with cookery and jewellery making.

The ladies came for fittings and were received in the Atelier, which is how Ewa now started referring to her front room. I would take you out in your pram and push you around the Common to make sure that no inappropriate baby screams would disturb the proceedings. Ewa and her two new assistants, fellow Poles, worked crazy hours at the three machines and sewing by hand in the back room to ensure that everything would be ready for Easter. There were times when I thought the Singers would go up in smoke. Meanwhile, Ewa started to plan her winter collection. She was living on black coffee, cigarettes, excitement, vitamin pills, adrenalin and ambition. I wonder if she would have eaten at all had Gerry not brought back meals for us consisting of left-overs from Notre Table every night.

I thought Ewa was joking when she told me how much she was charging per outfit.

'It's almost couture, Vitka. Not factory rubbish. I must pay my girls. We must work many hours. Materials are expensive. And remember, we have image to build. Atelier Eve Lewis is not Dorote Perkinks!'

The ladies did not demur, and the cheques duly started to arrive, though initially a lot of it went straight out again to pay suppliers and to pay off Astrid's loan. In addition to her high street bank account, Ewa had a Swiss one which Harry Lewis had opened in her name at some point while they were still wed. Let's just say that she banked rather creatively in those days. A good thing the Inland Revenue were not on to us. Atelier Eve Lewis didn't get officially registered until 1989, on Gerry's nervous insistence. Ewa reserved even more loathing for the taxman than for her ex-husband. She thought tax was a communist thing and didn't understand why Mrs T. didn't abolish it. Wasn't she in favour of entrepreneurship? Well then? Why this tax punishment?

Those first three years of your life I spent much of my time feeling shattered through lack of sleep. I had little energy left for creativity and neither the time nor the money to enrol on a jewellery design course. I ended up doing an informal apprenticeship in Islington with a craft jeweller I found through one of Astrid's old tutors at the Slade who in turn knew people at Goldsmith's. That is how I came to meet Susanna Di Maggio, who taught me pretty much everything I needed to know about working with precious metals. I insisted on working with artificial gemstones as well as recycled silver and gold, something which was deemed a bit eccentric in those days. This was for my own peace of mind. It had not occurred to me then that I might be able to exploit its business potential as an ethical brand.

Gerry's reputation at Notre Table went from strength to strength, and a visit by the *Evening Standard* restaurant critic resulted in fulsome praise for both the fare and the ambiance. It was followed by a profile in the *Sunday Times* magazine. The place became so sought-after that tables had to be booked weeks in advance. Your father was totally in his element, though almost permanently exhausted. I spent my days trying to tire you out, getting you to run around, taking you to the zoo and to adventure playgrounds in the hope that you would sleep through the night and not wake us. Sweet Senta, as a toddler you were a little tyrant of the first order, a demon of energy, of curiosity, of ceaseless motion. Your tantrums were beginning to ease off, but when they did occur, I feared that you would explode, that a lava of red hot anger would spurt forth from your furiously contorted mouth. Where, I used to ask myself, where oh where did all this volcanic anger spring from? What I did learn fairly quickly from experience and from observing Ewa was to cut you as much slack as possible. If you got into a tantrum, the best thing for me was not to get upset or try and hug you. On one memorable occasion when you were about three and we were in Sainsbury's, you actually bit and kicked me when I tried to pick you up and soothe you. No, I just had to keep my distance and let you holler your head off until your fit had passed. It was highly embarrassing at times, and would earn me reproachful looks and tut-tutting from people who thought they knew better how to deal with what they thought was an incompetent mother with just another spoilt brat that badly needed a clip round the ear. Your condition wasn't diagnosed until several years later.

Atelier Eve Lewis was slow to take off. Business ticked over for the first couple of years but nothing dramatic happened for quite a while. Still, it was enough to keep the wolf from the door. Ewa had thought that word of mouth would be enough, but London is no village and competition from upmarket off-the-peg retailers with status labels was and still is intense. What she needed was publicity, the kind of profile that Gerry had had. However, as the business didn't officially exist for fear of the tax man, this wasn't an option. Eventually, Gerry managed to convince her that she simply had to go legit. 'Think big, Ewa,' he said. 'It's the only way.'

When you turned three, we bundled you off to kindergarten with, I have to admit, a massive if guilty sigh of relief on my part, and our lives regained some semblance of normality. Gerry was making good money, and when the house next to Ewa's went up for sale, we bought it. It had been split into two large flats and needed a lot doing to it. We initially bought the ground floor apartment and I spent my days doing it up to the best of my ability, stripping the doors and sanding the floorboards, painting the walls white; a kind of 1980s mania.

There were all sorts of acronyms for various demographic groups at the time; yuppie, dinky and spoola – stripped pine, olive oil and Laura Ashley. I didn't care much for the twee nostalgic whimsy of Laura Ashley, preferring clean, uncluttered Scandinavian modernity, but I did have a weakness for stripped pine and olive oil. Your mother was the very epitome of spoo.

We were so fortunate to be able to buy that house, yet moving out of Ewa's place was a wrench. We had become a family unit and I had become much closer to Ewa than I ever have been to Grandma. Ewa is mother, aunt, older sister, grandmother and business partner all rolled into one. Above all, she is an inspiration, given the adversity she's had to overcome. She was sad to see us leave, but delighted that we would remain immediate next-door neighbours. She understood that we needed to build our own nest, but one of the first things we did after moving was to have that gate made in our back garden wall to ease access to each other's houses. Her two assistants became her new lodgers. She offered them board and lodging for free, but at reduced salaries. It was the only way she could make ends meet. Gerry continued to bring meals home for all of us to help keep her grocery bills down. It certainly wasn't an easy start...

6TH JANUARY 2009

It's your birthday next week, and I am dreading it. I want to spend it with your father and Ewa in Clapham. As Tris and Marcus are still on holiday for another week, I have decided to risk taking them with me. Tris has been bugging me about this for a while, and I have decided to relent, possibly against my better judgment. I have justified this to myself and to Gerry by pointing out that Tris has managed to stay out of trouble for the entire school term, though it is of course true that trouble has also stayed out of his way, so he has not exactly been put to the test. It was Astrid who suggested that Marcus go along too, as this would make it more difficult for Tris to slip the leash and get up to no good. However, when I suggested to Tris that we could also invite Lucy, he was less than enthusiastic. He doesn't want anyone thinking she's his girlfriend, because she's not quite 'hot' enough. This saddens me, all the more as Lucy has now passed her driving test. She has been handed the keys to an old blue Volvo estate and will be giving Marcus and Tris lifts to and from school next term. We will be paying for her petrol and MOT, but I can't help feeling that she is being used by Tristan.

10TH JANUARY 2009

It's Dylan's birthday today, which has plunged me into melancholy. He gets to turn twenty-three, while you, my lovely girl, are ashes in the wind.

I must not indulge this line of thought...

Gerry has presented Dylan and his girlfriend Irini, who also works at Citibank, with a champagne dinner at De Vlaaminck. The poor kids, both on graduate schemes apparently designed either to kill them or make them stronger, are far too knackered to go out during the week. They will be celebrating at the weekend.

16TH JANUARY 2009

Fortunately all went well in London. I think your brother realised just how much was at stake, so decided not to do anything stupid. I really do not know what I would have done if he had. For the first two days, we did not allow him out of our sight, but on the third day, we decided that we had to let him go out during the day, accompanied by Marcus. I feel bad about using Marcus as his minder. It really isn't fair on him, but he seems OK with it and I don't think Tristan would let him down. And yet... there was still an element of risk. Tristan is not exactly trustworthy.

It was wonderful to be in our own house again, to have our own space back. Your father moved out of Ewa's spare room and back into our bedroom, and there were brief moments when we could delude ourselves that life was almost normal again, when it seemed that the murders had never happened and you were about to kick off your muddy wellies at the back door and come inside, having tended the vegetable patch and the hens. But then one glimpse of the neglected wintry garden and deserted hen house would yank us out of our reverie and back to bleak reality.

Grandma joined us on the 14th. She did not want to be on her own then either. Ewa offered to host the dinner at her place, but we really wanted to have it in our own home. We decided that we were going to confront our pain and commemorate you properly rather than downplay your birthday by sinking into alcohol-induced oblivion, which is something you would have disapproved of anyway. Gerry took the day off work and prepared your favourite Flemish dish, *Poulet Waterzooi*. It was the only non-vegetarian dish that you would eat, providing the chicken had impeccable free range, organic credentials. Grandma brought one of her deliciously moist carrot cakes which you used to love. She then got nervous about it, worried that we would think it an unhealthy act of necrophilia to have something resembling a birthday cake for you.

'It's not a birthday cake,' she kept saying. 'It's just... you know, she loved carrot cake. She always used to ask me to make it for her when she came to Wimbledon.' She managed to get all upset at the possibility of upsetting us.

Senta, these days we are made of glass...

I think we did the right thing to remember you in this way, though I did have my doubts beforehand. I feared we might break down and not be able to pull ourselves together again. When I told Ewa of my reservations, she said an interesting thing. 'You know when you have little bit toothache and you press on tooth with finger? It make the pain stronger. Then you remove finger and pain is less than before.'

Well, I'm not sure it diminished the pain, but at least it was no worse. There were six of us that evening; Ewa, Salvatore, Tris, Marcus, your father and me. All day long, I had Wagner on, at full volume as it should be. I kept wondering how Isobel was coping in California. I worked through highlights of the operas that you used to try and tame your Asperger's-induced aversion to displays of emotion.. *Götterdämmerung* from *The Ring* and highlights from *Tristan and Isolde* and *The Flying Dutchman*. Your brother and Marcus fled the house and only reappeared in the late afternoon. Remember how Tristan loathes Wagner? Well, I don't think Marcus has the makings of a potential fan either. Anyway, they went off to the Tate Britain, to catch the last days of the Turner Exhibition, leaving us to our Wagnerian wallowing.

We dined late, without Wagner. His is hardly the kind of music you can have burbling gently in the background. Instead, I put on your beloved Philip Glass. You never had to force yourself to like him. On the contrary, the endless repetition of those diatonic arpeggios soothed you whenever you felt a fit of rage coming on. Gerry set a place for you at table, and Tristan and Marcus sat either side of it. I was very worried that Tristan would not be able to cope with this, but instead we decided to be totally un-British, raise a glass to you and talk about you. Nobody broke down. In fact, it was a tremendous release. The stories poured out, many familiar, but also quite a few I had never heard before. Grandma recalled a question you'd asked Sven when you were six or seven. 'Grandpa?' you'd asked, 'if I put my right leg over my left leg, is it still my right leg?'

Gerry and I both laughed and then stared at each other in amazement for having done so. That kind of question was so typical of you when you were that age. Marcus recalled an occasion when, one summer when you were staying at the farm, you all went skinny dipping in the river Wensum. You were ten or eleven at the time. 'Boys are so badly designed.' you had said to your brother and cousins, curling your lip at the sight of their nether regions. 'All these dangly bits on the outside. Ugh! It's so ugly and untidy. I'm so glad I'm a girl.'

I was familiar with this opinion of yours, but didn't know that you'd actually blurted it out to your cousins. Again, we all had a good laugh at this. Then Ewa told us something she's always kept to herself. You were twelve or thirteen at the time, and had just hit puberty. Ewa had shown you how to put darts in the bodice of a dress you were making, to accommodate your budding breasts. 'I don't want them to grow.' you'd said, staring at the darts she'd drawn on the pattern. 'I'm already weird enough, and now this.'

We laughed again, but this time it was bittersweet, a reminder of the struggle you had all your short life with your peculiar handicap. It changed the dinner table atmosphere into a gentle minor key, and eventually we stopped talking about you altogether. I suddenly realised that Gerry was talking about the restaurant, telling us about a waiter he had disciplined for asking an MP if the vintage champagne he'd just consumed was going to be put on his expense account. At first I felt annoyed, but then realised that it actually indicated a return to normality, the fact that we were no longer so totally obsessed by your death that we could actually talk about other things. As soon as I had the chance, I asked the boys about their impressions of the Turner exhibition, and so we steered away from introspection and back towards the present. The evening, which could easily have degenerated into an emotional meltdown, turned out surprisingly well.

I only hope we manage to cope half as well when the first anniversary of your murder comes round in April.

21ST JANUARY 2009 AND VERY VERY COLD

We were all glued to the TV for Obama's inauguration yesterday. You would have been delighted at his election, all the more because I remember you saying, about this time last year, that you didn't think he had a chance and that we shouldn't raise our hopes. Well, he's done it. Gerry is getting a little fed up with the constant references to Obama's skin colour and the assumption among some people that he should be pleased for Obama because he himself is of mixed race. The whole race thing annoys the hell out of him. As far as he's concerned, Obama is simply the best man for the job by a very long shot. Race should not come into it. Rhys said this race obsession is rather like a variation on that Dr Johnson quote about women preaching, except in this case it was about a mixed race president of the USA – *'Sir, a black man as president is like a dog's walking on his hind legs. It is not done well; but you are surprised to find it done at all.'*

Tristan has re-embraced his inner blackness with a vengeance and has been slouching around with his hair tucked in a beanie. It is odd that he should choose to identify racially with Obama, whereas Gerry totally refuses to. I suppose it's because Tristan is still in search of his identity, something neither you nor your father ever seemed to agonise over. Gerry is happy to see himself as a Flemish Belgian with a shot of Congolese blood. In many respects, your father is enviably uncomplicated. I once asked him if he was ever bullied at school. 'When you are my size, Vita – and I was a very big boy – nobody picks a fight wiss you!'

Back in 1989, we witnessed a cluster of historic events. In November, the Berlin Wall was breached. For months, East Germany had been twitching and bucking in its rusting Communist chains, straining at the rapidly weakening links, driven insane with rumours. When summer arrived, an endless procession of rinky-dink little Trabants with their spluttering, stinky two-stroke engines hauled their owners towards Dresden and into Czechoslovakia and from there to Hungary, under the thinly-veiled pretence of spending the holidays there. For most, however, it was a one-way trip with no intention of return, because news had reached them that the Austro-Hungarian border, the gateway to the West, was open. Driven frantic by suspicions that Honecker and his cronies were bound to clamp down again soon and seal the borders when they realised the extent of the exodus, they hurtled towards Austria as fast as their hiccoughing little Mickey Mouse cars could carry them.

On November 9th, Gerry, Ewa and I sat watching the news footage with amazement as East Berliners, some of them still in their pyjamas, tentatively wandered around the previously forbidden, demonised capitalist enclave of West Berlin, and long-separated families and friends were reunited amid hugs and tears of disbelief and joy. I wondered what Walter's reaction would have been, given that his mother had relatives in Leipzig. And how would Silke Nass feel? She, a hard-bitten product of the GDR, was an émigrée from Dresden. I couldn't help but search the crowds for their and other familiar faces, although I knew this was folly. You, my love, were sitting next to Ewa, and wanted to know what exactly those people were doing, climbing on top of the wall, trying to pull it down, whacking it with sledge hammers, milling around, laughing, crying, kissing, taking photographs. It was to become your earliest personal memory of a major historic event. How could we best answer your questions? You were only three and a half, but you knew exactly when you were being fobbed off with vague, fudgy answers when what you craved were clear, crisp facts. Still, how do you explain the history of the Cold War to a little girl, albeit a precocious one? Ewa simplified it for you – she told you that the Germans had started a big nasty war which finished just a few years before she was born, and that after this war, Germany was divided as punishment and a big wall was built between the two halves. And now, this wall was coming down, but it would probably be rebuilt very soon. This satisfied you for a while, but you remained as transfixed by the images as the rest of us. It did all seem utterly unbelievable.

I had been to Berlin once with Walter, back in 1983 or 1984. He had taken me to the graffiti-covered wall, a monstrously tattooed concrete snake of a thing, a monument to folly, and we had climbed onto one of the special viewing platforms on the Western side that enabled you to look over the top and into East Berlin. It was only then that I realised that in Berlin itself, the wall actually consisted of two parallel walls, separated by a heavily-guarded ribbon of land, patrolled by GDR border guards. Yet birds could fly freely from one side to the other, and little bunny rabbits, a most incongruous sight, hopped innocently among the grass and weeds between the two walls, presumably too light to trip any of the thousands of landmines which were said to protect the GDR and its inhabitants from the fatal contagion of freedom of speech and the evils of unfettered capitalism. When we came down from the platform, I wanted to touch the wall and examine the graffiti close up. I think we were within a foot or two of the thing when the head and shoulders of a border guard appeared over the top of the wall, took a photograph of us and barked something about illegal *Republiksübertretung* or trespass. Walter shrugged, waved him away nonchalantly and explained to me that the wall itself had been built not on the border, but just a foot or two inside the East German side. If you got too close to it on the Western side, you had set foot illegally on GDR soil. The guard took a photograph of us. It gave me a sick thrill.

We also spent a day in East Berlin. I went through Checkpoint Charlie with my Danish passport but Walter, being German, had to cross elsewhere. We exchanged the compulsory daily amount of hard currency Deutsche Mark for Ost Mark, but apart from a surprisingly good lunch, could not find anything to spend it on. East Berlin, architecturally a mixture of imposing but neglected, soot-blackened majestic pre-war splendour and hideous jerry-built post-war monstrosities, was drab, sad and thoroughly depressing. It was in sharp contrast with the decadent opulence of West Berlin, where shops overflowed with every imaginable luxury and expensive cars lined the streets. We went into a large bookshop, somewhere near Alexanderplatz, hoping to find at least something to spend our worthless and unconvertible Ost Mark on, but absolutely everything was propaganda, with the exception of scientific textbooks. I ended up buying that little guide to understanding western newspapers which you found so intriguing when you came across it a few years ago, because it defined western economic and political terminology in Marxist terms. I felt uncomfortable the whole time we were in East Berlin, like a privileged voyeur in an ideological zoo where the animals looked listless and resented my stares. I disapproved of the buzz it gave me to know I was free to escape.

We expected Ewa to be delighted at the demise of the wall, but instead her reaction was one of muted disbelief, almost as if she didn't really want it to happen. She thought that at any moment the troops would be sent in and there would be an almighty confrontation ending in a bloodbath. She kept referring to the Tiananmen Square massacre which had taken place that summer. She had convinced herself that the iron curtain was permanent, maybe to justify her exile. She had no faith in the Oder-Neisse line, or indeed in the permanence of any of Poland's other borders, and given the tragic history of the country, this was hardly surprising. It had been variously invaded and plundered from the north, the east and the west and partitioned by Prussia, Russia and Habsburg Austria. Now Gorbachev, conceding the economic failure of communism, was allowing things to change all over Eastern Europe. In June, Poland held a general election and Solidarity won a massive number of seats in Parliament. Ewa, though virulently anti-communist, was no supporter of Lech Wałesa. So now this plebby little moustachioed shipyard electrician, this barely-educated Catholic prole from Gdańsk who went about with an icon of the Black Madonna of Częstochowa pinned to his lapel, this butcher of the Polish language was to become Prime Minister?

You are jokink, no?

That night, in bed, I turned to your father.

'Our three-year-old is developing an interest in politics and world events.'

He chuckled. 'Vita Vita. She only wanted to know why all dose people were trying to climb over a woll. Dat's not showing an interest in politics. Come on!'

He wrapped his arms around me and squeezed me.

'My wife loves to exaggerate!'

'My husband loves to underaggerate!'

'Is that an English word?'

'Of course it is.'

'Vita. *Liegebeest!* Big liar! You teach me nonsense words again!'

We started horsing around, and one thing led to another. Will it ever be like that again?

23ʳᴰ JANUARY 2009

Tristan has been working on your portrait. Astrid tells me he works in fits and starts, with rather more fits than starts. I have just taken a peek. He has started on your eyes and eyebrows. Your eyelashes are a smudge of black as you gaze down at the page of the book you are reading. He has captured to perfection the arch of your eyebrows and the perfect oval of your delicate face, and has made a start on your nose. He's also been experimenting with skin tones. His palette bears witness to various attempts at the right shade of the palest café au lait. That's as far as he has got. Astrid is right – he has talent. Even from this small sample, it is unmistakeable. The essence of you is already there.

As for me, I am doodling and drawing less as I become more used to words as a means of expression, and haven't touched my sketchpad in months. Your uncle no longer asks me how I am getting on. I think I've become part of the furniture now. Maybe it's better that way.

It's bitterly cold outside. An arctic wind is blowing from Siberia, and there is snow in the air. Doobie doesn't seem to mind it, despite her arthritic joints, and her winter coat has grown much thicker than it ever did in Clapham. Poor Mutt is worse off, with his skinny body and thin fur. Astrid has improvised a coat for him by cutting up an old yellow jumper. It makes him look like a performing dog from some circus act.

In the historic year of 1989, Atelier Eve Lewis was finally registered with Companies House. I had repeatedly told Ewa of the success my humble jewellery collections had enjoyed in Munich, thanks almost entirely to a newspaper profile that Ulrike had secured for me through a friend of a friend. I got the impression that Ewa thought such publicity was in some way incompatible with the image that she wished to project of luxury and exclusivity. Gerry and I had quite a job persuading her otherwise, but eventually we won her over. We contacted Astrid and Rhys for advice. Your aunt was occasionally profiled in newspapers and magazines, and Rhys had a number of useful press contacts. Ewa only wanted to be in *The Daily Telegraph* or *The Times* – she considered *The Guardian* to be full of misguided commie twaddle, and as for the tabloids... In the end, *The Telegraph* Sunday magazine offered to do a feature on her, as one on a series of new Eastern European entrepreneurs in Britain.

Ewa worked feverishly on her winter collection designs, to consist of two dozen outfits. It was the first time that I did all the *accessoires* without supplementing them with extras sourced from various outlets. Shoes were kept as plain as possible; patent leather pumps in different shades. Sylvia was once more prevailed upon to model, but Ewa did not want to use Agnieszka again (too Polish!) and hired two professional models, contacts of Damian's, the hairdresser. This time the venue was Notre Table. We printed one hundred invitations and sent them to a very carefully-selected group who were required to RSVP. We got over eighty replies when we thought we'd get fifty or sixty at most. This meant it would be a bit of a crush, but I did not think that would be a bad thing, as it would create a heightened sense of desirability and excitement. Ewa, however, fretted that a bit of a jostle would in fact detract from her treasured image of rarefied exclusivity. It was the kind of thing we would argue about many times over the years.

In addition to the reporter and photographer from *The Telegraph*, we also had our own photographer, Astrid, to record the occasion. The tables in the large L-shaped room were stacked in a corner and a low catwalk was created. Instead of soulless background music, I persuaded Ewa that we should have film scores from the Grace Kelly and Audrey Hepburn films of the Fifties. I was spared the embarrassment of having to read out the design details of the garments. Ewa had little catalogues and order forms printed with Astrid's photographs of each garment, all modelled by Sylvia.

The show took place on a Monday, that being the only day the restaurant was closed. Grandma and Sven came to Clapham to keep you entertained, which was a great relief, as you would have been impossible to control in the restaurant. We started at one o'clock with champagne and a buffet lunch of Italian antipasti. It was late September, and we were fortunate to have a dry, sunny day. I'd had an idea; instead of models just walking in from the kitchen, doing their twirl and then disappearing again into the kitchen, I thought we could have them arriving through the main entrance and walking into the restaurant, pretending to be ladies who were meeting other ladies for lunch. This was possible as Notre Table was on a street corner, and the models could go from the kitchen, which doubled as a dressing room, through the little back yard with the bins, out through the side gate, up the side street and round to the front. This, of course, was weather-dependent. We'd have had to fall back on a less original plan if it rained, or supply them with large umbrellas.

At the end of the catwalk, we set up a table and chairs and laid it for four with the usual white linen and fine wine glasses. Astrid positioned herself on one of the chairs with her camera.

As the show kicked off to the strains of *Moon River*, Sylvia appeared through the front door in a knee-length pale blue silk cocktail dress with a chaste high neck but a daringly low cut back. She wore my necklace back to front, as intended for this outfit; a large teardrop-shaped synthetic sapphire suspended from a delicate gold chain nestled high between the very white skin of her shoulder blades. Her hair was swept up. She acted out her part so convincingly that for a moment I reckon the audience was fooled into mistaking her for a late guest. Then, in a sort of send-up of old-fashioned modelling style, she shimmied up the catwalk, sashayed to the short end of the L, twirled, hand on hip, turned round and slowly made her way towards the table at the far end, giving Astrid ample opportunity to click away. She then went over to Astrid, air-kissed her and sat down most elegantly, crossing her long legs. Astrid filled their glasses with champagne and they toasted each other, then turned sideways and raised another toast to the enthusiastic audience.

A minute or two later, the next model would enter the restaurant, pretend to look for her friend, twirl at the short end of the L, then, having spotted Sylvia at the other end of the room, make her way slinkily, hip-swayingly, to the table, while Astrid, on her haunches, released another barrage of clicks. Air kissing, mwah mwah, more pouring of champagne by Astrid, clinking of glasses, a few sips, applause from the audience. Sylvia then disappeared through the kitchen doors to get changed into her next outfit, while the previous model stayed at the table, in pretend rhubarb rhubarb conversation with Astrid.

It verged on the camp; the models were definitely taking the piss and I secretly, guiltily thought it was hilarious, but a small voice inside me did wonder what on earth I was doing there. This just wasn't my thing. How long would I be able to play along with it?

The subsequent feature in the *Sunday Telegraph* magazine wasn't entirely to Ewa's liking. What bothered her was that instead of concentrating on the clothes, the reporter had made quite a lot of what she called the powerful symbiosis of Ewa's collection with chef Gerry Steeneken's Notre Table, his wife Vita's classy jewellery designs and famous sister-in-law, artist Astrid Rasmussen's presence as photographer.

I think Ewa felt a little miffed, sensing the implication that she could not have made it without this powerful supporting cast. It was something that we were to encounter many times over, this being told that the sum of our combined talents was better than the parts. Ewa was more than happy with Astrid's photos, but didn't care for the ones that had been taken by *The Telegraph*'s own photographer and selected to accompany the interview. Gerry and I both thought they were rather good, but Ewa was disappointed that they did not focus more on the clothes. I tried to explain to her that the photographer had decided to capture the whole event, of which the clothes were only a part. This he'd done rather well. There was a particularly striking shot of a lady sucking on her little complementary silver pencil as she studied the catalogue while her friend fossicked in a Gucci handbag, trying to find her lipstick or her glasses. In the background, Sylvia was twirling in an evening gown, an out of focus blur. Another picture showed a discreetly yawning waiter by the plundered buffet, peering furtively at his watch. The three remaining photographs did focus more on the clothes, but in no way could it be said that they were *about* the clothes.

The article was light-hearted, tongue-in-cheek. Ewa has kept every single article or interview ever published about her, from that early *Telegraph* one to the most recent one, in *Hello!* in a series of scrapbooks. I don't think Ewa quite got the slightly condescending tone of the article because her English wasn't up to sensing such nuances. When the collection was described as *'about as far removed from Vivienne Westwood as one could possibly hope to imagine,'* Ewa took it as a compliment, but I saw the implied dig. This wasn't cutting edge, innovative stuff; this was Ladies Who Lunch stuff; Norman Hartnell, Jean Muir, Jaeger, Country Casuals. But that was fine with Ewa, as that was exactly the image she was aiming for.

She had no grounds for complaint. The particular symbiosis of Notre Table, Astrid, the article, and who knows, maybe in some minor way my jewellery, resulted in substantial orders. Ewa had to employ two more assistants. AEL's official launch was a success. She could sleep in peace.

You, on the other hand, were still an insomniac, even if things did get a little better once you started to go to kindergarten. You were hyperactive and never seemed to need much sleep. I worried about your tantrums, and didn't know whether to reveal these to your new teacher or not. Actually, I was scared stiff the school would refuse to take you. The place was oversubscribed as it was, so they could easily afford to be selective if they wished, and refuse to take a problem child. In the end, I went in for a bit of understatement. My daughter, I told them, could be a trifle difficult at times, just a teensy weensy bit wilful...

Your father and I were both amazed and relieved to discover that, far from being impossible, you were actually quite well-behaved at school. You had, so your teacher told us, an insatiable curiosity about almost everything. That much we knew already, but what was news to us was her observation that you showed scant interest in other children. Those foolish enough to try and play with you were at best ignored, and at worst pushed away or even kicked. You didn't care much for dolls or anything involving mummy and daddy games or cuddly toys. No, you liked complex jigsaw puzzles, train sets, Lego and anything you could take apart and put together again, anything that challenged your mind. You also liked making geometrical shapes out of wooden blocks and entertaining yourself with endless counting games. You would sit and count the pages of the nursery rhyme books. At the age of three and a half, you counted compulsively into the thousands and when you'd finished counting the pages of books, you'd count whatever else you could see; trees, cars, the number of steps on each staircase, the bobbins in Ewa's sewing boxes, the tiles on the bathroom walls, the petals on a flower; you name it. Miss Harris decided to help her precocious little oddball and got hold of some arithmetic primers. Within a matter of months, you had mastered addition, subtraction, multiplication and division, fractions and percentages. You insisted on taking the books home and doing all the exercises. Ewa joked that we had bred a little accountant for AEL. You had inherited your Grandpa Sven's mathematical aptitude but you looked very much like Gerry, just several shades paler. A further dilution of the exotic Congolese bloodline, this time with your mother's Nordic genes. Your great grandfather Steeneken was so pale on old photos that he looked almost albino. Your father used to joke that great grandpa must have been afraid his children would turn out pale as ghosts and simply disappear with a puff into the ether if he didn't marry a dark-skinned woman to reintroduce some melanin into his offspring. Your grandfather then added milk to the coffee by marrying a very blonde Flemish girl, and your father diluted his children's African roots even further by marrying me. This makes you and Tristan octoroons; an odd word that describes those who have one eighth black blood. 'Octoroon,' Tris once said, sounded racist and offensive, like some crazy cross between a baboon and an octagon. With you, the only trace of your racial heritage was your wavy black gypsy hair and Mediterranean skin tone. Tristan's hair turned out Afro frizzy but it was fair and his eyes were green, much to his disappointment. But both of you were lucky to have inherited your father's finely chiselled nose and fleshy, sensual mouth.

Your troubled brother. What can I do to help him? We are all birds with broken wings here, all just going through the motions of living since your murder, your slaughter, that ridiculous untimely death, that useless martyrdom, as we wait for time to heal us, as everybody assures us it surely will. Should we believe them? Haven't you effectively cursed us for the rest of our lives? I get angry about that sometimes, and then I feel bad about it, because I realise that you were not pursuing martyrdom at all, but were merely misguided. You thought, with your idiosyncratic logic and complete absence of emotional intelligence, that you were doing the right thing.

Nightmare last night. I'm giving birth, in terrible pain. A crumpled, slimy being is handed to me. I wipe its face. It has sightless eyes, like a weather-bleached statue from antiquity. White, no irises or pupils. I look up at the midwife, who smiles and shrugs. When I look down again, the creature in my arms has shrunk. You must feed it, urges the nurse. I put it down next to me on the bed and start to unbutton the complex highnecked gown that I am wearing. It has hundreds of buttons and some are impossible to open as the buttonholes are too small. I yank at them, try to tear the gown open. I glance at the creature. It has shrunk to the size of an orange, a peach, a walnut. When I am finally ready to offer it my breast, it is little more than a tiny ball of black threads which then changes into a spider and scurries away into a corner of the room. What could it all mean? Is it symbolic of my failure to nurture my children properly?

At the beginning of 1990, your father and his sous-chef, that lovable Belgian of Neapolitan parentage by the name of Salvatore Esposito, your uncle Sal, decided to set up on their own and take over the lease on an ailing restaurant in Great Peter Street in Westminster. It had been an undistinguished Italian eatery where Sal had worked when he first came to London. Perfect location but crap management and no imagination, Sal had said. When he heard that the lease was up, he persuaded Gerry that it was now or never. It was quite scary, as the overheads were huge and the deeds to our house and Sal's flat had to be used as collateral before they could secure the substantial loan required to refurbish the place.

Over a period of about three months, it was stripped bare of every last fishing net, plastic lobster and Chianti bottle. I furtively did the rounds of several dozen of the top London eateries of the Yuppie era. I snooped around Langan's Brasserie in Mayfair, but didn't much like its old-fashioned gentlemen's club interiors. I lunched at Conran's Bibendum in the beautifully-restored Michelin building and felt that we could not possibly hope to compete, as our premises did not possess that kind of architectural pedigree. Astrid and I also dined at her favourite, the River Café in Hammersmith. We were much taken with the clean, bright feel of the place and envied its lovely garden. However, we did not want to copy anyone; it was more an exercise to see the best of what was out there. Gerry was hell-bent on specialising in Belgian cuisine, even though a little market research showed that the average Londoner failed to associate Belgium with good food. In fact, they failed to associate it with anything much other than a kind of bad Euro joke, something which used to mystify and annoy both you and your father.

I drew up a questionnaire which required people to list the things they most associated with Belgium. We paid a dozen university students to stand outside supermarkets with clipboards and approach people for their opinions and reactions. The answers were predictable; Brussels sprouts, bureaucracy, the EU's definition of a banana, the Battle of Waterloo, that funny little detective from the Agatha Christie novels, what was his name again? Clouseau? Bardot? Maginot? But those responses were from people who'd never set foot in Belgium. The few adventurous souls who had ventured there mentioned *moules frites*, Ardennes pâté, *kriek* beer, good chocolate, delicious cakes, beautiful medieval cities, lace and great painters like Bruegel. When those who'd never been there were asked to rank the following types of cuisine in order of preference: French, Italian, English, Indian, Chinese and Belgian, it was Indian that almost invariably came out at number one, followed by Italian. When it came to Belgian food, people made comments like 'What do they eat, apart from sprouts?' All in all, it didn't seem very promising. Most people, I noticed, did not even know that 'Belgian' is the adjective of Belgium. Your father had told the bank that he and Sal were going to open a Mediterranean restaurant; he too realised the perceived risk he was taking. Sal was also in favour of the Belgian option. He thought that there were already more than enough Italian restaurants in Central London. Something new and different was needed.

Astrid offered her services as decor consultant. Your father claimed he had absolutely no eye for such things, and we had no money to employ an interior designer, so Astrid volunteered. She favoured a minimal and modern look with light colours and wooden floors. For some reason she wanted to start by designing the font for the name; she believed all else would flow from there.

The name... my God, how we argued over that. Right from the start, your father wanted De Vlaaminck, an old Dutch spelling for The Fleming, but worried about what he'd told the bank. Sal strongly favoured 'Chez Gérard' because he thought it was important to sound intimate and personal, but your father objected to being made to sound French. Astrid suggested something totally neutral and a bit whacky like Aardvark or Division Bell, because of the proximity to the Houses of Parliament. As for me, I thought something French-sounding would be our best bet; *Le* something or other. In the end, though, De Vlaminck won. Your father simply put his foot down. 'People won't know how to pronounce it.' I objected. 'Dat woss never a problem for Häagen Dasz.' he reminded me. 'So what if dey mispronounce it as Duh Flaymink!'

Your father wanted Astrid to do murals but she resisted the idea. Instead, she did three large paintings for him; one a sort of Brueghel pastiche showing him and Sal wielding carving knives, chasing after an enormous grinning pig. Astrid, Ewa and I were depicted as peasants in the crowd – Ewa was far from amused when she discovered this – with you and Dylan playing around our feet with a little dog. Another was a sort of tribute to Magritte's famous painting of a pipe; the one she painted was of a huge Brussels sprout, and underneath, in neat copperplate: *Ceci n'est pas un chou de Bruxelles.* The third was a map of Western Europe, painted in faux-naïve style on two planks of wood, with a large red arrow pointing at Belgium, and a caption that read 'Voilà - here it is.' Your father thought it was hilarious, but I'm not sure Sal was quite as amused. Given a chance, I reckon he'd have swapped all three for a large official portrait of King Baudouin and Queen Fabiola of the kind you'd find in any Belgian embassy.

We opted for plain Scandinavian furniture, and Astrid convinced us that we needed to counter the rather severe, modern nature of this look with half a dozen old-fashioned chandeliers. It took weeks and weeks of trawling flea markets and junk shops before we had them; three totally different sets of two. It was Astrid's idea to spray-paint the metal parts cobalt blue. I cleaned the crystals and restored the missing and broken ones by cannibalising a spare one we'd bought solely for that purpose. When we put them up, any misgivings we may have had vanished – they looked magnificent and added just the right amount of quirkiness and character.

De Vlaaminck opened for business at Easter of 1990. It quickly became popular with ministers, MPs and other assorted civil servants, and quite a few loyal Notre Table customers decided to try it too. Importantly, it found favour with the food critics and the waiting staff came in for much praise. They were loyal, not only because Gerry did not tolerate any shouting or abuse from the kitchen, but because all gratuities were divided fairly, and Gerry was scrupulous about ensuring that credit card tips were added to the wages. I was amazed to discover how many other places did not do this and routinely diddled their staff out of their hard-earned tips. Six months after opening, De Vlaaminck was featured in a BBC documentary on working conditions in the catering industry in London, and was rated among the top three best employers. Although it had nothing to do with the quality of the food, this further increased its popularity.

We breathed a huge sigh of financial relief.

And you, Senta? You were four and a half in the summer of 1990, and we normal mortals could hardly keep up with you. You had clocked up a year at kindergarten, and in addition to mastering arithmetic, had taught yourself to read. You were devouring books that most children twice your age were only just getting to grips with, but what interested you most, even then, was anything to do with numbers and with nature. You could spend hours in the garden with a magnifying glass, examining insects and plants. One sunny summer's day as I was drinking coffee in the garden, you were on your haunches next to the lavender bush with its old-fashioned grand-motherly fragrance, closely observing a huge bee as it bumbled and hummed around the flowers.

'Gosh,' I said, 'look at him, busy collecting honey. I wonder where he lives. Maybe someone keeps bees around here. Maybe we can buy honey from them. Wouldn't that be nice!'

You turned your face towards me and knitted your brow. I sensed a lecture coming.

'Mummy, this is a bumble bee. And it's a 'she', not a 'he.' Bumble bees make very little honey. It's honey bees that make lots of honey. They're much smaller. Honey bees get nectar from the flowers and that's what they use to make honey. They don't get honey from the flowers. And they carry the pollen from flower to flower. That is their other function.'

I tried to keep a straight face. Your knowledge and pedantry were impressive, scary and amusing, but it wouldn't do to laugh, as this could trigger a tantrum.

'What about her then? Mrs Bumble Bee. What's her function?'

'Oh, nothing much,' you said. 'Just pollination, I suppose, but that's very important. It sticks to their fur because of the electrostatic charge, and also in the little pollen basket on their hind legs.' At that, you got up and headed towards the back of the garden, to observe the carp in the little pond and the tortoises in their pen.

Around this time – it may well have been earlier – every sentence you uttered started with the words 'how' or 'why'. This is of course common in young children, but my answers were rarely detailed or accurate enough to satisfy you. You pulled things apart to see how they were made. You wanted to know how things worked; car engines, clocks, telephones, television, the fridge. One day you took the lid off the toilet cistern to just see what happened when you pushed the handle to activate the flush. It drove me crazy because more often than not I couldn't begin to answer your questions, and you were not content with vague answers or satisfied with confessions of ignorance. I really could have done with the internet, but access to that wonderful tool still lay five or six years in the future. Gerry had bought a little Amstrad word processor which we had to hide from you, as you would have wanted to know how it worked and would not have been able to resist taking it apart. This must have been when I first became aware of a certain look of yours, a look of amazed disappointment when I had to admit that I couldn't explain how electricity worked because I'd always hated physics and dropped it at fourteen. To my shame, I couldn't even begin to explain the workings of the television or the radio, and was forever telling you to ask Grandpa Sven. I felt totally inadequate. At the age of four and a half, you still assumed that adults had the answer to everything. By your fifth birthday, you had pretty much figured out what Gerry, Ewa and I were and were not likely to be able to explain. You discovered that most of us had simply long stopped asking ourselves certain questions. Not necessarily because we knew the answers, but rather because we'd started to take all these miraculous things like telephones, microwaves and cars for granted. Our curiosity had become blunted and we had got used to using and living and working with things we didn't understand.

I was concerned about your precociousness but aware that many parents think their children are geniuses, so one day I took you to visit Astrid in order to observe Dylan and compare your behaviour. Even you would have to admit that your cousin is no fool; he graduated from Cambridge last summer and got snapped up by Citibank on their milk round, but compared to you he was positively retarded at the age of four. He could count a bit and he spent a lot of time drawing farm animals. At least, that's what he told us they were. It required a considerable imagination to make out whether the wobbly little round body shapes with the stick legs were cows, sheep or pigs. He babbled happily to himself and was very affectionate. He tried to play with you, but you ignored him. You found a globe, spun it round and asked why the people who lived upside down at the bottom didn't fall off into space; Dylan walked a plastic dinosaur up and down the wall and asked for more chocolate ice-cream. He had quite a wide vocabulary, but it was nothing like yours, with your love of taxonomy. What is more, you could chatter away in Polish; you'd simply picked it up by hanging around Ewa in the sewing room. You knew the words for pin, needle, scissors, stitch, embroider, hem, thread, bobbin and pattern in Polish long before you learnt them in English. You and Ewa could chat away happily without Gerry and me understanding a word.

A case for Mensa, Rhys concluded. Miss Harris at your kindergarten had said the same, and was also the first to suspect Asperger's, a condition on the autism spectrum which afflicted her brother. I had never heard of it and at first I flatly refused to believe that there was anything wrong with you. Autism conjured up visions of children so deeply disturbed that they were locked up deep inside themselves, banging their heads against walls and floors, flapping their hands and rocking compulsively. You did none of these things. Your unusual behaviour was, I thought, just the result of your high intelligence, which led to your frustration with normal mortals. Your father, Astrid and I also had mixed feelings about subjecting you to any kind of IQ assessment. We did not want to create another Ruth Lawrence, to send you to Oxford at the age of twelve. What was the point? It would only have estranged you from your contemporaries. I didn't want to rob you of your childhood. And yet... what if you were bored stiff at infant school? Was that fair? Highly intelligent children can go off the rails if not sufficiently stimulated. I consulted your Grandpa

Sven, but he wasn't very helpful; his IQ, he reckoned, wasn't anything like as high as yours. He really couldn't remember whether he'd driven his mother crazy with questions. On his visits to us, he would take you to London Zoo and to the Natural History Museum and the Science Museum. You begged and pestered to be taken back time and again. Shortly after your fifth birthday, we caved in and had you assessed. Miss Harris found a psychologist specialised in assessing children's intelligence. He came along to the school and sat in class, unobtrusively observing your behaviour over several days. He noted your unusually advanced vocabulary, your ability to solve all manner of puzzles in no time, your insatiable curiosity about the way things work. He also saw that you were easily bored and that you showed no interest in other children. Those were all things that we already knew. He confirmed what we had suspected – that you had a very high IQ. He did not want to hazard a guess, and advised us to get you tested by Mensa when you were eleven or twelve, though he was not really a fan of what he called 'IQ pigeon holing. '

As for Asperger's, he went through a checklist with us and you certainly fitted aspects of the profile, yet I refused to believe it. But his confirmation of your exceptional intelligence didn't surprise anybody. When you were in your teens and finally took a Cattell test, you scored towards the top of the scale. You were to the far right of the IQ bell curve. I thought it explained everything. But to this day, I've never been totally convinced by the Asperger's diagnosis. Maybe I just resented the label it stuck on you. I was more comfortable thinking of you as an idiosyncratic, emotionally stunted oddball.

September 1990 came, and you moved from kindergarten to infants' school. We all, not least Miss Harris, had serious doubts about this move, but we were in a quandary. We felt that you needed to socialise with children of your own age. So far, attempts by Miss Harris to encourage this at kindergarten had been a failure. You could not care less about the other children and only spoke to them if you wanted something from them. You played alone, which normally involved taking things apart to see how they were made. You made yourself memorably unpopular by dismembering Chloë Hall's favourite baby doll and severing the elastic that held its head in place to see how the mechanism worked that closed the eyes when you held the doll horizontally. Apparently Chloë was traumatised for weeks, and her mother put it about that you were psychologically disturbed and needed treatment. Miss Harris was caught in the middle. She fixed the doll and tried hard to soothe Mrs Hall's hackles, but Chloë never went near you again and didn't come back after Christmas. I used to bump into Mrs Hall occasionally on Clapham High Street, and she'd glare at me as if I were some kind of psychopath. I'd nod and smile politely, but she'd just twitch her face at me and manage to make me feel terrible.

Miss Harris decided to find suitable things for you to take apart. Do you remember when she brought you an old wind-up alarm clock and challenged you to take it apart and put it together again? That kept you busy for about a week. You were not able to reassemble it, and Miss Harris told me she tried to get you to understand that you should never take anything apart if you couldn't put it back together again. It was a lesson that took quite a few more years to sink in.

When you weren't pulling things apart, you would sit and read books intended for much older children from the Junior School library or do sums and riddles with the ever-patient Miss Harris. The children you had spurned quickly learned to leave you alone. No doubt they also remembered the scene that Chloë had made when she saw her dismembered, decapitated doll. Instead of making friends with your classmates, you became devoted to the animals in the little petting zoo. Zara the goat,

Molly and Dolly the ducks, Bonzo the guinea pig, Boris the albino rabbit with the red eyes, the two hens, Dotty and Potty, and the cat that had been raised with them from orphaned kittenhood, Plonker the ginger tabby, who slept in the hen house and tried to groom Bonzo. You adored them all, and told us about them every day. You empathised easily with animals, but people were a huge problem.

Your new teacher, Miss Anderson, had been fully briefed. She had prepared some special worksheets for you from National Geographic about plants and animals. These were intended to keep you amused as the other children did addition and subtraction. But things she thought would keep you busy for a whole week only took you an hour or so to complete. Every break time you'd escape from the infants' playground by clambering over the dividing wall with the help of a plastic crate and going back to your beloved Miss Harris and to the petting zoo. On your third day, there was complete panic. After the mid-morning break, you had failed to come back to class. A frantic headmistress searched high and low for you and Miss Harris hadn't seen you either. Finally they conceded defeat and phoned me. Had you run away and gone home by any chance?

I went haring up to the school, a good mile away. I had a feeling I knew where you might be. A highly apologetic and nervous headmistress was waiting for me at the gates. I told her of my hunch. 'But that's impossible,' she said, almost offended.

'Allow me,' I pleaded.

Zara the goat had a little shelter. Behind it was a storage shed for tools, hay and animal feed. You had told me about it. The door had a big padlock on it.

'That's locked, so she can't be in there.'

'No it isn't,' I said. 'Mr Timms lost the key ages ago. It just looks locked. You can go in, pull the door closed, stick your hand through the little window and rearrange the padlock shackle so that it looks locked. Senta told me about it once.'

I removed the lock and opened the door. You already knew that your number was up. You were sitting there with Plonker the cat on your lap and a large school atlas. It was open on a double page about planets and stars. You looked both frightened and defiant, and I felt deeply sorry for you.

'Come, sweetheart, I'll take you home. '

That was to be your first and last experience of a normal school for another eight years.

It was Grandpa Sven who came to the rescue by offering to home-school you. We were steeling ourselves for a battle with the LEA to obtain permission, and were amazed to discover how shockingly easy it was. All we needed to do was inform your headmistress in writing of our intentions so that you could be taken off the school register. Sven had retired in March, and was looking forward to the challenge of educating you. He'd already taken you to the Science Museum half a dozen times, explained and demonstrated to you the workings of the internal combustion engine, (suck-squeeze-bang-blow!) let you take apart and then reassemble an old manual typewriter and visited a farm with you to see cows being milked. ('Grandpa, why do cows have milk all the time? Why do hens keep laying eggs?') He'd shown you the inside of his single lens reflex camera, let you take black and white pictures of snails, a dead sparrow, your own foot, and then the two of you developed, enlarged and printed them in the bathroom that also served as his dark room. You liked being with him because he was one of the few adults that you knew who could answer many of your questions in satisfactory detail. What is more, he was calm, unemotional and even-tempered; just perfect for you. He adored you, not only for your insatiable curiosity and search for knowledge, but because you provided a much-needed distraction from Grandma who was going through a phase of serious depression. You helped to give him a sense of purpose and a new focus to his retirement.

They lived in Wimbledon. The problem was that he could not travel up to Clapham every day and leave Grandma on her own, though he must at times have been tempted to do just that. Instead, you spent three days a week with them. On Monday morning after the early morning rush hour, I'd take you there on the tube and on Wednesday evening I'd travel down again, the four of us would have dinner, and I would take you back home to Clapham Common. He gave you copious quantities of homework, so you would spend hours poring over books and atlases and encyclopaedias and copies of National Geographic.

In June of 1991, when you were five and De Vlaaminck was beginning to turn a profit, your father and I finally got round to tying the knot. Somehow something which we had intended to be a very a low-key affair in a register office with just immediate family and some close friends just grew and grew until I felt the wedding preparations had been hijacked by outside forces beyond our control. Ewa worked secretively on my dress and matching outfits for you and Dylan, our flower girl and page boy. I had feared, initially, that she might want to go over the top with lace and frills and furbelows and dress me up like some frothy blancmange à la Princess Diana, but I was completely wrong and should have known better. She kept the dress very plain. It was a sleeveless ankle-length ivory silk shift with a low round neckline and a v-shaped back, and it flared coquettishly at mid-calf. It was stunning in its simplicity. Five years later, when those star-crossed lovers Carolyn Bessette and John Kennedy Junior got married, she wore a $40,000 pearl-coloured silk crepe dress by Narciso Rodriguez which was almost identical to Ewa's design. Ewa couldn't get over this, and it annoyed and flattered her in equal measure. 'I am ahead of time, Vitka.' she sighed, as she examined the Kennedy wedding photographs in some society mag. Orders for similar plain designs started rolling in, and for a while she was inundated with requests for knock-offs, which fattened her bank balance.

Rummaging on Portobello Road, I had found a pair of maroon satin flapper-era shoes, and made myself a matching necklace consisting of a thick rope of synthetic rubies and garnets. Gerry wore a cream-coloured Italian linen suit; one of the few times I've ever seen him wear one. On the photographs, we really do look striking, but that smiling bride just isn't me. I think it was the make-up and the swept-up hair. I'd wanted to wear my hair down. 'I'm tall enough already.' I'd moaned to Ewa.

'No problem, darlink. Gerry is very tall man. With hair up you show beautiful neck and necklace. Much more elegant, no?'

Somehow we almost forgot the wedding rings. It was Ewa who reminded me, less than a week before the big day. She'd assumed that Gerry and I had long sorted that out. I didn't think your father would want to wear one, as rings are a nuisance in his line of work, but he said he'd wear one round his neck, on a chain. It was too late to design anything, so we just bought some plain gold bands with the intention of replacing them later with a design of my own. Another thing I never got round to. I lost mine while swimming in the sea on honeymoon. Your father's still nestles in his chest hair.

Damian came to the house to do my hair. Your grandmother had interfered very little in the whole pre-nuptial period. Wedding preparations weren't really her scene, just as they weren't Astrid's, but your aunt Ewa more than made up for that. She had ordered a spray of miniature pink roses for me, and also wanted me to wear some in my hair, which I refused. I was getting more and more frustrated. Her intentions were only the best, but I felt I was being taken over and wanted to have some say in how I looked. In the end, not wanting to upset her too much, I consented to being made up. The face that stared back at me in the mirror was not me, but some window dummy. I sneakily toned it down a bit in the loo, blotting my lips with a tissue to get rid of some of the lipstick and removing blobs of thick mascara with a cotton bud.

How did we end up with more than fifty guests when I'd originally envisaged about a dozen? Only very close relatives and friends came to the Wandsworth Register Office; Ewa and Sal, and from my side your Grandpa Sven and Grandma and your great Aunt Jeanie, Astrid, Rhys and little Dylan, as well as assorted Danes. From the Belgian side there were Oma and Opa Steeneken, Tante Madeleine, Oom Johan and your cousins, Anneke and Marijne. Our own photographer took pictures of us in the magnificent marble-clad art deco hallway, but the press had been told they could snap us outside the building. The press – this was another bone of contention – I was very much against what I saw as an intrusion in a private family celebration, but your father and Ewa persuaded me to relent. He claimed it was really for Ewa's sake, so that she could get some publicity out of it; Ewa told me she thought it would be good for De Vlaaminck; after all, your father was fast becoming something of a minor celebrity. I rolled over, as usual.

The hacks trotted out the symbiosis thing again. Alluding to the title of a Peter Greenaway film, one picture bore the caption 'The artist, the couturier, the chef and his designer wife' under a shot of us on the steps of the register office. Ewa was flattered with this classy epithet. Your father joked that if Ewa was a couturier, he should have been elevated from chef to restaurateur, especially as he now had his own restaurant. I wasn't best pleased with being described ambiguously as a designer wife. Jewellery designer wife would have been acceptable, but 'designer wife?' It seemed bitchy and it really rankled. The last one on the list too, not much talent, but in the right place at the right time. I guess nobody really knew what I did in those days. My name was not publicly associated with Ewa's *accessoires*; not even Ewa's clients knew. Probably just as well.

De Vlaaminck was decked out in a riot of stephanotis, ivy and white roses. The guests included the entire restaurant staff, Ewa's Polish assistants, Damian and of course various old friends and their spouses and partners. I had sent an invitation to Ulrike in Munich. She had responded with warmest wishes and a beautiful silver teapot of her own creation. She regretted not being able to attend, but did not give a reason. I suspected torn loyalties. In a throwaway PS, she mentioned that Walter had finally passed the audition for the Bavarian State Opera.

Our wedding breakfast was a tribute to the best of Belgian and Scandinavian cuisine, with gravad laks from Denmark and fillet of roebuck with pear in red wine. Champagne corks popped freely, and to this day, some of them have been left where they lodged between the crystals of the chandeliers. You, Senta, drove our poor official photographer absolutely crazy. The only thing you were interested in was his camera equipment. You wanted to see inside the camera, understand how it worked, what all the buttons and dials did, hold the thing, take pictures yourself. You fired off your usual volley of 'Why? How? Can I...?' questions. You dogged him relentlessly as he crouched and clicked, trying to take the informal shots we'd asked him for, and I could sense his mounting frustration, but you would not be restrained. Ewa, Astrid and I both tried our damnedest to get you to sit down with your cousins. You'd manage for about five minutes, and then you would be off again. Meanwhile, Dylan played quietly with toy cars on the corner of the table. Grandpa Sven tried to entertain you with some napkin origami, but you weren't so easily distracted. You kept sneaking back to the photographer. In the end, your great-uncle Mikkel managed to hold your attention for a while by showing you the various functions of his complicated Breitling watch.

While you stayed with Grandpa and Grandma in Wimbledon, we honeymooned in Amalfi in a hotel that was managed by a nephew of Sal's. The exquisite fourteenth century building, originally a Franciscan convent, clung to a steep hillside and had sweeping views of the Mediterranean. There was a lemon tree near our balcony which bore fruit so large and so perfect that they looked like wax. At night, we'd sit there, breathe the scent of jasmine and honeysuckle and gaze at the enormous pale moon as it illuminated the vast black waters with a million dancing silver scales. Our days were lazy, making love, rising late, swimming, lolling around on the beach and in cafés, strolling around the town, eating seafood pasta and liberally quaffing wine. On one day when we felt particularly energetic, we visited neighbouring Positano, but we never did make any of the must-do trips to Pompeii and the Isle of Capri which Sal's nephew kept recommending to us. We were simply too happy being idle together. The sun brought out the melanin of your father's African heritage and he turned from cappuccino into espresso. I turned a golden brown and my hair became almost platinum.

That honeymoon, ten uninterrupted lazy days, is the longest we've ever spent together, just the two of us. Ridiculous. We should have made more time for each other. What am I saying? I had plenty of time to give; it was your father who had less and less, as the restaurant sucked up all his energy and passion. De Vlaaminck has become his temperamental, demanding, exhausting mistress, always prepared to threaten theatrical suicide at the merest suspicion of neglect. I grew to resent, even to hate the place. What do you expect when you marry a chef, an exasperated Astrid once asked me when I was having a bit of a bitch about the amount of time your father spent at work. In my ignorance of the reality, I envied the relationship she and Rhys had, the amount of time they were able to spend together. 'Come on, Veets!' she said. 'If you'd married a racing driver, you wouldn't expect him to give up racing, would you!' She was right, of course. The same is true for relationships with singers and actors. No matter what, you'll always have to play second fiddle to their main passion.

Not long after we'd returned to London, I realised that I was pregnant. Would it shock you to know that I was devastated? I flatly refused to believe the result of the little home test kit and went to see Dr Gupta for a second test. Alas; positive. I wept with rage when I got the confirmation. Alone in the kitchen, I banged my fists on the wall. This was one experience I never wanted to repeat. After more than five years of doing battle with your tantrums and insomnia, I was determined never to have another baby again. In fact, for the first four years of your life, you would only go to sleep properly if you could lie between us, but you didn't like to curl up against us. You wanted plenty of space. As a result, your father and I spent years sleeping uncomfortably on the outer edges of the bed, occasionally rolling onto the floor with a painful thump. I could not face a repeat of this, just as things were finally becoming so much easier with you. And now Tristan had snuck into my womb, somehow circumventing the barrier of the copper coil.

Who could I talk to? I thought of getting an abortion, but I knew Gerry would have been very unhappy. He wouldn't have stopped me, but he would have pleaded with me not to do it. And Ewa? Out of the question, for obvious reasons. Your grandparents? Forget it.

I caught the train to Norwich to consult your aunt, who was heavily pregnant with Marcus at the time. Being so tiny and slender, her bump seemed too big for the rest of her. Her pregnancy looked like an act of cruelty, as if she were an overloaded mule straining under a preposterous burden. The funny thing was that Astrid treated the whole business of being pregnant in a wonderfully casual way. She kind of ignored it and made very few concessions, one of which was not to touch her beloved weed.

It was a boiling hot summer day. She fixed us some Pimms with fresh mint and a lot of ice cubes and we went and sat outside in her newly-created sculpture garden, a little sun trap that she had made by partly demolishing the end pig sty. The roof had been removed and so had one of the long walls. She had planted creepers and placed some of her early period animal works there – the scrap metal herons, the stork, the driftwood fish, the bronze of the cat rolling on its back that you loved so much because it was warm and smooth to the touch in the sun. After a bit of chit chat about the exhibition she was preparing for, she turned to me: 'Go on then, spit it out!'

'Astrid, I... Oh God, I...'

'What?'

'I'm... I'm pregnant!'

'Congra...'

'No! I want an abortion. You don't understand. I don't want another Midwich Cuckoo. I'm just getting my life back, and now this.'

Astrid was silent for a long time and let me stew in my self-pity. Then she waddled off to fetch me a box of tissues and handed it to me silently.

'What am I going to do, Azzie? Nobody knows yet apart from you and the doctor... '

She sighed, cracked her knuckles, sipped her Pimms.

'Okay Veets, I'm going to take the liberty of getting something off my chest. Just promise you won't get mad.. Do we have a deal?'

'We do, I promise.'

'It's not the pregnancy that's your problem.'

'What?'

'It's your... your passivity. You just let things happen to you and then you complain about the consequences.'

'I didn't just let this happen to me.. It was a fucking accident!'

'Ha ha.. Yes, literally! That's a good one! No, I don't mean the pregnancy. I mean other things. You're... you're like a piece of driftwood. You're just letting everything and everyone control you. You're frittering your talent away designing boring jewellery for the Ladies of Leisure, Ewa's ladies who lunch, as you call them.'

'Ewa relies on me... '

'I'm not criticising your partnership with Ewa, Veets. It's just – I don't understand why you don't also want to... do your own thing.' She winced at her own cliché.

'I'm not much cop as an artist, Az. Please don't pretend otherwise.'

'As a painter, maybe, but that little collection you showed me ages ago, after you ran away from Munich. The one with the black and white photographs. That was inspirational.'

'*Erotik?*.

'Now I bet that's languishing in a drawer somewhere, gathering dust. Am I right?'

'It's in a suitcase in the attic, actually.'

'Why don't you start your own line of funky stuff? Under your own name? I'm always astonished at how utterly boring and conservative the average person's jewellery still is in this country. Remember the wonderful designs they have in

Denmark? Really imaginative, playful, different. All over Europe you see great stuff. Come back here and all you see is women wearing boring old wedding bands paired with equally boring diamond solitaires. It's a kind of uniform, as if it's some sacred tradition and there's no alternative. The High Street stuff is deadly dull. It's overdue for a shake-up, for new ideas.'

'The market is very conservative here, Az. I do know a bit about it, you know. There are plenty of really gifted craft jewellers around, but they're just not mainstream. In any case, I fail to see how this is going to solve my problem.'

'It would give you something else to focus on. You are not the maternal type. So what, that's not a crime. I'm not either. At the moment you're just...'

'...not fulfilling my potential?'

'Sounds like something from a school report.'

'Yes, it bloody does... *Could do better. Needs to apply herself. Has not reached a level commensurate with her ability... has not stretched herself... disappointing results.*'

'But it's true. You're coasting, idling. Letting Senta drive you nuts, using her as an excuse. You've got to...'

'I've got to take control?'

'Uhuh.'

'You know how to design the stuff. You know how to make it, too. Just... fucking *go* for it.'

'But I still don't want this baby. What if I produce another semi-autistic insomniac screamer?' (Oh God, Senta, it's true. Forgive me, but that's how I felt.)

'Come on, Veets! You know that's extremely unlikely.'

'About as unlikely as producing a child like Senta. But it can happen, and knowing my luck...'

'Don't do it. Don't have an abortion. Have the baby. And pour your energy into your designs. That's my advice. Oh, and suggest to Gerry that he gets the snip or else you go and get your tubes tied.'

On the train back to Liverpool Street I brooded. Would I ever have gone ahead with an abortion? I very much doubt it. I mulled over your aunt's advice, and when I got home, I retrieved the dusty little suitcase with Claudio's photographs and took the heavily tarnished 'Erotik' collection out of its pouch and wondered who would wear such things. The Yuppie era of Cartier tank watches and diamond solitaire earrings was in its death throes, but I had not been able to spot the birth of any new trend to take its place. Everything just seemed very low key, very minimal. If I was to persuade the public to buy my somewhat retro baubles, I'd have to create an identity, a name for myself. Cartier, Rolex, Rasmussen. Ah, but Rasmussen was already taken, associated with your aunt, AzRaz, the artist. I didn't want to ride on her coat tails. Steeneken then? An apt name for a jeweller, as it means little stone in Dutch. But then I'd risk riding on your father's coattails. Hmm, can't have that either.

Driftwood. That's what Astrid had called me.

Brilliant.

Driftwood it would be. Suitably anti-Yuppie and unfocused.

I never did confess my wish for an abortion to your father, but I did tell him that I wasn't exactly over the moon either. He on the other hand simply couldn't hide his joy, and tried his utmost to reassure me that a repeat of the experience we'd had with you would be very unlikely. As for Ewa, her face lit up when I told her. She hugged me tight and grew a little teary. It made me feel deeply ungrateful and ashamed of my misgivings.

Grandma's reaction was odd. There was a silence after I had broken the news to her over the phone. I had hoped that the news would cheer her up, but all I got was a tired-sounding response. 'That's nice, dear, that'll be good for Senta. Is Gerry pleased?' She spoke in what I'd come to call her pharma-voice, drugged, flat, automaton-like. I could picture her sitting by the phone, a zonked expression on her face, probably still in her dressing gown and slippers, or maybe in something ill-matched, grabbed at random out of the wardrobe at Sven's urging. It is a good thing that you barely remember those days and really only got to know her once the correct balance of medication had finally been found to put her back on an even keel. Even then, she was never again the feisty little terrier of a woman that Astrid and I remember from our childhood, full of energy, a bohemian eccentric who painted prolifically but unremarkably, smoked roll-ups, painted her toenails green and laughed raucously, a great raconteuse of risqué anecdotes.

And you? I decided not to wait until the bump appeared because I wanted you to hear it from me, not from some snatch of conversation gleaned in the sewing room.

'Senta, you're going to have a little brother or sister.'

You stopped doing whatever you were doing or examining – I think you were pulling the kitchen scales apart. Or it might have been the toaster.

'A boy or a girl?'

'I don't know yet, darling.'

'Why not? Why don't you know?'

'It's too early.'

'Why?'

'The baby is inside me and it is too soon to tell if it's a boy or a girl.'

'Inside you? Did you ... like... swallow it?'

'Hmmm... sort of, yes.'

'How? With water?'

'No... '

'Tea?... '

'No!'

'Coca Cola?'

'Er, no... '

'You swallowed a whole BABY without any LIQUID?'

'Well, not exactly. Let me try and explain... '

You sighed. 'Try and explain.' In your experience, that's not something I was very good at.

'You remember being in the paddling pool with Dylan?'

'Yes. He didn't have any swimming trunks on..'

'Exactly.'

'Dylan has a willy.'

'Yes.' '

'It's very funny. Like a little finger.'

'Well, all boys and men have a willy.'

'Yeah, daddy has one. Big, with hairy bits, ugh!'

'Now then, girls and women are different. They... '

'It's a good system for peeing, but it should be retractable, like the head of a tortoise. Then it would be less vulnerable and it wouldn't look so silly.'

'Hmm... yes, but we can't all have one, because... '

'Because?'

And so you had your introduction to the facts of life. I thought the topic would never go away. You were fascinated. Do you remember how we looked at anatomical diagrams of pregnant women in the encyclopaedia, at pictures that showed the progress of gestation from embryo to foetus over the nine-month period and at detailed drawings of the human reproductive system? In no time, you had learnt a whole new anatomical vocabulary and started to sound like a mini gynaecologist. You couldn't be doing with childish language. None of this 'The lickle baby grows in Mummy's tummy' stuff. No, for you it had to be 'The foetus gestates in the mother's uterus.' As you studied the diagram of the female reproductive organs, you looked puzzled. With your index finger, you traced a line from the ovary along the fallopian tube to the womb.

'It's complicated, Mummy, isn't it.'

I laughed. You didn't like that. You didn't think that what you said was funny. It was not meant to be funny.

'Yes,' I said, to appease you. 'Yes, it's very complicated, darling.'

'It's kind of stupid. I think I could make a much better design. Simpler.'

It was so hard to keep a straight face. I had to look away, feign a coughing fit and pretend I needed a glass of water.

'What would you change?' I asked, having regained control of my face.

'Well, the men and women. Why have two? Why not one?'

'Ah, like some fish... '

'Really there are fish like that? Where? What are they called?'

'Jellyfish, I think. Not sure...'

For the time being I was off the hook. You were now looking up parthenogenesis and single-celled organisms. The amoeba and the euglena and their associated vocabulary kept you absorbed for days.

I felt exhausted, inadequate and nauseous.

You scared me. *Please,* I prayed to Lady Luck, *please let this next baby be utterly average.*

30ᵀᴴ JANUARY 2009

My God it's cold... it dropped to minus 8 centigrade last night according to the max-min thermometer outside the kitchen window. Even though the heating is on full blast, the only really warm place is the kitchen. Siberian weather is heading this way, with heavy snow forecast for tomorrow. This morning over breakfast, your brother told me he wore his socks and two T shirts in bed last night. He seems to be getting vain about his skin – this morning my moisturiser had disappeared from the bathroom. Later, I found it on his bedside cabinet, along with a roll of cling film. I dare not ask, but the mind truly boggles.

Your aunt is delighted with the cold snap. She is in the process of updating her website – the one that you redesigned for her three years ago – with some new photographs, and wants me to take shots of her in the sculpture garden if it does snow. She has shown me a whole series of pictures that have been taken there at different times of the year and in varying weather conditions. She normally sets up the camera on a tripod and uses the remote control or gets Rhys or one of the boys to press the shutter. There are hundreds of these photographs from the pre-digital era, stashed away in rough chronological order in two shoe boxes. Did you ever look at them? Astrid isn't sure. You were always at liberty to rummage around, but normally your curiosity was about processes and machinery. The way Astrid would make a cast for a bronze sculpture and the setting and controls of her camera equipment interested you much more than her artwork or photographs. In fact, when you were little, you used to find some of Astrid's art very disconcerting. Remember that famous photograph of her where she is standing in the pouring rain, wearing a tacky, sodden bridal gown she'd found in a charity shop, her mascara smudged into panda eyes? Mutt's predecessor, a fat black poodle named Rasta because Astrid didn't believe in getting his coat clipped, is sitting next to her, sheltering under a huge golf umbrella, looking puzzled, head cocked to one side, probably listening to the whirring and clicking of the camera. He has a bunch of wilted roses at his feet. You must have been nine or ten when this photograph was used on a poster for one of Astrid's exhibitions.

'Why is Aunt Astrid outside in the rain? Why isn't *she* using that umbrella?'

Those were the sorts of incredibly logical, sensible questions you would ask. Actually, they would probably be the kinds of questions most children your age as well as quite a few adults would have asked.

'Why don't you ask her yourself?' I suggested.

You immediately ran to the phone, dialled the number and without any preamble, blurted out your question. It took years before you finally understood that you were supposed to preface such requests for information with a little introduction: 'Hello, this is Senta. How are you? I'm fine, thank you. I was just wondering... ' This wasn't such a problem when you were little, but as you grew into your teens, it became a bit of an embarrassment. I finally resorted to writing a notice with this polite little intro in large letters on a piece of paper and Blu-Tacking it to the wall by the phone. You would rattle it off in a robotic monotone, as if it were a foreign phrase you'd learned by heart, without understanding its meaning.

Fortunately Astrid did not confuse you with stuff about irony and her rather cynical views on marriage, so she told you that she was just playing dress-up that day and had got caught in the rain.

'But why didn't you use the umbrella,' you persisted. 'Why is Rasta under the umbrella?'

She told you it was because his long shaggy fur took ages to dry and smelled really bad when it got wet.

'But why don't you get his coat clipped?' I could hear Astrid laugh at the other end of the line. I don't know what she told you, but somehow she managed to wind up the conversation. You had been known to go on and on with ever more *but why...* questions because your curiosity knew no limits, and you were quite unable to sense when others were getting exasperated with your interrogations.

Still, at least the sodden bride photograph didn't actually freak you out, unlike that other one, Astrid's iconic pastiche of Botticelli's Birth of Venus. That one was taken at least fifteen years ago on a warm spring day, and made into a poster which sold by the thousands. I've just Googled it to refresh my memory of the details. Astrid is standing nude in that same golf umbrella which here, turned upside down, represents Venus's shell. She mimics Venus's virginal pose, but for the long flowing golden locks she has substituted a large quantity of ivy which she has fashioned into a wig and draped over her shoulder and down to her pubes. However, there is nothing virginal about Astrid's lean body with its sagging breasts and slack belly. Marcus, a toddler at the time, and Dylan, aged six or seven, are the zephyrs, making little whistle mouths at their mother. Marcus is naked, his chin and nose chocolate-smeared. Dylan insisted on keeping his shorts on and looks slightly cross. It is a gloriously bizarre photograph, and it totally spooked you. When it first came out, we put up a framed copy of it in the sitting room, but it disturbed you so much when you saw it that you promptly had a screaming fit, so I took it down and hid it in my studio. When I told your aunt, she was saddened.

'It's not Senta who is mad, Veets,' she said. 'It's me.'

2ND FEBRUARY 2009

I am inclined to agree with your aunt's assessment of her mental state after yesterday's experience. There is a blurry twilight zone that separates eccentricity from lunacy, and I think she pretty much inhabits that place itself most of the time, with occasional forays into territory either side.

As predicted, thick snow fell during the night, coating the world around us in a sparkly, crunchy duvet. Tristan and Marcus were mightily pissed off at having to go to school, and Lucy phoned to say she did not dare drive up to the farm to collect them in case her car slithered off the track and into one of Astrid's artworks. So they had to hoof it down to the end of the drive to meet her at the main road, which had been gritted. Predictably, they had several snowball fights on the way.

The dogs are perplexed and frustrated, as their all-important olfactory world has suddenly vanished. Mutt, in his fraying yellow sweater coat, was actually frowning as he ventured forth cautiously into the yard. Mid-morning, your aunt and I accompanied them down the long driveway and watched them truffle away in the snow, trying to get their scent bearings. The venerable Doobie was not amused. You should have seen her. She looked at me as if to say 'What kind of cruel joke is this? Can't you make it go away?' Mutt, who at the age of two still has reserves of puppyish energy, was amused at first, and leapt around in the stuff, but soon started limping. The snow had compacted into lumps of ice, caught between the pads of his paws. We had to prize them out. I took the dogs back to the farm where they made a beeline for the fireplace, while Astrid photographed her snow-clad driveway sculptures.

I was making cappuccino when she came back, stomping the snow off her boots. We sat and sipped our drinks by the fire, in an odour of damp dog fur. Astrid poked at the logs.

'I want to be a daffodil this time.'

'You what?' I said, not following her train of thoughts.

'For the photograph. A daffodil. I'll use green body paint – you'll have to help me with that. And an old lampshade for the trumpet part of the flower. I've got one I can paint yellow. Can you Google me a good picture of a daffodil on the internet?'

'Azzie, are you telling me that you are planning to pose starkers in the snow with a lampshade on your head, covered only in green body paint?'

'Hmmm... ' she said, mind elsewhere. 'Yeah... What do you think – should I shave my pubes?'

We spent a couple of hours bending lengths of wire into six triangular shapes to make the petals of the perianth, as the internet informs us they are called. Astrid twisted them round the base of the lampshade and then stretched old tights over them. She spread newspapers on the floor, rummaged around among the chaos of boxes at the far end of the studio and produced a can of aerosol paint, which she tried out on the newspaper. Gordon Brown turned a satisfying shade of deep saffron.

'Perfect..' she declared. She placed the daffodil frame on the floor and handed me the can.

'Here, Veets. You do it. I'll search out some body paint. Don't inhale. Use a mask. There's one on the table.'

She disappeared upstairs. I slipped the mask on and started to spray the frame. Life is never dull with your aunt, and I was actually having fun. Isn't that amazing? Shouldn't I feel bad about that? You were murdered less than a year ago, and here I was, behaving like a silly teenager with your mad aunt. Isn't it a little... unseemly? What would you have made of it?

When Astrid reappeared, she was in an old dressing gown and had tied her hair back into a bun.

'Got rid of the pubes. Now for the body paint.' She examined my daffodil. 'You're doing a fine job there,' she says.

She rootled among her supplies again and came back with cakes of body paint which she mixed with tap water.

'If you help me with this, we can do it twice as fast,' she says, tossing me a brush. She slips out of her dressing gown.

'Wouldn't it be better to do this in the kitchen, where it's warm?' I ask.

She laughed. 'Nah! Better here. Then it won't be quite such a shock when I go outside.'

It took us about forty-five minutes to cover her in what was described on the tin as Kelly green, all this to the music of the Kings of Leon on Marcus's iPod, plugged into the studio sound system. When she was ready, I handed her the dressing gown.

'I'm not putting that on. It'll get paint on it. It's Rhys's.'

'You'll catch your death!'

'You don't catch a cold from getting cold, Veets. That's just an old wives' tale.'

'No, but you can get hypothermia.'

'Not if you are quick about it.'

'Me?'

'Well, I need *you* to take the photograph. Doh... I can't go out like this and fiddle about setting up the tripod, can I?'

She picks up the yellow lampshade and pops it on her head. It is still tacky and her hair sticks to it.

'How do I look?' she asks.

'Totally fucking ridiculous!'

'Good. Let's go for it. Here's the camera. It's on automatic. All you have to do is point and shoot.'

It is lunchtime, the sun is out and it's just above freezing. I am wearing woolly tights under my jeans, a T- shirt under my sweater and a navy blue Michelin Man anorak. Your aunt is naked except for a pair of wellies and a lampshade on her head. She quickly takes up position in the sculpture garden and I click away as she strikes a number of poses, including a birth - flowering - wilting - death sequence. A couple of minutes and over a hundred clicks later, she admits to feeling a tad chilly and we rush indoors. She makes a dash for a hot shower while I download the pictures onto her paint-smeared laptop, desperately hoping that they will pass muster so we won't have to repeat the whole exercise again.

Fortunately she likes at least some of them. It's supposed to be about contradiction. Her own autumnal body representing a spring flower. 'I feel like a daffodil inside, Veets, but the mirror tells me I am deceiving myself. We'll call this series *Self-delusion*.'

We have the leftovers of last night's vegetable soup for lunch and then go back to the studio to share a joint on the bean bag.

'How's the Olympic sculpture coming on?' I ask, after a while.

'It's not. That's why I'm indulging in all these displacement activities. I'm blocked. I can't do what I want to do because it would be offensive. I should never have accepted the bloody commission. This sort of thing is perfect for Anish Kapoor or Gormley or Susan Forsyth or. . or. . Ackroyd and Harvey. To me, it's like being Poet Laureate and having to compose poems about royal weddings when you actually despise the whole institution of the monarchy.'

'What are you going to do?'

'Dunno. I want to go and see Maggi Hambling. Might go tomorrow if she's around. Might stay in London a couple of days. See Mother at the same time. Get some more weed. Would you mind holding the fort here?'

Maggi Hambling... Astrid's guru. Last summer, we'd been to Aldeburgh beach with Tristan to see her wonderful sculpture, a huge steel scallop, dedicated to Benjamin Britten. I think you would have liked it because it actually looks like a shell. I'd met Maggi once, years ago, and found her rather formidable. Astrid adores her.

'No problem,' I say, but my heart sinks. I don't like being with your uncle Rhys when Astrid isn't around. Not that I don't trust him after all those years, but I just don't feel comfortable with him. Still, he's out most of the day, and in the evenings the boys are there, so it shouldn't be too awkward.

Just had a look at my own website. It is the first time I have looked at it since May of last year, when I put up my message to potential customers about Driftwood's temporary suspension of trading, and uploaded a series of In Memoriam photographs of you. Email messages of sympathy still come in from complete strangers. I have just checked the folder; over six hundred of them to date, and the most recent one was only two days ago, from someone in Australia. They range from the illiterate to the whacky and include one memorable one with advice on how to deal with your death from an Irish woman, an art teacher, who lost both her teenage daughters six years ago when a drunk driver crashed into their car. 'The pain never goes away but you must now save yourself if you don't want to become the third victim. You will need to become more selfish,' she wrote.

I'm still not sure what to make of that.

4TH FEBRUARY 2009

These last couple of days you would probably either have found deeply disturbing because you would not have understood what was happening, or else totally normal because you did not pick up the undercurrents, the body language, the moods. I still can't predict after all those years how you would have reacted in certain situations. Anyway, it was a day that gave me a sleepless night and a powerful attack of longing for your father, Ewa and being back in my own space in our own house.

I dropped your aunt off at Norwich station, where she caught the 9 o'clock train to Liverpool Street. She still had some traces of yellow paint on the nape of her neck, which I dabbed at in vain with a tissue. She laughed and told me not to fuss.

Envious of her escape, I consoled myself with an overdue visit to the hairdresser's and some clothes shopping in an ever lovely but bitterly cold Norwich. Then I headed for the Eaton Centre and, in my capacity as Catering Manager for Wensum, raided Waitrose, filling two trolleys to overflowing with groceries. It is staggering how much food the boys get through.

The afternoon was peaceful; the lull before the storm. The hens were huddling in the barn, feathers fluffed up. Only Godfrey had ventured forth and hopped onto the fence, cocking his head this way and that at the strange white world. I piled more logs onto the fire, caught up with email and phone calls, talking at length to Ewa, and even did some cleaning. It was all set to be an unremarkable, humdrum sort of day. The boys came home and Lucy stayed to help them clear the yard of the fresh snow that had fallen. Then, as we were sitting round the table drinking cocoa and Tristan was teasing Marcus about his unsuccessful pursuit of a certain Sarah, your uncle appeared unexpectedly early with a young girl in tow.

'This is Emily,' he said, tossing his car keys onto the window sill and offering no further explanation. She was vaguely familiar; pretty, with long red hair and skin of a ghostly bluish white pallor. Mid-twenties at most. She looked at him and then at us, an embarrassed smile: 'I'm one of Rhys's students,' she said. Very Welsh, I noted.

We must have looked non-plussed. 'On his Creative Writing course,' she added, unnecessarily. A blush started to appear, so she turned round and shrugged off her coat, handing it to Rhys. Marcus and Tris exchanged glances. Lucy stared at me. I tried to keep my face in neutral, but I was twitching. Rhys disappeared into his study, leaving Emily momentarily stranded in social limbo. Marcus was the first among us to remember his manners, inviting her to sit down at the table. We introduced ourselves and I offered to make her some cocoa.

'Oh, that would be...' she said, and then ground to a halt as Rhys reappeared, holding up a DVD of Fellini's *La Dolce Vita*. 'Emily tells me she's never seen this,' he said, implying that this was a major gap in the girl's education. 'And I don't think you boys have either, have you?'

Marcus shook his head. Tristan just stared.

'How about you, Lucy? Would you like to watch it? It's an amazing film. One of the all-time greats.'

'Is it in Italian?' she asks, looking alarmed.

Rhys chuckles. 'It's subtitled.'

Lucy looks at me with a mildly panicked expression. 'I'll have to phone Dad to let him know that I'll be late.'

I feel myself getting very annoyed, as I sense that it is assumed that I can just magic up dinner for two extra people at zero notice. Fortunately this is not a problem as I had just replenished both the fridge and the larder, but being expected to cook for your uncle Rhys's little Welsh flower while your aunt is in London really rankles. What must the boys and Lucy make of this? It also suddenly came back to me why Emily looked familiar. All those photos Astrid and I found on Rhys's camera last December when we were searching for pictures of you to finish the portrait that Grandma had started. At least Astrid knows about the affair, though I believe she thought it was over. I am furious, though, and I glower at Rhys.

'So... spag.bol. in half an hour, with *La Dolce Vita* for dessert?' I say, as coolly as possible.

'That would be very appropriate,' says Rhys, full of bonhomie and apparently oblivious to my tone. 'Emily, would you like a glass of wine?'

The poor girl looks mortified and the boys and Lucy are trying not to look saucer-eyed. He doesn't wait for her answer but retrieves a bottle of Australian Chardonnay from the fridge. 'How about some of this?'

'Hmmm...' she mumbles, and twiddles with the gold ring on her right index finger. For a moment, the jeweller in me is distracted by the Celtic design of intertwined loops. I want to ask her if it is Welsh gold, but can't get myself to do so. Her nails are bitten down to the quick.

Rhys uncorks the bottle and pours her a glass. 'How about you guys?' he says, addressing the rest of us. He is met by a mixture of mumblings and head shakes. He turns to me.

'Vita?'

'No thank you,' I say, icily. What I wanted to say was *shove it up your arse, you bastard!*

He smiles a patronising little smile. He's actually registered my disapproval. He shrugs, pours himself a glass and invites Emily into his study, supposedly to discuss something relating to one of her assignments.

'Jesus!' mutters Tris, as the door closes behind them. Marcus says nothing but drums his fingers on the table. He grabs the remote and turns the TV on to watch the news and strangle any further uncomfortable discussion. I get up to make a start on the meal and Lucy offers to help chop onions and mushrooms. Just as well, as in my agitation I might have chopped the tips off my fingers. I delegate the onions to Lucy and slice the mushrooms with a very blunt knife. Sweet, sweet Lucy...

In the middle of a monumentally awkward dinner, the phone rings. I answer it, and it's your aunt. She's at Mother's. I am raging inside, but try to keep it light. Everything is fine. How's Mother? When are you seeing Maggi Hambling? And Dylan? The temptation to hand the phone to your uncle to see how he would cope is almost overwhelming, but I manage to resist. Nor does Astrid ask to speak to him. Emily's face is an inscrutable mask as she battles clumsily with the spaghetti. 'Wind it round your fork as you push it against your spoon.' I hear Lucy advise her gently.

We eat our apple crumble and custard without uttering a word, to the clinking and scraping of spoons in bowls and the sound of Doobie making whiny noises and wagging her tail against the floor in her sleep.

Marcus excuses himself, saying he has maths homework to do, and thunders up the stairs. I suspect Tristan stayed simply because Lucy was there, or maybe out of curiosity to see how things would develop. I made coffee and Rhys slipped the DVD in the slot. I was tempted to follow Marcus's example and go upstairs to my bedroom, but felt obliged to stay with Tristan and Lucy. Rhys settles himself in his fireside armchair while the rest of us stay less comfortably seated around the table. Jaffa jumps onto Emily's lap, and I notice how his fur matches her beautiful hair. She strokes him lovingly, no doubt relieved that at least one other being in this hostile household is well-disposed towards her. He purrs loudly and dribbles on her jeans.

I watch Mastroianni and Ekberg, but without taking anything in, spending the time trying to sort out my feelings and figure out the best way to deal with this outrage. Emily, Tristan and Lucy have become absorbed in the film, but after about an hour or so I decide I can't stand it any more and go upstairs to bed. *La Dolce Vita* had once been one of my favourite films too, but now it just seems a pretentious, rambling celebration of the lives of a bunch of rich, vapid degenerates. You would have hated it, with its lack of storyline and its cast of bored, corrupt characters. In bed, I try to distract myself by reading for a while. I'm halfway through Hari Kunzru's wonderful novel *Transmission*, but I just can't concentrate. I couldn't phone your father until after midnight, when he gets home from the restaurant. It would have been a rather selfish thing to do anyway, as it probably would mean that he too would have a sleepless night.

It was that strange time – mid-week and just after nine thirty – edging uncomfortably close to the time reserved for making emergency calls only. I knew Ewa was away on business in the States. Finally, I phone Susanna as I know her to be an insomniac who rarely goes to bed before three in the morning. I got Alan on the phone. Susanna was in bed with the 'flu. I was stuck with nobody to talk to and found myself getting more and more worked up. It's the frustration at being a guest at Wensum and being gagged by gratitude. I had black thoughts about your uncle and fantasised about various nasty things I'd like to happen to him. Being run over by an articulated lorry or slowly flattened by a steam roller, that kind of thing. Nothing painless.

I hear Lucy drive home at about ten o'clock, but Rhys's old Jaguar stayed in the same place in the yard all night.

I must have succumbed to sleep around dawn, and was woken by a worried Tristan.

'You awright, Mum?'

'Oh God! Is that the time? Oh shit! Breakfast! I'm sorry – I've overslept... couldn't sleep last night.'

'You weren't the only one.' he grumbled, darkly. 'Don't worry about breakfast. We'll sort something out ourselves.'

A few minutes later, he brings me a mug of tea. I mumble more apologies.

'No worries, mum,' he says, with a touching flash of maturity and consideration.

I fell asleep after that, and finally awoke around midday to an eerily empty house, the usual farmyard noises muffled by the snow.

I was sitting by the fire with Mutt and Doobie, numbly cradling a bowl of soup, when both dogs leapt up and started barking. I heard the crunch of car tyres on the snow, then the slamming of a door. It was just after three in the afternoon; too early for the boys or your uncle, yet Rhys it was. I steeled myself. Bite your tongue, Vita. It is none of your business. You are a guest in his house.

'Hello Vita.'

'Hello Rhys. You're early.' I continue to stare at the fire. I hear him pull a kitchen chair back and plonk something on it. His briefcase, probably. He unzips his jacket, then fills the kettle and switches it on. He rummages in the fridge and I hear the sound of a lid being removed from something. More rummaging in the cutlery drawer. He is standing by the range, eating something – yoghurt possibly, waiting for the water to boil.

'Tea?' he asks.

'I have soup.'

He pours the water in the pot and gets a mug out of the cupboard. I concentrate on controlling myself. Please *please* go to your study. Please stop pretending that everything is as normal. Please...

He sits down in the armchair opposite me and rests his feet on the edge of the log basket.

I sigh.

Silence, for a while.

'Get it off your chest,' he says, eventually. We are both staring at the fire.

'It's none of my business.'

'So you censure me with your tone of voice and your silences.'

'Oh I'm sorry,' I say, sarcastically. 'I really must learn to dissimulate better. I'll work on it.'

'You really hate me, don't you.' He says this very quietly and sips his tea.

'You have given me plenty of reason to.'

'Are you referring to December 1984?'

'Well, that rather set the tone. Let's say it hasn't done much for our relationship.'

He sighs. A deep sigh.

'Vita, I am deeply, deeply sorry about what happened then. I can't undo it. I can't deny it, erase it, make light of it. I hate myself for it. I wish it had never happened. I apologise unreservedly for it.'

'You want me to play priest at your confessional? Absolve you? Clean slate?'

'Vita. What more can I do than grovel apologies? For God's sake! I hate what I did.'

Mutt lifts his head and peers at Rhys, alarmed at the sudden raised pitch of his voice. He swivels his ears back and rests his head on his front paws. Doobie opens one rheumy eye.

'Look, the atmosphere between us is pretty poisonous. I came home early today to try and straighten things out with you. I find this ... this ... disapproval of me that oozes out of your every pore very wearing. Here we are, living under the same roof,' he says.

'*Your* roof. Which is very kind of you.'

'Which is not the point.'

'Which doesn't help.'

'Which means we've got to find a modus vivendi.'

'A modus vivendi. OK, Rhys. Your move.'

'Last night...'

'Last night is not my business. Who you screw when Astrid is away is not my business. Your life. Your house. Your relationship. Or should that be *relationships*?'

'Then don't jump to conclusions.'

'I'm trying not to, but you know what, I'm human. I'm fucking human! As soon as Astrid's back is turned, you bring home some bimbo who could be your granddaughter. What about Marcus and Tristan? At least have the decency to take her to a hotel. Ah, but I'm forgetting the fact that this is your house. I *do* apologise.'

Doobie has started to whine. Jaffa jumps off the footstool and heads for Rhys's study. We are disturbing his nap.

'It is not what you think,' he says, very quietly.

'Surprise me.'

'Emily needs me.'

'Oh? Does she have a grandfather fixation?'

He ignores my sarcasm and sips his tea.

'She's doing this course as a kind of therapy. A bit like your writing. Just under a year ago she was abducted – dragged into a car in Swansea by two men, driven off to some isolated place and raped. They kept her there for ten days. Dreadful ordeal.'

He gets up, goes over to the kitchen table, picks up my laptop, unplugs it and hands it to me. 'Just Google *Emily Griffiths abduction*.'

My hands are trembling. 'You do it.'

He taps away, and up pops a string of references from the online broadsheets and tabloids. 'Swansea woman in abduction horror.' 'Young woman's tale of terror.' 'Bound, gagged and raped.'

'I don't remember any of this,' I mutter.

'Look at the date, Vita. April 6th 2008.'

That was two days after your murder. Small wonder this news story never registered with me. I put the laptop back on the table. I did not have the stomach to read the details of Emily's horrific experience. I did not know what to say to your uncle. My mind was in complete turmoil. We sat like that a while, sipping our drinks. Mutt broke the silence by whining at the kitchen door, asking to be let out. It was his 'Lemme out, I must have a pee' whine. Rhys got up to open the door for him.

'So where did she sleep?' I asked, as I continued to stare at the fire.

He stopped in his tracks. 'In my bed.'

'What?'

'Musical beds, Vita. I slept in Marcus's room. The bed that Tristan used to sleep in. Poor Marcus can't have got much sleep because I'm a serious snorer.'

But I wasn't about to give up. 'Why, if all this is so innocent, did you wait till Astrid was gone to bring her round here?'

He comes back and sits down again in the fireside armchair.

'Jesus, Vita, I didn't know Astrid wasn't going to be here. I got a text from her at three o'clock yesterday afternoon to say she was in London. By then, I'd already invited Emily. I told Astrid about it over the phone.'

I shook my head and buried my face in my hands: 'I'm sorry, Rhys. I'm so sorry.'

He eased my hand away from my face and held it, which made me feel very uncomfortable.

'I couldn't very well explain the Emily thing to Marcus and co. last night in her presence. I'll tell them this evening.'

My tears started to flow. 'I feel so stupid. You have a talent for making me feel stupid.'

'That's what my students say about me too,' he sighed. 'You should see the evaluations I get at the end of each course. I've lost count of the number of times I've seen the word 'pompous'. Recently there was a nice one from a girl: "Dr Jones often comes across as intimidating and pompous, though he is in fact well-meaning and helpful."

'I always have the feeling that you think I'm just a dilettante, that my Driftwood stuff is just a self-indulgent little vanity project kept afloat on the back of Gerry and Ewa's profits.'

Rhys looked me in the eye, and I realised for the first time that we have avoided eye contact for many many months. His eyes are tired, and the left one looks a little milky, as if he might be developing a cataract.

'That's your perception. It is certainly not what I think. Your designs are beautiful and your writing isn't bad either.'

When the implication sank in, I yanked my hand away and let out a shriek, making Doobie jump up and bark.

'You haven't read my stuff, have you? Tell me you haven't. That's private.'

'Vita, I may as well come clean. Yes, I have. Some time ago I read about ten pages while you were out with the dogs.'

I was speechless. I wanted to yell at him all over again. But he looked so tired and genuinely apologetic that I just closed my mouth.

'I'm sorry.' he mumbled. 'I really am. But curiosity just got the better of me. Please put a password on your laptop so I don't succumb to temptation again.'

'My God! That stuff is so personal,' I say.

'I realise that...'

'How would you feel if I snooped around your study and looked at your stuff?'

'Unfortunately there's nothing to look at. I haven't been able to write anything decent for two or three years now. I'm spent. I've been working on some poetry, but it just looks like inferior Dylan Thomas. *Rage, rage against the lack of inspiration!*'

'Jesus!' I say.

'I feel like a stiff drink. Care to join me?'

He gets up, disappears into his study and comes back with a bottle of Glenfiddich.

By the time the boys come home, we are three sheets to the wind, and dinner has to be a freezer-to-microwave shepherd's pie.

I slept like the proverbial log last night, a long, dreamless, whisky-induced slumber, and have spent much of today mulling over the events of yesterday. Misunderstandings and misreadings seem to be something of a *leitmotiv* in my life, and I don't seem able to break the pattern. Maybe I have a touch of Asperger's too, or am I just making excuses for my stupidity? It is very confusing to have to reappraise my opinion of your uncle after all those years, but I am mightily relieved that we have lanced this festering boil.

At breakfast this morning, he briefly put his arm around my shoulder and asked me if I'd had a good night. I froze and flinched before I remembered to relax and smile. My distrust of him has become habitual, fossilised over the years. It is going to take some time before I manage to change.

The snow has started melting and is turning into a horrible muddy slush in the yard. The dogs are ecstatic at the return of their familiar scent world. I just long for it all to melt away now.

I've put a password on my laptop – SENTA22. Not very imaginative of me, is it?

Spent the late morning fiddling with bits of copper coil and chicken mesh that I found among Astrid's supplies. The urge to make things has come back. I played around at the kitchen table with the wire mesh and moulded it into a hare on its hind legs, weaving copper wire in and out of it, to give it a sense of movement. It's rather good, even if I say so myself.

The dogs are barking. Lucy's old Volvo has appeared in the driveway. Time to put the kettle on.

6TH FEBRUARY 2009

When Marcus and Tris came home yesterday, we sat around drinking tea with Lucy, who has of late got into the habit of spending a little time with us most afternoons before driving home. Marcus brought up the subject of Emily. Rhys has told the boys about her background and they had looked up the gory details of the abduction on the internet. Marcus had initially been confused about Emily, as he thought Rhys had a long-standing relationship with a colleague. ('That mad poet woman with the long grey hair – can't remember her name.') I didn't know what to say, so I didn't say anything. I'm certainly not going to ask your uncle.

Lucy was fingering the hare I'd made of chicken mesh and copper wire. 'It's so lovely,' she kept saying. 'So ... true. Essence of hare. *Natura artis magistra.*'

'You what?' says Tris.

'Nature is art's master, something like that,' mumbles Lucy, suddenly embarrassed, possibly regretting this uncool display of erudition.

'It's yours,' I say.

She is about to protest. She is cradling the thing in both hands. 'I couldn't...'

'Yes you could. I promised myself that I would give it to the first person who admired it,' I say. That was a complete lie – but an inspired one.

'Oh!' she says. 'Thank you, thank you *so* much.'

She gets up and gives me a hug, and I promptly burst into tears, which I try to choke back.

The poor girl looks shocked and embarrassed.

'You are thinking of ... your daughter?'

I nod. But of course you would never have hugged me. I get up to blow my nose. Lucy is still holding the hare, and the boys are staring into their mugs. Too much raw emotion for them.

'Are you awright now, Mum?' Tristan asks gently.

'Yes, darling. Just sometimes I get these... these waves of grief.'

I sit down again and Lucy puts the hare back on the table. She has accidentally bent its hind legs out of shape, so it keeps falling over. I pick it up and rework the mesh.

'You should mount him on a piece of driftwood,' I tell her.

'Driftwood, that's the brand name of your jewellery designs, isn't it? How did you get into the ethical jewellery thing, Mrs Steeneken?' says Lucy.

'Please call me Vita,' I say.

'I'll try,' she smiles. 'Vita... that's the Latin word for life.'

Not long after that visit to your aunt in the summer of 1991, when I was in a funk about my pregnancy, I received a letter from Carla Geyer Dos Santos whom I hadn't seen in eight years. She had seen pictures of your parents' wedding in some society magazine that had made it across the Atlantic. She complimented me on how handsome we looked and sent the customary best wishes for a long and happy life together. She told me she had taken over the running of Geyer Dos Santos. Ernesto had died not six months after I had left Brazil and Raoul, having fallen out with his mother, the Empress Luciana, had returned to Paris to resume his life as a musician and trust fund bum. No surprises there. Carla had gathered from the magazine article that I'd become a jewellery designer. She was planning a trip to London at the beginning of December and would love to meet up with me. Maybe we could even do some business? She'd sent the letter to De Vlaaminck, having called a friend in London to look up the address in the telephone directory. Our home number in Clapham was ex-directory.

I sat in the garden, nursing my nausea, reading and re-reading the letter. Yes, of course I wanted to see her again, but do business with her? I recalled the squalor of the shanties where the mineworkers' families lived. The animals in your kindergarten petting zoo were much better off with their solid brick shelters, tiled roofs, loving care and plentiful, nutritious diet. I imagined that Carla was probably coming to do a spot of Christmas shopping and would stay at the Dorchester or some such, popping into Harrods and Harvey Nicks for suitable presents while these poor souls back in the mines lacked all but the most basic necessities. Still, I wrote back, told her I was delighted to hear from her, how sad I was to hear about Ernesto's death and yes, please do contact me when you are in London so we can meet up. I didn't mention business; I'd think of some excuse nearer the time.

As the nausea wore off, towards the end of September, I suddenly felt a surge of energy and creativity. Atelier Eve Lewis was inundated with orders and had a waiting list. Women wanted copies of my wedding dress and Ewa was often up late, working till 2 a.m. I produced another collection of safe but elegant costume jewellery for her winter collection, but my mind was on other things. Do your own thing, Astrid had said. This kept echoing in my head. Damn, they were all doing their own thing; Carla, Ewa, Gerry and, of course, Astrid. As Atelier Eve Lewis's bauble maker I had no separate identity. In fact, Ewa had asked if I wanted to give my name to the line, but I didn't really want to because of the constraints the AEL image placed on my creativity. Astrid was right. I should do my own thing, and I had no excuse now you were spending half the week in Wimbledon with Sven and Grandma. I'd had an idea, not initially for jewellery, but for decorative wall panels. I'd been for a walk on the Common and had marvelled at the autumnal shades of the trees and of the glistening silvery cobwebs on the tree bark. It was when I started making my wall panels that we decided that the time had come for my own studio in the back garden. I needed a place where I could have all my stuff and make a mess to my heart's content. Even though your father is very tolerant of my chronic untidiness, the presence of my materials all over the sitting room, dining table and kitchen had started to get on his nerves.

The shed came in a flat pack with instructions for assembly which appeared to have been translated from Chinese via Arabic into English. The written instructions made no sense, so we were left trying to figure out the little diagrams. It was a Monday in early autumn, and you couldn't go to Wimbledon that week because Grandpa Sven was laid up with a cold. As your father and I unpacked the box and laid the planks and parts all over the garden, we tried to understand what was supposed to go where. Using common sense, Gerry and I figured out the flooring and frame, but then got stuck trying to assemble the rest. We were both getting grumpy and frustrated when it began to drizzle, and what had started as a gloriously sunny morning suddenly turned grey. We were standing by the French windows with our fists on our hips, watching the scattered panels and shelves get damp when you appeared. You had been sitting at the dining table with a book about the Wright Brothers, studying diagrams that explained drag and lift.

'Hello sweetie, hef you fickered out how de planes fly yet?'

You looked at your father and signalled the tiniest of affirmatives, little more than a slight nod and a blink, the way you tended to do when people asked you stupid questions.

'Are these all the components, Pappie?' Yes, seriously, components, not bits.

'Yes, but we can't work out how to put them together. The instructions are in gobbledegook,' I confessed.

'Where are they?'

Gerry and I smiled at each other. I handed the piece of paper to you.

'It's in English too.'

'Yes, but it's badly translated. We can't make it out.'

You studied the paper and looked at the diagram.

'Can you help us, sweetie?' Gerry smiled, winked at me and stroked your curls. 'If you can understand flight, den essembling a shet should be a piece of cake.'

'The flight diagrams are a lot clearer,' you said, without taking your eyes off the paper. Then, with complete confidence, you started telling us which bits should go where. You never hedged anything with words like 'I think', or 'I reckon' or 'I guess', or heaven forbid: 'Let's see if...' Not once. It was quite a sight; little five-year-old you, now standing inside the dining room by the open French windows to keep out of the rain, telling your parents where various parts went as you peered at the diagram and we clambered about, obediently following your instructions and picking up posts, panels and shelves. With a couple of breaks for lunch and tea, it took most of the day, but by early evening the shed was more or less assembled, only lacking the door.

We were exhausted. Over dinner, Gerry asked you what you would like as a present for your help.

'A kitten, Pappie,' you said, without a flicker of hesitation. You'd obviously already given it some thought.

A few weeks later, you were out on the Common with Grandpa Sven, having a botany lesson. Old Mr Innes was out there with his spaniel, Mandy, which had slipped its leash. No matter how hard he called and blew the dog whistle, she would not tear herself away from something irresistible in a distant hedgerow. It turned out to be a small ball of grey and black striped fur, a tabby so tiny that it still had its eyes closed. That is how little Maggie Scratcher came into our lives. That name, you'll recall, was Grandma's idea. Ewa wasn't amused, and never used the name. She rather admired the Iron Lady, besides which, she didn't much care for cats. And soon enough Maggie Scratcher simply became known as Maggie.

Once the shed had been assembled, I headed for Walsh in Hatton Garden where I spent a small fortune on a special bench and a selection of essential jewellery-making equipment. I then set about experimenting on a flat sheet of rusty metal, roughly two feet by three. It was the first of what eventually became my 'four seasons' series. Your father loved them, Ewa was polite about them and you, well, you just wanted to know how I'd got the silver to go into that cobweb configuration. Was it like Plasticine? Did it come out of a tube? Was it poisonous, like mercury? You were dying to be allowed into my studio shed, but it had to remain strictly off limits, as there were far too many dangerous things in there, not least of which was a slow cooker full of sulphuric acid. A most unsuitable play area for a curious child, especially one like you. I bolted the window, padlocked the door and kept the key on a chain around my neck.

The panels were hung in De Vlaaminck. I'd just signed them by etching my maiden name initials, VR, and the date, October 1991. To my surprise, but not, apparently to your father's, the customers liked them and wanted to know who VR was. 'My wife, Vita Rasmussen,' he chuckled, proudly.

'Aha! Must be Astrid Rasmussen's sister. Small wonder, then,' somebody said.

I phoned Astrid and told her about this. She just laughed: 'You know, stop fighting it and just use it instead. We're so different in what we do – you work with metal and stones. Why don't we just exploit it? Symbiosis!'

'I don't want to be your Dannii Minogue.'

'Don't knock it Veets. I've got an exhibition coming up early next year. The body paintings. How about doing some stuff for that? Or even exhibiting those sexy silver genitalia things from your Munich days? With the photographs?'

Carla Geyer Dos Santos phoned me in early December 1991. She was at a *pied à terre* in Knightsbridge that her mother had bought so she would have somewhere to stay on her shopping sprees. I invited her round for morning coffee so that she could meet your father, and then for dinner at De Vlaaminck. The intervening eight years had matured her a great deal; so much so that she now looked rather older than her twenty-nine years. She was striking in a very severe, natural way, unlike her surgically-enhanced mother, and now had the same surprising lock of silver grey hair on one side of her head that I had noticed on photographs of her late father. You were fascinated. 'How did you get that silver streak in your black hair? Is it natural?' you asked.

Carla just laughed. 'It's a family thing, honey. My daddy had it too, and my granddaddy.'

'So you mean it's hereditary, like my hair.' (Here you pulled at your springy black ringlets) 'I inherited this from my father. He got it from his father who got it from Africa a long time ago. From the Congo.'

Carla admired your hair, said nice things about your amber eyes, told you that in her country many people looked like you. Mixed race, she meant, without saying it. I feared this might trigger a whole volley of questions, but fortunately you decided it was time to do something more interesting. Your latest thing at the time was playing chess on a little computer which Grandpa Sven had given you.

Carla told me she'd taken over the family business four years ago, when it became obvious that Raoul risked running it into the ground if something drastic wasn't done. She bought him out and, after an audit, set about a radical overhaul. The finances were in a complete mess, salaries had not been paid on time, but worst of all, important relations with major clients – something her father had always taken the greatest pains to cultivate and maintain – had been neglected. Despite being blessed with the natural advantage of being the eldest son and heir, Raoul had quickly managed to destroy his credibility. After a massive argument over Raoul's mounting personal expenses, the manager, Ricardo, finally resigned and told him to his face that he was a disgrace to the memory of his late father and grandfather and to the Geyer Dos Santos name.

Carla said she spent a lot of time and energy on reputation damage limitation, bridge building and financial restructuring. The gratifying thing was that people who had known her father and grandfather kept telling her that she was a chip off the old block, the only offspring capable and worthy of running the business. Ernesto had been regarded by most to be sweet but useless; an ineffectual mummy's boy, and Raoul, though very different, wasn't much better; a wastrel, a pseudo bohemian of very little musical talent but with a tremendous sense of entitlement, not to mention a very expensive cocaine habit. Mama Luciana too was a high maintenance lady, with her addiction to the scalpel and penchant for designer goods and long-distance shopping trips to New York, Paris and London. In the end, she was only too happy to let Carla get on with the rescue of the family business.

It wasn't until the evening over at De Vlaaminck that the dreaded topic of doing business with Geyer Dos Santos came up. I had tried to avoid it as much as possible during the day, and steered away from it every time Carla threatened to broach it. I was wearing the amber and silver necklace which Ewa had given me for my thirty-fifth birthday. Carla complimented me on it. Polish amber, I told her. 'No exploitation, darlink,' Ewa had assured me. 'It washes up on beach. No dirty dangerous mine.' Now I blurted this out to Carla and immediately felt awkward. She looked at me and shook her head. Yes, the mining conditions were terrible in Brazil, but she had been busy trying to improve things in the GDS mine in Itabira. So far, she'd had the miners' shanties knocked down and replaced with little wooden structures that had proper roofs. There were twenty of them in total, housing nearly a hundred people. She'd had latrines dug and ten shower cubicles built, as well as a wash house where the women could do the laundry. Mains electricity was next on the agenda, to be followed by a proper waste disposal system. In the final phase, she wanted to build a little school house and a clinic. 'My God! These people must be over the moon,' I said. 'They're happy but the competition is not,' she replied.

Apparently the workers in other mines were agitating for similar improvements, and there were quite a few people who wanted Carla's head on a plate for setting this new standard of employee care. She'd had death threats and had to employ bodyguards. Twice, the brakes on her car had been tampered with. 'It's shocking,' she said. 'It makes me hate Brazil, but what can I do? I cannot exploit these people the way my father did. It is inexcusable. I cannot, will not do it. It is not civilised. It is just not right.'

I told Carla about the frustrations of my partnership with Ewa, of being constrained to design what I had come to think of as Muzak jewellery. She admired the wall panels in the restaurant. Did I think I'd ever design my own line of jewellery using real stones?

'Only if they were to come with a certificate of origin from your mine. But at the moment, I'm preoccupied with this' – I pointed at my baby bump – 'and with an exhibition of some old stuff from my time in Munich.'

'Well, bear me in mind. People are becoming more and more eco-minded,' she said.

Eco mines for the eco-minded...

The Rasmussen sisters' exhibition opened in February 1992 at Gagliardi's on the King's Road. I was so nervous at the vernissage, trying to read the expressions of the art critics, that I nearly threw up. Your aunt loathed them, and I remembered how much damage certain critics had done to Rhys's confidence when they'd compared his novel *Ashes* unfavourably to the film. I was eight and a half months pregnant with Tristan. This made for a bizarre contrast, which every single critic present that evening remarked upon – that the Rasmussen sisters couldn't look more different. There was the petite, wild-haired, nervy, bird-like Astrid with her startled blue eyes, and her six foot tall, languid, enormously pregnant Brunnhilde of a sister. Little and Large, said *The Telegraph*. It hurt, but it was accurate. We really did look like a comedy duo. We would have been perfect material for a French and Saunders sketch.

I had tracked down Claudio via the Bavaria Film Studios, and had obtained an address in Rome, where he had been working in Cinecittà. I wanted to ask him for his permission to use his pictures. 'My God, Vita, of course you can use them. I gave you the negatives, didn't I? *Come stai, bella?*'

'*Molto* pregnant,' I told him.

For the exhibition, I had nine of Claudio's best black and white photographs blown up to A1 size, mounted in thin, shiny dark red frames. There was the problematic matter of how best to display the actual jewellery itself. I agonised over this for a while, and recalled jewellery exhibitions where I had been handed a magnifying glass to examine the items. Then it came to me. A few days before, while we were in the kitchen, you were intrigued by the fact that the serving spoon you had been dangling in a carafe of water appeared bigger. 'Look, Mummy. The spoon appears almost double its size when I immerse it.' Once again, no age-appropriate vocabulary for you. I remember wishing I had the kind of six-year-old who might have been satisfied with some non-scientific explanation. (Yes, darling. It's magic, isn't it!) All I could tell you was that water somehow magnified objects. Something to do with refraction.

'Yes, I can *see* that, Mummy, but why?' you had said. This was followed by a deep sigh of exasperation. I told you to ask Grandpa Sven to explain, and off you went, straight to the phone. It was this little episode that gave me the idea of suspending pendants and earrings in water. After successfully trying this out in the kitchen with a pendant in the same carafe, I scouted out a dozen plain crystal vases and jugs, filled the bottom with black pebbles from a garden centre and hung the pieces in still mineral water just above the pebbles, using nylon fishing line and fine silver chains. The rings I placed on pieces of slate. Each container was placed at eye level on a shelf near the photograph that displayed it, and had a spotlight trained on it. The water had the desired effect of magnifying the items, and with the spotlights on, the result was striking as the silver twinkled and shimmered. It was very effective, and for once I felt really pleased with myself.

The reviews were slightly embarrassing in that I unexpectedly upstaged your aunt. I suppose this was inevitable; she was so well-established by then, that maybe the critics thought it was time to give her a few knocks in the time-honoured British 'build'em up, then knock 'em down' tradition. 'Unoriginal,' was one scathing assessment of her paintings. 'Tired clichés,' said another. Your mother on the other hand, had apparently come out of nowhere, the new kid on the block, and was the big surprise. It wasn't quite 'a star is born', but it was a bit painful nonetheless. However, Astrid, secure in her talent, did not appear to be in the least bothered about it and seemed genuinely pleased for me.

Your aunt Ewa's reaction was funny. She was a little miffed that I'd never shown these pieces to her before. I told her I thought she'd be embarrassed by them. 'You are jokink, Vitka, after what I've been through. These thinks not exactly suitable for my clientele, but I can admire them as art, no?'

Of course I had to bite the bullet and show them to you too, because everybody was talking about the exhibition. I was worried about this. You'd just turned six, and although you knew a lot about anatomy – we all, especially Grandpa Sven, thought that you were a surgeon in the making at this stage – what would you make of this depiction of eroticism? Grandpa Sven, having seen (and admired) the things, reckoned that you'd just see them as little anatomical sculptures because you didn't have the necessary maturity to fathom their eroticism. I wasn't totally convinced. I don't think children are ever as innocent as we often like to make them out to be. I believe that within even very young ones there slumbers some latent sense, some suspicion of the sexual and the erotic. As it turned out, it was hard to make out what you thought. Your main interest, which we should have anticipated, lay in knowing how I had made these funny little silver shapes. The photographs also intrigued you. 'Mummy, who are these people?' you asked. Then, pointing at Eboa: 'Are we related? Is he one of Daddy's cousins from the Congo?'

I had laughed nervously when the gallery owner suggested appropriate prices for my things. Two hundred pounds for a pair of silver breast earrings? It seemed exorbitant. To my mind, they were worth about twenty quid. Ah, he said, but these items are one-offs, not some mass-produced junk. They are unique. Besides which, they are quite exquisite. He fished the breast pendant out of the vase, dried it on his shirt and lovingly rubbed the tiny silver nipples with his thumb. It occurred to me that I could have used synthetic rubies or garnets for them.

Every last item of the *Erotik* collection was sold within a week, though they remained on display for another two months. Harper's Bazaar did an interview a day before I went into labour. Suddenly everything was completely insane. Your father, Astrid, Ewa and I were caught in a sort of vortex and we couldn't stop spinning. I felt taken over by success and all the attention it suddenly brought in its wake. Your brother's arrival was the perfect excuse to keep everything at bay for a while and catch my breath.

Tristan was born on February 28th 1992 after a labour of less than three hours. A big, contented, calm baby. He was an exceptionally ugly newborn, but my goodness was he ever an easy child. It was as if the heavens had decided that you'd given me enough of a hard time. Tris suckled, slept, shat and peed like a dream. He was placid and even-tempered. He soon smiled a lot, and only ever seemed to cry when he was hungry. By six months, the ugly duckling had become stunningly beautiful with large blue-green eyes like Gerry's and a halo of frizzy blond afro fuzz. 'Whatever heppened to my Congolese genes with dis one,' Gerry would joke, as he played with your cackling, googooing little brother. The last faint trace of the Congo was evident only in the frizzy hair and the ease with which his skin would tan after even the slightest exposure to the sun.

We had worried that you might be jealous of the competition, but once again we got it all wrong. To you, Tris was an object of immense curiosity, an instantly accessible biological case study. You were fascinated by his bodily functions, his development, and at all the various things he could and couldn't do at three months, at six months, at one year. You were sweet and patient in a way I'd only ever witnessed at the petting zoo, and constantly tried to play little games with him to see if his development was on track. You would then bring out a full progress report at the dinner table. We struggled to keep straight faces. You so hated being laughed at.

That summer, Grandpa Sven decided to find out if you had any aptitude for music. He himself was not especially musical, so he found you a piano teacher. He did not tell the teacher anything about you because he didn't want her to have any pre-conceived notions or expectations.

When he came to pick you up after your second or third lesson, Mrs Rippon had a little chat with Grandpa while you were poking around in her front garden, examining the flora and fauna. Apparently she had never known a pupil remotely like you. Not that you were particularly musical; far from it. Your interest had been purely in the piano itself. How did it work? Could she please open the lid and show you the inside? What did the pedals do? Why did middle C sound the same as all the other Cs, yet didn't? Why was a major scale made up of tones and semitones? Why not all semitones or all whole tones? What actually made the sound? What were vibrations? What was resonance? What are overtones? That cello in the corner, why did it sound different from a violin? Who invented music? Why was musical notation so weird? Surely there had to be a better way of writing it down? Anyway, it transpired that you'd driven the poor woman nuts with your questions. You'd extracted a lot of information about acoustics, but had not shown the slightest bit of interest in learning to play. You had thought of music purely as a form of physics. When you discovered that you would just be learning how to read and play other people's compositions you immediately lost interest.

That was it. No little Mozart in the making, then. You never had any more music lessons after that, but ever after, you remained fascinated with acoustics and with the physics of music, and in time you came to like first Bach, then Mozart and eventually, in your teens, you subjected yourself to Wagner to work on your self-control. You forced yourself to stay calm as you tortured yourself with hours of *The Ring* and *Parsifal* which you played through headphones. You were trying to rewire your faulty Aspie brain, trying to tame it and get it not to freak out at displays of emotion. You succeeded only in that you learned to control yourself and not scream or throw tantrums in public, but your relationship with the great Wagner always remained ambivalent.

I had contacted Ulrike and sent her a copy of the Harper's Bazaar interview and various press cuttings of the Rasmussen exhibition. I felt that I really had to let her know about this, as she had been instrumental in setting me on my unlikely path to jewellery making and had helped a lot with the *Erotik* collection. I also wrote to Claudio to ask him if he'd come and take more photographs of the remaining thirteen items. In the end, you'll remember, they came together in the spring of 1992 and stayed with us for a week. Neither seemed to have changed much. We were in the sitting room, sipping wine and nibbling olives, catching up on the intervening years. Ulrike was still based in Munich, doing what sounded like more of the same. Claudio had moved to Rome and had been doing post-production work on a Taviani brothers film. Silke Nass had scaled the heights of divadom, which was no surprise to any of us. In 1999, she had won the prestigious Operalia prize in Hamburg.

'And Walter?' I asked. 'How is he getting on at the Bavarian State Opera?'

'Well, he's getting good reviews,' said Ulrike.

She guessed my next question. 'Yes, and he's married. A Japanese violinist.'

There was a bit of a silence. I tried to hide my confusion by passing round the bottle for a top-up, but I caught them glancing at each other. Then Claudio said how much he liked Gerry and how happy I seemed in this lovely house with you, my beautiful Senta, and with little Tristan. Much happier than I ever would have been with Walter.

'You reckon?' I said.

'I should know, Vita. I had a relationship with Walter once. It lasted six months. At the end he decided to opt for women, but I was never completely convinced.'

I think my mouth must have been hanging open.

'Jesus, Claudio, why the fuck did you never tell me that?'

It took me a day or two to digest this. After the shock, I just felt stupid, as in retrospect it all seemed rather obvious. I asked Ulrike, who'd also known all along, why she'd never told me. 'Ach Weeta,' she said. 'I wanted to, but I didn't think you two were going to last anyway. And I also felt it wasn't really my business.' It was difficult. You know... Walter is a friend.'

We hired a photographic studio. Claudio didn't want human models this time. No, he wanted... a dog, oh, and preferably a cat too. No, not necessarily together, but wouldn't it just be great if they did get on – more possibilities that way. Oh, and the dog had to be black. And have short hair. The cat too, preferably. Maggie Scratcher, being a tabby, was unsuitable. Plain dark fur would provide the desired contrast.

I just laughed. 'Where on earth do you expect me to find those at such short notice?' I said to him.

'But Vita, England is full of dogs and cats. Look at this park outside your house – it is full of people walking their dogs. England is an animal lover's *paradiso, non è vero?*'

'Yes, but... we can't just go up to the first person we spot walking a black dog on the Common and ask them if they'd lend us their doggie or kitty to model some erotic jewellery.'

Ulrike was laughing now.

'But Vita, don't you know anyone with a suitable black dog or cat?' said Claudio. He was genuinely astonished that I didn't.

I consulted Ewa. 'Well, one of my ladies she have little black poodle, but I don't think she lend him to you to model naughty jewels, Vitka.'

Plan B; visit Battersea Dogs' Home. Having got Maggie Scratcher, you had been begging your father and me for a dog for the past year, but I kept putting it off, knowing full well that I would be the one who'd have to walk the dog three times a day. You were in Wimbledon when Claudio, Ulrike and I went to look for a suitable canine model, which is just as well, as you would have wanted to adopt them all, these poor barking, howling, snarling, tail-wagging buggers. However, we hadn't reckoned with the bureaucracy and the need for a home visit to check out our suitability as canine adopters. That wouldn't have been a problem, but we didn't have much time, and the earliest possibility for a home inspection was in a week's time.

'It's for my daughter's birthday, in three days' time,' I lied, which deservedly earned me a frown and a bit of a lecture about this being a major decision, and a dog being a serious commitment, not just an ill-considered quick fix for a birthday or Christmas present. In the end, we managed to persuade the woman to come and check us out the following evening.

Snoopy was just a big pup then. They reckoned she was about eight months old. A Labrador cross of some kind, coal black, short haired, lovable and gentle but very much into chewing everything in sight. Snoopy was the name she'd been given at the dogs' home. I thought it was rather naff, and in any case I had always thought that Snoopy from Peanuts was meant to be a male beagle. In the end, we renamed her Bella because that's what Claudio kept calling her. *Ciao Bella! Vieni qua, Bella! Brava, Bella!*

Bella turned out to be a most uncooperative model. She was full of energy and just wanted to play and chew things all the time. We could not get her to sit still for more than a few seconds. She wriggled and grinned and panted, she yapped and raced around the studio and tried to lick Claudio's lenses. She peed on the carpet and chewed some electric flex. To top it all, she actually managed to swallow one of the rings, shaped like a pregnant belly. We'd taken her for an hour's walk on the Common, hoping to exhaust her. Then we went back to the studio and tried to lull her to sleep. Good girl, Bella, I said, stroking her head and ears. Gooood girl. She wagged her little tail a couple of times and closed her eyes with a theatrical sigh. Very carefully, I followed Claudio's instructions and positioned the ring on her head, then continued to stroke her and shush her. Claudio was about to press the shutter when Bella suddenly shook her head, flapping her ears. The ring fell on the carpet and she snaffled it. Within seconds, it was bedlam. We chased her around the studio, but it was too late – she'd swallowed it. 'You can always get that back,' said Ulrike, ever practical. Did she really think I was going to poke around with a stick in Bella's turds on Clapham Common?

'*Nah, warom denn nicht?*' Why ever not?

After that, we gave up on the Bella experiment and didn't even try to find a suitable cat. We'd hired the studio for two days, and you would remember only too well what happened next. Claudio asked me if I'd like him to take some photos of you and Bella. Of course you didn't even know about Bella; you were in Wimbledon with Grandpa Sven. I phoned him up, explained the situation to him and swore him to secrecy. He travelled up on the underground with you that same day, telling you only that some big surprise awaited you, and that calculus or astronomy or whatever you were doing at the time would have to wait.

You were ecstatic, and so was Bella. (It led to much overexcited peeing on the carpet, alas.) Later that afternoon we all went back to the studio, with me pushing your little brother in his pram. Unfortunately your father had to go back to De Vlaaminck. The black and white photos that Claudio took are among our most precious possessions now. There is that magical one of you with Bella, who is trying to lick your face, and another of you, Grandpa Sven and Bella. I have just been looking at them on my laptop photo gallery. In that second one, Sven is sitting in the middle, his left arm around you and his right arm around a goofy-looking Bella, one ear cocked and the other flopped, tongue lolling with excitement. You are smiling, a gummy gap where you'd just lost your milk teeth incisors. We had several prints made of that one, one of which hung in De Vlaaminck until Gerry took it down a few months ago and brought it home because he couldn't bear the daily reminder of his loss.

9TH FEBRUARY 2009

Can't wait for Astrid to come back. Yesterday, Sunday, was one of those days where I really felt I was going stir crazy and longed for our house in Clapham. The problem is the bloody television, and the fact that it is in the kitchen, which is basically where I spend my days. Before, when we had the old one, it wasn't quite such a distraction, but now we have that flat screen monstrosity, it has started to dominate our lives. Thursday nights it's '*Skins*', eagerly awaited by Tristan but pooh poohed as infantile and unrepresentative by Marcus. Yesterday afternoon I was hoping to do some writing, but Rhys and Marcus wanted to watch the Wales vs. Scotland rugby match, which seemed to be on all afternoon. All I can say is thank Lady Luck that Wales won. This, of course, had to be duly celebrated, so Rhys opened a bottle of Cava and then another one, and soon I was convinced that the best thing was just to get pissed rather than pissed off. Meanwhile, the television simply stayed on. Lucy turned up with a Tupperware full of chocolate fudge that she'd just made, and stayed to watch *Lark Rise to Candleford*, which was followed by the British Academy Film Awards. I think I went to bed halfway through, leaving them glued to the screen.

I need a study of my own. Maybe I could ask Astrid and Rhys if I could build a shed somewhere round the back of the sculpture garden? Something that could eventually double up as a summer house when I leave?

It's Tristan's seventeenth birthday in a little under three weeks. A few days ago I asked him how he wanted to celebrate. He seemed surprised at the question.

'Celebrate?' he said, as if the idea were quite outlandish.

'Yes, I think that would be a normal, healthy thing to do. Celebrate.'

'OK, well... ' He feigns a great interest in his fingernails for a while. 'Well, ... I'd quite like to go... paintballing?'

'Paintballing?' I say. (Pure Lady Bracknell: 'A *handbag?*')

'Yeah, there's a really good place near Plumstead. Or would that be... like... inappropriate?'

Jesus, I think. Your brother wants to play Rambo with paint. Pretend to shoot his friends with paint.

'No. If that's what you want to do, I'm cool with it. Who do you want to invite?'

'You need like a minimum of like ten people? So... like... Marcus, Lucy, ... can I ask my London mates?'

'You can. OK, look, you make the arrangements for the booking, and find out who is able to come up from London. They can sleep over here if they want.'

He pulls a face at that. This is clearly not a cool place to stay over if you are a London teen, despite your aunt's whacky art. Or maybe because of it?

10TH FEBRUARY 2009

Last night, I noticed a distinct tension around the dinner table. Marcus was in a strange mood, which is unusual, and Tris was kind of twitchy. After an unimaginative dessert of chocolate and vanilla ice cream, Tristan disappeared into the studio, which is where he has taken to doing his homework of late, leaving Rhys and me alone with Marcus, who was moving the salt and pepper pots around on the table like toy soldiers, bashing them against each other.

'Have you two had a fight?' asks Rhys.

'No.'

'So... everything's fine between you and Tristan?' I prompt.

'Hmmm...'

'Woman trouble?' suggests Rhys.

'Oh, for God's sake, Dad!' At this, he rolls his eyes, gets up and makes for the stairs.

'Marcus, don't run away. Let's sort this out,' I plead.

'You need to talk to Tristan, I've got homework to do,' he says.

'Is he in trouble?' asks Rhys.

'Talk to him. It's his problem. Don't make it mine.' And with that, he is off upstairs, taking the steps two at a time.

Rhys and I stare at each other.

'Oh shit! What now?'

'Do you want me to talk to him?'

'No, I think I need to sort this out myself.'

Tristan is in the freezing cold studio. He has put my blue Michelin Man anorak on and is sitting in front of the easel, staring at your unfinished portrait. He has recently been working on the wavy dark waterfall of your hair. I put an arm round his shoulder and kiss his forehead.

'What's with you, my love? Problems at school?'

He shakes his head. 'No, fine. I'm good.'

'That's what I thought. But something is definitely up. Have you had a row with Marcus?'

'Not exactly.'

'Well, what then?'

'He's mad with me. It's my fault. I don't blame him.'

'What for?'

'I'll show you...' He starts to take off his jacket.

'Oh God! Don't tell me you've been cutting yourself again.'

'Well, no... but it was bloody painful.' He pulls his sweatshirt over his head and shows me his upper right arm. And damn it, he's got himself another tattoo. In gothic navy blue letters about an inch high, intertwined with an eglantine branch sprouting three pale pink roses, it reads 'Senta, RIP.' The eglantine winds through the letters and has sharp thorns that have ruby red drops of blood on the end. I can't help thinking that you would have been horrified. Still, although I was shocked and disappointed, I was also strangely relieved not to be looking at razor slashes or needle tracks. And at least the thing wasn't septic, which is what had happened to the one he got on his shoulder a year ago. I force myself to stay calm, as I shake my head slowly and gently trace the outline of the tattoo with my index finger.

'When did you get this done?'

'About 10 days ago? On a Saturday?... aren't you mad at me?' he asks.

'Is that why you did it?'

'No.'

'Do you want me to be angry?'

'No.'

'Not even a little?'

He shrugs and pulls his sweatshirt back on.

'So that's why Marcus is mad with you?'

'Yeah, he knew about it and he wanted me to tell you.'

'He didn't want to cover for you.'

'He's very straight.'

'Don't make it sound like a character flaw.'

'No... he's great, really.'

I hug him and he lets out a sigh.

'Dad won't like it...'

'Better not show it to him then.'

'But I want him to see it.'

'You want him to be angry.'

'No, I don't!'

'Yes, you do!'

I am holding both his hands. For no logical reason, we are speaking in whispers.

'I know what he'll say.'

'What?'

'That it's just a cheap theatrical attention-seeking gesture.'

'Is it? Do you think that's what it is?'

'Dunno. Maybe that's part of it.'

'Well, you must know why you had it done... '

'It was an impulse...'

'Really?'

'Yeah, I'd doodled the design on the cover of an exercise book. Lucy said it would make a good tattoo.'

'Lucy?'

'Yeah!'

'So it was Lucy's idea?'

'No, I mean, all she said was, like, it'd make a good tattoo.'

'Hmmm... Where did you get it done?'

He smiles, shakes his head. 'Can't tell you that.'

'They're only supposed to do people over the age of eighteen. Didn't they ask for some form of ID?'

'Yeah, but I told the guy I didn't have any. Told him I was like nineteen and showed him my other tattoo. That was good enough for him.'

'It could have gone septic.'

'Nah. His equipment is disinfected. And I was careful afterwards this time. I put face cream on it and wrapped cling film around it.'

The other tattoo – that was the one he'd had done somewhere in Peckham last year, on his left arm. 'Proud Nigger'. Gerry had been incandescent. You, on the other hand, just wanted Tristan to tell you about the process; you had no interest in the message or in his motives. Your brother with his black man fantasy. How he would have loved a dark skin and black eyes.

What am I supposed to do? I am in uncharted parental territory. Part of me wants to track down the tattooist and give him a piece of my mind, then have him reported for offering his services to an underage teenager. I dare not tell Gerry about this. He'd probably lose it completely and duff the guy up, after losing it with Tris.

Thank heavens Astrid is back tomorrow.

11TH FEBRUARY 2009

Astrid is on fine form once again, having decided to withdraw from the Olympics commission. Instead, she wants to do something for London that is not connected with the Olympics, but doesn't know what yet. She thinks there is something sinister and deeply philistine about the whole circus, and does not want to be associated with it.

'Did Maggi Hambling help you reach that decision?' I ask.

She shakes her head. 'Nope, I decided it on my way into London, on the train. It just came as a huge relief.'

I fill her in about your brother's tattoo, but dare not ask the one thing I'm burning to find out. Did she or did she not know about Emily's visit? If it turns out that your uncle has lied to me, he and I will be back to square one again. On the whole, I'd rather stick my head in the sand.

'So how are you getting on?' she asks.

I tell her about the hare. 'I want to make things again, Azzie. My hands are restless.'

'What's stopping you?'

'I don't have my stuff here. My bench. My equipment...'

'We can fetch it with my van.'

'Hmmm. but I don't want to make jewellery. I want to sculpt. Chicken mesh, papier maché. Junk sculpture.'

'Help yourself.' She gestures towards the disorderly pile of materials against the end wall. 'But first, time to relax. I have fresh supplies from London. Good old-fashioned Mary Jane.

None of that dreadful skunk stuff.' She produces a little zip lock bag full of brownish black lumps and rolls a generous joint. We snuggle up on the beanbag sofa to the sounds of Krystle Warren, Astrid's latest musical infatuation. She has been on an iTunes download spree.

'So... ' she says, after a while, 'How did it go with our little redhead the other night?'

'Emily?'

'That's the one.'

'Well, to be honest, I made a complete tit of myself, because I assumed Rhys had invited her because you weren't here.'

'Oh crap! I should have told you.'

'Hmmm. A sad case, really. Rhys told me about the abduction the next day. Of course I thought he was having a thing with her.'

'Yeah, that's what I thought too, initially, but he's still got a thing with Mary Allingham. That's been going on for years.'

'The poetry woman?'

'Yeah...'

'And it doesn't bother you? How can it *not* bother you?'

'Oh come on Veets. You know Rhys and I have never believed in monogamy.'

'I know, but doesn't it bother you nonetheless? Jealousy is a human emotion. Surely you're not immune to that?'

'I show it the door, Veets. I kick its arse right down the driveway.'

At this, we both collapse into giggles.

You would have been totally mystified.

I spent the afternoon messing around with wire mesh, persuading it into the shape of a duck. Don't ask me why I chose a duck, of all things. I can only think that this must, subconsciously, have something to do with my dog walks along the river, where I see lots of them. It has occurred to me that I might be able to dip it in silver and use gems for the eyes. Maybe this is the way to go for me, away from jewellery, at least for the time being. It is yet another example of how circumstances have come to determine what I do. Back in 1992, the failure of the experiment with Bella as a doggie model for my little silver *Erotik* collection had also forced me to think of new ideas. After Claudio and Ulrike's return to Germany, I sat at the dining table with all the little silver items spread out on a cloth in front of me. I played around with them and waited for inspiration. I concluded we'd been quite wrong to try and go down the photographic route a second time. What was needed was a totally fresh approach. What I wanted was contrast; the shiny smoothness of the silver against a rough background texture. I asked your father to bring home some of the big jute sacks in which Brakes delivers rice in bulk to restaurants. I washed them and dyed them with Dylon in dark tints that would provide a strong contrast with the silver; aubergine, racing green, maroon, deep purple. Then I made a number of wooden panels, all slightly different in their dimensions, but all roughly two feet by three. Using plaster of Paris, I made relief moulds of the female torso, buttocks, thighs, breasts and neck on the panels. Once the plaster had set, I glued the tinted jute over them, crunching it and folding it, and colour-washed the background. I positioned the jewellery on the bodies. It really did look effective, and well-positioned spotlights in a gallery would highlight the silver to perfection.

Your aunt came down from Norfolk to have a look and liked my idea, but more than anything, I suspect she was pleased that

I was finally doing something creative after all those years in the doldrums. We debated whether to exhibit some of the pieces at De Vlaaminck, but in the end decided that Astrid's gallery in Norwich would be a more suitable venue, in order to reinforce the idea of them as little works of art rather than restaurant wallpaper.

Once again, they sold well, and the trade reviews were flattering. What amused us both, something neither of us had anticipated, was that several buyers wanted the wood, plaster of Paris and jute display boards too. When they weren't wearing the jewellery, they wanted to be able to put it on show on a wall in their house. This unexpected development eventually led to the next step.

There followed a period of artistic and commercial success for all of us. De Vlaaminck continued to get glowing reviews. It was the beginning of my phase of multimedia wall hangings which combined wood, paint, jute, silk, rusty metal, silver and paste stones to depict moods and scenes in various degrees of abstraction. I went back to Hatton Garden and bought more jewellery-making equipment, things like a saw frame, a bench pin, a ring mandrel and a hide mallet, as well as a collection of files. I started making simple items of silver jewellery which I would add to the wall hangings. Little silver earrings shaped like leaves hanging off tree branches, rings mounted on twigs, squirrel pendants pinned against tree bark. In this way, jewellery did not need to sit in a box when not being worn, but could become part of a permanent but changeable display. Commissions came rolling in from architects and interior designers, often at the behest of the older generation of rock stars.

Your father's BBC series *'Not just Sprouts!'* had just started and we suddenly found ourselves catapulted into the celebrity social scene. This time round, I was no longer just the designer wife appendage. We could have gone to a different party each night had we wished, but fortunately this was not possible for Gerry. I say fortunately, because after attending a couple of such parties to satisfy my curiosity about the behaviour of the rich and famous, I decided that this was most definitely not my scene, and became highly selective. We were even invited to Downing Street and to one of the Queen's garden parties. Our popularity, I am convinced, owed a lot to your father's sociable personality. I am much more awkward and often have to make a conscious effort to act the part at functions, though I'm much better at it than your aunt. I can never quite shake off the Vita who is watching me perform from the sidelines, mocking me as I jump through various social hoops. To this day, I still have stage fright every time there is an award ceremony or woman of the year thing, especially when I'm required to make some witty speech. Your father, on the other hand, is a complete natural. People love him and he is exactly the same with everyone. At the Queen's garden party, he asked her what her Corgis were fed on. Canned or fresh meat? This got her talking about her beloved dogs and their different dietary preferences. In the end, some flunkey had to lead Gerry away by the elbow, because he was monopolising Her Maj... Did I imagine a fleeting look of regret on her face as he was moved on?

It was an epidemic of fame, and our photos appeared regularly in the society columns of the gossip magazines. *'Spitting Image'* made a giant Gerry puppet and Rory Bremner cruelly but oh so accurately impersonated his Flemish accent. ('My Gott,' your father grumbled, more flattered than annoyed, 'I don't really shpeak like det, do I?') They wrote a series of John Major and Gerry sketches, in which a gigantic Gerry in his signature red pirate headscarf – your father never wore a chef's hat – with a necklace of Brussels sprouts, was cast as Major's secret advisor on all things European, a sort of Virgil to Major's bumbling Dante, roaring up to Number 10 on his Harley, holding kitchen cabinet meetings at De Vlaaminck to knock out foreign policy and poke fun at EU bureaucracy. Edwina Currie was portrayed as your father's besotted lover, her eyes flashing heart-shaped beams and her enormously long tongue licking him all over while she whispered suitably idiotic endearments. ('Ah, Gerry, my little chocolate coated Manikin Piss!') It made us cringe, yet it was also hysterically funny. You watched the programmes but were far too young to understand the political allusions, and I don't know if later, when you were older, you ever watched the videotaped recordings we made. Humour was never really something that you were able to understand, and you had no sense of the absurd. You would sometimes say that you found something funny, but you generally meant it in the sense of peculiar. I don't ever recall hearing you laughing out loud at anything. At most you managed a wry smile or a chuckle, but I think even that was a concession to perceived appropriate social behaviour. It always made me wonder what it must be like to lack a sense of humour. Most mortals need theirs for survival, to stay sane, to cope with stress and not least to bond with friends.

I found all the fame and attention a little frightening and would rather have flown under the notoriously fickle media radar. The higher you fly... I remembered how the press had slighted Astrid at our joint exhibition, and steeled myself against the inevitability of today's darling becoming tomorrow's has-been. Astrid had proven to be a feisty survivor. The critics have always been ambivalent about her paintings, but as a sculptor she remains pre-eminent, well on the way to sanctification, that dubious 'national treasure' category, though maybe not quite in the pantheon with Epstein, Hepworth and Moore.

I had just started producing things for Driftwood when economic disaster struck in September 1992. Black Wednesday, they called it. The pound had to be withdrawn from the ERM. In the aftermath, house prices, which had been shooting up, stagnated and then slumped. The stock market plummeted and presaged the end of the Yuppie era. I recall a joke from that period:

Q: What's the difference between and yuppie and a pigeon?

A: A pigeon can still leave a deposit on a Porsche.

You understood the pun but did not react. I taught you the accepted British social response to a pun; groan theatrically and say 'God, that's awful.' or words to that effect. You applied this diligently, conning a number of people, your uncle Rhys among them, into believing that you really did understand a certain kind of humour.

Ewa, Gerry and I were fortunate in that the crash didn't affect us that much. Ewa's clients were mainly nouveau riche, whereas De Vlaaminck's tended to come from the higher echelons of political power and from the media. Even though most would have been affected to some extent, it did not greatly alter their dining and clothing habits. My own things under the Driftwood name continued to sell nicely, but I suspect that my reasonable prices combined with publicity reaped as a result of some features in *Vogue* and *Marie Claire* may have had quite a lot to do with it.

And you, my eternal enigma? I seem to recall that you were heavily into chess by then. Grandpa Sven, himself once Denmark's Junior Chess Champion, was soon no longer able to provide enough of a challenge for you. He asked around and found a ten-year-old boy in Wimbledon whom you could play against. His name was Paul Lewan, and he was a tiny little nerd in the making; skinny, pale and asthmatic, with glasses in big tortoiseshell frames. His Polish mother was neurotically overprotective and single, though whether widowed, divorced or just plain unwed, we never did find out. We invited Paul to your seventh birthday party, along with half a dozen other little Mensa monsters, and although Grandpa Sven was to accompany you and Paul from Wimbledon to Clapham on the Tube, Mrs Lewan insisted on coming too. I thought it would be nice for her to meet Ewa, but I couldn't have been more mistaken. The sharply elegant, ever more highly-groomed Ewa, and the dowdy, awkward, twitchy Mrs Lewan chatted politely for a few minutes in their mother tongue, then I noticed Mrs L. get up from the sofa to find the loo. She sought refuge in the kitchen after that, where Gerry managed to soothe her a little. The only thing she would drink was peppermint tea.

Much later, we discovered that Mrs Lewan was the only child of parents who had survived the holocaust and had come to England after the war had ended. Her parents never learnt much English, and at home she heard both Polish and Yiddish. She was a peripatetic cello teacher.

When I asked Ewa what she made of her, she pulled a face. 'Jewish,' she said, as if that were some kind of social disease. 'Jews are very strange people, Vitka...'

In fact, this was not the first time I'd caught a strong whiff of racial prejudice from Ewa. Over the years it has unfortunately become clear that she doesn't like or trust anyone who isn't white and at the very least middle class. She once confessed to me that she even distrusted our Indian GP, the lovely Dr Gupta, and she is terrified of black people, especially teenagers. It is a wonder that she should be so fond of your father, but then again his African genes are quite diluted. His charm must have blinded her. Right now she's having difficulties with Barack Obama. 'Can a black man really run a country, Vitka? Look at

Mugabe. And that Idi Amin. And Africa – a big mess, no? They don't know what they doink.'

Oh dear... and Tristan adores Obama. Your little brother, who has never shown the slightest interest in politics before, has become mesmerised by Mr Charisma. He monitors his every move, reads every speech, Googles him constantly and has read both his autobiographies. What would you make of Obama? And of Hockey Mom, the absurd Sarah Palin, the Republican Party's greatest vote loser? How the Democrats must love her.

Looking back, I think of the period from 1992 till 2007 as a sort of golden age. Of course there were ups and downs, but on the whole, everything hummed along nicely. De Vlaaminck became one of the Establishment's favourite haunts and was frequently alluded to in Private Eye. I was interviewed by Vogue, and explained my refusal to work with anything other than recycled gold and stones that originated from the GDS mines. It was the accidental birth of the ethical eco image that is now associated with everything I produce, and which has secured me what marketing people call a niche.

Ewa was so pleased for me. 'Now you have USP, Vitka. Unique Sales Point.' Your aunt Astrid, despite knocks from certain critics, nevertheless continued to have exhibitions at the Tate Modern, the New York Guggenheim and the Musée Georges Pompidou. As for Atelier Eve Lewis, it made more money than the rest of us put together. As you grew up, it developed into a super exclusive little fashion house with its own lucrative sideline in cosmetics and perfume. Ewa never had a shop, and never went in for off-the-peg collections, though she added a line of *accessoires*; silk scarves, sunglasses, handbags and shoes which are available at Harvey Nic's. Eventually the paste jewellery I designed for her was also sold in this way, though I never put my name to it. She had a waiting list a mile long for her quasi couture, which even now is particularly sought after by ultra-chic South Americans and the new breed of Russian women one encounters in all the world's most exclusive hot spots these days. Some of the Russians come to Ewa for advice on how *not* to look nouveau and trashy. She is none too fond of them, but can't get herself to turn them away because they pay through the nose. And of course, like many Poles, she can get by in Russian, which is very useful.

I don't know how much of this you would have been aware of. Once Sven started teaching you, you spent less and less time with Ewa and more with your nose in your books. You knew the basics of couture; how patterns were cut, the characteristics of different types of material and the average amount of time it took to create an item from design to final fitting. All this came from bombarding Ewa with questions which she never brushed aside, but answered as if talking to an adult. In Polish. My God, you were all of seven or eight at the time, and scarily precocious. Yet once you'd extracted the information you wanted, you lost interest and moved on to other things. More and more this involved probing the secrets of the natural world. I had to remind you to go and see Ewa every now and then, and explain to you that she missed you and loved you. You'd look at me with that puzzled frown of yours that made me feel I was talking to a little Martian disguised as a human child, and then you'd do as I'd asked. I'm sure Ewa sensed that these visits were at my instigation – you may even have told her so, as your emotional intelligence was as abnormally low as your IQ was high. Ewa just accepted you as you were, though. Once or twice, when I bemoaned your inability to show anything remotely resembling affection for me, she'd come to your defence and say that you were deserving, if not of pity, then at least of our sympathy, because you could not help the way you were, and you were surely cursed with a future of solitude and unhappiness for which no amount of brilliance could compensate. Although I never said it to her face, I did not think Ewa's point was valid because people who do not need others presumably do not suffer from solitude either. Yet in the bleak days that followed your murder, I sought consolation in Ewa's theory, telling myself that you had at least been spared such a fate.

14TH FEBRUARY. VALENTINE'S DAY.

Although professing complete indifference, I think Tris was a bit miffed when Marcus revealed that he'd received a slew of Valentine messages on his Facebook page, as well as a load of texts. He tried to downplay Marcus's success by saying that they were probably all from the same girl, but Marcus was riding high and having none of it. Tristan was quite annoyed. He has been minus a mobile – a great bone of contention – ever since I confiscated it as a rather pointless punishment when we left Clapham for Wensum last summer. When I last spoke to your father, he actually suggested that we get him some kind of smart phone for his birthday, as a token of trust.

Your father sent flowers. Red roses, which made me cry. Not a sentimental reaction at his old-fashioned, corny romantic gesture, but a breach of the walls that contain my grief.

We miss you so much...

15TH FEBRUARY 2009

Have just re-read yesterday's entry, and have concluded that I must have been under the influence of Mr Hallmark when I wrote that last sentence. To be brutally honest, what I really yearn for is our normal life *before* you decided to track down your brother's dope dealer and get yourself killed.

You were not an easy child to love, because you gave so little back, and I had to remind myself constantly that this was not your fault. In a dark way, your death is a relief, but this is a feeling I am ashamed of and dare not admit to anyone. Ewa was a much better mother for you, because she simply accepted you the way you were. Maybe that is easier to do when you are not dealing with your own kin.

When I think of our family – and your aunt Ewa is of course an honorary member – as well as of people like Carla Geyer Dos Santos, I consider Ewa to be the most remarkable. Unlike Gerry, Rhys, Astrid or myself, she's had to overcome the disadvantage of being a poorly-educated immigrant with very little English, only to fight off poverty all over again when her husband left her and start up a business from scratch in middle age. You know how she hates the 'rags to riches' tag that the press like to give her – 'I was never in rags. Poor, yes, but rags, no!' She takes it too literally, imagining herself down at heel and clad like some soot-smeared Cinderella in filthy, torn tatters. This tendency towards literalism is in fact something that you two have in common. Her change of fortune parallels that of Silke Nass, who also succeeded against the odds on that same unreliable cocktail of talent and perseverance which depends for its success on the timely intervention of Lady Luck. Atelier Eve Lewis is thriving now, and has become a tight-knit family business. From being her stepmother's some-time model, Sylvia has become her full-time PA and Andrew has for some years now been her accountant and financial advisor. A few years ago he also took over the management of De Vlaaminck's accounts and those of Driftwood. Together the 'steppies' make up Ewa's English establishment façade. At the time of writing she has half a dozen assistants, all Polish, all highly skilled, beavering away behind the scenes. Most of them you would remember, except for Anya, who only joined last summer.

Here's something I bet you didn't know. You'll recall that three years ago, your father's partner, Uncle Sal, split up with his girlfriend, sold his flat and came to lodge with Ewa. Well, somewhere along the line, he changed status from lodger to lover. Ewa is coy and very secretive about this, and I only found out because Uncle Sal confided in your father. One day, before I knew, I had made some frivolous remark about toy boys as Ewa and I came across a photo of Demi Moore and Ashton Kutcher while flicking through a copy of *Hello!* magazine. Poor Ewa stiffened, pulling a face. Sal is more than fifteen years her junior. How would you have reacted to this information? With a blank look? With incredulity? With a 'so what' reaction? Probably the latter. You would have reacted the same way had she taken up with the dustman. It was an emotional matter after all, and as such, quite beyond your ken.

As for Driftwood, in the mid-nineties I stopped making those mixed media decorative wall panels on which you could hang items of silver jewellery and started concentrating exclusively on rings. You hung around in the studio shed – now you were a little older, I allowed you access, though only while I was present. You were eager to know all about the properties of metals and stones. At least I was on familiar territory there, and was able to give you reasonably satisfying answers. I remember telling you all about my experiences with the Geyer Dos Santos family in Brazil, my visit to the mine in Itabira and the plight of the workers. You were nine or ten and you listened with wide open eyes because the subject of mining had captured your attention. 'But Mummy,' you said. 'Why do people pay all that money for these stones when you say fakes are just as good and look the same?'

I had to go into the whole business of status symbols and the gem industry's own image spinning. I told you about De Beers' brilliant *A Diamond is Forever* slogan and the careful marketing of these stones as some kind of magic symbol of love and commitment. You found it incomprehensible that people should be so stupid as to think that ownership of some artificially overpriced stones should confer status and distinction on them.

'Mummy, you should only make green jewellery from Carla's mine,' you said.

'That's what I'm doing, darling.'

'And Mummy, you should tell everybody that the stones come from a special mine where the workers are treated well. Like with free range chickens. Then everybody will want to buy your jewellery. Even the Queen. And Princess Diana.'

I had to struggle not to laugh at the comparison. To you, cruelty to chickens was just as unacceptable as cruelty to people. Not, I think, out of any deep sense of empathy, as that was an unknown emotion to you, but rather because it didn't make any sense to you. Suffering and pain were simply bad because they stopped sentient beings from functioning properly. Therefore this should be prevented. Pure Mr Spock-style logic.

For a while, I was in turmoil. I was going through a transitional phase, a periodic shifting of gears. I wanted to rethink my whole business strategy. The jewellery I had been making as a part of the wall pieces had become more and more unwearable. One that comes to mind, because the buyer complained about it, was a silver cobweb necklace which looked good on the branches of the tree, but when removed and hung around the neck, it would not mould to the wearer's body and stuck out awkwardly. I wondered whether I should go down a more commercial high street path and launch a so-called high end collection that traded heavily on my 'green' credentials, something I had not really pushed that hard before. It could consist of limited-number editions of items consisting exclusively of politically correct materials like recycled gold and silver, using only ethically-sourced stones from the GDS mine. For a while I dithered because I didn't have the confidence to go ahead. Ewa confessed she had no idea whether there would be a market for it – her own clientele were not interested in such matters. Astrid thought there would be, as did Rhys and Gerry, but none of them thought it would ever account for a significant market segment.

In the end, I followed my instincts and stayed away from the High Street, selling instead through art galleries and by advertising in the back pages of glossy fashion magazines. Enough commissions came in to keep me fully occupied, and my reputation spread further by word of mouth. I have never aspired to anything more. Unlike Ewa, I have never wanted to build an empire. I am not much of a business woman, but then again, I have had the luxury of being cushioned by De Vlaaminck's financial success. Ewa had no such safety net.

In time, I started doing less and less work for Ewa. I persuaded her that she no longer required new jewellery for each collection. The same plain, unfussy, understated things could be used two or three years on the trot. I did some designs for her silk scarves; shells and ostrich feathers but the constraints of having to stay within the confines of the ultra-conservative AEL image had turned from a challenge into an irritation, and I resented the time it took.

Ostrich feathers...that reminds me. I remember sitting in the garden one balmy autumn day, while little Tristan was googoo-gagaing in his pram and playing with his pink plastic duck rattle. Grandpa Sven had just brought you back from your weekly sessions of tuition and was giving me the usual surreal progress update when you came up to us with a pigeon feather you'd found. You disappeared into the house and returned with a magnifying glass to study the system of barbules and hooklets. I could see that my conversation with Grandpa was about to be interrupted by questions about the physics of bird flight, but for once you just gazed through the glass at the feather. Grandpa smiled.

'I think my girl has found a design that she can't improve.'

'Grandpa,' you said, 'God has done a good job here. It's really intelligent.'

I looked at Sven. 'God? Intelligent design? Did I hear right?' I muttered.

He sighed and shook his head: 'Don't look at me, Vita. She found God all by herself. She thinks He's pretty clever. Most of the time, anyway.'

As an out-and-out atheist, I initially found your belief in God a complete mystery. There isn't a believer to be found in our entire family, with the exception of Oma Steeneken, who suffers from a form of chronic hereditary Catholicism. However, at that point in your life you'd had very little contact with her. On the few occasions that you two had met, you had not shared a common language. No chance of contagion from those quarters, I concluded. I have always suspected that your father was something of a closet believer, but he swears he never mentioned God to you, except when accidentally taking the Lord's name in vain in Flemish with a loud *Godverdomme* while you were within earshot. Maybe it was your intense analytical interest in the natural world that led you to believe in some supernatural engineer. Whatever the cause, at the time, I just dismissed it as a childish phase. Grandpa Sven advised me to ignore it and not enter into theological debates with a seven-year-old, however precocious you might have been in other ways. Yet somehow your God business rattled me. You could understand so many things that most mortals didn't have the faintest inkling of. Could it be that we atheists simply lacked the right kind of intelligence to understand God? Was there some vital component missing in our brains? Is religious belief the result of a particular genetic predisposition, as has been claimed by some?

It took a while to realise that your idea of God was quite idiosyncratic and certainly did not involve any primitive vision of some benign old man with a flowing white beard on a throne in the heavens, surrounded by cherubim and seraphim. For you, he was neither good nor bad in the moral sense; his morality, you told me years later, had a neutral pH value, like that of distilled water, but he was extremely clever. He would have a Mensa score of a billion to the power of n. However, even this genius value-free God of yours sometimes got tired or distracted – after all, he'd obviously seriously screwed up on a number of fronts. This resulted in things like cancer and mildew and Siamese twins and poorly-designed knee joints and hips like Grandma's, which needed replacing. God got a big fat zero for those things. He was naughty and had serious lapses of attention to detail, but when he was on form, like with the design of a feather, he was unbeatable and then your admiration knew no bounds.

As well as being exceptionally bright, you were also an unusually beautiful child with your Botticelli madonna face and cascade of loose black ringlets. This wasn't just the opinion of a biased mother. On several occasions, I was approached by agency scouts on the look-out for child models, but I always gave them the brush-off. I knew the whole business of posing would have bored you rigid, and that you would have been a complete nightmare in a studio, given your curiosity about camera equipment. Quite apart from that, the whole child modelling scene struck me as unhealthy and I wanted no part of it for you.

It was the colour of your hair that made me want to work with jet, and your eyes that inspired me to pair it with amber. In the jewellery trade, amber had undergone something of a comeback after the release of the film Jurassic Park, which you'd been to see in the cinema with Grandpa Sven, obsessed as you were at the time with dinosaurs. I had long been attracted to the unusual qualities of amber and it was Ewa who told me that the amber from Poland and Russia had formed from the petrifaction of pine resin under the Baltic in the last ice age, and washed up on the shores of countries that line the Baltic Sea. Although there are places where amber is actually mined, it is quite easy to source the type that has washed up on the beach, which doesn't require men to risk their health and their lives hacking away under the ground. Amber is infinitely varied. We typically associate it with a rich golden-brown colour, but in fact it comes in a wide spectrum from pitch black to milky white, as well as shades of yellow and green. There is even a rare form from the Caribbean which is blue. It can be clear, contain fish scales or insects, or be opaque. You loved it, because it was never boring and had no standard shape, cut or size. Along with lapis lazuli and turquoise, it was one of the few gems you cared for and would wear. There was something magical about it. Ewa was convinced of its healing powers, and always wore an amber bracelet.

Astrid, who had once been into the whole hippy trippy crystals and birthstones nonsense, had told me that jet was the 'opposite' of amber. Some stuff about positive and negative polarities. When I asked her yesterday to remind me of her theory, she just smiled and seemed a bit embarrassed, which is very unlike your aunt. All that shaman and High Priestess nonsense is behind her now, but she definitely used to believe that amber cleansed your chakras while jet was supposed to stimulate your kundalini and keep you balanced. There was some kind of yin and yang thing, some kind of static versus kinetic principle involved. Anyway, she thoroughly approved of the pairing, and as usual, her approval boosted my ever-fragile confidence.

My first collection, the Senta collection, was inspired by you and dedicated to you. It consisted of brooches, necklaces and earrings of amber and silver, set on a background of flat pieces of jet which I had scoured lightly with the finest grade of emery paper to give them a dullish, brushed finish. The pieces were exhibited at the Markham Gallery, as well as at Astrid's gallery in Norwich. They were reasonably priced, as amber, jet and silver are not particularly expensive and I didn't want to seem greedy. The little flyer that went with the collection had that wonderful portrait of you, taken by Astrid. She'd faded everything to shades of sepia, except for your black ringlets and your luminous eyes. You thought it was great, and I made a little jet and amber necklace just for you, which you loved. When you grew into your teens and it got too small, I offered to enlarge it for you, but you chose to double it round your wrist instead and wear it as a bracelet.

That is where it was, bloodstained, when I saw you in the mortuary.

20TH FEBRUARY 2009

Have been unable to write for a while. That memory of you at the mortuary sent me plummeting down a bottomless chasm and back into the foggy state of numb shock I was in just after your murder. It's little more than ten months ago now, and I wonder how we are going to cope with the anniversary. I have been to London for a couple of days to be with your father and Ewa and to see Grandma. We have been trying to imagine how you would best like to be remembered, yet we know that you would have had no thoughts on this at all. Why would any healthy twenty-two-year-old have such thoughts? In the end, we are doing this for us, not for you. We are doing it to help heal ourselves and cope with our new circumstances. When I mentioned this, Gerry looked a little taken aback, but Ewa nodded slowly. We agreed that our commemoration should include a visit to the Unitarian Church in Kensington and a contribution to your favourite charity, Earthwatch, followed by a meal together. What we cannot agree on is whether or to what extent Tristan should be involved. I am scared that it will upset his precarious emotional equilibrium. I need to talk to Astrid about this.

Back at Wensum yesterday, there was an email from Isobel. She plans to come back to England to consult her supervisor at Imperial about resuming her research in September, and wants to see us. I have replied, inviting her and her father to join us on April 4th. I hope she accepts.

Having been back home has made me more homesick than ever. I am now desperately hoping that Tristan will not stray too far from the parameters of acceptable behaviour, which he has just about managed so far. This would then allow me to return to Clapham in June and to resume some kind of semblance of a normal life. Astrid and I would be doing a 'son' swap – she would have Tris for another year, while Marcus moves in with us, always providing he actually gets into LSE. Astrid seems to get on better with Tris than with Marcus, and it's more than just a connection through art. They just seem to have a natural rapport. I don't of course know what Marcus makes of me, and somehow I'd rather not know.

The urge to create things has definitely returned, and it was playing around with chicken mesh the other day that did it. I think that's the direction I'll pursue for a while, making objects rather than jewellery. I have brought some of my storage boxes to Wensum, filled with a selection of the equipment essential for the work I plan to do; pliers, clamps, tweezers and snips, as well as supplies of beads. As I was poking through the stuff, seated at Astrid's trestle table, she was standing in front of the full-length mirror which she uses for self portraits. With her index fingers, she was giving herself a facelift and examining the topography of late middle age from various angles.

'You know, Veets, I never used to be vain, but in my dotage I'm getting this morbid fascination with the loss of my looks. I can't pass a mirror without checking on the latest damage. Liver spots. Wrinkles. Hairs sprouting where they have no business.'

'Don't tell me you're thinking of plastic surgery.'

'No. Plastic surgery is for plastic people. At least, if it's just a silly vanity thing to stave off the inevitable. I'm just fascinated by my own decline. And by other changes. My complete lack of interest in sex. That's a kind of liberation. It allows you to stand back and look at sex with a sort of puzzled detachment, like, what the fuck was all that fuss about? By the way, how is it for you these days? Still hot for Gerry?'

'Mainly in the sense of hot flushes these days. But I find it comforting. Sex keeps you close, even if the fireworks have long gone.'

'Yeah, well, Rhys and I haven't been close for years.'

I look at your aunt. Barefoot, she is now doing stretching exercises on the floor in little more than shorts and a T shirt, even though it's freezing in the studio. She's amazingly supple and can not only touch her toes, she can do the splits. I decide to ask the question that's been burning on my lips for ages: 'Why are you two still together?'

She stops her exercises, lies flat on her back and stares at the ceiling. 'Convenience, habit and a shared past. Plus this place.'

I don't really know what to say to that.

'Do you think that's shallow?' she asks the ceiling. 'Am I selling out?'

'Are you happy?' I ask.

'Mostly, yes. It suits me. It suits Rhys.'

'Then shallow is the wrong word. Just... I never had you down as such a pragmatist.'

'Not everybody is as lucky as you, Veets.'

'What do you mean?'

'You have Gerry. He has to be one of the nicest human beings on this planet.'

I just stared at her, speechless, amazed at how much I still do not know about your aunt.

Apparently insignificant events can become unexpected triggers for fresh inspiration. In 1995, I started working with emeralds as a result of such an event. I wanted to design a new collection, but with something other than amber and jet. I was vaguely considering lapis lazuli, but the muse was on holiday, and I was in limbo for a while. Your brother was a delightful three-year-old at the time, sweet-tempered and full of energy. He was much into running around and screaming for joy, and I would take both him and Bella out for walks on the Common so they could burn off some of that boundless, life-affirming energy.

Bella and Maggie Scratcher were never exactly the best of pals, and Maggie would scarper whenever the dog came anywhere near her, hissing and hiding high up on top of the kitchen cupboards. One day while I was on the phone to your father, Tristan seized the chance to toddle into the kitchen unsupervised to help himself to some ice cream. Maggie must have leapt onto the counter and up onto the wall cupboards to escape him, and in doing so, knocked over an empty wine bottle, which shattered onto the floor. Tristan burst into tears and I cut short my phone call to see what had happened. He was rooted to the spot, sobbing, his fists in his eyes, while a terrified pop-eyed Maggie crouched up above, tail twitching.

'Maggie,' he sobbed, pointing at her. 'Bad cat!'

I knew it had to be her, as he couldn't have reached the bottle by himself. I comforted him as best I could and set about cleaning up the lethal shards. As I squatted on my haunches with dustpan and brush, a beam of sunlight caught the glass on its jagged edges. For a moment I was mesmerised. I salvaged some of the bigger pieces and disposed of the rest, then mopped the floor. I put the pieces in the sun on the kitchen window sill and looked at them. The rough edges were beautiful. Eureka, I thought, that's what I want. Rough-cut emeralds, not the conventional emerald cut. Rough cut and asymmetrically cut emeralds, together with jet and gold. And I knew just the right source for the emeralds.

I faxed Carla Geyer Dos Santos in Brazil to find out if she could send me supplies and examine the possibility of getting some kind of Fair Trade certification, and this was the start of our business partnership. She was delighted, and over the phone we popped champagne corks to seal the deal. I could hear her husband laughing in the background as the cork shot across their living room and the bubbles fizzed into the glasses.

The emeralds – a selection of rough and cut stones in different sizes – arrived with a certificate of origin printed on recycled paper. It explained, in Portuguese and English, the new GDS philanthropic philosophy. It took another year or so for the operation to get its Fair Trade certification. There was also a hand-written note from Carla, expressing her wish that this shipment might presage the first step in a long and successful collaboration. The leaflet contained photographs of the little miners' settlement. Neat little wooden log cabins around a paved square had replaced the ramshackle shanties. Instead of the filthy, malnourished urchins I remembered from my visit, there were smiling children in clean clothes on swings in a little playground. A woman in a bright orange dress was shown tending vegetables in an allotment. A little group of older children posed with their teacher in a classroom. It was impressive, especially if you knew what conditions these people had lived in before, and it made me feel good about what I was doing.

The whole ethical jewellery thing may seem like old hat now that so many others have jumped on the bandwagon, but in the mid-nineties there seemed to be very little awareness among most consumers in affluent countries of the conditions under which their luxuries were obtained or produced. The only thing that appeared to upset most people in Britain at the time was practices that involved cruelty to animals. If you wore a fur coat in London, you risked invoking the wrath of PETA activists and having red paint daubed on you. Lab experiments using animals were also widely condemned, and the Animal Liberation Front regularly went about threatening the lives of anyone involved in such research, as well as breaking into labs and 'liberating' animals which, having been bred in captivity, were mostly incapable of surviving in the wild. However, although the British like to think of themselves as a nation of animal lovers, most people are still not prepared to pay the price for organic produce and continue to buy factory-farmed meat and eggs. Can't afford the organic stuff? I'm sure there are those who genuinely can't, but for most people it's a choice. Spend less on beer, cigarettes, junk food and other processed crap. This, popularised by Jamie Oliver, has been Gerry's credo all along, and one which you endorsed one hundred percent.

It was around this time that I started buying free-range eggs, Astrid having graphically described to me the conditions of the battery hens that she'd witnessed at her neighbours' farm, but it was still considered a bit of a weird thing to worry about. I didn't think it right that any animal should have to suffer in such dreadful conditions, but I was equally worried about the effect of ingesting their hormone and antibiotics-fed flesh and eggs. Then you decided that you wanted to be vegetarian. You were nine or ten at the time, and the whole idea of eating dead animals suddenly disgusted you, though you became a bit more flexible as time wore on, as long as the meat was organic. Grandpa Sven had been doing environmental studies stuff with you, and you had found out that it takes sixteen kilos of grain and heaven knows how much water to produce just one kilo of meat.

'Mummy,' you said, 'if we grew food crops for people instead, nobody would have to be hungry. And the meat industry is one of the biggest causes of global warming.' Then you would reel off more guilt-inducing statistics. With your amazing memory, you could recite hundreds of figures. In the end, I begged you to stop and agreed to put you on a vegetarian diet, while cursing your Grandpa Sven, who remained an unrepentant meat eater to the end. You bugged your father too, remember? You wanted him to change the menu at De Vlaaminck so it only contained organic vegetarian fare, but he told you he would go out of business if he did that. He did, however, add some vegetarian options. Senta's Choice, they were called.

25TH FEBRUARY 2009

I feel emotionally exhausted. Just when I was thinking that, with the exception of the tattoo episode, all was going reasonably well with Tristan, and that I might actually be able to return to Clapham in the summer, he goes and screws up again, very nearly destroying my fragile trust in him.

It started when he had the mother of all nightmares the night before last; the first in almost two months. At around four in the morning I was woken up with a jolt by a combination of screams and thumping on the wall that separates our rooms. It didn't even occur to me that this might be a nightmare, because it sounded more as if he were being attacked. He'd actually succeeded in something long considered impossible – waking your aunt up. The four of us – Marcus had woken up too – emerged bleary-eyed from our rooms onto the landing, and your uncle was the first to open the door to your brother's room. He was sitting bolt upright in bed, pale and shaking. The bedclothes were tangled and twisted, and his pillow was on the floor.

'Christ!' said Rhys, 'I thought you were being strangled by a burglar!'

'It's... I had... just a nightmare,' he mumbles. I sit down next to him and put my arm around him. I look at the others and give them my *please go away, I'll deal with this* expression. They take the hint and retreat to their beds.

'What was it?' I ask him gently, as I stroke his sweaty hair.

'Buried alive. They buried me alive...' 'I...I couldn't... breathe,' he mutters.

'I'll get you a glass of water. Or would you like a cup of tea instead?'

'S-awright. Gotta go to the bog anyway. I'll have a drink of water in the bathroom.'

While he is gone, I remake his bed and find a BlackBerry on the floor, under the pillow. Tristan hasn't had a mobile since we've been at Wensum, partly as a kind of punishment but also to make it more difficult for him to contact his bad-ass friends back in London and to be contacted by drug dealers who have his number. It has been a bone of great contention and he has argued that, if he really wanted to, he could call them from a payphone or using a friend's mobile, but Gerry and I both felt that this would be less tempting if we made it all just a bit more difficult. There was no way that we could completely render him incommunicado, especially as we had allowed him to keep his laptop, but we felt that having a mobile was a privilege that we wanted to revoke for a while. Of course it has also made it more inconvenient for me. If I need to contact him at school, I have to do it via Marcus. But this BlackBerry isn't Marcus's phone. He has a scratchy old Nokia. I only know one person here who has a shiny new BlackBerry.

'Oh crap...' says Tristan, when he comes back and sees me looking at the phone.

'Whose is this?' I ask, as gently as possible.

He lowers his eyes.

'Tristan?'

'It's Lucy's.'

'You stole her mobile?'

'No, I, er... I ... borrowed it.'

'You borrowed it? She lent you her phone? For real?'

'OK, no, I, er... I took it from her bag yesterday, on the way home.'

'You did what?'

'I ... took it from her bag. The side pocket. I was going to put it back today.'

'Tristan, you can't do things like that. That's theft!'

'It's not. It's ... borrowing.'

'Without her permission. She's probably been searching high and low for the thing. It was a Christmas present from her dad.'

He looks at me, genuinely bewildered. I am becoming more and more convinced that he doesn't actually understand the difference between right and wrong. Either that, or he deserves an Oscar for his consummate performance.

'She is one of your best friends, and she dotes on you. Your behaviour is...' I was starting to lose it and had to rein myself in by reminding myself that it was 4:15am on a school day morning, and that your disturbed brother had just had one hell of a nightmare.

'The nightmare was a punishment.'

'Maybe. So who have you been speaking to? Do I have to check the call log?'

'Texting.' he says, as he sinks down on the bed next to me. 'Texting Martin and Sam...'

'Tris, for God's sake! You still have your laptop. Why can't you use MSN? Or Facebook? Why the hell do you have to go and nick Lucy's phone?'

'It's a BlackBerry... it's different... it's more fun... I wanted to play with the functions.'

'That is a pathetic excuse.'

'OK, I know... I'm really sorry. I just wanted to play around with it.'

'Should I read these messages?'

'I can't stop you.'

'Anything about drugs?'

'No! Just... stuff. Like what they're doing. What the others are doing.'

'Delete the messages and give me the phone.'

He clears the inbox and sent log messages and passes it back to me.

'Tomorrow morning, when Lucy comes to pick you up, you are going to give this back to her and you are going to apologise to her, OK?'

Tris nods and buries his face in his hands.

'You're going to be seventeen in three days time, and Dad and I were going to give you a new phone.'

'Oh shit... no...'

'Come, get back into bed. I'll nip down to the kitchen and make us both a cup of tea. Then I'll sit with you a while.'

When I came back ten minutes later with two mugs of tea, he was asleep. I stayed a while to make sure, but he really was. As if nothing had happened.

Here's something I can't figure out. Would your brother have behaved in this way if your murder had never happened? Is he just inherently, genetically dishonest, lacking a sense of right and wrong, just as you lacked empathy? Or are my ideas about what constitutes acceptable teenage behaviour simply out of whack with modern reality?

After I'd gone back to bed, I thought about it some more. I could not get back to sleep for fretting about your brother's behaviour and trying to think of the best way to deal with it. I felt this mixture of shame and disappointment, but it was sullied by something rather selfish – the realisation that he was still not trustworthy and that my hopes of being able to return to Clapham and leave him entirely in the care of Astrid and Rhys for his final year at school were most probably dashed by this event.

As soon as I heard his alarm clock go off, I went and knocked on his door and told him to phone Lucy, to save her from wasting any more time looking for her phone. I stood next to him as he called the Bligh family landline from the paint splattered phone in the freezing cold studio. She sounded incredulous, then angry. She'd driven all the way back to school late yesterday afternoon and searched high and low for it. She hadn't dared tell her father. She'd called the phone a couple of times, but Tris had ignored the calls. The bastard...

'She may not want to give you a lift to school today,' I say to him over breakfast.

'She wouldn't do that,' he says, genuinely surprised.

'Why not? It would be perfectly understandable.'

'But... we pay for her petrol and stuff, don't we?'

'For God's sake, Tristan! She's not just some paid chauffeur!' I was about to lose it and have a real go at him when Marcus came in. I had to bite my tongue.

At seven thirty, the headlights of Lucy's old Volvo appeared as usual at the end of the driveway. I turned to Tristan.

'Go and give her back her phone and apologise to her. Then come back. I don't want her to have to give you a lift to school today.'

I watch from the kitchen window as he walks towards the car. She lowers the window, her face a dark cloud. He hands the phone to her. He has his back to me, but I can see Lucy's face quite clearly. She shakes her head and says something. I want her to show some backbone, to tell him he's a bastard, but that's not her style. She rolls the window up and Tristan slowly makes his way back towards us, slouching, eyes on the ground. Marcus picks up his bag and goes out. He thumps Tristan on the shoulder in passing. Not a friendly thump. Tris almost loses his balance.

I watch the car's rear lights disappear, bobbing down the potholed driveway.

'You going to take me in to school?'

'Hmmm... for today, I have other plans. What kind of day have you got at school?'

'Just a random shit day.'

'Right. You are going to do some supervised skiving. Finish your breakfast, put some warm clothes on, and you'll need to wear your walking boots.'

I left a note for Astrid and Rhys, and just after eight thirty we set out.

'Am I allowed to know where we are going?' asks Tristan in a voice that hovers between the perplexed and the peevish.

'For a drive,' I say.

'For a drive... Ohhhkaaay.'

I decided to try a totally new tactic with your brother. Let's call it the silent approach. Given that he invariably clams up and shies away whenever I try to initiate any kind of meaningful discussion with him, and by that I mean anything more profound than the banalities of everyday life, I thought I'd try and see what would happen if we spent a day together, just the two of us, with no other distractions apart from the wintry Norwich countryside. I would not ask him any probing questions. I would simply wait for him to talk and ask me questions. Would it work? I had no idea, but I was frustrated with our lack of communication and thought this bit of reverse psychology would be worth a try. I needed to know if he was actually changing and maturing, and if so, what direction these changes were taking.

For seemingly ages, he said nothing. I drove eastwards on those little B roads through Drayton, Horsham and past the airport until I hit the main road and headed towards Wroxham and the Broads. Somewhere past Hoveton, he turned to me.

'I get it. We're going to Sea Palling.'

I nod.

'Why?'

'Why do you think?'

'Well, not to build sandcastles, presumably.'

'No.'

There is silence for a while.

'It wasn't stealing, Mum. I was going to give it back to her today?'

'So... that makes it alright, then?'

He cracks his fingers. 'No... but... I didn't think she'd even notice.'

'Yeah, such a trivial little thing, a BlackBerry. She's probably got three spare ones at home.'

'Mum!'

'You didn't really think that, did you?'

'Well, it's what I told myself.'

'It's what you told yourself. To justify what you did.'

'Lucy's not the little angel you think she is, Mum.'

'That's irrelevant.'

'She's got this tramp stamp, and her Dad doesn't even know about it?'

'A what?'

'A tramp stamp. You know, a slag tag, a whatsit, a lumbar tattoo?'

'So now you're ratting on her to make yourself look better?'

'No, but, you know ... neither of us is pure as the driven snow.'

'Do you regret what you've done, or are you just pissed off at being found out?'

He shrugs. 'Both, if that's possible. Maybe that's not the answer you want, but it's the truth.'

There followed a silence, pretty much to where you come off the main road at Stalham and find yourself on the B road and the final stretch to the coast. I was surprised that he didn't ask me if he could have the radio on. I found myself thinking about my own many and various teenage sins. They were the usual ones; shop-lifting for a dare from Woolworths when I was about fourteen; being suspended from school for cheating in a mock history 'O' level; aged fifteen, lying to mother and Sven about spending the night at my best friend Karen's parents' house when in fact we'd gone off to some dodgy disco with a couple of older boys, got horribly drunk and ended up being taken home by the police. Were any of them as bad as 'borrowing' your sort of girlfriend's mobile? I suppose the caper with Karen was, because I lied to your grandparents, and Grandpa Sven in particular was both shocked and hurt. I spent months trying to mend fences with him. Tristan, on the other hand, doesn't seem to care that he's hurt Lucy or upset me, and that worries me more than anything.

I parked the car near a jet ski rental place and we headed for the beach. I had absolutely no plans at this stage. I was just going to play it by ear and keep walking until your brother started talking. There was a biting east wind, and we pulled up our hoods, muffling our faces in woollen scarves and thrusting our hands deep into our pockets. Beyond the wide, pale, deserted beach, the sea was rippled pewter, a humourless, grim, don't-mess-with-me kind of sea.

We walked north a little way along the beach and I stopped to stare out at the strange, scalloped shapes created by the breakwaters that lie offshore, parallel to the coast. A lone fisherman was trying his luck on the northernmost one. I remember clearly when they were built, these breakwaters, in the mid-nineties, to stop further coastal erosion. Those were the days when your aunt and uncle still had a beach hut here, and I would travel up on hot summer's days with you and Tris so you and your cousins could do the bucket and spade thing while Astrid and I sat in the sun behind a very necessary canvas windbreak and quaffed quantities of wine. When construction started, you were fascinated and full of the kind of questions only a marine engineer could have answered properly. Were they going to build them all along the east coast? What were they made of? How come they didn't get washed away? What happened to the fish?

Astrid and I answered as best we could, but you had that little frown, that expression which showed that you only half believed our answers. Dylan did not share your interest, and you played together less and less often. He found other little boys to play football with, while Tristan and Marcus were still at the bucket and spade stage. Eventually you discovered that old Mr Hodson, three huts down, knew the answers to many of your questions. He was a retired marine biologist. You bugged him mercilessly, and although he was both amused and impressed with your questions, it did reach a point where I had to rein you in, so that the poor man could have the peace and quiet he sought to read his books and do his cryptic crosswords.

As I was smiling at these memories, I became aware of Tristan muttering into his scarf: (I've just had to Google this to get it right.)

'*...brass eternal slave to mortal rage;*

When I have seen the hungry ocean gain

Advantage on the kingdom of the shore,

And the firm soil win of the wat'ry main,

Increasing store with loss; and loss with store... '

He stopped and I urged him to continue, but he shook his head: 'Can't remember the rest. We did it at school last week. A Shakespeare sonnet. It's like ... it's about this,' he says, pointing at the breakwaters. 'The futility of this. It's all just going to disappear when the polar ice cap melts anyway.'

It seemed pointless to contradict his bleak view of the future with some trite *look on the bright side* comment.

'That's what your sister thought too... but she was determined to fight it with all her might.'

'My sister, always tilting at windmills.'

I bit my tongue to avoid an argument.

We cut across the dunes to see what had become of the beach hut. There was a row of them along a little road that ran behind the dunes. Under Astrid's stewardship, the hut had been painted bright blue. It was now a faded green, and the name, Guano Cottage – Astrid's idea, obviously – had been changed to Sea Breezes. A pity, as Astrid had even dribbled blobby white paint on the sign to simulate seagull shit.

We clambered back onto the dunes and I sat down on a little hillock. After a moment's hesitation, Tristan joined me. A gust of icy wind flattened the marram grass and revealed the decomposing remains of a seagull, about ten feet away. I wanted to ask Tris if he was feeling depressed, even suicidal, but remembered my resolution not to probe.

'You can't see where the sea ends and the sky starts,' I observed, neutrally. He ignored this and tugged at a blade of grass.

'At least his troubles are over...'

'What?'

'The bird. The seagull. It's dead.'

Sod it, I think. He's dropping hints. I can't just ignore them.

'Do you envy the gull?' I say, quietly, while staring at the invisible horizon.

'Hmm... in a way... yeah. You know that speech of Hamlet's? I feel I can kind of identify with that, with his sea of troubles, to die, to sleep, perchance to dream, all that. Hamlet's pretty random.'

I willed myself not to overreact.

'You know, when I was your age, I also went through a very dark phase. I read French existentialist novels and Baudelaire's *Fleurs du Mal* and wore a lot of black and smoked *Gitanes*.'

'Did you ever think of committing suicide?'

'I thought of drowning myself once, when I was sixteen.'

'Really?'

'Really. I'd been dumped by a boyfriend, but what really ate my soul was that your aunt had just won the Wilks Art Prize. I was consumed with jealousy. I was on some God-awful rain-soaked geography field trip in the Lake District and my teacher came and told me the news. I had to pretend to be really proud and pleased, then I went out for a walk to the shore of lake Windermere or Ullswater or whatever piddly little water it was and thought that I could just put an end to all the unfairness there and then.'

'What stopped you?'

'I don't think I really wanted to do it. I think I liked the idea, flirting with the idea. And it was a kind of comfort in a weird way, knowing that I could always opt out if I really couldn't stand it any more.'

He turns and looks me in the eye, his expression doing battle between surprise and disbelief. I hook my arm through his, and he leans his head on my shoulder. We sit in silence a while, huddled against the cold, but our silence is warm.

We walked as far as Eccles-on-Sea. We hadn't been there for at least five or six years, and never before in mid-winter. It looked forlorn and windswept, little more than a deserted caravan site and a sprinkling of little bungalows, but I remember your fascination with the place, with the fact that most of what had once been Eccles-on-Sea was now Eccles-under-the-Sea, having fallen victim to coastal erosion. When you were little and we first went there, Astrid told you about the village church that was now under the waves. She had some spooky tale of local people claiming that they could still hear the church bells pealing at night during a storm. You were eight or nine, and this made a huge impression on you. It was your first realisation that nature has forces which are way beyond the control of man, and that the world was not as cosy and safe as you had thought.

'Christ, what a fucking dump!' mutters Tristan with heartfelt teenage disdain. 'Not even a bloody café.'

I have to agree with him that Eccles is rather lacking in appeal for young people. It wasn't doing a lot for me either, so we trudged back to Sea Palling and had a cup of tea in the little café next to the jet ski place. When Astrid and Rhys were house hunting back in 1984, they used to stay at nearby Church Farm, once a much-favoured haunt of artists like Henry Moore, Barbara Hepworth and Ben Nicholson. I mention this to Tristan, who is re-shaping the Demerara sugar in the little white plastic bowl with his spoon, moulding it into little ripples.

'I want to be a sculptor, I think.' He flattens the sugar with the back of the spoon. 'I like making shapes. Even better than painting or drawing.'

'Well, you know who to talk to about that.'

'Yeah, Aunt Az. She's pretty cool. I used to think she was really mad?'

'She is.'

'Yeah, but it's kind of cool mad. I want to do stuff with that chicken mesh you've been working with. Like caves, with like these little objects dangling off the inside?'

'Lucy liked that hare I made,' I say. 'Maybe you could make her something.'

'Another token of my contrition.'

'Do you feel contrite?' I ask, as nonchalantly as possible, while poking around in my bag for my purse. I realise I am getting dangerously close to breaking my promise, and am ready to change tack as soon as I detect the merest hint of clamming up.

'I feel like... awkward? Like it was a stupid thing to do, right? But contrite, dunno. It doesn't seem a big enough deal. Taking her mobile? OK, it was wrong, but...'

'It's not about the mobile, darling, it's about the abuse of trust. She trusted you. And she's in love with you, so that makes her very vulnerable. If you'd nicked Marcus's phone, that would have been a different matter.'

'Marcus has a code on his mobile.'

'That's not the point.'

'You're right, I know, but it's not my fault if she's got this thing about me. I wish she didn't. I find it a bit creepy. Like she has no pride?' He stabs his spoon into the sugar.

'Are there really no other girls for you at that school?'

'They're all so... white... so... oh, I dunno, like country girls? It's all horse riding and hockey and stuff. Their legs go this mottled pink in the cold. Not like London girls. I like dark girls, not these piggy-coloured ones.'

At that moment, as if on cue, two plump, blue-eyed, pink-faced teenage girls enter the café and sit down at the table in the corner. One of them smiles in our direction and gives Tristan the once over. He turns towards me and rolls his eyes.

It is gone one o'clock by the time we leave, and we have both worked up an appetite from the fresh air. Tris actually looks healthy, his cheeks rosy from the biting wind, and his eyes clear. I propose a pub lunch, which gets the 'cool' stamp of approval, so we head for South Walsham and the Ship Inn. I buy him half a pint of lager, reluctantly sticking to water myself. Then, as we find ourselves a fireside table, a stunning long-legged black girl approaches us with a menu. Your brother's eyes pop as he gawps at her and she smiled back playfully, revealing perfect, very white teeth. 'Alice', reads the little red name tag on her white blouse. She reels off the day's specials with all the glottal stops and *f*'s replacing *th*'s that are the hallmark of pure estuary, and Tris tries to compose himself. He ends up ordering steak and chips in a slightly quivery voice, while I opt for something virtuously vegetarian.

'Nice girl,' I say.

'Jesus... she's hot. What's she doing here? Must feel like a fly in a fucking milk jug!'

'Why don't you ask her?'

'What, with you here, Mum?'

'Oh – am I cramping your style?'

He shrugs and sips his half-pint.

'Can I still go paintballing on Saturday?'

'Yes... why, do you want to invite her?'

'Mum!'

'Only teasing, darling.'

'You know Dad wants to come? And Uncle Rhys?'

'Paintballing? Are you kidding?'

He nods and sighs: 'Yeah... '

'Do you find that embarrassing?'

'Well ... it's a bit like... weird... having your Dad there and all.'

'Look, it's your birthday. If you don't want him to come paintballing, just say so.'

'I couldn't do that, could I. He sounded really keen.'

Funny, I think. Gerry hadn't mentioned any of this to me. I knew he was coming up at the weekend, but not that he was planning to join in the paintballing. Rhys hadn't said anything either. Probably too embarrassed.

The meal over, Tris delays our departure by asking for another half pint so he can ogle Alice for a little longer. I keep him company with a coffee.

'I wish I was older,' he says.

'So you could ask her for a date?'

'So I'd have a car and my own money, yeah... But also to... to have more distance between the present and last April?'

He's brought the topic of your death up himself. A very small voice inside me whispers the word 'hurrah!' I want to say something and am trying to rephrase it so it doesn't sound like a probe, but he doesn't need prompting.

'I wish it was further behind me? It's never going to go away, obviously, but...' He's spinning the beer mat and suddenly looks tired. 'You know what's weird? I feel resentful of her. Like I really hate her at times for fucking my life up, for making me live with this... mess? And then I feel guilty about feeling like that? Like I shouldn't feel like that about her? And it really like does my head in? What's going to happen on April 4th?'

'I'm not sure. Isobel is coming over from California to see her tutor at Imperial about resuming her research. I've asked her to join us on that day. Her father may come too.'

'And what am I supposed to do? They hate me, Izzy and her Dad. They think it's my fault.'

'No, they don't. You're imagining that. You know you are not to blame for this. Senta did a strange thing. She and Toby were in the wrong place at the wrong time.'

'Yeah, no kidding,' he says, not sounding at all convinced.

'Anyway, we'll be going home. April 4th is a Saturday. I think we should do something at the Unitarian Church.'

He nods and suddenly looks weary beyond his years. I put my hand on his and then I notice the tears.

Sensing the likelihood of an imminent meltdown, I settle the bill at the bar and we make a hasty exit. In the car park, Tristan delivers a vicious kick to the wall. He is suddenly furious and sobbing, angrily wiping the tears away with the back of his hand.

'My life is totally fucked up!'

I put my hand on his elbow and gently guide him towards the car.

'It's not, darling,' I say quietly. 'You have been doing fine. Amazingly well, actually.'

'Oh Mum! Save me the positive reinforcement crap. Please. Don't fucking patronise me.'

'I'm not patro...'

'You can't possibly know what it's like to be me.'

I decide not to argue with that. I mean, what can I say? Just let him be angry. At least that's better than bottling it up. This kind of anger is cathartic. He hasn't been like this for months. I remember the words from the bereavement counsellor who was assigned to us by the police. Expect setbacks, she told us. You will have flare-ups and moments of black despair when you are least expecting them, when all has been going well for months. Grieving is a jagged process. The loss of your child does not, will not fade away smoothly. That is all to be expected.

As we drive back to Wensum, he slowly calms down and even apologises for his outburst. We get home before the others, and Astrid is out too. The dogs are all over us, welcoming us with yappy barks, licking our faces and wiggling their bottoms. I fill the kettle and Tristan picks Jaffa up from the fireside armchair and cuddles him.

'What am I going to tell them at school about my absence?' he asks.

'I'll think of something. Don't worry.'

'Mum...' he says.

'Yeah?'

'Thanks for... today.'

I resist the urge – a very powerful urge – to give him a massive bear hug. This is because I fear I might crack up if I do. At the same time, something inside me tells me to stop being so bloody British. Now if we were American, by this stage we would both be hugging like mad and saying how much we loved each other. Instead, I just go over to him. He is cradling the cat in his arms, like a baby. Jaffa is purring loudly and I scratch him under the chin.

'You are welcome, my darling,' I say, apparently addressing Jaffa. I hear the kettle switch click off.

'I'll just go and make us a nice cup of tea.'

'That would be great,' says Tris, as he sits down in the armchair.

This family may be a mix of Belgian, Danish, Congolese and Yorkshire, but in some ways we couldn't be more British.

SUNDAY 1ST MARCH.

Your brother's birthday celebration was a success, though both your father and your uncle can barely walk today, following a particularly aggressive session of paintballing yesterday afternoon. Serves them right. They have massive bruises and are aching all over. Tristan proudly showed me his skin damage this morning and it really did look like he'd done ten rounds in the ring with Frank Bruno. The bruises are quite spectacular, all over his chest and upper arms, and apparently on his bottom too, though he spared me that sight. Marcus seems to have got off lightly, or perhaps he simply doesn't bruise much. Apparently Lucy was largely responsible for the drubbing of Tristan's posterior. When he tripped at one point and fell over, she leapt on him and blasted him pretty much at point blank range. I can't say I blame her.

I must admit that I was uneasy about this paintballing thing, but I didn't want to be a killjoy. Nonetheless, this is simulated Rambo stuff, pure fantasy violence, where you get to dress up and pretend to shoot each other. I couldn't get myself to go along, but I didn't want to deprive them of their fun either, so kept my reservations to myself, feigned a bit of a headache and stayed home with your aunt. I never even got to see Sam and Josh, who travelled up from London on the train, were met at the station, immediately whisked off to Plumstead and afterwards taken straight back to the station to catch their train back to Liverpool Street. I did wonder whether it was because Tris feared I might grill them about having been in contact with him, but this is a potential can of worms I really do not want to open. Or maybe it was at their own behest; a London teen phobia mixed with contempt for all things rural. Heaven forbid that their London 'cool' should be contaminated by the countryside.

In the evening, the six of us went to the Red Lion in Drayton. This was your brother's choice because, as you know, he likes the carvery. Your father was dreading being recognised. People round here are used to Astrid and don't bother her, but then again she doesn't suffer from celebrity status syndrome because she is rarely on telly. (Half a dozen times in forty years hardly qualifies as overexposure.) Unfortunately there are always some people who just don't seem to realise that we don't like to be interrupted on private family occasions by complete strangers asking for autographs or recipes or off-the-cuff interviews. To his great relief, Gerry got off lightly yesterday. Just a bit of banter at the bar, a handshake from the chef and some nervous chatter from a young waiter. The other diners shot us a few curious looks, but left it at that. Your murder, which was in the news for days on end, has had this unexpected effect of making most people think twice about approaching us.

Tristan is thrilled with his iPhone, but poor Marcus looked slightly put out. His own jealously-guarded Nokia, long the object of Tristan's desire, now suddenly seems old and shabby. He probably also thinks Tris doesn't deserve this shiny new toy, but he doesn't know what lies behind the decision. They spent a lot of time trying out the various apps, and Tris is already bugging us for permission (and money) to download something called Brushes, which turns the screen into a mini canvas and allows you to draw on it.

I have not said anything to your father about the incident with Lucy's BlackBerry, nor does he know about the new tattoo yet. I feel a bit bad about this, but I don't want him flaring up at

Tris so close to the anniversary of your death. I am just dreading the possibility of your brother going right off the rails.

Astrid gave him a voucher she'd designed herself, entitling him to ten weekly two-hour sessions every Saturday afternoon of what she called 'Sculpture 101,' starting with polymer clay, metal and plaster, and graduating to fabric, latex, and random found objects. I may be mistaken, but I don't think he really appreciated the value of her offer, and I couldn't help but think of all those aspiring sculptors who would have killed for such an opportunity. He did thank her – he even kissed her – but then went straight back to playing with his new mobile. If Astrid was put out, she didn't show it.

4TH MARCH 2009

Dreadful nightmare last night. I found myself first travelling in tiny dimly-lit lifts that moved diagonally, bumping and swaying over endless distances, then walking along winding passages that became narrower and narrower, with walls that oozed a sweaty dampness. There were doors, some very small, little more than hatches, others not more than a foot wide, but none had functioning door handles. Eventually I managed to open a sort of fire door and found myself on a stage in a theatre, with thousands of people staring at me in complete silence. At this point I suddenly realised that I was stark naked and with my back to a wall, the fire door having vanished, and confronted by a blindfolded man who had raised his arm to hurl a monstrous knife at me. I ducked and heard the sickening sound of the blade as it thwacked and twanged into the wall just inches from my head, at which point I woke up, having knocked the Angle-poise off the bedside table. No more sleep for me after that.

This dream may well have been triggered by something that happened yesterday when I accidentally cut myself in the index finger while chopping onions, and it just wouldn't stop bleeding. It will not surprise you to learn that I have a serious problem with knives these days, but I have yet to master the art of cooking without using one. I know that life without the use of knives is almost impossible, so I have, right from the start, forced myself to keep using them. Your father has the same thing, but in his profession, working without knives is out of the question. Yet every time I hold one in my hand, images of your final moments flash before my eyes. Two of your attackers had bog standard cook's knives, which did their share of damage, but the one that did for you, right through the aorta, just below the heart, that turned out to have been inflicted by Laron Grant's American army knife. It's been eleven months to the day, and I wonder if this association will ever fade.

6TH MARCH 2009

Writing this in bed, as all the others are watching *House MD* in the kitchen. Hugh Laurie is brilliant, but I find his portrayal very unsettling as he has so many uncanny Aspie characteristics that remind me of you, though you had taught yourself much better social skills. I wonder what you would have made of him? I don't think you ever saw a single episode as you had little interest in fiction.

Had a chat with your brother's teachers today, and all seems reasonably well, though late coursework submissions for English and History of Art were mentioned. The only teachers to be unconditionally enthusiastic about his performance are his art teachers. In their opinion, Tristan has genuine talent. Hannah Critchley seems half in love with him and was almost gushingly complimentary, which seemed to embarrass the others a little.

Your 'A' level performance, by contrast, was in an entirely different league. At the age of twelve, back in 1998, you took Pure and Applied Maths and got top grades. So certain were you of your success that you didn't even bother to open the envelope when the results arrived.

Grandpa Sven was characteristically modest. Teaching you maths was like teaching a duckling to swim, he told us.

What worried your father and me was that you had no friends. Nerdy little Paul Lewan may have had his uses as a challenging chess opponent, but that was all. Your friends from Mensa, the Mensa Monsters we called them, were good for competitive games, but as far as I could see, there was no real bonding going on there. Nothing that could compare with the friendships I'd had at that age; intense, full of mischief, shared secrets and monumental sulks about slights, real or imagined. It might have been better if, instead of a brother who was five years younger, you'd had a sister closer in age. Then again, if she'd not been blessed with your freakish IQ, that might have been even worse. Did I say blessed? I think I mean cursed. When you were twelve, you considered your seven-year-old brother to be a complete moron. *My God, he was still counting on his fingers.* Your father and I had to sit you down and have the first in a number of talks with you about *normal* human intellectual development.

We longed for you to be protective of Tris, as you had been when he was little. Not critical, not mocking or disparaging. You did rein yourself in after that, but I could often see that peculiar mix of puzzlement and disdain on your face whenever you deemed Tristan to be slow-witted about something. Increasingly, you turned away from people and started to focus your laser brain on understanding computers and software programmes. Your affection, your hugs and cuddles, rare at the best of times, were reserved for Bella and Maggie Scratcher. You'd go to bed without saying good night, and I'd go up to your room to check on you. You'd be asleep, or else pretend to be, Maggie curled up at your feet. I'd stroke your curls and kiss your forehead. I felt I was losing you. You'd cut loose from us, if indeed you'd ever been truly attached. It seemed that what you wanted from us was not affection but rather answers to your many questions, and being mere average mortals, we must have been a source of great disappointment.

In the autumn of 1996, Bella was hit by a car while chasing a cat across the road, and had to be put down. Tristan cried a river, but you remained dry-eyed. It was this reaction that made me realise I'd been in a state of denial about your Asperger's.

Yours was definitely not a normal reaction. Ewa looked after you and Tristan while I took the poor whimpering dog to the vet, driven there by the mortified man who had hit her. When I came back, I was seriously upset and fighting back the tears with great difficulty. I had stroked Bella's head and held her paws as she succumbed to the fatal injection. Ewa poured me a large whisky and put an arm around me. And you? You wanted to know how the vet had put Bella down.

'He gave her an injection to make her go to sleep.'

'Go to sleep?' (You took everything very literally.)

'Well, yes, but forever. Bella's not coming back, darling.'

You stared at me with your amber orbs: 'Mummy?'

'Yes, darling?'

'Can we get another dog?'

Not having access to a science lab, Grandpa Sven couldn't teach you much in the way of physics or chemistry, so he suggested that we enrol you in a suitable Sixth Form College. The Headmaster of William Harvey Sixth Form College had some reservations about this when I explained the situation over the phone. Two things worried him; firstly that you were only twelve, and secondly, that you might intimidate not only the other students but also his teaching staff. The latter concern was something he only confessed to me much later.

You would no doubt remember the interview. At twelve and a half, you were almost as tall as me, and puberty had begun to draw its curves on your lanky frame. At first sight, therefore, you could easily have passed for a sixteen or seventeen-year-old with zero fashion sense. I think Mr Cairns was initially relieved to see that you didn't arrive at his office sucking a lollipop, your hair in bunches and a teddy bear tucked under your arm. Then he started to ask you questions. What did you want to study? What were you hoping to do eventually? We were used to you, and no longer remotely surprised by frequently lengthy, detailed, well-informed, eloquently expressed opinions and discourses, but Mr Cairns, used as he was to the shy, semi-literate, mono-syllabic grunts from many of his charges, had difficulty believing his ears and keeping a straight face. You told him the world was going to hell in a handcart, and that you wanted to save the planet. Your particular thing was water; for nearly twenty minutes you held forth, citing grim statistical projections for the twenty-first century, rising birth rates, water wars and climate change, scarcely pausing to draw breath.

'I see,' he said, at the end of it, trying to look serious. As he saw us out, you disappeared to the loo.

'Extraordinary girl, Mrs Staynickers.'

'Takes all sorts, Mr Cairns.'

'Hugh, please. And yes, it certainly does.'

You started in September with physics, chemistry and biology. You wanted to take history as well, but they couldn't fit that into the timetable, so you just did that on your own in one year. By the age of fourteen, you had collected a total of six top grade 'A' levels but you still didn't have any friends. We were advised to wait until you were at least sixteen before letting you go to university. This left us with the problem of finding something useful for you to do in the intervening two gap years. Just hanging around at home, waiting for the time to pass did not seem very appealing, but as it turned out, you had plenty of ideas to fill your days. First, you turned our back garden into a miniature organic farm, then you decided that you wanted to learn about the restaurant business. You really wanted to hang out in the kitchen and observe the various chefs at work. This put your father in a quandary. Much as he adored you, he did not see how he could let you do this, and had to explain to you that a restaurant kitchen is a highly stressful environment full of people working in close cooperation to meet tight deadlines. You pointed out that you'd only be observing them, and he had to explain that this would still cause a problem because the kitchen was small, with no spare stations. I don't think I've ever seen you so disappointed, but I understood his objections. He tried to make it up to you by taking you to Smithfield and Billingsgate, and when he made his first television series, he made a point of involving you, taking you along to the studio and on trips to Belgium. You designed complex spreadsheets that accurately tracked the profitability of the restaurant and annoyed the hell out of the official accountant whom you classified damningly as a rather dim life form. Not long afterwards, he was replaced by Andrew.

You also hung out with Ewa. From your earliest childhood you had absorbed the secrets of tailoring and you knew about boning, hand-stitched overcasting and blind hem stitches, as well as the behaviours of dozens of different kinds of materials and the whole dressmaking process, from design right through to the final fitting. Funnily enough, you yourself were not at all interested in wearing nice clothes, much to Ewa's chagrin. Once again, it was the process that interested you; how exactly things were made. You begged to be allowed to make a spreadsheet for Ewa, but she put her foot down. She didn't want you upsetting Andrew the way you'd upset Gerry's accountant.

Just after your fifteenth birthday, you spent six months in Denmark, on your Great Uncle Mikkel's pig farm. What you didn't know about pig-farming in Denmark when you came back to London could have been written on a postage stamp. You'd also managed to pick up fluent Danish, and from that moment on would only speak to Grandpa Sven in his mother tongue. Much as we were in favour of multilingualism, it annoyed your father and me, because we hadn't a clue what you were talking about when you had your long conversations with Grandpa on the phone. Mikkel said you worked hard and did not mind performing the muckiest of farm tasks, that you loved the pigs and spent hours observing them, and seemed to prefer their company to that of your second cousins.

You were in Aarhus when 9/11 happened. When we phoned you a few days after the event, your reaction was very typically Aspie. You couldn't understand why people were making such a song and dance over it. *Didn't buildings get bombed in different parts of the world every day? Well?*

Great Uncle Mikkel and Great Aunt Grete never did invite you back...

Next, you developed an obsession about wanting to go to the Congo, to do the *Roots* thing. We had a hell of a job talking you out of that, and in the end, Opa Steeneken had rashly promised to take you there when you were a bit older, preferably once you'd graduated. You never did get the chance, as he cheated you by dying most inconveniently just as he was actually in the process of planning the trip, scheduled for September 2007. We were indecently relieved. The Congo is not exactly a safe destination.

For your sixteenth birthday, I had promised to take you to South America during the summer holiday, and among other things, to the Geyer Dos Santos mines in Itabira. You still had all your usual curiosity about my craft. The design element meant very little to you, but you were fascinated with the processes involved in assembling the pieces, much as you were eager to learn about couture whilst not giving a stuff about fashion. I showed you how to solder and how to anneal. You made and kept just one single item – a rather distorted silver ring which you made one day and always wore on the middle finger of your left hand. You loved that dull clanging sound of the hide hammer as you hit the silver into shape on the mandrel. In preparation for the trip, you had mugged up on emeralds and their properties, turning yourself into an overnight gemmologist. I contacted Carla, sketched out a 6-week trip that would include a week in Peru to see one of the places I had always wanted to see – Machu Picchu – and off we went.

You suffered from serious claustrophobia, particularly if crowds were involved. A trip on public transport during the rush hour could trigger a terrifying meltdown, and for the entire time that you were at Imperial College, you insisted, in fair weather and in foul, on cycling there rather than taking the tube. Airports and planes also scared you, but such was the strength of your curiosity that you simply forced yourself to overcome your fears. On the flight to Rio, you were so full of sedatives that you slept most of the way and then cursed yourself for missing the experience of seeing the earth from the air.

When we landed in Rio, I had a hell of a job to wake you up, and was worried that your woozy state and unsteady walk would arouse the suspicions of the immigration officers. You swallowed some Pocket Coffee sweets and clutched my arm so tightly that I had bruises for days afterwards. Rio was not a success, as you were too scared most of the time to be able to relax, and the kind of things that helped to take your mind off your fear of the unfamiliar were not there. I soon learned that this was the way to cope with your phobias. If there was something that stimulated your curiosity sufficiently, then all your fears of strange people, a strange language and strange places would simply fade as you concentrated on the object of your curiosity. I learned this to my cost, after persuading you to go up Sugarloaf Mountain and Corcovado. The stunning panoramic views of Rio meant nothing to you, and your nervous twitches and darting looks caused other tourists to give us a wide berth as you clung to me. Back in the hotel, you were so upset with yourself that you sobbed hysterically. I could do nothing. You did not want to be touched or soothed. You lay on the bed, face down, and I feared you would asphyxiate yourself with your face in the pillow. You were writhing, convulsed with frustration at yourself. I was scared, and tempted to check out and take you straight back to London on the first available flight. I couldn't understand at first how I hadn't realised that you would react in this way. You had travelled before, to Denmark and Great Uncle Mikkel's farm near Aarhus. Sven had accompanied you on that occasion, and although he told us that you were a nervous traveller, he never mentioned anything as dramatic as your behaviour in Rio. Was it because you were not in a big city in Denmark, but on a farm outside a village? From a very young age you had been to Belgium with us for the holidays, so that particular trip and that destination no longer frightened you because you had become familiar with the route and the places. But Rio was totally unfamiliar and quite intimidating, even for a fearless, seasoned traveller like myself. You hated being touched, especially by strangers, and the bustle of the city terrified you.

As these thoughts were racing through my mind, I was flicking through our *Lonely Planet* guide book to see what we could do in Rio that might possibly be of sufficient interest to you to take your mind off your phobias. Most of the things on offer would not have ticked the boxes, but there was one thing I thought you would like. It was a day trip to the Tijuca Rain Forest in an open Jeep. I read the description of the trip to you and waited for a reaction. There was nothing for the longest while, but at least your sobbing was beginning to subside. Then you turned on your side and looked at me: 'Mummy, I'm so sorry...'

I wanted to snuggle up to you and comfort you, but I knew better.

'That's alright, darling. I know this is very difficult for you. So... what do you think? Shall I book this trip?'

'Yes please,' you said in your smallest voice. 'Do you think we could get the Jeep just for ourselves, without other people? Just you, me and the driver?'

'I'll try and find out for you.'

'And ... do you think we can move to a room on the ground floor? I feel trapped here, and we're a long way from the fire escape.'

That was another phobia you had. Being in a tall building. It wasn't a case of vertigo, but rather one of not being able to escape in case of fire. I can't remember what floor we were on, in the Rio Othon, but it was high up and had a great view of Copacabana Beach. I managed to get us moved to a room on the first floor next to the fire escape. You went and checked the fire doors to see if they would open.

The trip, the following day, was a complete success. At reception, they had looked at me as if I was completely nuts when I offered to pay whatever it took to have the jeep to ourselves. It was expensive, but your delight and fascination in the rainforest, the monkeys, the birds and the butterflies made it all worthwhile. Your questions were never ending, but the guide, who had good English, was both patient and extremely knowledgeable, and talked to you at length in his nasal sing-song accent about reforestation programmes. I was amused by his interest in you. He was clearly both taken with your looks and intrigued by your extraordinary curiosity. You seemed totally oblivious of the admiring glances and the playful flirtatiousness. At one point, when you'd wandered off ahead on our hike, he asked me if your father was Brazilian. This is the kind of question I had grown used to over the years. The Belgian Congolese thing impressed him, but when I told him that you were only sixteen and gave him a good old-fashioned 'don't-get-any-funny-ideas-young-man' look, he reverted to a more formal, distant behaviour. It was my first experience of the effect that you now had on the opposite sex, of which you appeared totally unaware. Yet another thing to worry about.

After this experience, I rearranged our tour to suit your interests and minimise stress-inducing situations. It wasn't easy. Basically we had to avoid, as much as possible, anything that could trigger attacks of claustrophobia or anxiety. This meant avoiding, whenever we could, big cities, crowds, public transport and hotel rooms that were higher than the first floor and not right next to a fire exit. After your taste of the Tijuca rain forest, you wanted to see more of the jungle, so we flew to Manaus , took a long boat trip up the Rio Negro and went on an eco-tour of the Jau National Park. Most of the time you were in your element, though not all of the guides were as knowledgeable and as patient as the man who had shown us round Tijuca, nor was their English particularly good, often verging on the unintelligible, but you were not deterred. You scribbled notes, recorded birdsong on your phone and took thousands of photographs. I had never seen you happier or more relaxed.

You would have loved to spend many more months in the jungle, but we had promised to see Carla. On the flight to Belo Horizonte, I felt you stiffen up and become fearful again. Our arrival was a little traumatic as our luggage had gone astray, and I thought you were going to throw a fit. You were pacing around like a lunatic, and I mean that in the most literal sense. You paced up and down along the luggage belt, digging your nails into the palms of your hand and muttering. People moved out of your way. I had to forget about reporting the loss of our bags at the '*bagagem perdida.*' I grabbed you by the arm and marched you through customs and to the exit, where Carla was waiting for us. She went back in and filled in the requisite forms while I walked up and down the arrivals hall with you. At least you'd met Carla before, and I had warned her over the phone from Manaus what to expect.

The Geyer Dos Santos clan, what was left of it, had moved from the penthouse in the downtown Savassi district to a brand new villa on a hillside, overlooking the city. In the past, it had been the poor whose *favelas* sprawled up the hills, but at a certain point, the rich of Belo Horizonte had decided that they too rather fancied houses with panoramic views. Carla laughingly told us that the locals referred to her area as the '*favelas dos ricos,*' the slums of the rich. She now lived there in gated splendour with her husband and two children. Mama Luciana, my harridan of a near-miss mother-in-law, was incapacitated with Alzheimer's and drifted around in a dense fog. I had loathed her imperious manner and lack of compassion when I had stayed in the old penthouse with Raoul all those years ago, yet I was saddened to see her reduced to such a pitiful state, with a nurse in tow to act as minder and see to her needs. I think my feeling was not one of compassion so much as of fear at this reminder of what we may all eventually be reduced to. Her grooming was still immaculate, her hair dyed honey blonde, her talon-like nails still blood red and without the slightest chip, her designer clothes hanging off her gaunt frame, but her eyes were dull and vacant, and her swept up hair exposed the facelift scars behind her ears. She did not, of course, recognise me, but went through the motions of greeting me and kissing me on the cheek. She stroked your hair and I saw you flinch, but you mustered enough self-control not to freak out.

Carla took you on a tour of the villa – I had advised her to do this because this kind of reconnaissance always helped to put you at ease. In particular, you needed to know how to make a quick getaway from any new place. She put us in guest quarters on the ground floor and which, much to your relief, opened onto a large terrace.

The rest of our time in Belo Horizonte, you were fine. Carla took us to the workshops downtown where your fear of the unknown city was outweighed by your curiosity about stone cutting. While I marvelled at the improvements in working conditions, which included better lighting, new toilets and showers, a recreation room with a ping pong table and a bank of computers, you asked the workers dozens of questions about their craft, with Carla acting as translator. You had absolutely no interest in the people, just in their skills and knowledge, and as usual I wondered what they made of you.

Later that week, we went to Itabira by helicopter to visit the Geyer Dos Santos mine, and once again, you were scared white-knuckle witless, but so fascinated by the view of the landscape scrolling past beneath us that you managed to keep your composure. Nothing much appeared to have changed in Itabira itself, except that there was more of it. It was largely as I had remembered it, the air polluted by iron ore dust, a functional, ugly place which spoke eloquently of human greed and heedless exploitation. Carla mentioned that it had become notorious for two grim statistics – the high incidence of both asthma and suicide, which seems to have risen following the privatisation of some of the mines in the 1990s. At least the GDS mine offered a glimmer of hope in all this grimness. I could not wait to see for myself the new accommodation that Carla had built for the miners and their families. You were asking her endless questions about the mine, so that is where the two of you went first with the new manager, while I stayed behind and visited the little settlement.

To someone who had not seen the conditions that had so shocked me on my previous visit in 1983, it might well have looked nothing special, but to me the transformation was amazing. The improvised slummy shelters made of plastic sheets and rusty corrugated iron had given way to neat rows of little log cabins built around a paved, tree-lined square, in the middle of which was a little playground with swings, a climbing frame and a slide. It was deserted, because the children were at school, in a red-roofed building off to the right of the settlement. I peeked in through the windows and saw them - about two dozen in all, of different ages, being taught by two women. One group of little ones was seated in a circle in the corner, listening to a teacher reading a story, whilst the older ones, under the supervision of the other teacher, were scribbling away in exercise books. I had a powerful attack of the warm fuzzies, something I don't think you would have understood even if you had seen what the place was like before. Behind the log cabins there was a new wash house where a group of women were doing the laundry. They stopped to look at me, and I went over for a chat, using what little Portuguese I could dredge up.

They had heard the chopper land - it had thrown up clouds of dust, which is why they were rinsing the washing that had been drying on the line, but they seemed far from resentful. I told them I was a friend of Carla's, but I could not muster enough Portuguese to let them know that I had been there before, let alone what conditions had been like, so we just smiled and nodded at each other and I indicated that I wanted to have a look round. I asked them where the toilets were, and followed the direction that they indicated. Toilets and showers were a little further down the hill; basic latrines, but clean enough. A girl of about twelve in a yellow dress was on her haunches, washing a shrieking toddler with a hand shower. She stood up to greet me, and I realised that she was likely to be the mother rather than the older sister. She beamed a gap-toothed smile at me, while her charge saw his chance to escape. She ran off in pursuit, grabbed the squealing child and dragged him back to his ablutions, laughing and scolding him at the same time.

I took some photographs and made my way back to the offices, which still had the same old framed posters of the Swiss Alps on the walls. When eventually you reappeared with Carla and the manager, you were deep in conversation with Carla, who was doing her utmost to answer all your questions. The manager wandered over to me. 'So many questions, your daughter. Never anybody ask so many difficult questions!' He looked rather exasperated, poor man. I hope you did not make him look stupid in front of Carla, but I suspect that is precisely what did happen.

We spent the final week of our South American jaunt in Peru, indulging my lifetime wish to see Machu Picchu. It turned out to be a monumental mistake, but what I learned about you was most revealing. With the benefit of hindsight, I can now see that your fateful decision to pursue your brother's dope dealer in Peckham was entirely consistent with your Aspie way of thinking.

You were, I know, none too keen on seeing Machu Picchu. You'd read about it in our guide book, studied photographs and Googled it on the Internet, and felt you knew enough. You were much more interested in the natural world than in ancient civilisations. I gave you the option of staying behind in the hotel in the ugly little town of Aguas Calientes, but you said you did not feel safe, and preferred to come with me. I tried to put you off – I had heard about the crowded buses, the queues and the hundreds of tourists to be found swarming the site like ants. 'Mummy,' you said, (it was just before you switched to calling me Mum, which coincided with your going to university) I have to learn to overcome my phobias. I *have* to.'

'That's very brave of you, my darling.'

'No, it's a necessity. I've got to learn to deal with it.'

Your jaw was set, your expression grim and determined. It obviously was not a challenge that you relished, and I cursed myself for not cancelling this leg of the trip.

The main way to reach Machu Picchu from Aguas Calientes is by bus, up a steep, narrow dirt track, the Bingham Road, with a dozen or more hairpin bends, not suitable for those of a nervous disposition. This was clearly going to be a trial for you, but the only other way of getting there is on foot along one of the Inca trails, which would have taken a couple of days and involved camping en route. You might have been fit enough to do so, but I certainly wasn't, so it had to be the bus or nothing.

We left the hotel shortly after five in the morning and were surprised to see a crowd of people waiting at the appointed place. An old rattletrap of a bus appeared, wheezing and panting, and we boarded along with our yawning and shivering fellow travellers from all corners of the globe, including a number of young Israelis, who seem to be ubiquitous in South America. It was still dark and very cold. We set off, and you opened the guidebook to try and distract yourself. We had not been gone long when we were startled out of our early morning stupor by the unmistakeable sound of gunfire. The bus juddered to a halt. We could hear angry voices shouting outside – later I realised that they were threatening to shoot the driver if he didn't open the door. Three masked gunmen in balaclavas stormed onto the bus, screaming orders that we could not understand. They pistol-whipped the driver, who slumped over the steering wheel, then they came round with a bucket and a couple of gunny sacks and commanded us to hand over our cameras, wallets, watches and mobiles. When one of the Israelis sitting in front of us showed a moment's reluctance, he was punched in the face. I remember the sickening sound of cracking bone. You started to say something to the robber who was grabbing my camera, but I clapped my hand over your mouth to shut you up. They made their way down the bus, cleaning us out, then retreated, walking backwards, keeping their guns pointed at us, and vanished into the pre-dawn darkness. The whole thing can't have lasted more than a couple of minutes. After a few seconds of stunned silence, the bus suddenly came alive with a crescendo of swearing and indignation. Somebody got up and went to the front of the bus to tend to the driver, who was out cold. The Israeli had a broken nose, but apart from that, there were, it seemed, no injuries.

'Well, I guess we got off lightly. That could have been a lot worse,' said an elderly female American voice. The comment was met with a certain amount of muttering. I looked at you and realised that you had been shocked into silence.

'Anyone still have a cell? So we can call the cops?' shouted another American.

Somebody laughed mirthlessly. 'Honey, that probably was the cops!'

By now, some people had got off and were vomiting by the roadside. A stench of excrement was spreading around the bus.

We got off, stood by the bus and wondered what to do next, while I asked myself how this little adventure was going to affect your resolve to fight your phobias. All around us the gratitude at not having been mown down in a hail of bullets was now giving way to people wondering how they were going to get home, never mind continue their holiday, minus their wallets, credit cards and plane tickets. 'Well, ah thank the Lord they didn't want mah weddin' band 'cause it don't come off,' said one of the American women with a Texan drawl. 'They'd have to hack off mah finger.'

Fortunately our only loss had been my Canon Eos and my mobile. The plane tickets were in the hotel safe, along with our passports, most of my cash and my credit cards.

As we stood waiting for some kind of rescue, I asked you if you were alright. You did not answer my question, but fixed me with your amber headlights: 'Mummy, why didn't you let me talk to that robber?'

'Because he might have shot you. They were jumpy as hell, these boys. Probably stoked themselves up on cocaine. Not in the mood for negotiation.'

'But ... I could have reasoned with them. I mean, it doesn't make sense robbing tourists. It's like killing the goose that lays the golden eggs. It's... it doesn't make economic sense.'

Oh dear, I remember thinking. Oh dear oh dear... there we were, at imminent risk of having our brains blown out, and you wanted to teach an armed robber a lesson on economics. Your Asperger's opened before me like an unbridgeable, unfathomable dark chasm.

We never did make it up Machu Picchu, and flew back to England two days later.

In October 2002, aged sixteen and nine months, you started your BSc in Physics with Theoretical Physics at Imperial College. Your father and I worried about your ability to cope. Not with the academic demands, but with the social side of university life. We went to see your tutor, Dr Fanshawe, who promised to monitor your progress. He took this very seriously, and you became highly dependent on him, all but monopolising him. I felt bad, and I imagined that at times he had to hide from you to be able to get on with his work. You would visit his office every day to talk about some scientific issue or other, oblivious of the fact that he had dozens of other students to supervise.

After a couple of months, your father and I had to take you aside and ask you to restrict your visits to once a week. I can still picture the look of surprise and incomprehension on your face.

'But... Dr Fanshawe never told me he didn't have time.'

You overcompensated by going to the opposite extreme and avoiding him altogether. He phoned us to find out what was going on, and to propose a solution. You were to have one fixed individual tutorial per week, and he was to have no compunction about telling you that time was up at the end of the allotted hour. I was tempted to give him a kitchen timer.

In my memory, the remainder of your undergraduate days at Imperial have telescoped into a blur of routine. You cycled in every day, no matter how foul the weather, even though there was a chemistry lecturer who lived in Tooting and who had offered you a daily lift in. At home, you withdrew almost completely from us to study in your room. We only saw you when you were tending the vegetable patch, and feeding the hens or at meal times, and even then, you would have preferred to take your plate to your room, had we not insisted that you eat with us. You sailed through your assignments and exams, but, predictably, your social life was non-existent. You had, as far as I could gather, no friends on the course, though there were students that you worked with on certain projects. I imagine they found you weird and intimidating, and you probably made them feel like idiots. You were very beautiful, but this gift was entirely negated by your nerdiness, your gauche body language, your awkward behaviour and lack of social graces. Our only consolation was that you did not seem to care. You were not, as far as we could gather, unhappy in your isolation.

Did I miss having any meaningful communication with you? The truth is that by that stage I did not. Your father and I had got used to it, and we were heavily involved in our separate career ventures. What I did have was a selfish sense of despair at the prospect of having you living with us for the rest of our lives, because I could not imagine that you would ever want to leave home, let alone embark on anything resembling a relationship with someone. This unmaternal sentiment still shocks me, but I cannot lie to you now, and it is at the root of my feelings of guilt towards you. Shouldn't I have shown more understanding for the combined handicap of your IQ and your Asperger's? Was it your fault that you couldn't relate to people? At the time, your pre-pubescent brother more than made up for your emotional remoteness. Tristan was affectionate. He sought and thrived on parental approval and praise; two things that seemingly meant nothing to you. He had lots of friends who came to the house, made a lot of noise, played Super Mario, watched cartoons and wore Ninja Turtle T shirts. He was angelically beautiful, and dozens of little girls were in love with him. He did well at school, and was popular with his teachers. I doted on him, and because your father worked such long hours, it was inevitable that Tristan should grow much closer to me, as I worked entirely from home. Thank heavens, I thought to myself, for this normal child.

10TH MARCH 2009

The first real hint of spring today. Astrid swept the sun trap clean of leaves and twigs and sundry dead things of animal and vegetable nature, got the cushions for the swing from the barn, hoovered the crap out of them and persuaded me to join her there for a coffee and a spliff. At midday, the temperature had risen to 20°C, and your aunt the Inuit was in shorts and a sleeveless T-shirt, while I just about felt comfortable in my jeans, woolly jumper and socks. Some of the metal sculptures are beginning to rust quite badly, but she likes it that way. Here and there, early signs of plant life herald the arrival of spring. I only hope they are right, and don't get punished for their optimism with a heavy night frost. Weeds are beginning to poke through crevices and between the brick pavers. There is a sprinkling of snowdrops, and one or two etiolated stripy mauve crocuses have opened up around the stork statue. In the fat, squat terracotta pot in the corner, the hellebore has started to flower, and next to the swing, the magnolia bush has sprouted confident, furry white buds. Even the stick-like stalks of the clematis are beginning to sprout tiny green shoots.

We were joined by the dogs. Mutt frolics around and cocks a leg against the stork statue, while an arthritically waddling Doobie flops down on the brick pavers and rolls on her back, wiggling with delight, tongue lolling out of her mouth.

Doobie... we got her a few months after Bella was put down. It was strange. You did not shed a tear for Bella, yet you had seemingly been very fond of her, and she of you. Doobie was another Battersea Dogs Home orphan, who had been given the naff name Scooby Doo. Scooby Doobie Doo, your father would sing, to the tune of Sinatra's *Strangers in the Night*. Soon, it degenerated to Doobie Doo, and somewhere along the line, it just became Doobie, with all sorts of variations including Doobs, Doodle Dog, Donald Dog, Donald Duck, DoDo and Doris Day. Tristan was responsible for most of these variations. You always faithfully stuck with Doobie, though I think I may have heard you call her Doobs once or twice.

Astrid asks me what I've been writing about, so I tell her about my recollections of your withdrawal from us during your undergrad years.

'We had a total stranger in the house. It was like having a lodger rather than a daughter. She was completely introverted, and Tris was the polar opposite; affectionate, emotional, an open book of a boy.'

Astrid inhaled and closed her eyes.

'You know, Veets,' she said after a while, 'I can honestly say that I don't know my own boys that well. I think that maybe you are guilty of wanting to know too much. You have to let people decide how much of themselves they wish to reveal, to share. It's going to vary enormously. Take Marcus. I look at him sometimes and think how the fuck did he spring from Rhys and me? Just like you once said about Senta. He can't draw, he despises the humanities and he thinks we are a bunch of deluded old hippies. He'll probably vote Conservative in the next election. He doesn't have Asperger's, but at best I reckon he reveals about ten percent of himself to us. But that's his choice. Forcing him to open up more would be pointless. Dylan is more open, but even Dylan is very private. And sometimes I look at Rhys and I think Jesus, we've been together for nearly forty years, but how well do I really know you? There is stuff about me he doesn't know, so I imagine the same must go for him.'

It's funny. Until I moved to Wensum last year, I always thought that your aunt's family was much closer than ours. I have come to realise now that this is little more than an illusion, and that in fact they exist largely in their own private spheres, albeit under the same roof. Astrid and I appear to be the only ones who can really claim to know each other well. Your aunt does not seem to feel the need to penetrate anyone's psyche, maybe because she is so much more confident in herself than I am, and quite happy to be an island surrounded by other islands. By contrast, I am pathetically needy. I crave access to private thoughts and feelings. I like to think that Gerry and I are close and have no secrets from each other, but I know I am deluding myself. I only have to think back to that foolish business with Walter two years ago, when I was contemplating a sneaky little fling to lift my middle-aged spirits.

This afternoon, Tristan asked Astrid if Lucy could come along to the sculpture classes she'd promised him for his birthday. When Astrid mentioned this to me after dinner, I found myself getting very cross. This was a cheap way of making up to Lucy for the BlackBerry business, and I told her I thought he had a nerve. She just laughed and told me to lighten up. She is quite happy to teach Lucy too.

Lucky Lucy, but I still want to strangle Tristan.

12TH MARCH 2009

A deranged seventeen-year-old German kid has gone on a shooting spree in his old school, killing sixteen people, mainly girls and female teachers, before committing suicide. This in a sleepy little village in Baden-Württemberg! As we watched this evening's news coverage of the carnage, I caught myself looking at Tristan and Marcus, trying to imagine whether either of them would be capable of such an act. It's the after effect of that conversation with Astrid the other day.

How well do we really know each other?

THE IDES OF MARCH 2009

Can't seem to focus on the last couple of years of your life. The post-grad days, the Hobbs twins, the double murder. I sit down to write, but nothing comes out. I have been fidgeting, watching DVDs of '*Not just Sprouts!*,' phoning Ewa, phoning mother, emailing Carla and Susanna, looking up recipes online, driving into Norwich with no other purpose than to walk around, have a coffee and browse distractedly through rails of clothes at Jarrolds without bothering to buy anything. Yesterday, I had to fight the impulse to catch the next train to London, but it was Saturday, Gerry's busiest day, and Ewa was in New York, so it seemed a bit pointless.

When I got home, Tristan and Lucy were in the studio, having their first sculpture lesson with polymer clay. Astrid had been showing them how to make armatures from chicken mesh, and they were absorbed in bending and snipping the metal. Astrid wanted them to make a basic shape, just to get their hands used to sculpting, to the adding, subtracting and pushing around of the clay into and around the wire. You have to teach your hands to sculpt; you have to get a feel for what you can do with the clay. She invited me to join them, but I didn't want to intrude, besides which, I was restless. I knew I wouldn't have been able to produce anything.

I was just sitting in the kitchen with a mug of tea and the paper, trying to concentrate on a Sudoku, when Rhys appeared from his study.

'What's happened to your love affair with the laptop?' he asks.

'Writer's block. Can't focus on the last two years. I just... baulk at it...'

He sits down in the armchair and faces the grate, piled high with fresh logs.

'Well, don't torture yourself... '

'But I set myself this goal... '

'That being?'

'To cover her whole life before the first anniversary of her murder.'

He takes his eyes off the logs and turns towards me.

'Maybe you should let someone else have a go at finishing it for you if it's too painful.'

'Are you offering...?' I ask.

He shakes his head. 'No, but I know someone who could do it for you. Correction; I know several people who would probably like to do it for you.'

I stare in dull incomprehension. He is talking in riddles.

'My students, Vita. I have three in my class who show distinct promise. Three out of fifteen is not bad going, I guess.'

'And how,' I counter, 'would they know what to write about? They don't know the facts for a start. I mean, even I don't know all the facts. There is stuff we will never know. Like what exactly happened in that kebab shop.'

'Vita, all they need to do is Google *Steeneken Hobbs murder*, to find dozens of links to newspaper articles. They can use that as a framework. The rest they can make up.'

I shake my head. 'You are missing the point, Rhys. I have been writing as an act of catharsis, remember? That was your idea. It is something that I have to do myself. Nobody else can do it for me.'

'Just a thought,' he sighed.

19TH MARCH 2009

Have given in, after four more days of writerly constipation and insomnia. Rhys is almost indecently delighted and will propose the idea to his select group tomorrow. I have mentioned none of this to your father, whom I am going to see next week. He'll probably think Rhys's suggestion is insensitive, to put it mildly.

20TH MARCH 2009

Rhys's three students have accepted the challenge, and will be doing it in the form of a special project. They have, however, asked to meet me, so we have invited them round for dinner on Saturday. I have told Rhys that I really do not want to talk about the murder, but that I don't mind answering questions about your earlier life. What the fuck have I let myself in for here? Can I still back out of this?

22ND MARCH 2009

Not as traumatic or weird as I had feared. I made a huge moussaka and a salad, and got more and more nervous as the evening approached. I could not settle to anything, and ended up taking the dogs out for a long walk along the river. Should I lay down certain preconditions about the kind of questions they could ask? Or should I just rely on their common sense and on whatever no-go areas Rhys had stipulated?

When they arrived with Rhys, just after seven, I had already knocked back several glasses of wine. I had declined Astrid's panacea of a large spliff, as it tends to make me slightly paranoid when I am already worked up. In they came, rather awkwardly. Ethereal Emily, pale as a ghost, handed me a bunch of cellophaned and beribboned red tulips. I kissed her on her marble cheek, in an attempt to make up for the undeservedly frosty reception she had suffered the last time she came to the farm. Rhys then introduced me to Gina McKenzie, an older woman in her forties with sensible shoes and baggy clothes, who smiled apologetically and launched straight into a 'thank-you-for-consenting-to-this' speech, as she handed me a bottle of Freixenet. Then there was Julian Symes, dark haired and beetle browed, whose age was difficult to guess, but whose nasal estuary accent placed him firmly in Sarf Lannen. We shook hands and he gave me an anthology of Pablo Neruda poems, while he mumbled something about his choice being 'a bit of a risk', because he had tried to extrapolate my taste in poetry from the jewellery designs that he had seen on the Driftwood website.

As we were standing around in the kitchen while I poured the drinks, Tristan and Marcus appeared and submitted to quick cursory introductions before making their excuses. They were off to a party at Lucy's. There had been a bit of an argument about borrowing Astrid's van, but she put her foot down, anticipating the inevitability of inebriation and offering instead to provide a taxi service. She was out in the yard, waiting by the van, fiddling with a lame wing mirror. Gina McKenzie followed my gaze.

'Handsome lads you've got there. And so tall. Hard to believe they're only sixteen.'

She is pure Morningside, mild, mellow and rounded, a bit like her own physique, but there's a sharpness in her pale blue eyes, something that tells you that although she may look a little mumsy and harmless, she does not miss much. She has the hooded eyes of a hawk.

What did we talk about? I found myself taking control by asking lots of questions to stop them from interrogating me. Gina McKenzie is a librarian who had already written three novels which have been rejected by dozens of literary agents. Julian is an English teacher and a musician with his own funk/soul/jazz band. Emily... well, you already know about her. It was Julian who eventually nudged open the door to The Topic by asking me if or when I planned to resume my work as a jeweller. This involved talking about Tristan's state of mind and performance at school. I found myself clamming up, giving the briefest possible answer. There was an embarrassed silence, broken by Rhys.

'I expect you'll be moving your equipment up here if you do decide to stay another year.' He picked up the bottle of Sauvignon and offered to top up our glasses.

'Hmmm... yes... I suppose,' I mumbled.

Gill reached for the water jug, filled her glass and took a long draught.

'I really enjoy '*Not just Sprouts!*' she said, looking me straight in the eye. It was such an abrupt and awkward change of subject that the whole table seemed to lurch suddenly to the left. It was then that I realised that I'd had too much to drink.

We never went anywhere near The Topic after that. We just stuck to safe ones; food, Norwich, the university, books they had enjoyed, authors they admired. David Mitchell has cast a spell over all of them with his *Cloud Atlas*. Rhys is envious of him, I know. Commercial Richard and Judy success *and* praise from the critics.

Your name was not mentioned once all evening, but you were there throughout; the elephant in the room.

Diploma in Creative Writing
Attn: Dr Rhys Jones
Senta Project (Special assignment)
Submitted by: G. W. McKenzie

Extract from Isobel Hobbs' statement at Peckham police station.

Detective Constable Gillian Barton: Isobel, please can you describe your relationship with the victims?

Isobel Hobbs: Yes... I am Toby Hobbs's twin sister.

G.B: And, er, Senta Steinekeen?

I.H: Steeneken, pronounced Stayneken. Like the TV Chef? He's Senta's father. She's ... was... a close friend of ours.

G.B: Your brother's girlfriend?

I.H: Ah no... no, just a very er... special friend.

G.B: Right, I see, now, can you explain what your brother and his... friend... er...Senta... were ... doing in Peckham yesterday afternoon? Why had they gone there?

I.H: Yes, well, that's a long story.

G.B: Uhuh. Please go ahead. Bear in mind that any information you give us about Senta and Toby's movements could help us bring these murderers to justice.

I.H: Well, Senta has ... had a younger brother, Tristan. He... he was... had been in trouble... in and out of trouble for some time, and...

G.B: How old is he... this brother?

I.H: Fifteen... He'd been suspended from school for... dabbling in drugs.

G.B: Dabbling? What was he doing exactly?

I.H: I don't know the exact details, but he'd been playing truant with a couple of friends and one of them, Martin, was getting into hard drugs, heroin, I believe. So they all... the three of them... went to some place in Peckham – the flat of a friend of Martin's older brother, a guy called Spider. He is a small-time dealer and a junkie himself. They bought some heroin there and they injected it in his flat. Tristan and

Martin got high, but the other boy, Sam, lost consciousness... I don't think they'd realised this for quite some time, because they were out of it and Sam had gone to the bathroom to throw up. Then, according to Tristan, Spider's flatmate came home, found Sam half-unconscious on the bathroom floor, and panicked. He didn't want to call an ambulance, because he knew the police would end up being involved, so he dragged the three of them – they had to carry Sam – into his van and drove them to Kings College Hospital and just kind of dumped them there outside accident and emergency. Sam survived, but I'm told it was a close call.

G.B: When was this, exactly?

I.H: About two weeks ago. March 20th or 21st.

G.B: I see. Right. And what's that got to do with your brother and his friend?

I.H: Senta, Toby and I all belong to the same church. We all felt we had – we wanted to do something, but Toby and I disagreed with Senta. She... wanted to find this dealer and talk to him. She was convinced that all she needed to do was make him see the error of his ways, the damage he was doing. I don't know, it all sounds so ridiculously naïve...

G.B: Please go on.

I.H: But you'd have to understand Senta. She's... she's a very unusual person.

G.B: In what way?

I.H: She's... was highly intelligent. You know, off the scale. Went to university at sixteen, graduated at nineteen with a First and is...was working on her doctorate. A brilliant mind, but hopeless at understanding normal mortals. As if she couldn't empathise with people. Toby and I eventually figured she had Asperger's Syndrome, you know, like being kind of autistic?

G.B: Uhuh.

I.H: Toby and I were her only friends. She made like this huge effort with us, almost as if she'd read a book about how to behave with friends, or had behavioural therapy and was desperate to put it into practice. The friendship thing didn't come naturally to her. She had to ... learn about it. You know, Teach Yourself Friendship. That kinda thing.

G.B: Where did you meet?

I.H: At Imperial College. We are ... were... post-graduates there. The three of us were specialising in the effects of global warming on the Greenland glaciers. We were all interested in ecological issues and especially in means of combating climate change. We met on this trip to Greenland two summers ago. That's what brought us together. Senta was lonely. She seemed to be completely without friends. She latched on to us. When we got back, we started taking her along to our Unitarian Church meetings, and she seemed to get this real buzz out of being part of a community.

G.B: Unitarian Church did you say? What kind of church is that? Like a Born Again type thing?

I.H: No... We are anti-trinitarian, monotheistic... we don't believe... I mean, we don't have a creed.

G.B: Hang on, you've lost me there. I'm afraid I don't know very much about religion. What do you mean by antitri... trin... trinism?

I.H: Antitrinitarianism. Oh, it just means that we believe in God as one single being...

G.B: Oh, right...

I.H: Our... my mother is American. The Unitarian Church is well-known in the United States. Much more so than here in England.

G.B: I see.

I.H: Erm, well, anyway, we took her along to our local church in Kensington...

G. B: Kensington?

I. H: Yes, the Kensington Unitarians, and she made us promise not to tell anyone there about what she called her 'freak status.' She soon became totally fascinated by Unitarianism. She was an obsessive sort of person. It was kind of strange, because she remained this staunch atheist and supporter of Dawkins, but what she wanted, I think, was to belong to an organization that could provide her with an intelligent moral compass. Religion without God. Actually, I think Jesus was probably dispensable too. What she craved was a set of moral guidelines for herself and a like-minded supportive community. She had no time for preaching. She had no time for metaphysical speculation or ivory tower academia. She could have pursued the most complex scientific or mathematical studies if she'd wanted, but she decided to do something which would be of more immediate tangible benefit to humanity, that's why she was so interested in things like climate change research. Then, recently, she'd been talking about establishing a new community movement. She wanted it to be driven by secular humanist values, but she felt it needed a charismatic leader, and she knew that she didn't fit the bill. She wanted it to be truly post-Christian, free of the shadow of the church. She really didn't like the word 'church'. Felt it had too much ugly baggage. We had several big arguments about walking the talk. She accused us – Toby and me – of not putting our principles into practice, of not doing enough community work, of... of staying too much within the boundaries of our own comfort zone... She was all fired up and wanted to go out there into the sink estates and the deprived areas and talk to people, but the problem was, she didn't have a clue how to go about it. She had no personal experience of deprivation. Quite the opposite, in fact. Her parents are well-off. Like I said, her father is the TV chef, Gerry Steeneken. He also owns that restaurant in Westminster; De Vlaaminck. Her mother is a jeweller who makes weird artistic stuff. Her aunt is the sculptor, Astrid Rasmussen. It's a pretty amazing family. Toby and me, well, our family isn't famous, but there's no shortage of money on our... my father's side. The three of us are from privileged backgrounds. We simply don't have any street credibility in places like Peckham. We sound wrong, we look wrong, but you know, at least we – Toby and I are... were... aware of that. Senta wasn't. She just didn't get it. I don't think she really 'got' people at all. What happened yesterday just proves all that... I'm sorry... I'm...

G.B: Shall I get you some more tea?

I.H: Oh yes please. Yes, tea... would be good...

G.B: So now that you've given me some background information, could you tell me a little more about yesterday? Did you know that your brother was going to Peckham with Senta to ... confront this dealer?

I.H: Well, Toby and I both knew that's what Senta wanted to do, and we'd both tried to talk her out of it. It led to a huge row. We were in our house in Notting Hill.

G.B: The three of you share a house?

I.H: No, I share that ... shared that house with Toby. It belongs to our father.

G.B: Right...

I.H: Senta was on her high horse about practising what you preach, and we were all the time trying to get her to tell us what she thought such a confrontation with a guy like Spider would achieve.

She couldn't see it. She just thought our attitude was a form of moral cowardice. In the end, she left in a huff and went back to her parents' home. They live on Clapham Common. At least, we thought that's what she did. Toby called her about an hour after she'd stormed out. He was worried about her. He... was kind of in love with her, though he always denied it and she seemed unaware of it... She didn't really understand normal human emotions very well at all.

G.B: So what happened after that?

I.H: He told me that she sounded very upset and that he'd decided to go after her. He hated arguments, especially with her.

G.B: So he went to Clapham Common?

I.H: I doubt it. I'm pretty sure he lied to me. I figure that when he called her, she was already on her way to Peckham, and he wanted to follow her and try to talk her out of it. But he didn't want to tell me that. But you know, we are twins, and I just know when he is lying. He's not good at it...

G.B: So at what point did you decide to act?

I.H: Well, after a while, I tried to call them on their cells... their mobiles, but they were both switched off? Then I tried Senta's parents' home and her mother answered. When I asked to speak to Senta, she said she wasn't at home, and that she thought Senta was with us in Notting Hill. That's when I got really freaked, but I didn't want to worry Senta's mother at this stage in case I was mistaken, so I just ended the call with some kind of excuse. I was totally freaking out and didn't know what to do. Then a few hours later my phone rang. It was Senta's mother, in a complete state. She was calling me from King's College accident and emergency. She told me Senta and Toby had been...

G.B: You're doing fine. This is very helpful information. Take your time. Would you like a break?

I.H: I... no... er... they... they had been stabbed... stabbed for God's sakes! In some kebab take-out on Peckham High Street by a gang of hoodlums. Senta died of her injuries shortly after arriving at the hospital – she'd lost a massive amount of blood because they'd sliced through her aorta and my brother ... he... they'd stabbed him in the heart... he died before the ambulance had even arrived...

G.B: I'm sorry, that must have been a terrible way to hear such news. Were you alone?

I.H: Yes. I ran next door to my neighbour. She drove me to the hospital. I... oh Jesus... please tell me this is a nightmare and I'm dreaming this... It's gonna kill my mother.

G.B: Are you sure you wouldn't like to have a break? I appreciate how difficult this must be for you.

I.H: No... I'd prefer... just get this over and done with. There's not much more to tell. You know the rest.

G.B: I understand.

Diploma in Creative Writing
Attn: Dr Rhys Jones
Senta Project (Special Assignment)
Submitted by: Julian Symes.

Scene: a non-descript pub on Peckham High Street. It is mid-afternoon, and three men are nursing pints of bitter in a corner. Nikos Demitriou, a dark-haired, thickset young man in his late twenties in jeans and a pale blue Lacoste polo shirt comes in and heads straight for the bar, where the barman is drying glasses.

'Pint of Stella, please, mate.'

'Looks like you need one.'

'You can say that again.'

'Looks like you need one.'

'Yeah, funny...'

The barman shoves the frothy pint through the slops on the counter.

'So, bit of trouble then?'

'Christ...'

'Been to the Bill again?'

'Yeah...'

'So what happened then?'

Nikos absent-mindedly tamps a Marlboro Red on the counter. The barman raises his eyebrows and shakes his head.

'Sod it! I really need one right now.'

'Sorry mate...'

'It's not a free country any more, is it. Nanny state. Anyway, this was yesterday around five o'clock, right? These three kids come in. Hoodies. Beanies. All twitchy and fired up, been at the skunk or somefink. Got the munchies. Two go and sit at the back. One, the leader, I recognise him, I seen him before. He orders shawarmas and Cokes. Pay you tomowwa, he says. What can I say. Don't argue, right? Never seen the others before. The leader I recognised 'cos he's got a bloody great scar across his face, from the corner of his mouth to his left ear lobe. He's trouble. One of them Peckham Boys. The others – dunno. Maybe Scarface was recruiting. They looked about thirteen. Maybe he needed new members, rate at which they slaughter each avva, know what I mean? Lifespan of a fruit fly, them kids.'

'Yeah, come and go, don't they. And it ain't getting any better.'

'Well, in comes this young couple, and I'm thinking to meself, hello, what have we here, visitors from Planet Poshville looking for a bit of rough? You know, the girl was this like charity shop type? But dead posh when she opened her mouth. And him, well, he was a right geek. Glasses, anorak. He kinda shoved her inside. She didn't want to be there. Didn't want to eat naffink or drink naffink. He orders a doner kebab and a can of Sprite. She was just like sat there, fuming. They start arguing about the food. She's saying stuff like (Attempts a posh voice) 'You shouldn't be eating that rubbish, you know.'

They was arguing like mad, but keeping their voices down, so I couldn't tell you what it was about. Then bugger me, she gets up and tries to leave, but he's holding her arm and won't let go. She loses it and starts shouting. Then the boys at the back get interested. Scarface goes over to them. 'Oi, matey, leave the lady alone, awright.' This right in the geeky kid's face, you know, like eyeball to eyeball. The geek gets it all wrong. 'Mind your own business!' he says. I'm thinking Oh Christ, a fucking Yank! Here we go. Second fight in a mamf coming up. So I'm trying to stay calm behind the counter. 'Easy now, mate.' I says. So Scarface eyeballs me: 'You keep out of it, matey.' And I'm thinking Thank God me carving knife's safe under the counter...'

(Nikos sips his lager and fiddles with his cigarette packet. The barman wipes the counter and nods at him to carry on.)

'Then Scarface turns to the geek and he's like 'What did you say, young man?' You know, putting on a posh accent. And then: 'Did you say this was your business?'

Now he's got the geek by the collar and he's pulled a fancy knife on him. He's holding it right against the kid's jugular.' Then he's like 'Well, I don't fink you've got any business here, matey.' And he nicks him wiv the knife. There's this bright red blood trickling down his neck. 'Now let the lady go.' But the geek is still clutching this girl's arm, and she's shouting at him to let her go. But he keeps hanging on to her arm. With his free hand, he's trying to staunch the blood from his neck wound. Behind the counter, I'm punching 999 on me mobile and hoping they don't notice. Next everything happens dead fast. The two other kids appear, knives out. One of them stabs the geek's arm, right through his jacket. So he has to let go of the girl. He's yelping now. There's this blood welling up inside his sleeve like. And the girl, she just loses it. 'What the fuck are you doing? Leave him alone.' But it's like the kids have scented blood and they want more. They jump on the geek. They're stabbing him in the lower back. I've got through to 999 and I go outside into the backyard, lock the door behind me and tell them I need police and an ambulance. I stay out there until I hear the siren five minutes later. I go back into the café and it's fucking carnage, man. A fucking slaughterhouse ...

'Yeah?'

'They're on the floor, the boy and the girl. He's lifeless. In a pool of blood. She's still alive, curled up, clutching her belly. There's blood coming out her mouth. No sign of the troublemaker and his two little mates. They've legged it.'

'Christ...'

'Yeah... So then the police and ambulance men come. Put them on stretchers and off they go. Fuzz stay behind to question me. Had to close the place for the forensics, then go to the police station to make a statement. It's becoming a bad joke, you know. That's the third time this year I've had to go to Peckham Nick. It's getting to be home from home. And you know what, I've bloody well had enough of this place. I was finking to meself that's it, Nikos me boy. Outta here. Time to go. I'm witness to a fucking double murder, and I'm gonna have to pick Scarface out in an identity parade and give evidence in court. I ain't safe no more. Daren't even go back to me own place. I'm couch-surfing at a mate's place in Tooting.'

'Where are you thinking of going, then?'

'Dunno, mate. Maybe back to Cyprus after the trial. Chill out a bit. Got an uncle wiv a restaurant in Agia Napa. At least over there you ain't got half the population going round with knives trying to kill the avva half. It's totally fucked up here. And anyway, like I said, I ain't safe no more here. It'll be me next if I hang around. I've been offered witness protection, but I still don't feel safe. They know who I am.'

'Good luck, bruv. Can't say I blame you. Here.'

He pushes another pint toward Nikos. 'This one's on the house.'

For: Dr Rhys Jones
Senta Project (Special Assignment)
Submitted by: Emily Griffiths

Toby Hobbs – the Spirit's View.

They are gathering in clusters and hugging each other on the sloping walkway that leads to the front door of the church where our memorial service is about to be held. Hands on shoulders and condolatory handshakes for the men, embraces and soothing noises and patting gestures for the women. I'm watching them from my vantage point diagonally across the road, hovering outside the Broadway Court building. It's like I'm looking at a movie instead of the actual thing. I'm still getting used to my spirit state, and this is one of its features; I myself feel real, even though it is a non-physical reality, but everything else I observe seems like a scene from a movie, and I can no more communicate with the people I see than I could in the past with actors on the screen. As time passes, the picture is becoming fainter and the sound too is beginning to fade. This worries me. Just after I died and my spirit birthed itself, colors were almost frighteningly vivid and sounds were so loud that they distorted. Then the picture quality and the sound improved, as if adjusted by an invisible projectionist. I totally freaked just after the stabbing, as I transformed into this ethereal form and just hovered, helplessly watching as Senta bled and writhed in agony and our killers slipped away. I simply had no time to marvel at my unexpected mutation – I who had always arrogantly dismissed the very idea of life after death – because I was simply overwhelmed with frustration and worry. She lay dying and there was nothing, absolutely nothing that I could do for her except hang around like a dumb cloud and wait for an ambulance to arrive.

At first, I couldn't figure out how to move around, and I just kind of hung where I first found myself, about six feet above our bloodied bodies. Then I realized that I could relocate myself by simply looking at another place and thinking 'I want to go there.' But this only works if the place I want to move to is within view. Later on, I experimented by thinking of places further afield, but no luck. I could not, for example, teleport myself to California. I can go through solid objects – one of the first things I tried, but it is a slow process, so I just mainly use doors instead. In some respects, my spirit state is rather disappointing. To visit Mom in San Diego, I actually had to take the plane, which if you think about it is quite funny. In case you are wondering, I travelled in the hold, as I was curious to see the conditions under which animals are transported. Unlike most people, who seem to lack the right antennae for the supernatural, animals, I've discovered, can see or sense spirits. There was an Alsatian which growled at me, and three cats, which showed only a passing flicker of interest before going back to sleep. Kittens are the best, as they are still new to the phenomenon. Once, after I'd visited Izzy in our little house in Denbigh Terrace, about a week after my death, I went and hung out in some of the neighboring gardens I'd always been curious to see. Our next-door neighbors have a kitten which can't be more than three months old, and it was outside on the lawn with Mrs Pozcu and her little girl. The kitten went completely nuts when it saw me. I flitted around, teasing it, and it leapt high in the air, spun around, clawed at me and ran in crazy spazzy jagged circles. 'What's he doing, mommy?' asked the little girl. 'Oh, just playing darling, chasing an imaginary butterfly maybe.' An imaginary butterfly, my ass! I've tried several times to provoke older cats, but they just blink at you. I deduce from this that they may simply be blasé because spirits are commonplace and of no more interest to them than shadows. Yet the only other spirit I have seen since I died is Senta's, so in this respect, animals would seem to be more privileged than humans. I guess they deserve some kind of compensation for the servitude we've reduced so many of them to.

It sure is weird, this non-physical state. Senta and I are invisible to people, yet we can see ourselves and each other. I can see my body – I am still wearing the clothes I died in – but like a vampire, I do not produce a reflection in a mirror. I can see and hear, but have no sense of smell or touch, and I do not experience hunger, thirst, pain, lust, heat, cold or tiredness. I have emotions, but they're kind of muted, without extremes. Like I said, in the last week or two, everything has begun to fade, leaving me to wonder what will happen when the picture vanishes completely. The strange thing is that my spirit self feels as strong as ever. Is this limbo? Will there be a transition to another state once the world is tuned out? So far, Senta and I have not undergone anything resembling a conventionally religious experience. No choirs of heavenly angels, no pearly gates or any of that stuff. No meeting with deceased family members or friends either, which is kind of disappointing. I thought I might see Gramps or Carl, my buddy from High School who died in a car crash a few years back, but all I can see is Senta, and even she is beginning to fade. The scientist in me is curious as hell to find out. Senta is totally blown away by it. It pretty much conclusively proves that the conventional laws of physics don't hold in this particular dimension.

When Senta died, from blood loss caused by vicious knife wounds to her stomach, I watched as her spirit form materialized in the ambulance, and her amazement was far stronger than any horror at what had happened. It was almost indecent. She wanted immediately to find out what she could and could not do. I too was curious, but I wanted to stay with our bodies at least until our parents had seen us and we'd been placed in the morgue. But Senta thought our spirit state might not last long, and that it would be stupid not to make the most of it. I don't know where she went, but she eventually reappeared at Denbigh Terrace in the early hours of the morning. Izzy was not there – Senta and I tracked her down in Clapham at Senta's parents' place. They were all there, in a terrible state, as Mr. Steeneken and Dad had just returned that evening from identifying our bodies. There were six of them in the front room – Senta's parents, her brother, Izzy, Dad and an elderly blond lady I initially took to be Senta's grandmother, but who seems to be a neighbor. When Senta and I arrived, they were just sitting there in silence, cradling glasses of brandy and cups of tea or coffee, staring dully into space. Izzy had a purplish aura of shock about her. The elderly blonde lady was holding her hand, and Dad had his arm around Izzy's shoulders. Mr. Steeneken was sitting on the floor, his back against the sofa, holding Doobie. Mrs. Steeneken was trying to comfort Tristan, stroking his hair. He'd curled up into a fetal ball next to her. I discovered that my loathing for him, which had been powerful enough to turn my gut into knots ever since Senta had told me of her plan to talk to the dealer guy, that this powerful loathing had simply evaporated. I was fully expecting to feel it, but it was like I couldn't reach the emotion. Access denied. I lingered uneasily near Izzy. How would she, my closest friend, my mirror, manage life as a single after more than twenty years of being my twin? Was there any truth in the commonly-held belief that the surviving twin gains the strength of the dead one? I know I would be totally devastated in her shoes. It would have been hard enough if we'd done the sensible thing we'd been advised to do and gone to separate universities instead of opting to do research at the same college. I concede that Aunt Julia was right when she urged us to split after high school to find our separate identities or else risk facing problems in our relationships with others later on. Instead, we'd only grown more dependent on each other, more inseparable. And then Senta came into our lives.

That evening after our murder, Senta did not want to hang around her family and went into the garden to seek comfort among her chickens and vegetables. I stayed near Izzy and felt useless. I hung around until she and Dad fell asleep, towards dawn.

They've started entering the church. Mrs Steeneken is leaning heavily on her husband. Another woman, small and wiry with crazy hair and a lime green coat – the strongest splash of color in an otherwise near achromatic scene – is standing next to a thickset guy with wavy gray hair. I figure the woman must be Senta's aunt, the artist. Senta is not here to confirm any of this. She has no intention of attending. There are two blank-faced young guys with the aunt, probably brothers, though very different in build. One, short and slight, in a business suit, readjusting the knot in his necktie, the other, tall and broad-shouldered, in a black leather jacket, jeans and sneakers, examining his feet. The suit says something to the tall guy in the leather jacket, who yanks out his ear buds and slips them in his pocket. The neighbor lady, stick thin and very blond, eyes hidden behind huge shades, is leaning on the arm of a dark-haired younger man. There is no sign of Tristan. I figure the little shit couldn't face the trauma of a memorial service and the blame that, rightly or wrongly, attaches to him. A cab pulls up and Dad gets out. I am shocked at how old he looks all of a sudden. He seems to have shrunk in his suit. He is alone; no sign of Grandma or Judy. I was expecting him to arrive with Mom, Aunt Julia and Izzy but I guess that was asking too much. He goes up to Mr. and Mrs. Steeneken, and they embrace briefly, awkwardly. Nobody has spotted the lone paparazzo who, half hidden behind a plant, has been clicking away non-stop from a window on the second floor in the Broadway Court building. I wish I could tip them off.

They enter the building and I decide to move to the wooden benches outside the church and linger a little while till Mom arrives. More and more people appear in dribs and drabs – here come Dr Fanshawe and Senta's doctoral supervisor, Professor Leibowitz, as well as various other faces from Imperial. I spot my buddy Chris Howard. He's with a girl I don't know, maybe a new girlfriend. Their body language gives nothing away. And here's Renata, a musician friend of Izzy's. I'm about to give up on Mom, Aunt Julia and Izzy when they arrive on foot, looking a little flustered. They have been staying in our house, just five minutes' walk from here. It is so typical of Mom to be late for such an occasion. I can see the tension on Izzy's face, she's trying not to lose it with Mom, who has found a pair of shades so enormous that they cover half her face. She has made no effort to tone down her eccentric vintage hippy dress style. An ankle length black cape with silver stars, flip-flops and purple toenails, for Chrissakes... Izzy looks very pale and there is an aura of anger about her. Maybe it's as well that Tristan isn't here. Aunt Julia looks calm, as always. She is professionally trained to dissimulate her emotions.

I follow them into the church where Renata has just launched into the opening bars of *Jesu Joy of Man's Desiring* on the grand piano, and I position myself in the top right-hand corner of the room against the ceiling. As far as I know, none of the mourners, apart from Mom, Aunt Julia and Izzy, has ever been inside a Unitarian church before. They probably know nothing about Unitarians and assume that we are a bunch of non-conformist weirdos. They are looking around, taking in the room which is much more like a functional, scuffed community meeting hall than a traditional church. The elderly blonde lady removes her shades and frowns as she glances round at the unpretentious plainness. Maybe she longs for the mumbo jumbo of Catholicism, for incense, tinkling bells, robed priests, stained glass saints and soaring gothic pillars. The chairs have been set out in a semi circle on the parquet floor and the candle flickers in the chalice, atop the black pillar, towards the front of the room. Mr. Steeneken, who is sitting in the middle, has spotted Mom and Izzy and beckons them over to sit next to him. Mom hesitates and glances at Dad who is seated next to a man I take to be the husband of Senta's aunt Astrid, and who is talking with him. He looks up at her, but gives her no sign of encouragement, just loaded blankness. Izzy decides for her and guides her towards the seats next to Senta's dad. Our parents' mutual loathing is undiminished, even at their son's memorial service. Raw with shock and grief, they managed a show of tolerance and support at the cremation, but have now reverted to their habitual ill-disguised festering animosity.

I am curious to see what shape this service will take. Memorial services generally try to celebrate the life of the deceased rather than mourn their passing, but in our case the circumstances make any kind of celebration rather difficult. When Gramps died last year in San Diego, there was plenty to celebrate about his life and his achievements. It must have been easy to write his eulogy, but with Senta and me it is very different. Our lives, which people are sure to say were 'full of promise' and similar clichés, were, to use another cliché, 'brutally cut short.' For those who mourn us, there isn't the consolation of a long life well-lived. Instead, there is just the pain of senseless, violent, premature loss. Our murder was partly due to us being in the wrong place at the wrong time, and partly due to my own boneheaded stupidity. I should have contacted the police as soon as I realized that Senta had lied and gone to Peckham to talk sense to Spider. Instead, I didn't think fast enough and went after her alone. People like to point a finger at Tristan. Sure, he is undeniably the ultimate cause of it all, yet it was our – Senta and my – lack of judgment that is really to blame. Of course the sad little shit has the vanity to think it is all his fault. What I know of him, he'll probably milk it to garner sympathy and get laid. As for Senta, how can you blame someone who is completely incapable of reading human emotions? Can you blame the blind for not seeing? It wasn't as if she didn't try to feel and understand. Wasn't that how our whole 'friendship' came about? This beautiful weirdo, desperately trying to understand and experience a 'relationship?' And of course I lost my head, being arrogant and ignorant and immature enough to believe that I could 'cure' her.

This past year with Senta has been one of toxic tension and argument between me and Izzy. My poor twin was battling with two blind people; one Aspo-autistic and the other besotted with the former. It was the first time Izz and I had ever fallen out. All our lives we'd been close and some folks would even insinuate that there was something a little 'unhealthy' about our closeness. Maybe it gave them a thrill to think that we had something incestuous going on, but we did not. It just so happened that we understood each other perfectly and shared the same opinions and interests. Our brains were wired the same way, for math and the sciences. For much of the time while we were growing up, our parents – two more incompatible individuals would be hard to imagine – were at war. It started when we were just toddlers and living in London. After an initial infatuation, Mom, a Germanic-looking ex-Miss California, had grown to hate everything about drizzly cold England and longed for the sunshine. Her homesickness might have been bearable but for Dad's infidelities. She had become addicted to alcohol as well as all sorts of prescription pills and was letting herself go to seed, which then further increased her depression.

The summer of our ninth birthday, she took us to her old home in San Diego for the long vacation, and refused to return. We soon ditched our British accents and behaviors, and grew up in a rambling house in North Park, where we lived with our bipolar pill-head alcoholic mother, our Aunt Julia, who is a psychiatric nurse and our anchor to sanity, and a succession of their lovers, often female in Julia's case. A custody battle ensued, which dragged on for years. Dad eventually lost, but got Mom to agree to send us to Francis Parker, an exclusive private prep school on Linda Vista, for which he stumped up the fees and where we, as the children from an unorthodox background – but not of the kind that might give us some cred – led a socially schizoid existence, trying to fit in at school, mocked both openly and (worse) silently by many of our classmates for our unfashionable clothes, our crazy mother in her beat-up Chevvy and our apparent lack of money. It was, of course, only apparent, as Dad was wealthy, yet we always seemed short of cash and it showed in our clothes. Only years later did we discover that he had sent regular maintenance checks, but Mom was hopeless with money and drank it or lost it or gave it away instead of spending it on us. Amid the conspicuous wealth that was flaunted at school, in the form of expensive cars, clothes and jewellery, Izzy and I clung to each other for support like two orphans in a consumer war zone of one-upmanship and mindless materialist snobbery. If we managed to weather the experience, it was only because we were straight- A students and excelled at sport. Both were qualities which were highly valued by the school. It was Dad who enticed us back to England after we graduated summa cum laude from Berkeley. Not that we needed much enticing, as we'd spent every summer with him in London since he and Mom split, and had grown to love our big, maternal stepmother, conservative Judy who possessed the greatest virtue of all in our eyes – she was, unlike Mom, totally unembarrassing, warm and wonderfully sane. Dad, a merchant banker, owns a house in Kensington. When we were accepted to do doctoral research at Imperial, he bought us the little house on Denbigh Terrace in Notting Hill, just off Portobello Road. Izzy and I are trust fund children and Izzy will never have to worry about money, which is an amazing blessing and also a strange sort of curse. We were determined not to let it affect our ambitions, and have lived on self-imposed student budgets, though always with the knowledge of having a financial safety net beneath us. Privileged and fortunate certainly, but spoilt, no, definitely not.

Then Senta happened to us, and everything changed. To start with, we were both fascinated and a little in awe of her. She was real tall and most un-English looking. We thought she was some kind of South American or Indian mix. Her accent was posh English and her clothes were definitely careless Brit, not a studied style at all. It was just a mess, but it didn't matter because she just had this amazing body and beautiful face with red-brown eyes like a fox, and long very dark wavy hair. We thought she was forbidding because she never smiled, so that, despite her coloring, she seemed cold and distant. When we met at Imperial in the summer of 2006, it was she who, very awkwardly, approached us one afternoon in the Library Café. I guess we were flattered at first, Izzy and I, but things were weird even at the start. Just we didn't want to admit it. She didn't understand about giving people space. She kind of imposed herself and wanted to be with us one hundred percent of the time. She could talk for hours about her pet interests. Then she would remind herself that she should show an interest in us too, and toss a few questions our way. She would feign attention, but you could tell she wasn't really taking in what you were saying.

We didn't have the heart to tell her to give us a bit of breathing space. She would call round at the house at weekends, oblivious to our own need to have time to study. Dropping hints did not work, nor did switching off our cells or not answering texts. The only way was to spell it out to her – please go now; we have to study / meet a deadline / go to bed. Then she'd look surprised. 'Oh, oh, yes, er, right, I'll be off then. Bye.' She seemed neither embarrassed nor offended, and often she'd suggest the next meeting as she headed for the front door. 'Chess tomorrow evening?' was a favorite. Even though we played two against one, Izzy and I could never win. The whole thing started to affect our relationship, and Izzy got more and more agitated by it. In the end, we confided in our Unitarian pastor, Jane. She suggested bringing Senta along to the Sunday service, so that she could meet this extraordinary person for herself. And so began Senta's Unitarian phase...

All the seats are taken now, and Judy has appeared too, with Grandma. Poor Grandma. She is struggling with a walking stick, ankles badly swollen, shuffling along, arm in arm with Judy. I wish she hadn't come. It is simply the wrong way round for a grandparent to be attending the memorial service of a grandson, and in this case her only grandson. Of course it's not the natural order for our parents either, but it is more extreme in the case of grandparents. I don't think Senta's grandmother is here; at least I cannot see anyone who might fit that description.

Jane walks over to Renata, who nods at her and stops playing after a couple more bars.

Jane stands at the front, tall, flame-haired and imposing as ever. For the first time I get to see the congregation from her physical point of view. I do a quick head count – around one hundred have come. She is addressing them now in her informal London accent, and I'm kind of tuning out. Not deliberately; no, it's like there's something wrong with the sound, like a poor connection on a cell phone. A succession of phrases and blanks.'... welcome you today... this sad occasion... two young people... great promise... cut short... the honor... Senta and Toby... struggle ... intention... eulogy... Senta's uncle.' I don't know if it's my imagination, but the picture is getting fainter too, as if someone is tinkering with brightness and contrast.

Senta's uncle, the thickset man with the lion's mane of gray hair, now comes forward. He has a powerful, lilting voice, that of a trained actor or a teacher, and is obviously at ease addressing large audiences. Even so, I can only catch odd phrases and the blanks between are getting longer. He starts by talking about Senta's childhood. 'Endowed with a freakishly high IQ... insatiable curiosity... Mensa... math and the natural world... Ewa... the Polish language... her grandfather Sven... Asperger's... brilliant... solitude... passion for conservation... friendship... Toby... (Hang on. He's talking about me and the guy's never even met me!) Toby and Isobel... Our hearts go out to her... so full of promise ... the prime of life.'

I look at the faces. Dad has buried his face in his hands. Mrs. S. is weeping silently, trying to blink away the tears. Mr. S., a great bear of a man, is sitting next to her, his hand on hers. He just looks exhausted. Senta's aunt sits sphinx-like. Mom... I can only speculate what might be going on behind her shades. Izzy stares blankly, I don't think she has any tears left. Aunt Julia, calm as ever, sits between Mom and Izzy and is holding their hands. Judy is crying, making no attempt to hide it. Grandma is expressionless and looks numb. Chris Howard is staring at a sheet of A4 on his lap. He looks tense.

Senta's uncle winds up and takes his seat. Jane takes over briefly, thanking him, and then calls Chris Howard to the front. Holy shit! Chris is going to talk about me. I am touched and amazed, because Chris is a shy guy, a classic science nerd who freaks out when he has to speak in public. This must be torture for him.

He stands, holding his crib sheet which betrays his nerves by trembling. He clears his throat several times, and Jane hands him a glass of water. His voice is a complete contrast to the confident, powerfully-projected speech of Senta's uncle. People lean forward to hear better as he stumbles and coughs, but after a short while he gets himself together and manages to conquer some of his stage fright. I did not think he had it in him to do this kind of thing. Did he volunteer, or did someone ask him to do it? Either way, it is a great thing that he's doing for us. I only wish I could show my gratitude. Izzy has found some tears and everybody looks kind of nervous and touched, like when parents watch their kids in a school play and pray they don't screw up. Chris seems to acquit himself well, though. I can barely hear what he's saying, but I can tell from his body language and from the expressions on people's faces. I can only catch occasional words and phrases now: 'Imperial... Isobel... strength... support and friendship... courage... much missed...' When he returns to his seat, there is a ripple of applause and the girl he came with gives him a proud look.

The sound has almost completely gone now, and the picture has turned sepia. Jane is speaking again, but I cannot hear her words. I notice a shimmering over behind the window in the door to the small garden at the back. It is Senta. Has she been there all along? I move towards her. No, she's only just arrived and won't come into the church, so I join her among the plants and bushes where our ashes were strewn. To me, she is still as clear and bright as if she were physically alive, but the world is vanishing for her too. Our time here is over, I say. Yes, she answers, that's why I came. Let's stay together. I think we're entering another phase.

3RD APRIL 2009

It is the eve of the first anniversary of your murder. Early tomorrow morning I will be making my way to London and to the Unitarian Church in Kensington with Rhys, Astrid, Tristan and Marcus to meet up with your father, Ewa, Sal, Mother, Isobel, her father and her stepmother Judy. Isobel's mother has decided to stay in San Diego. Lucy has kindly offered to stay at the farm to tend the animals.

We will be taking Tristan's portrait of you with us. He has been working at it on and off since January, sometimes leaving it for weeks on end, then suddenly finished it last weekend. The maturity of the work is curiously at odds with the immaturity of the painter. I know it sounds unkind, but quite how he could have produced such a sensitive piece of work is a mystery to me. He has seen right into your soul, your essence, in a way I would never have credited him with. It is, frankly, unnerving, and made me realise that I really absolutely do NOT have the measure of your brother.

He has used Grandma's original outline sketch of you, which portrayed you reading your book, legs curled up under your long green skirt. Only your face and neck, and the book you are reading are in the light, which comes from diagonally above you, creating a *chiaroscuro* effect. There is an uncanny eidetic perception at work here, because he has done so much more than capture your features; he has caught that air you often had of being totally deaf to the world, remote and utterly absorbed in what you were reading. Astrid has this too, sometimes, when she is very caught up in what she is doing. Your beautiful unruly hair foams over your shoulders, trailing off into a faint aura of light, as if a candle were burning behind you. Astrid swears blind that she has had nothing to do with the portrait, and that Tris had never once even asked her for advice, though he had spent hours looking at Italian renaissance paintings in Astrid's art books. He said he had tried to capture your self-contained unknowableness, your remoteness. He's signed the painting TriSte, the first three letters of his first and surname. In the dot of the 'i' was the only hint that this was the work of a sixteen-year-old. It contained the tiniest sad smiley. On the back, he'd written: Portrait of my sister, Senta Eva Steeneken. 14-01-1986 4-04-2008.

Forever an Enigma.

We will clear a wall in the living room for you.

ABOUT THE AUTHOR
LV Madsen

L.V. Madsen is a rootless European, born in India and raised in Holland and England. She has lived and worked, mainly as a teacher, in France, Italy and Germany and spent 17 years in the United Arab Emirates.

She now lives with her husband and a cat named Mrs Jones in a small village in the mountains of Andalucia, where, free at last from the constraints of timetables, lesson preparation and marking homework, she is able to read and write to her heart's content.

Author's Note

This is a work of fiction. It is often assumed that a first novel is a thinly-disguised autobiography. However, in this case there are very few resemblances between my life and that of the narrator and her family. To wit, I did live in Munich for a couple of years where I worked at the Canadian Consulate, knew people who were involved in opera and attended some evening classes on Wagner which may or may not have been held on a Wednesday evening, but that is about the extent of any overlap with my own life. I have never lived in Clapham, been married to a chef or had children, let alone a genius with Asperger's who gets murdered. I do not have a sister, nor have I ever designed jewellery and I cannot abide Wagner's operas!

Acknowledgements

Many people have helped me with support, encouragement, background research and feedback. All errors, as ever, are the sole responsibility of the author.

Serafina Clarke, retired literary agent and my friend and neighbour in Spain. Serafina loved and believed in this novel right from the start, which gave me the much-needed confidence to get it self-published, after all the literary agents we contacted shook their heads, deeming it variously 'too introspective,' too slow' and even in one case 'too classy for our list.'

David Rory O'Neill of davidrory-publishing. A fellow author, for advice and guidance. For copy-editing, design and formatting my manuscript and beating it into a publishable shape.

Pilar Osborn, key catalyst, for introducing me to Serafina Clarke.

Bjørn Veseth, for reading the manuscript and giving it the thumbs up. I had feared that a novel with a female narrator reflecting on her life and the murder of her daughter might not appeal to a male readership, so I was delighted that it should find favour with Bjørn, a hard-boiled Norwegian political journalist who would not have pulled his punches.

Jenny Vorwerk for editing the manuscript and pointing out a number of gaps and inconsistencies.

Callum Sutherland, former murder squad detective, once based at Peckham police station and now police advisor to Lynda La Plante, for taking the time to comment on relevant sections of my manuscript and sharing some of his vast knowledge of forensics and knife-crime in that area.

Susan May, the London-based jeweller, who gave her time to a complete stranger and patiently showed me some of the processes involved and equipment used in jewelry making. She is fictionalised as Suzanna Di Maggio in the novel.

Oytun Camcigil, a Dubai-based architect turned jeweller, who likewise was kind enough to give up some of her time to explain her craft to me.

Julian Symes, for his advice on the correct 'Sarf Lannenfication' of Peckham speech. Julian has a cameo role in the novel and Julian's late wife, the lovely Carla, for supplying information about Belo Horizonte.

Konrad Cedro, my Polish Canadian colleague at Dubai Men's College, for 'polishing' my character Ewa's 'Polski English' speech patterns by basing them on those of his own mother.

Anita Sheehan, for help with the German

Penelope 'Koukla' Doyle, for help with the Greek.

Romulo Miclat, for turning my awful sketches into professional drawings. As a professional graphic artist, he had the perverse brief of producing artwork that had to look less amateurish than mine, yet much less professional than his own. A bit like asking a concert pianist to hit a few bum notes.

Emma Pathare, for producing the painting used for the cover; a stunning interpretation of the Portrait of an Enigma, and for Einat, her model.

The Bavarian State Opera PR office, for kindly photocopying and mailing the entire program list from September 1983 to May 1985 on A3 paper. You must have cursed me under your breath!

Helen Kamioner and Anne Midgette who helped me push the right buttons to obtain the above information.

Jane Blackall, for being welcoming and most helpful at the Essex Unitarian Church in Kensington. Jane has a cameo part towards the end of the novel.

Maggi Hambling, sculptor and painter, for consenting to play a small part in the novel.

R-J Barth, who opened my ears to opera back in the 1980's.

Three 'borrowed' Dubai-based teenagers helped to give me insights into their concerns:

- **Dominic Palubiski** on music, girls and other teen preoccupations.
- **Srei Mom Rae**, who talked me through her A Level art and showed me her portfolio.
- **Sherif Salem**, who, via his mother, gave me his unvarnished opinions on his 'A' level Eng. Lit. syllabus, though not in the language attributed to my character Tristan!

Gerry Moore, the librarian in Taverham, Norfolk, for answering my questions about the area.

Amanda Howard, for her insights into the catering industry.

Paul and Sarah Brocklehurst, for letting me know what was flowering in their garden in Kent at given times of the year. (This novel was written in Dubai and Spain.)

Last but not least, my ever-patient husband, **Peter Foster**, for proof-reading the manuscript, tweaking commas and incorrect spacing, as well as pointing out infelicities of style and putting up with the many hours I spent at my computer, lost in my fantasy world.

Made in the USA
Lexington, KY
23 December 2016